Ace Books by Linda Poitevin

SINS OF THE ANGELS
SINS OF THE SON

SINS OF THE SON

THE GRIGORI LEGACY

LINDA POITEVIN

ACE BOOKS, NEW YORK

THE BERKLEY PUBLISHING GROUP
Published by the Penguin Group
Penguin Group (USA) Inc.
375 Hudson Street, New York, New York 10014, USA

Penguin Group (Canada), 90 Eglinton Avenue East, Suite 700, Toronto, Ontario M4P 2Y3, Canada
(a division of Pearson Penguin Canada Inc.) • Penguin Books Ltd., 80 Strand, London WC2R 0RL,
England • Penguin Group Ireland, 25 St. Stephen's Green, Dublin 2, Ireland (a division of Penguin
Books Ltd.) • Penguin Group (Australia), 250 Camberwell Road, Camberwell, Victoria 3124, Australia
(a division of Pearson Australia Group Pty. Ltd.) • Penguin Books India Pvt. Ltd., 11 Community
Centre, Panchsheel Park, New Delhi—110 017, India • Penguin Group (NZ), 67 Apollo Drive,
Rosedale, Auckland 0632, New Zealand (a division of Pearson New Zealand Ltd.) • Penguin Books
(South Africa) (Pty.) Ltd., 24 Sturdee Avenue, Rosebank, Johannesburg 2196, South Africa

Penguin Books Ltd., Registered Offices: 80 Strand, London WC2R 0RL, England

This is a work of fiction. Names, characters, places, and incidents either are the product of the author's
imagination or are used fictitiously, and any resemblance to actual persons, living or dead, business
establishments, events, or locales is entirely coincidental. The publisher does not have any control over
and does not assume any responsibility for author or third-party websites or their content.

SINS OF THE SON

An Ace Book / published by arrangement with the author

PUBLISHING HISTORY
Ace mass-market edition / April 2012

Copyright © 2012 by Linda Poitevin.
Cover art by Mike Heath.
Cover design by Annette Fiore.
Interior text design by Kristin del Rosario.

ISBN: 978-1-937007-37-9

ACE
Ace Books are published by The Berkley Publishing Group,
a division of Penguin Group (USA) Inc.,
375 Hudson Street, New York, New York 10014.
ACE and the "A" design are trademarks of Penguin Group (USA) Inc.

PRINTED IN THE UNITED STATES OF AMERICA

10 9 8 7 6 5 4 3 2 1

ALWAYS LEARNING   **PEARSON**

For my husband, Pat,
who believed in me before I believed in myself

ACKNOWLEDGMENTS

Most people think of writing as a solitary endeavor, but the truth is, it's kind of like raising a child . . . It truly takes a village. While a story certainly begins with me, turning it into a book that I can put into the hands of you, the reader, is very much a group effort. Here, then, are some of the inhabitants of my village who deserve special mention:

My husband, who acts as my sounding board, my police procedural encyclopedia, and my head cheerleader—*and* who uncomplainingly picks up the slack around the house when I'm facing a deadline.

My daughters, whose belief in me carries me through my not-infrequent moments of self-doubt—and who, for the most part, don't complain too much about the lack of groceries in the house when I become a little too wrapped up in a story.

My many friends who have patiently endured the ups and downs of my becoming a published author, and who share so generously and enthusiastically in my excitement.

My editor, Michelle Vega, who has provided a calm, steady guidance through the whole publishing process and is as excited about my story as I am.

My agent, Becca Stumpf, whose perfectionism rivals my own and keeps me honest to myself, my story, and my readers.

PROLOGUE

Five thousand years ago

"Do we have an agreement?" the One asked.

"You're serious." Lucifer turned from the window, a scowl etched between his brows, eyes clouded with suspicion. "You would do this to your own son, burden him with this destiny."

"*We* would do this to *our* son," the One corrected, "because we have run out of other options. We both know the pact between us won't last forever. There are too many variables. And if we go to war again, it will never end. Think of it, Lucifer: you wish the annihilation of the mortals, I wish their survival. When the peace now between us comes to an end, let our son decide which of our wishes will be granted. Seth is equal parts each of us. Who better to decide who is right about the mortal race?"

"How do I know I can trust you? How do I know you'll abide by the agreement if he chooses against you?"

"Because I am the One," she said simply. She met her former helpmeet's gaze with an unflinching one of her own. His mouth drew almost imperceptibly tighter. She felt her heartbeat catch. For a moment, she wondered if he might have guessed at her secret. Then, deep within him, she sensed his desire to accept her words, his longing to believe her. She offered him a small smile.

Lucifer's gaze flicked to the wall and then returned to her. He rocked back on his heels, hands tucked into his pockets.

"You've always said my mortal children are worthless," she pressed. "That there was no point to their existence. If you truly believe that, if you're certain you're right, then this is your chance to redeem your views. Our son, reborn into the mortal world to live as one of them, raised by them, growing to adulthood—and then, by his own choices, deciding their fate. If he chooses to live a life of good, to live up to his potential by mortal standards, then you acknowledge the inherent worth of all humans and withdraw fully from their realm. If he chooses otherwise, then I accept defeat. And if either of us does anything to interfere with him once the contract is signed, we forfeit. Do we have an agreement?"

"Forfeit how?"

"We accept defeat according to the terms."

Nostrils flaring and jaw tight, Lucifer stared at her, hovering on the edge of decision. "And us?" he asked at last. "What of us?"

The One hesitated. She had anticipated this question and agonized over it for days before coming up with a response that would satisfy Lucifer without being a lie. Vague as the words were, however, they still proved difficult to utter. She straightened, finding resolve in the certainty that she did what was right. That it was the only way.

Without meeting his eyes, she recited the words she had rehearsed. "One way or the other, my mortal children will no longer stand in our way."

"That's not much of an answer."

"It is the best I can give. A great deal of betrayal has passed between us."

"Betrayal on both sides." Bitterness edged Lucifer's words.

The One inclined her head, acknowledging his perspective without commenting on its truth—or lack thereof.

Lucifer's jaw hardened. "What is to stop me from breaking the pact now and triggering this agreement you propose? If the decision will be that final, perhaps we should just get it over with."

"We could. But with an equal chance that Seth might take my path, are you willing to take the risk before you must? I don't propose this as an alternative, Lucifer, but as a last possible resort."

He stared at her for a long moment without speaking. Then, suddenly, hostility fell away to reveal raw agony shining from his eyes. "Is there any hope?" he asked. "Can you ever love me again?"

The One stared at him, her most beautiful of all creations, wrought from desire and longing and her own infinite capacity for love. She had not laid eyes on him since his departure from Heaven more than a thousand years before, had refused even to call his image to mind, and so allowed herself a moment now to study him. To remember all he had been . . . see all he still was.

He stood before her, tall and fair, his eyes the pure, crystalline color of amethyst, his magnificent wings pulsing with a glow that had faded only slightly in the years apart from her. The One's heart contracted in a spasm of pain a hundred thousand times greater than his would ever be. *Could* ever be. Even now, even after all he had done, all he had become, it seemed light itself originated within him.

Lucifer, her Light-Bearer, stared back at her, waiting.

She answered with the truth. "I never stopped."

The hope she needed to inspire within him sparked in his eyes at last. He held her gaze a moment longer, then crossed the room to the desk. Pulling the parchment toward him, he plucked a feather from his wing, dipped it into an inkpot, and signed his name. The scratch of quill tip against paper was loud in the silence that had fallen. He held the feather out to her.

"We have an agreement," he said.

With all her heart, she wanted to believe him.

ONE

"Yo, Jarvis!"

Alexandra Jarvis lifted her forehead from the hand supporting it and peered over the jumble of files strewn across her desk. Raymond Joly stood in the entrance to the elevator hallway.

"You got company." The other detective jabbed his thumb at the woman beside him before strolling away, coffee cup in hand.

Even before Alex's gaze settled on her sister, she remembered. After three weeks of hedging, she'd finally given in and promised to meet Jen for an early lunch—she shot a look at the clock above Jen's head and winced—half an hour ago. Great. The entire morning had dragged by in thirty-second increments, and still she'd managed to lose track of time, giving her older sibling yet one more lecture topic.

Heaving a sigh, she climbed to her feet and grimaced at the stiffness of a body unaccustomed to week after week of desk duty. Three files slid off the pile, heading for the floor. Alex grabbed, missed, and with another sigh, stooped to retrieve the waterfall of paper.

Her sister arrived desk-side as she dropped the wayward files on top of the others.

"I think you're losing."

"I think I lost before I even started," Alex replied. This lunch date was a bad idea. She and Jen had so little to say to one another these days, with both of them skirting the issue of what had happened. What might have happened. What Alex knew to be true and Jen preferred not to know at all.

Jen waved at the files. "What do they have you doing?"

"Cold cases. Making calls to see if anything new has turned up. Some of these go back thirty years. You can imagine my success rate so far." Alex grimaced. She paused, then added, "And you can see how far behind I am."

"Are you trying to get out of lunch, by any chance?"

"I wouldn't if I didn't have so much—" Meeting her sister's brown eyes, she stopped. She couldn't lie. Not to Jen. Not after what she'd put her sister through. And her niece. She swallowed. "I just don't want to get into anything with you, that's all."

Jen lifted her chin. "And I don't want to start anything, but you have to know I'm worried about you, Alex." She crossed her arms and looked away, biting at her lip. "You haven't been over to the house, you never call Nina . . ."

"I'm sorry, I've just been so busy with the insurance and the repairs and—" Again the lies stuck in Alex's throat. Aware of far too many ears in the vicinity, she jerked her head toward the conference room. "Let's go somewhere quieter."

She led the way into the windowed room, closing the door behind them. Pasting a smile onto her face, she turned to Jen. "So how is Nina, anyway?"

"You could call her yourself and ask."

"Jen."

Her sister sighed. "She's okay. We found a great therapist and Nina seems to like her. She still won't sleep alone, but the nightmares aren't as frequent."

"That's good. I'm glad."

It *was* good—and nothing short of miraculous, given that Nina had witnessed the mass murder of twenty-one people, seen a Fallen Angel in his demonic form, and very nearly been driven to suicide by the experience. A shudder rippled through Alex at the stir of memories. She crossed her arms over herself and perched on the edge of the conference table. *Not going there, Jarvis. Not now. Not with Jen watching.*

"The real question is how are *you*?" Jen asked. Her gaze moved to the scar at Alex's throat, then dropped to the three additional ridges slashed across her chest.

Alex tightened her arms against the urge to pull her blouse closed over the remains of the gashes that had so nearly ended her life. "Surviving."

"Are you still seeing the department psychiatrist?"

"Not by choice"—Alex grimaced—"but yes. It's force policy. Roberts tried to pull some strings, but he didn't get far."

Her staff inspector had been amazing, in fact, doing everything he could to have the usual post-traumatic-event evaluation waived for her. Roberts might not know exactly what had happened in Alex's house the night she'd almost died, but the careful way he didn't ask too much told Alex that he had his suspicions. And that, like Jen, he would rather *not* know about the reality of Heaven and Hell, or angels and demons, or the impending war between them. A war almost certain to wipe out humanity.

"Is it helping?" Jen asked. "Have you told him what happened?"

Alex snorted at the idea of confiding in the pompous, irritating Dr. Bell. He'd restricted her to desk duty based on what little he *did* know. If she told him just a fraction of what she carried around in her head these days, he'd slap her into a psych ward and throw away the key.

Well, you see, Doc, it turns out my soulmate is an angel and he's been cast out of Heaven because he fell in love with me and killed his twin brother. That was the demon who tried to do me in, by the way, and the whole mess may well have triggered the Apocalypse, and . . .

Oh, yeah. She could just imagine how fast the department shrink would draw up those commitment papers. Alex squeezed her eyelids shut against the ache in her right temple, a dull throb that never quite went away. Another leftover from her near-fatal confrontation with Aramael's twin.

Opening her eyes, she met her sister's frown. "Bell isn't the confiding type."

"Then ask for someone else. You need to talk to someone, Alex. I wish it could be me, but—" Jen broke off and looked away, her lips tight and her eyes suspiciously shiny.

"Hey." Alex reached out and clasped her sister's shoulders. "Would you stop? You have enough to worry about with Nina. I'm a big girl. Let me deal with my own issues, will you?"

"But that's the problem, isn't it? You're *not* dealing with them. You're pretending they're not there."

Alex let her arms drop and curled her fingers over the edge of the table on either side of her. Knuckles aching, she stared at the light switch on the wall.

"If you can't work with this Dr. Bell," Jen continued, "ask him to refer you. Or let me give you some names. You need to keep looking until you find someone you're comfortable with. Someone who can help."

Alex almost laughed at the idea any human being could help her deal with the kind of evil she had faced, the kind of evil that might be unleashed on the world. Except it wasn't funny, and it wasn't going to happen. She didn't care what Jen or Bell or anyone said. Even if she *could* talk about the secrets she had come to know, she wouldn't. Because when it came right down to it, she didn't want to relive it. Didn't want to think about it. Not any of it.

Not about Aramael, lost to her forever; not about Caim or a broken pact between Heaven and Hell; not about Heaven's contingency plan or the Apocalypse waiting for humanity if that plan failed.

She slid off the table. "Look, Jen, I know you want to help, and I appreciate it. Really I do. But as much as *you* don't want to talk about it, neither do I. Can we please just leave it at that?"

Jen stalked the length of the conference room. "No, Alex, we can't just leave it at that, because you can't continue like *this*. You're stretched so thin right now I'm afraid you'll fly apart if someone sneezes too close. And I can't help!"

"Is that what's bugging you? That you can't fix me again?"

"I never fixed you in the first place," Jen muttered.

"Because it was never your responsibility. What Mom did—what Mom was—" Alex swallowed and pressed on. "What happened was horrific, Jen, but it's over. Done. We both survived. It's time to stop trying to compensate for something that happened twenty-three years ago and wasn't your fault to begin with."

A tear slid down Jennifer's cheek.

Alex sighed. She went to Jen and hugged her, crossed arms and all. "You're not responsible," she said softly.

"I know. I just don't know what I'll do if you—I can't lose you, Alex."

Alex leaned her forehead against her sister's. "You won't lose me. I'm not Mom and I'm not that easy to get rid of."

Jen sniffed. "Promise?"

Perhaps some lies weren't all bad.

"Promise. Now I really do have to get back to work before I lose my desk under the mess. How about I come by for dinner on Saturday? I'll bring a movie and ice cream."

LEVERING HIMSELF OFF the filthy pavement, Aramael swiped the back of his hand across his bottom lip and spat out a mouthful of blood. He forced his spine straight against a spark of pain and glared at the Fallen One perched on the fire escape above him. He really needed to stop taking back-alley shortcuts.

His attacker grinned back. "I didn't believe it when they told me you were here," he said. "Thought I'd see for my-self."

Aramael spat again. A weapon would be nice right now—something to compensate for the things he could no longer do—but he didn't dare look away from his enemy long enough to find one. Even without using their supernatural powers, Fallen Ones moved way faster than he did in his new reality. They hit harder, too.

"You've seen," he retorted. "Now you can go."

The Fallen One uncoiled, stretched, and dropped lightly to the ground beside him. He linked his fingers and cracked his knuckles. "I don't think so, Power. Your kind has caused a great deal of suffering among us. It seems only fair one of you should pay for some of it."

Aramael scowled at the leather-clad figure. Bloody Hell, he was getting tired of this. The discovery of his presence had been inevitable, of course; he'd known he would become a target at some point. One of their nemeses, stripped of his angelic powers and cast from Heaven—what Fallen One wouldn't want a shot at that? But word had spread, the attacks came with increasing frequency, and Aramael's plans disintegrated further with each.

His path had seemed so clear at first. Find Alexandra Jarvis, the soulmate from whom Mittron had taken such care to separate him, and rekindle the connection between them. If Mittron were right about Alex once inspiring Aramael to abilities beyond what he should have had, perhaps she might do so again. Perhaps he might, through her, stretch beyond his current capacity and find a way to stop Mittron. To stop Armageddon.

With the Fallen Ones dogging his every step, however, it would take him an entire mortal lifetime just to reach Alex—and by then, with his memory of her fading a little more with each rise and fall of the sun, there might be nothing left to salvage. Nothing he could do.

He eyed his present tormentor, now circling just out of arm's reach. Despite what the Fallen One may have heard about Aramael's vulnerability, thousands of years of caution apparently died hard. Aramael was, after all, one of the select few angels capable of imprisoning Fallen Ones in Limbo. Or *had* been one of those angels until Mittron orchestrated his downfall.

Now, however, he was wingless, powerless, reduced to the same physical strength as a mortal, and sentenced to an eternity of having the crap kicked out of him by his former prey. And, worse, to watching from the sidelines as Heaven and Hell went to war.

Gritting his teeth, he rolled his shoulders to ease the tension building in them. It wasn't in his nature to lie down and play dead, so he'd fight back as best he could. He might even land a few hits of his own. But if the three previous encounters were anything to go by, he didn't expect to remain standing for long.

The Fallen One stepped in with a jab; Aramael blocked him and struck a glancing blow on his shoulder—a blow that, even to him, felt feeble. The Fallen One smirked.

A feral cat, scrounging through a pile of garbage, slunk out of sight behind a row of battered cans. Aramael braced himself. His enemy could take him down in a heartbeat, but it wouldn't happen that way. There would be pain involved first. A lot of pain.

The Fallen One's knuckles connected with his cheekbone and a starburst exploded behind his eyes. Reeling back, he staggered and shook his head, trying to locate his aggressor through flashes of light. Another hit, this one to the gut. He grunted and doubled over, staying on his feet through sheer willpower. He would *not* fall this easily. A fist drove into his kidney and agony sheared through him, obliterating his resolve. His lungs sucked for air as all sense of his enemy's whereabouts disappeared. Dropping to his hands and knees, he waited for the next blows. They came quickly. Kicks, now, from which no amount of curling up could protect him.

Lying in the alley's grunge, he endured the punishment. Grimly, resolutely, and with growing bitterness. He might not be able to stop Mittron, but if it took him the rest of his existence, the Highest Seraph would somehow answer for this. For the pain and humiliation; for the loss of what Armael had so briefly found with Alexandra Jarvis; for the treason that had brought it all to bear.

A booted foot crashed into Aramael's skull, sending a

wash of red across his vision. Awareness receded down a darkening tunnel. Sound faded. Sensation died away.

Deep inside, the life spark of the weakened vessel he had become snuffed out yet again.

TWO

This was it.

Time to decide.

Seth leaned his forehead against the cool oak door of the office of Heaven's executive administrator. The Highest Seraph didn't expect him until tomorrow. He could still leave and no one would ever know he'd been here. What he considered doing. He clenched his fist. Felt the same clench in his gut. One way or the other, he had to decide; if he was going to do this, he had to do it now.

The quiet confidence of his mother's words came back to him. *You will do everything you must, my son. I have never doubted that.* He'd been so certain she was right. His love for her had overwhelmed him—as had the desire to fulfill his destiny.

And then he thought about *her*.

Alexandra Jarvis. The name surged upward in his mind, dragging with it the dark morass he'd been avoiding for days. The doubts. The desires. Seth's palms went damp and sweat beaded on his forehead. Doubts and desires so new to him, so foreign, that he had kept them carefully tucked away as the time of his transition crept ever closer, afraid to examine them for fear he might be tempted to do the very thing that brought him to Mittron's door now.

He thought back to when he'd stood in Alex's living room, witness to her pain at losing her soulmate. He remembered how he'd wanted to reach out and comfort her. To hold her. To know her as Aramael had, only better.

If he followed the path set for him by his parents, he would never have that chance. Never even see her again unless . . .

Unless.

His fist tightened on the roll of papers he held. Two sheets of parchment: one in the handwriting and language of a Principality—a list of dates and events that would condemn the Highest Seraph to eternal Limbo; the other a note in his own handwriting that would absolve Mittron from responsibility. *If* he complied with Seth's request. Given the evidence against him, Mittron would almost certainly see the benefit of the latter.

Which brought Seth back to his own choice, within his grasp but still unmade.

Lifting his head, he stared at the dark oak grain of the door. The responsibility that had been his from infancy sat like a mantle of lead across his shoulders. If he walked away, he would give up everything. His parentage, his immortality, his destiny, his power . . .

Everything but a handful of years with a mortal woman soulmated to another, yet irrevocably his.

Desire uncoiled in his belly. Ever since Alex's hand had first closed over his arm in a silent plea for help, ever since that first, undeniable frisson of awareness had flared between them, he had been consumed by her. Had known that, ultimately, she belonged to him. Known it, fought it, and now . . .

Now he would forfeit his destiny to prove it.

Separating the papers, Seth rolled each individually and tucked them inside his sleeves.

Accusation in one, absolution in the other.

He raised his hand and knocked at Mittron's door.

THE GREENHOUSE DOOR opened and the One looked up from tamping the soil around the roots of a newly transplanted geranium. "Verchiel. Thank you for coming."

The Dominion inclined her head, tucking her hands into the folds of her robe. "I was already on my way when Kaziel gave me your message. I thought you might want an update."

"You read my mind." Setting the pot aside, the One brushed soil from her fingertips. "And? Is everything ready?"

"It is. The transition will take place as scheduled tomorrow." Verchiel's voice trailed off into hesitance.

"But?" The One raised an eyebrow.

Verchiel shook her head. "It's nothing, One. It really isn't my place—"

"Look at me."

Pale blue eyes met hers in response to the command, misery shadowing their depths, underscored by doubt. The One shook her head and sighed.

"You think too much, Dominion."

"I know. But Mittron, One? I know we have no proof, but—"

"And do we not have faith, either?"

Verchiel whitened, and the One curled hands into fists where they rested on the potting bench. For a breath of an instant, she thought about telling the Dominion what she knew, what she planned, what she had no choice but to do. The depth of her aloneness sat like a vast, infinite pit at her center, and suddenly—desperately—she wanted to share her burden with another. To admit she was undeserving of the faith she demanded; that she sensed an indecision in her own son that jeopardized her agreement with Lucifer and the very existence of humanity. That she had failed yet again to see what was before her, and would now forfeit her own son's life in a desperate attempt to remedy that failure.

For a breath of an instant, she wanted to confess all that and more, and then, because she was the One, she made herself voice a reassurance she did not feel. "Everything has a purpose, Verchiel. A reason."

"Even what Mittron has done? What he might still do?"

"Even that."

Verchiel stood by her for another moment, her doubt so loud in the silence it needed no voice. Then, without a word, the Dominion reached out and covered the One's fisted hand with her own, squeezed gently, and departed.

"YOU'VE LOST YOUR mind." Mittron stared at the Appointed.

Seth halted his pacing by the window and scowled back at him. "Just answer the question. Can you do it or not?"

"It isn't a question of ability. I simply won't go against the One's wishes like that."

"Oh, spare me." Seth gave a short, humorless bark of laughter. "We both know you're way past caring about the One's wishes, Seraph. You started this whole mess, remember? Don't insult my intelligence."

Mittron's breath snagged in his throat. He didn't pretend not to understand the Appointed, but neither did he intend to admit anything. For three weeks, he had lived with the razor-edged threat of discovery hanging over him, wondering how much Seth had figured out, how much he might have taken to his mother. Only when there had been no repercussions had he begun to relax, but never to the point of his original careless arrogance.

He wasn't interested in returning to that state of crippling anxiety again.

No matter how intriguing he found Seth's request.

Or how much he would like to see his own plans resurrected.

He shook his head. "Be that as it may, I am not entirely without instinct for self-preservation. Verchiel has only just stopped dogging my every step. I dare not—" he halted as

Seth tugged at the sleeve of his black tunic and produced a rolled paper. A very old paper.

Suddenly, vividly, Mittron remembered where he had last seen the Appointed. Seated in the Archives, surrounded by the records through which he searched. Had Seth found something? A shiver slid through Mittron's chest. Impossible. He had gone through every single file in the archive himself; had made sure there was nothing *to* find. The Appointed was bluffing.

But Seth's casual stroll across the room said otherwise.

The yellowed parchment dropped from Seth's hand onto the desk. A film of perspiration cooled Mittron's forehead. He swallowed.

"It's all there," the Appointed said. His words were as harsh as they were precise, the syllables dropping like gravel onto metal, one chunk of granite at a time. "Your deceit. Your manipulations. Bethiel recorded everything."

Mittron reached with trembling fingers to pick up the paper. Spidery handwriting peeked out from the top edge. The air hissed from his lungs.

It couldn't be. He'd been so careful. So certain.

"I know how you failed to cleanse Aramael properly," Seth continued. "How you plotted for him to know his soul-mate when he met her, how you arranged for a Nephilim descendant to be that soulmate. I know all of it."

Mittron's tongue darted out to moisten desert-dry lips. Outside the office door, footsteps and voices approached. He waited until they receded, fading into silence, and then, hands less than steady, unrolled the parchment.

The words of his long-gone accuser leapt off the page. The facts with which the Principality Bethiel had once confronted him, proving accurate all that Seth had said. Laying the groundwork for connections to be made, conclusions to be drawn, Mittron's treachery to be known.

He half dropped, half flung the roll across the desk and laced his fingers in his lap, squeezing until his knuckles protested.

"Where did you find it?"

It. Such a tiny word for something so monumental.

"Among Bethiel's personal effects. The ones put into storage after his exile to Limbo."

So the Appointed knew about that, too.

Seth settled onto a corner of the desk. "Tell me, how many others have there been, *Highest*? How many angels have you sacrificed in the name of your grand scheme? I know of Aramael, of course, and now Bethiel, but how many more? Two? Four? A dozen?"

"It was a long time ago," Mittron said, despising the tremor in his voice. Detesting the arrogance of the being who triggered it. "It means nothing."

"Doesn't it?" The Appointed reached out and set the roll spinning. "I think you're wrong. I think it might be considered evidence of treason. Especially when one considers the fortuitousness of Caim's escape from Limbo. The only escape to ever occur and it just happened to be a Fallen One exiled because of his propensity for murder, who just happened to be the twin brother of the Power *you* sent to hunt him. In the city where that Power's soulmate—a soulmate you engineered—just happened to work as a homicide detective." Seth *tsk*ed softly. "That's an awful lot of coincidence, don't you think?"

The scroll revolved lazily on the desktop. Slowed. Stopped.

"I don't know why you did it," Seth continued, "and personally, I don't care. But she will. All she has to do is look into your soul, and she will know everything. And when she sees what is in here—"

Mittron jumped as a hand reached down to flick the parchment roll toward him. He swallowed. "What do you want?"

"I told you what I want."

Pushing back from the desk, Mittron rose and went to stare out the window Seth had vacated. He needed time to think, to figure out what lay behind the Appointed's request. Was it a test of loyalty? Had Seth already showed the One the evidence, and now she placed temptation in his path to see what he might do? For an instant, blind panic obliterated coherence. Then reason asserted itself. No, if the One knew what was in that parchment, Mittron would not be having this conversation with Seth—would never converse with another soul again.

Which meant Seth was serious. He wanted to defy the One's wishes. Mittron's heart rate quickened. Despite his earlier intentions, he wavered. If he agreed to the Appointed's proposal, Seth would become a willing participant in plans he had thought abandoned. Plans that might be resurrected, that might unleash all kinds of new potential.

But even if he wanted to do what Seth asked, *could* he?

Removing the Appointed's powers, taking his immortality . . . it would require enormous energy and skill well beyond the normal purview of Heaven's executive administrator. He would have to tap into Heaven itself, working fast enough to complete the transition before anyone realized what he did. The risks were enormous.

So were the possibilities.

A thrill of excitement whispered through him. If he managed to pull it off, if he *did* transition Seth to true mortality, it would change everything. The agreement between Lucifer and the One would be null and void, and things might yet play out the way he had planned, might yet bear the fruit he had desired for so many years.

"An adult," he said.

"Yes."

"Fully mortal. Without power."

"Are you capable?"

Mittron looked over his shoulder. "I'm capable. If you're certain."

"Then we have an understanding."

"I'll require a letter claiming the responsibility as your own."

Seth withdrew a second parchment from a sleeve and set it on the desk beside the other.

Mittron stared at it. "And Bethiel's notes?" he asked. "They remain unrevealed?"

In response, the first paper's edges curled, blackened, and caught fire. The evidence of Mittron's transgressions drifted away in the breeze from the open window.

"For eternity," the Appointed agreed. "Shall we get started?"

Brushing a bit of lint from his robes and lingering doubt from his mind, Mittron returned to the desk. He tucked Seth's letter into a bookshelf. "I'm ready when you are."

The Appointed nodded and then frowned. "Before we begin, I'm curious about something. When you tried to stop me from searching the Archives, you spoke about secrets. About something being kept from me."

Mittron went still. *Emmanuelle.* "I remember."

"Is it something I need to know before I do this?"

Mittron eyed the One's son. Would knowing he wasn't an only child change the Appointed's mind about what he'd decided to do? Chances were good that Seth might simply acknowledge the information and then carry on with his plans. But there was also a possibility his conscience would kick in, sending him in search of his own replacement and perpetuating this Heavenly farce the One insisted on playing out. Mittron made himself smile. "No," he said. "It's nothing."

Seth wavered for a moment. Mittron saw the brief internal struggle he waged with himself, the hesitation—and then the dark head dipped once in agreement. The One's son had accepted his words.

He had made his choice.

THREE

"Well?"

Dr. Elizabeth Riley looked up from her notes and ran a sharp gaze over the man on the other side of the counter at the nurses' station. Weariness lined his face and, while he had shaved and his shirt looked clean and pressed, she recognized the rumpled suit from the day before.

"You didn't go home," she accused, ignoring his question.

Detective Hugh Henderson shrugged. "It's been a busy week."

"You need to sleep."

Hugh sighed. "For your information, *Mom*, I got four hours on the cot in the back office." He jerked his head toward the corridor. "How is she?"

Elizabeth pursed her lips. "She's a mess, is how she is. Which is what you'll be if you don't go home soon."

A heavy gray brow lifted. "Is that your professional shrink opinion? About her, not me."

She favored him with a glare and then peered through her glasses at the chart, scanning the neat, precise handwriting that made her a favorite among nurses: Melanie Chiu, age twenty-two, in the mid- to late stage of pregnancy despite her claim she had been a virgin until two weeks before. Suffering from an obvious psychotic break, unable or unwilling to detail actual sexual history.

"She's complaining of abdominal and pelvic pain, but they're still waiting for an ultrasound," she told Hugh. "Based on the initial exam, they estimate she's between five and six months along. There's obviously been a severe emotional trauma, but until she's more coherent, I can't tell you what it was. I've sedated her for the moment, and I'm hoping she'll be calmer when she wakes."

Rubbing a hand over his short-cropped, graying head, Hugh sighed. "So we really have no idea whether she was raped or not."

"Not yet. It would appear you were called prematurely."

Hugh's brow furled. "Don't go shitting on ER over this, Liz. They were only doing their job. Someone even breathes the possibility and they have no choice but to notify us."

Elizabeth closed Melanie Chiu's chart with a snap. "I wish you wouldn't call me that."

"So you keep telling me."

"Then why do it?"

He grinned. "Keeps you humble, Dr. Riley." Nodding at the chart on the counter, he added, "So now what?"

"Now we wait. I've left instructions to be called when she wakes. As soon as I have anything, I'll let you know."

"That works. You heading to the cabin tomorrow?"

"I'll see how Melanie is doing first, but probably."

"Well, the weather is supposed to be fantastic, so you should go if you can. No telling how many more nice weekends we'll get." Hugh ambled in the direction of the elevators, wiggling fingers over shoulder. "Talk to you tomorrow, *Liz*."

WAS IT SUPPOSED to hurt this much?

Or had Mittron gone back on his word?

Seth curled into a ball against the force crushing in on him, squeezing until he couldn't breathe, couldn't move, couldn't even blink. Fighting to detach from the pain, he gritted his teeth and swallowed against the nausea, then arched back as a sudden, sharper agony tore through him like a thousand unseen claws shredding body and mind.

It subsided an eternity later, leaving him drifting, hovering at the edge of consciousness, pulsing with aftershock. Remnants of pain jangled along his nerves until, little by little, they subsided and he could reach again for his thoughts, collect them, hold them steady where he could focus on them. Focus on what lay ahead. Mortal life. Alexandra. An end to his part in the struggle between Heaven and Hell.

If he survived.

Another spasm twisted through his belly and Seth curled into himself once more, jaw clenched. Had he been wrong to trust Mittron? The Seraph had appeared willing enough, but maybe Seth had underestimated him. Maybe Mittron's willingness had hidden his intention to rid himself of a potential problem once and for all. Maybe—

A new agony sliced through him, white-hot, swelling to fill his entire being, deftly excising bits of consciousness, threatening sanity itself. Seth struggled against it, fighting to hold the memory of Alex, to retain his vanishing sense of self. Deep in his mind, fear sparked. Something was seriously wrong. What if this wasn't Mittron's doing? What if the One had discovered her son's betrayal? What if she intervened?

Before Seth could register the consequences inherent in the possibility, agony exploded through his every atom, erasing lucidity in a brutal decimation of all that he was. His life code, his soul, his consciousness, all disappeared into a vortex that swallowed him, rearranged him to fit its immensity, made him one with it . . .

And then spat him out into nothingness.

THE ONE FELT the shock of her son's absence like a sudden, vast emptiness. One second he was there, in her consciousness where he had been from the moment of his conception, and then, simply, he was not. She drew a breath, startled at the change in the state of her own being. The unexpected shift.

Then she shook her head at her own naïveté. After all these millennia, after all that had passed, the most surprising thing about this entire mess was that she could still be surprised.

Setting down the pot of soil, she went to wash her hands. So. Seth was gone, dead at the hands of an angel she had known would kill him. An angel she had *allowed* to kill him. She found little comfort in the fact she hadn't actually condoned Mittron's actions, had only permitted the unfolding of the free will he had never given up. Because however she looked at it, she'd known, and the decision to end Seth's life belonged to no one but her.

A tiny whisper of doubt threaded through her. She closed her eyes, gripping the edge of the sink.

What if I was wrong?

When she had looked into Seth's soul and seen the potential for betrayal written there, the weakness, what if she had overreacted? Perhaps she had been too quick to judge what she considered a fatal flaw, an unacceptable threat to her agreement with Lucifer. And even if she had been right, even if she had prevented outright annihilation of the human race, this—what she had triggered in its place—would be nearly as bad.

War between Heaven and Hell. Between her beloved angels and their fallen kin. War that Lucifer would ensure was fought on mortal soil, taking out as much of humanity as he could in the process. Her fingers curled over the cool porcelain. *So many lives . . . so much grief . . . and all because I couldn't trust my own son.*

Flicking water from her hands, the One reached for a towel hanging by the sink. Her lips drew as tight as the band around her heart. She had either set the universe on the only possible path to be taken, or she had just made another in a line of monumental errors. Either way, it was too late now to change her mind.

Either way, she would still mourn the first life to be lost in this new conflict—that of her own child.

MITTRON STARED AT the space Seth had occupied, and then at his hands. Hands that should have held the pulsing, living energy of the Appointed's immortal power but were instead empty—stunningly, impossibly empty. He'd expected it to be difficult, but he'd been confident he could do as Seth asked. Certain. What in Heaven's name had gone wrong?

He raised his gaze to the Dominion who stood in the doorway. Met the betrayal in her pale blue eyes. The horror.

"What have you done?"

He flinched from Verchiel's whisper, a sound more harsh than any shout could have been, and returned his gaze to his hands. They trembled now, and a sickness had begun to wind through his chest. Mittron swayed. He needed to sit down before he fell down. But he didn't have time. All of Heaven would have felt this. *They* would already be on their way. How long did he have? Minutes? Seconds?

"Mittron!"

Verchiel's voice cut across his thoughts, startling him and then sparking annoyance. Wiping clammy palms against his robe, Mittron met the accusation in the other angel's eyes. He held himself upright, defying the weakness spreading outward from his core. He was the Highest Seraph; he would not stumble before a Dominion.

He lifted his chin. "Don't look at me like that. It wasn't my fault."

"Not your—" Verchiel's mouth hung open.

Mittron tried to wave away the Dominion, but his hand lay against his robe as if disconnected from its owner. The tremor reached his belly and continued spreading, an odd weakness following in its wake. He swallowed. He needed to get out of here while he still could—his breath caught. Get out. Is that what he was going to do? What he wanted to do?

Did he have a choice?

Why won't my hands move?

"I did only what I was told to do," he said to Verchiel, focusing his entire being on moving just one finger.

Nothing.

"You were to transition the Appointed to infancy and place him among the mortals."

"That was what the One wanted. Not Seth."

"Seth—*Seth* asked you to destroy him? But why?"

"Not destroy. Transition as an adult. As a mortal. And I didn't ask."

Hadn't asked because it hadn't mattered. Not once he'd understood Seth's proposal and its implications: refuse and face exile; agree and the dominoes he'd set in place might still fall as planned. There might still be a chance the One would call on him to rule at her side in the final conflict.

It seemed so clear, so certain.

Then Seth's life force had slipped from Mittron's grasp and he hadn't been able to catch it back. All his carefully arranged dominoes had randomly, irretrievably scattered, and the accusation in Verchiel's eyes marked only the beginning of what he would face.

Stiffening, the Dominion looked over his shoulder. Mittron's gaze tried to follow, but he couldn't move his head. Was that them? Did she sense their approach? Why didn't he? He fought to calm himself, to assess his state of being. Shaky. Everything in him felt so shaky. Verchiel's gaze flicked back to him, softened with pity.

The air around Mittron stilled. Panic clutched at his throat. They were nearly here, and he couldn't make so much as his little finger twitch. The angel who had once been his soulmate crossed the room and placed a gentle hand beneath his chin, held him so he would meet her eyes.

"Tell me," she said. "Tell me now—everything—and I will speak to her. Perhaps I can spare you some of what you—" She looked past him and broke off, her face going white. Her head inclined in unhesitating supplication. Her hand dropped to her side.

Mittron heard the rustle of feathers and his bowel filled

with ice water. His heartbeat slowed until it was a bare thread of rhythm. *No.*

Verchiel's gaze met his again, horror behind her expression. Horror not for what he had done this time, but for what she knew was coming. What they all knew was coming. *No.*

"There's a letter!" his mind screamed, but the words remained locked inside him, unable to pass through lips now frozen into the same stillness as the rest of his body. The rustle of feathers grew louder, filling his head with a noise so great the rest of the universe faded into nothingness. Then, silence.

And a new female voice, devoid of expression, devoid of warmth. "Mittron of the Seraphim," the Archangel Gabriel said, "you have been called to Judgment."

Please, no . . .

FOUR

Elizabeth lifted her hand from the SUV's horn and waited as the forest's nighttime stillness swallowed the blast. Not a creature stirred in response.

Not even the naked man in her high beams.

Well. She exhaled, breath fogging in the chill air from the half-open driver's window. Well. She studied the figure sprawled across the porch of the cabin. Male, a good twenty years younger than she, well-developed musculature, unmoving, and bare as the day he was born.

Altogether as out of place here as a grizzly would be on her verandah in the city.

She tapped a finger against the leather wheel. Part of her wanted to go to him, to see if he was all right. He hadn't so much as twitched in the five or so minutes since she'd arrived, and while she couldn't see any sign of obvious injury, neither could she tell from here whether he even breathed. Another part of her, the consulting-police-psychiatrist side, urged extreme caution. She found it damned difficult to argue with almost thirty years of experience.

Tap, tap, tap. Cell phone service didn't exist up here, and while the landline that ran to the cabin might have survived the unpredicted storm, the stranger lay between her and it. Her only other option was to drive back down the mountain to the nearest pay phone, a good hour away. With the road partially washed out in places, help would take another hour to get up the mountain, then they'd have to drive back here . . . Hell, it would be at least three hours before anyone even put a blanket over the guy. If he hadn't already succumbed to hypothermia, he certainly would by the time she returned.

Brushing back a strand of hair that had come loose from its customary coil at her nape, Elizabeth went back to studying the form sprawled in front of the cabin door. Where in God's name had he come from? Hers was the only human habitat for miles, she'd seen no sign of another vehicle on her way in on the former logging road, and he certainly couldn't have walked far without clothes in this weather. Had someone dropped him in the area? Left him for dead?

She considered the possibilities. Drug related, maybe. Or the Russian mafia, so active in human trafficking along the coast. She grimaced and shook her head at herself. Caution was one thing, an overactive imagination quite another. Opening the door, she slid out from behind the wheel, leaving the headlights on.

The car's open-door reminder chimed behind her as she walked toward the cabin, feet squelching in the thick, wet carpet of evergreen needles. The forest damp crept through the gaps in her clothing and she shivered, wrapping her cardigan around her. The retreating storm grumbled in the distance.

Still the man didn't move.

She stopped at the bottom of the stairs and, balancing humanity with common sense, picked up a broom propped nearby. Hefting it, she reached out to poke the figure on the porch. Nothing. She prodded a second time, and then a third, with increasing vigor. The man's chest rose and fell in a steady rhythm, but he displayed no other sign of life.

So. Alive, but out cold and not an immediate danger.

Elizabeth went up the stairs, stepped across the prone form, unlocked the door, and switched on the porch light.

Then, taking a deep breath, she faced the problem of moving a large naked man into the cabin.

THE WORLD RETURNED in millisecond bits.

Cold.

Wet.

Something jabbing into him. A lightening of the darkness. Footsteps, silence, more footsteps. Hands running over his limbs, sliding under his shoulders, lifting him, tugging at him. Movement. Something soft beneath him. Warmth.

With great effort, he forced his eyelids open. Stared at the face looking down at him. Lines appeared above the eyes that stared back. A mouth opened and sounds issued forth. Unintelligible sounds.

Consciousness fractured again.

Faded.

Ended.

ELIZABETH DIDN'T KNOW how long she stared down at the man in her arms before her knees, pressed against the floor, began to protest. He'd opened his eyes so unexpectedly. Not a groan, not a murmur, not even a catch in his breath. Just those eyes. Blacker, deeper, and emptier than she'd ever seen. As if they opened onto a void rather than a person.

And then he'd been gone again. She'd spoken one sentence, a single reassurance, and then—nothing. A closing of eyelids as abrupt as their opening had been, and she once more faced the task of caring for an unconscious stranger.

She pushed herself to her feet and surveyed her guest in his makeshift bed on the floor, waiting for her breathing to return to normal. Morning runs and yoga aside, she was too old for this kind of exertion. She'd tried to get him into the actual bed, but when she'd nearly dropped him—twice—she'd resorted to building a pad out of blankets, rolling him onto it, and covering him with a spare duvet.

At least she'd managed to get him off her porch and out of the elements. She studied him, deciding her first age estimate had been relatively accurate. He looked to be in his early thirties, black hair, at least six two, and powerfully built. Even in his unconscious state, he had an aura of coiled strength about him that made her wonder what he would be like when awake.

A shiver of unease slipped down her spine. It wasn't something she cared to find out on her own. Reaching for the phone on the bedside table, she felt her heart calm a fraction at the sound of the reassuring dial tone. She punched in a number.

"Sex Crimes. Henderson," a gruff voice announced after the third ring.

"Hugh? It's Elizabeth. You're not going to believe what I found on my front porch."

"WELL, MITTRON OF the Seraphim, are you satisfied with what you have achieved?"

The One's words fell like small, hard pebbles into the silence that filled the Great Hall, sending ripples of movement through the gathering. Mittron swallowed, his throat tightening against any chance of responding.

Had the Creator's voice ever been this flat? This cold? He shivered as a thousand eyes bored into him with shock and accusation and dismay. Only the One did not look upon him, and he felt the absence of her gaze as he would his own heart.

A door opened at the side of the vaulted space and Verchiel rushed in. Skirting the assembled angels, she hurried to the One, who stood by one of the soaring windows, shunning—as she always did—the plain, high-backed wooden throne from which she had once ruled the universe. The seat unused since Lucifer had left his place at her side.

The One took a paper offered by the Dominion and Mittron's heart gave a tiny leap. Seth's confession. Verchiel had found it, and now the One would understand. She would know why he had done it; know it hadn't been he who betrayed her. His Creator scanned the letter. Not so much as a flicker of expression gave away her thoughts. His fingers grew numb from the bonds around his wrists.

The One handed the paper back to Verchiel. Mittron waited for her to look upon him, waited for her understanding to fill him. Her forgiveness to wash him clean. Instead, she closed her eyes and lifted her face toward the ceiling. Fresh panic trickled through him, stealing the oxygen from his lungs, the strength from his limbs. He locked his knees against their need to buckle. His brain screamed at him to say something, to defend himself, but his throat refused passage to the words churning within.

It was Seth's idea. He wanted this, chose it. It was he who abandoned you, just like his father. It wasn't me. I would never leave your side like they did. Never. I want only to remain with you, fight with you, rule with you as I should have from the beginning.

At last the One lowered her head and looked upon him. The sadness in her eyes cleaved his soul in two. He shook his head, denying the reflection of himself he saw here. The words in him descended into an endless babble.

I didn't betray you I didn't I love you too much better than Lucifer did better purer it wasn't my fault it wasn't—

"Mittron of the Seraphim, you stand accused of treason. Will you answer to the charges?"

Despair held him mute.

"Then you will kneel for Judgment."

He tried to shake his head, to resist, but an unseen force gathered around his shoulders, weighed him down, and felled him to his knees on the stone floor. The gathered audience inhaled as one, waiting.

And then he felt her.

The full, unadulterated power of his Creator, meshing with his very existence. Exposing his every thought, his every memory, his every covetous desire. Exposing, examining . . .

Judging.

Finding him wanting.

Agony wracked his heart and tears coursed down his face. *I didn't mean it I'm sorry I'm so sorry . . .*

The One's presence withdrew abruptly. Emptier than he'd ever imagined it possible to be, Mittron collapsed to the floor and curled into a ball as the One began to speak. He tried to shut her out, tried not to listen, but her words reverberated inside his skull. Inside his very core.

"I find you guilty of treason, Seraph. You have betrayed both Heaven and Earth, and you have condemned the entire mortal race to unbearable suffering. I therefore sentence you to witness the consequences of your actions. You will live among the mortals you have failed and feel the agony of each and every soul lost to the Fallen Ones as if that agony were your own. Your suffering will be cumulative, and will continue as long as Heaven and Hell battle for dominion." Her voice dropped to a whisper. "And, too, you will feel the pain your betrayal has caused *me*. Feel it, remember it, and never escape it."

FIVE

Dropping a paper onto the cafeteria table in front of Liz, Hugh lowered himself into the chair across from her. "I've handed the file over to Missing Persons," he said. "That's the detective who'll be handling it. I told him there was no point coming over here to interview Doe, and said you'd let him know if there's any change."

Liz glanced at the paper and then favored him with a jaundiced eye. "Could you not have found *any*one else to take it?"

"Daniels is a good cop."

"He's a pig."

"You know, for a shrink, you sure do have some issues," Hugh observed dryly.

She arched a brow high above her wire-framed glasses. "Because I prefer to converse with people who shower more than once a month and don't wear their breakfasts on their ties?"

"He's not that bad. You're just getting crotchety in your old age."

"And I still don't see why you can't just handle this your-self. It's not like it will take a lot of time to put out a bulletin."

Hugh heaved a sigh. "Because unless John Doe is a vic-tim of rape or a suspect in one, he's not my problem. And no, finding him naked doesn't count. Daniels will make sure his photo is released to the media today, and he's already sent out a Canada-wide bulletin. Now stop being so bloody difficult and tell me what's going on with Melanie Chiu."

Liz compressed her lips. "Nothing new beyond what I've already told you. She still maintains she was raped, but she can't give me any details."

"Can't, or won't?" Hugh reached across the table and helped himself to a carrot stick from Liz's plate.

"Can't. I'm certain she doesn't have any conscious mem-ory of what happened, although whatever it was has upset her deeply enough we have her on suicide watch."

Hugh chewed the carrot rhythmically, then swallowed. "And you still think she's six months along in the pregnancy?"

"The ultrasound confirmed it on Friday."

"Any chance I can interview her yet?"

"You're welcome to try, but don't expect much. She's still on the heaviest meds they can give her for the pain she's in. And no, they haven't figured out why she's in pain, and no, I don't think it's psychosomatic. At least, not entirely." Liz pushed the plate of vegetables toward him and rose. "I'll let Psych know to expect you."

"You're forgetting something." Hugh held up the paper he'd given her.

Liz ignored the note. "I'm not forgetting anything. If something changes with Doe, I'll call you and *you* let Dan-iels know."

Tucking Daniels's number into his shirt pocket, Hugh shook his head. "You don't give up easily, do you?"

"Job requirement." Patting his shoulder, Liz bestowed one of her rare smiles on him and then departed the cafete-ria, sandals slapping against her feet.

* * *

VERCHIEL FOUND THE One in the rose garden, seated beneath an arbor, eyes closed and hands folded in her lap. She hesitated near a crimson-leafed hedge, loath to disturb her Creator's moment of peace, but the One's voice stopped her when she would have left.

"You're not disturbing me, Verchiel. Come. Sit."

Settling onto the arbor seat beside the One, Verchiel cleared her throat softly. "I just wanted to see how you're doing."

The One's eyes remained closed, but her lips curved upward. "I'm fine, thank you. Or as fine as one might expect, given all that has happened recently. What about the others? How are they?"

"They are—shaken."

A tiny frown shadowed the One's brow.

"I'm sure they must be." Eyes as silver as the One's hair opened to meet Verchiel's. "And you? Are you shaken as well?"

Verchiel looked down to where her fingers twisted into her robes. "Yes. And worried."

"Again? Why am I not surprised?" The One settled back against the bench. "What worries you?"

"You, One."

Verchiel sensed the Creator's gaze but couldn't bring herself to raise her own to meet it any more than she could make herself breathe. She waited for the One's response.

"My decision to allow Mittron to transition my son."

"Yes. If you knew—"

"I didn't know," the One interrupted. "Not for certain. But I hoped."

Her eyes flashed up to meet her Creator's, and Verchiel's jaw went slack. The One had *hoped* her son would—? A chill seeped through her, at odds with the warmth of the day.

"I don't understand."

"Something in Seth had changed. There was a weakness in him—a doubt—that would have made him an unacceptable risk within the agreement. I couldn't allow him to continue, and I knew Mittron wanted him gone. I counted on it."

An eternity dragged by as Verchiel digested the information. Weighed what the One said against what had been left unsaid. The risk—if the One had been right about Seth—of human annihilation versus the certainty of war. "And if Mittron hadn't—?"

"Thankfully we need not go there."

Still struggling to accept her Creator's words, never mind all that lay behind them, Verchiel shook her head. "You judged him for something you might have prevented."

"I judged him for his actions," the One corrected, her face going hard. "Five thousand years ago, Mittron chose to retain his free will and begin a chain of events meant to once again bring war between me and Lucifer. He could have abandoned his plans at any time during those years. He did not."

"And Seth's letter? The fact he chose to abdicate his responsibility? That didn't mitigate Mittron's involvement?"

"It only proved I was right about my son's weakness."

Silence fell, broken only by the hum of hundreds of bees gathering pollen from the flowers in the arbor above them.

At last Verchiel looked back to her Creator. "And now?" she asked. "What now?"

The One sighed and rose to her feet, brushing rose petals and yellow pollen dust from her robes. "Now we prepare for war, Verchiel, and we wait for Lucifer to strike the first blow."

ALEX THREADED HER way across the office to Roberts's door. Tapping on the frame, she held up the note she'd found on her desk when she'd arrived for yet another day of *not* being permitted to do her job. "You summoned?"

He waved her in, not looking up from the paper in his hands. "Close the door."

Alex's heart gave a little kick. Hell. Was that a report from Bell? Their session this morning hadn't gone at all well, ending with the shrink throwing her out of his office and telling her not to come back until she was ready to admit her issues—and to forget about returning to active duty until then. She eyed the paper Roberts held, wondering how bad it would be. Suspecting she hadn't helped matters by telling Bell to go fuck himself.

She closed the door and leaned back against it. "If this is about Dr. Bell, I can explain."

Roberts waved her to silence. "It's not about Bell unless that sentence is going where I think it is, in which case I'd rather not know." He laid the paper facedown on the desk and folded his hands across it. "Sit."

Alex sat.

Her supervisor cleared his throat and stared down at his hands. "We haven't talked much since you came back to work."

"We haven't had much reason. The files you gave me don't exactly require me to seek a lot of direction."

Roberts ignored the jab. "I don't mean about work. I mean about what happened."

Alex went still. "I didn't realize there was anything to talk about."

"There's a lot to talk about, Detective. There just didn't seem to be a way—or a reason—to bring it up."

"And that's changed how?"

Roberts picked up the paper and held it out to her. She hesitated, then took it and flipped it faceup. The air in her throat turned solid and the world faded to a buzzing in her ears.

It couldn't be.

Alex stared at the photo in the center of the page. At the black, shoulder-length hair, the strong, stubborn chin—and those eyes. Those black, seemingly bottomless eyes. They were what convinced her, because she could never mistake them. Never forget them.

It couldn't be him, but it was.

Seth Benjamin.

Aramael's fellow angel.

Her savior.

Alex raised her gaze to the letterhead at the top of the paper and the words emblazoned in bold above the photo: *Do you know this man?*

She knew him all right. But what the hell was Heaven's contingency plan doing in Vancouver police custody? She scanned the print at the bottom of the page. And how the hell had he ended up with amnesia?

"It is him, then," Roberts said quietly.

Placing the bulletin on the desk between them, Alex sat back. "Yes." Her voice came out as a bare whisper and she cleared the shock from her throat. "Yes," she said again, stronger this time. "It's him."

"You never introduced us."

"You never asked." She hadn't even been sure Roberts had noticed the angel's presence, either at the church murder scene or at the hospital after Nina's attempted suicide. Her supervisor had never mentioned Seth, and neither had she— part of their unspoken agreement not to talk about the surreal elements of that day.

Roberts grunted and sat back in his chair, leaning against one of the armrests. "I don't think I wanted to know then," he said, confirming her suspicions.

"And now?"

"You tell me."

"Staff, *I* don't want to know."

Her supervisor passed a hand over his face, palm rasping against stubble to create the only sound between them while he weighed her words. "Can you at least tell me what this is about?" he asked at last, gesturing at the poster. "Why he's there?"

"He's supposed to stop a war."

Roberts snapped upright. "Gangs?"

"Not on the scale you mean."

Frustration etched between his brows, her supervisor slumped even lower in his chair than he'd been before. "Damn it, Alex, I'm having a hard time wrapping my head around what's going on. None of what happened—nothing about that fucking serial case was normal. Hell, it wasn't *natural.* But the alternative—" He broke off and waved his hand again at the paper. "And now that. What the fuck am I supposed to do with that? I can't very well call Vancouver and tell them I've seen the guy. I'd have to say where, and when, and under what circumstances . . . They'd think I was out of my tree."

She rubbed an aching temple and muttered, "Trust me, I know the feeling."

"But we're not."

More question than statement. Dr. Bell would get a real thrill from this exchange.

"No. We're not crazy."

Not that she didn't consider the idea a viable alternative. Even taking into account her family history, insanity made more sense than reality seemed to these days.

Roberts nodded. "I didn't think so. But I still can't call Vancouver."

"No."

"And I can't send you out there. Not officially."

Sensing more to come, she waited. Roberts reached out and snagged a form sitting on the corner of the desk. He slid it toward her so it covered Seth Benjamin's photo. Her name was at the top and Roberts's familiar, scrawled signature at the bottom. She raised her gaze to his.

"A leave of absence?"

"Two weeks paid. If you want more time, pull vacation. And, Alex—if you need help, call. I'll do what I can."

SIX

Hugh Henderson stared at Katherine Gray, digesting her bizarre story. The young woman seated across the interview table from him didn't *seem* hysterical. Seemed cool as a cucumber, in fact. But her story? Fucking nuts. He swallowed a sigh. It was just his luck to be the one to catch this. Served him right for working so much overtime lately and being the only one here.

Still, if she wanted to lay a complaint, his job required he take it. Regardless of his personal opinion. "All right," he said. "Why don't we start from the top? Do you mind if I record this? I want to make sure I get it right, because it's kind of—"

"Crazy?" Gray suggested. "Believe me, I know."

"Out of the ordinary," Hugh supplied instead, and the young woman rewarded him with a tiny smile. Her first since entering the Sex Crimes office twenty minutes earlier.

"I don't mind," she said, responding to his question about the recording.

Hugh reached for the digital recorder that never left the

room. He checked to make sure it was plugged in, and then pushed the record button and pulled a pad of paper toward him. "Right. Let's start with your name and occupation."

"Katherine Gray," the woman said. Her voice quivered slightly and she paused to clear her throat. "I'm a doctoral student at UBC. The University of British Columbia . . . or don't I have to explain that?"

"It's fine. Tell me why you're here."

"I think I've been raped."

"You think?"

She sat up straighter in the chair. "I *have* been raped. But I don't know by whom."

"Go on."

"My boyfriend works at the oil sands in Alberta—doing environmental impact studies on the rivers near them, I mean, not working for the oil companies. Jared wouldn't do that. Work for the oil companies. He's—"

"Let's just stick with why you're here, okay?" Hugh prompted.

"Oh. Of course. Sorry." Gray took a deep breath. "This is harder than I thought."

The second repetition of a story often was, especially when that story was fabricated and the teller had to remember all those details already given. Hugh gave an inward wince at the uncharitable thought. Christ, he was becoming jaded.

He made himself smile. "You're doing fine."

Gray didn't look convinced but continued nonetheless. "So anyway, like I said, I hadn't seen him in more than eight months and then, one night, out of the blue, he turns up at my apartment. I had two essays due that week, but I was thrilled to see him. One thing led to another and—" She cast a pained look at the recorder. "Do I have to, you know, *say* what we did?"

"You had sex," Hugh supplied the words in his best professional voice.

Gray blushed. "Yes." Another throat clearing. "When I woke up the next morning, he was gone."

She gave a sudden gasp, face going pale, and pressed a hand against her swollen belly.

"Are you okay?" Hugh asked. "Would you like some water?"

Gray shook her head. "Sorry. It just hurts sometimes, like things are being stretched too fast. I'm fine now."

"All right. Let's get back to your boyfriend. Did he leave you a note when he left?"

"No. Nothing. I was worried he might have gone out for something and had an accident, but I called the police and the hospital and there was nothing. I couldn't call him because he doesn't believe in cell phones. He thinks they cause—sorry, I'm getting sidetracked again, aren't I?" She took another breath, fingers massaging her side. "Anyway, I left messages for him with his supervisor, but all I could do was wait for him to call me. About a week later, I started puking my guts out. I thought I had food poisoning, so I went to the hospital. They told me I was pregnant. About twelve weeks along. I said it was impossible, but they insisted. I told them they were fucking insane"—she cast a quick look of apology at Hugh, making him feel like a doddering old man from a generation shocked by such language—"and I left. Two days later, I couldn't do up the zipper on my jeans anymore."

"And then?"

Gray's face crumpled. Her voice dropped to a whisper. "And then Jared called. He'd just gotten back from three weeks at one of their remote camps, he said, and he'd called right away. He wanted to know what was wrong, why I'd left so many messages. He said—" She hiccupped. "He said he hadn't seen me or been to Vancouver since March."

The classic it-couldn't-have-been-me avoidance technique? Hugh kept the idea to himself for the moment. "What about the pregnancy?" he indicated her belly. "How far along are you?"

Gray compressed her lips until they whitened. She swallowed three times before she spoke. "Six months, according to the ultrasound this morning."

"And you've never—?"

"No," she cut him off fiercely. "I've never cheated on Jared."

Hugh tipped back in his chair and linked his fingers behind his head. He regarded her for a long time without speaking, then sighed and let the chair's front legs drop to the floor again. He returned pen to pad. "So you're saying you've only known about the pregnancy for two weeks?"

"I'm saying I've only *been* pregnant for two weeks."

"But you just said—"

"Detective Henderson." Gray's hands curled into fists on the table. "Someone came to my apartment two weeks ago, posing as my boyfriend. A week later, I was told I was pregnant. As of this morning, I'm six months along."

Same story she'd told initially. Just as crazy as it sounded the first time. The woman was either lying or delusional. Hugh's money was on the latter. He laid pen across paper and folded his hands atop both. "Ms. Gray, you know that's impossible."

"Oh, I know it, all right." Gray's laugh was short and high-pitched. "But that doesn't change the fact it happened."

Christ. Wait'll his colleagues heard this one. What was it with goddamn weird stories lately? Hugh rubbed a hand over his short-cropped hair. He eyed Gray. "You wouldn't happen to know a Melanie Chiu, would you?"

"I don't think so. Should I?"

"No. It was just an idea." He slid the pad of paper toward the young woman and began the process of extricating himself from the interview. "I think I have everything I need for the moment. If you'll just write your phone number at the top, I'll let you know if I have any more questions."

Gray made no move to accept the proffered pen. "You don't believe me."

Hugh had been at this far too many years to beat around the bush. He met her gaze squarely. "No. I don't. What you're telling me not only doesn't make sense, Katherine, it isn't physically possible. You do understand that, right?"

Tears filled green eyes, overflowed, trickled down Gray's cheeks. "So you're not going to do anything?"

"There's nothing I can do."

She nodded and swiped at her cheek with the back of one hand. "And that?" She pointed at her belly. "What am I supposed to do with that?"

Hugh hesitated. Liz might kill him for this, but given her recent experience with Melanie Chiu, she was the best person he could think of to help Gray. And in his opinion, the woman definitely needed help. Taking back the pad of paper, he ripped off a sheet and jotted down Liz's office number. "This is the number for a doctor who might be able to help you."

"It's too late for an abortion. I tried to get one as soon as I found out, but they said I was already too far along. After one week."

Hugh handed the paper to Gray. "Elizabeth Riley isn't that kind of doctor. She's a psychiatrist. It might help for you to talk to her."

Gray stared at the paper in her hand. Then, crumpling it, she dropped it on the table and pushed to her feet. Without another word, she walked out the door.

"WHAT DO YOU mean he's alive?" The One stared at Verchiel. "He can't be. I am the Creator. I would have felt the presence of my own son."

Verchiel tightened her fingers on the sheet of paper she held. "I don't know what to tell you except the man the Guardians have reported matches Seth's description." Verchiel glanced at the notes she'd hastily scribbled as details had filtered in. "He is in a place the mortals call Vancouver, British Columbia. In a hospital."

The barest flicker of something touched the One's countenance, gone before Verchiel could put a name to it. "Is he injured?" the One asked.

"Not physically."

"Explain."

"The man in question has no soul. At least, not a complete one. There is still something there, but it is too badly damaged for identification. And he has no memory of who he is. It is for that reason the mortals hold him."

Only a subtle shift in the air around the One gave evidence she had heard. Long seconds ticked by.

"What about powers?" she asked at last, her voice neutral but carrying an underlying thread of something that sent a shiver down Verchiel's spine.

"We're not sure, but—" The One stayed silent and Verchiel mustered her courage, forcing herself to speak the unthinkable. "He seems to have abilities beyond those of a mortal."

The air around the One pulsed again and her lips drew tight. "My son is loose in the mortal realm as an adult, with his powers intact and no memory of who he is or what he is to do," she clarified.

"We aren't certain—" Verchiel began, but a single raised eyebrow stopped her. She swallowed. "Yes, One. We believe so."

The One turned away and Verchiel stared at a back gone rigid with thoughts and emotions she couldn't begin to guess at. How did a mother deal with the knowledge her son lived but, for the good of the universe, would be better off dead?

"Damnation!" the One whispered, her voice laced with equal parts fury and pain.

That was how.

Verchiel closed her eyes. It made her heart ache, but the One was right: it would have been infinitely better for all if Seth had been killed outright. Far from being a good thing, the Appointed's survival held serious consequences. Potentially catastrophic ones, because the agreement contained no fine print stating Seth had to arrive among humanity in infant form. No clause regarding what age or condition he was to be in when he made his choice. Nothing that nullified the contract due to Heavenly treason.

Despite Mittron's attempt to alter Seth's existence, the

Appointed was still very much immortal. Very much the son of Lucifer and the One. And very much involved in the agreement between them. Except, instead of transitioning as an infant with years to absorb all that the One treasured and Lucifer despised in mortals, instead of growing into the role for which he'd been destined, Seth was an adult with divine powers, a damaged soul, and no memory. Heaven's last chance at peace could, through a single decision, hand over the entire world to Lucifer.

Could decimate humanity without even knowing he'd done so.

As awful as the specter of impending war had been, the consequences of Seth's continued survival were far, far worse.

"Find out."

Verchiel jumped at the abrupt command. "Pardon?"

"Find out if it's him."

"And if it is?"

The One's face became tight, drawn. "Just find out."

Verchiel swallowed. "Of course."

"Does anyone else know about this?"

"No. The Guardians reported directly to me and I have spoken to no one but you."

"See it remains that way."

Inclining her head, Verchiel opened the door to leave. She was halfway out when the One's voice stopped her.

"There is one more thing."

Verchiel looked over her shoulder, her gaze settling on the One's hands, clasped behind the Creator. No, not clasped. Clutched. Tightly. Verchiel's pulse skipped a beat. She stepped back inside.

The One's silver stare met hers. "I need you to find Mika'el," she said. "Quietly."

SEVEN

Michael Dominic looked up as his young patient tapped him on the shoulder. Following Joseph's dark, solemn gaze, he glanced toward the tent opening and the figure silhouetted against the afternoon glare.

The winged figure.

Wings only he could see.

His heart skipped a beat. He stared for a long moment before lifting the boy off the table and depositing him on the plank floor. Taking his stethoscope from his ears and slinging it around his neck, he dug finger and thumb into his shirt pocket. The boy's dark face split into a wide grin, and both he and the butterscotch Michael produced disappeared out the door. Michael reached for the chart, made his notes, and tried to still the quake in his center.

"You are not pleased to see me?" the figure asked. The voice told Michael what the silhouette had not. It was Raphael.

"Pleased doesn't enter into it, Raphael. Suffice it to say I'm surprised." Michael leaned against the table. The wood structure gave slightly beneath his weight and he made a mental note to ask Abraham to look at it later, before it collapsed beneath a patient. "Forty-five hundred years is a long time."

"It is." Raphael moved farther into the tent, ebony skin nearly as dark as his silhouette had been, and examined his surroundings with curiosity. "You appear to have found ways to occupy your time, however. What is this place?"

"It's a clinic. I'm a doctor."

"A healer?" The Archangel shot him a sharp look.

"Yes."

"Is that wise?"

"I'm careful." Very careful. His clinic, in the heart of Africa, held more hope and better health than many others, but no miracles. No angelic interference with mortals that might contravene the cardinal rule. Michael had strayed far enough from the One already; he would not abandon the path completely. He folded his arms across his chest. "But I don't think you're here to discuss my Earthly profession."

"No." Raphael left his examination of the photo collage on a sheet of plywood leaning against the canvas wall. "No, I'm not. You are being summoned, Mika'el of the Archangels."

It had been the only reason one of the others would come to him, of course. Michael knew that. But knowing didn't ease the shock of hearing the words.

He watched a beetle make its way across the wooden floor toward the tent wall. Summoned. After four and a half millennia. Long after he'd given up hope of being called back to fulfill his promise; given up hope of ever being a part of Heaven again. Of being part of her. He tried to take a deep breath but found his chest too constricted to accept air.

"Mika'el? Did you hear me?"

"Michael. I am called Michael here. And yes, I heard you." The beetle reached the wall and disappeared into the crevice at the bottom. Michael raised his gaze to meet Raphael's. "Am I to know why?"

"The Appointed's transition has gone wrong."

"His—" Michael's very heart seemed to still. "The agreement has been triggered?"

"One of the Powers killed a Fallen One."

The universe itself seemed to shift beneath Michael. If he hadn't had the support of the table, he might have toppled over. "Killed? As in dead?"

"As in committed the ultimate sin, yes."

"Who was the Power?"

"Aramael. His last hunt was for his brother, Caim."

Michael nodded. "I know of Caim. The seeker of a Nephilim soul." He frowned suddenly. While he had never intervened, knowing the Powers would take care of matters, he hadn't been able to escape the part of himself that knew when a Fallen One had become active on Earth. "The serial killer in Toronto last month?"

"Yes. One of the mortals investigating his crimes was of Nephilim descent. Mittron assigned Aramael to act as her Guardian at the same time as he hunted Caim."

"A Power made to act as a Guardian. I'm sure that was a huge success."

"It gets worse. The woman was Aramael's soulmate, and apparently his cleansing was incomplete. He recognized her."

Michael braced his hands against the table on either side of himself, absorbing the impact of Raphael's words. A Power, without doubt the most unstable of all angels, had met his soulmate? Known her? In retrospect, Heaven was lucky that all this Aramael had done was kill a Fallen One.

He scowled at Raphael. "How did this Power escape the cleansing? And how the hell did his soulmate end up as a mortal?"

Raphael's mouth tightened. "Mittron. The fool attempted to trigger Armageddon. He thought the One would invite him to rule beside her in a war."

"He thought *what*? Wait, you said the Appointed's transition went wrong. Who was in charge of it?"

Another grimace. "Mittron. From what we can piece together, the Appointed was born into the mortal realm as an adult rather than an infant, without memory of who he is or what he is to do."

"The Highest was allowed to oversee—after what had already happened?"

A shadow crossed the other Archangel's face. "Yes. We're not sure why. The One has not shared her reasons with any but the Dominion Verchiel, who looks as if she carries the weight of the universe on her shoulders but will say nothing."

"The One has to have told you something."

Raphael hesitated. Looked away. "She said—" He paused and cleared his throat. "She said Mittron had been undecided about his path, and as long as he remained so, she would honor his potential."

The words cut into Michael like a blade of cold steel. Precise, deep, just short of lethal. He curled his fingers into his palms against the pain and gritted his teeth. She would keep the undecided with her, but send away the one who remained fiercely, eternally loyal. Send him away, and then dispatch another to speak for her when she needed his help.

"But he has since been punished," Raphael hastened to add. "He was called to Judgment two days ago and—"

Michael cut him off with the lift of a hand. "And the Power?" he grated.

Raphael took a deep breath and put another few feet of space between them. "Banished. To the mortal realm."

Fuck.

While Michael generally avoided using the more colorful human vernacular, it was the only word that seemed to sum up all he'd heard, all he felt.

Fuck.

He glowered at the other Archangel. "Let me get this straight. I question a decision and she stops speaking to me for four and a half thousand years and then sends you to collect on the promise I made her. Mittron orchestrates a chain of events that may yet trigger war between Heaven and Hell, but he remains as her administrator until *after* he loses the Appointed; and a Power commits the ultimate sin and is merely banished to the mortal realm instead of being exiled to Limbo. Does that about cover it?"

Mouth twisting, Raphael nodded. "In a word, yes."

"And the rest of you are okay with this."

"She is the One, Mika'el."

Michael groaned and rubbed a hand over his eyes. Yes, that was what it still came down to, wasn't it? She was the One. The Creator. The others might question her actions, but after the example he'd set all those millennia ago, their reservations would remain unvoiced.

As would his. This time.

Because all those millennia ago, he had also given her his word. Had vowed his undying devotion and allegiance, sworn he would return without question in her time of need, promised he would always remain the Archangel Mika'el— her most powerful warrior.

He lifted his head, straightened his shoulders, and, for the first time since leaving Heaven, unfurled his massive wings. They stretched open, spanning the width of the clinic, a full double-arm's-length wider than those of his fellow warriors—at once his power, his glory, and his eternal burden.

Flexing the great supporting muscles, he shook out the feathers and stood for a moment, absorbing his own unspoken acceptance of the role he had never thought to play again. Coming to terms with all he would have to become. All he would give up.

Then Michael, once more Mika'el, turned to his messenger. "Where is she?"

"She waits for you in the gardens."

EIGHT

Lucifer leaned back in his chair and put his feet on the desk, crossing them at the ankles. He linked his fingers behind his head and regarded Samael narrowly. "You're certain."

The former Archangel, standing across from him, shrugged. "Ninety-nine percent."

"As an adult. In a psychiatric ward."

"With amnesia," Samael agreed.

Lucifer twisted his head to stare out the window. He scowled at the gardens intended to be more glorious than those of Heaven, but which had instead become a sad caricature. A perversion of what he'd had to leave behind. His eyes traveled the awkward, aimless curves of a path meant to be graceful; stone walls that had crumbled with decay the moment he created them; trees and shrubs and beds of plants caught in a perpetually failing struggle for life. All mocking his failure to equal the One's glory.

Jaw going tight, he looked away, back at Sam. "Something must have gone wrong. It makes no sense this would have been deliberate. The risk is too great."

"For both sides," Samael pointed out. "He could make his choice any minute, rather than in the years we thought we'd have."

Lucifer shot him a quelling glare. "If you're thinking what I think you are, forget it. The Appointed might not have his own Guardian, but you can bet those around him will be watching. Any move against him and we forfeit, remember? Besides, given enough time, mortals are more than capable of turning him against them."

"Except we don't have time because he's an *adult*. A highly unstable one, if I'm understanding the mortal concerns right. He could just as easily choose against us and then everything we've been working toward would go to shit."

"If we try to take him out, the exact same thing happens. That risk is greater than letting him live." Lucifer shook his head. "I'm not ready for war, Sam. No matter how much training you've done or how prepared you think we are, the fact remains we're outnumbered three to one. We need time to build the Nephilim numbers and every second the Appointed lives is a second in our favor. Leave him alone. That's an order."

"That's it, then. Your solution is to sit around and wait for your son and a handful of half-breeds to decide our future. Damn it, Lucifer, be reasonable. We'd be better off without him at this point. And without that ludicrous—" Samael stopped short as Lucifer's booted feet crashed to the floor.

"You'll want to be careful how you finish that," Lucifer drawled. Strolling around the desk, he towered over his aide. "The agreement originated between her and me and it remains between her and me. Understand?"

Samael clamped his lips together and ruffled his wings. "Frankly?" he shot back. "No, I don't understand. I never did. We already had a pact with her, one we'd all agreed on. The first strike by either side was to result in war and an end to all this bullshit—and it should have done so when that idiot Power took out his own brother. Outnumbered or not, we could still force her hand and take out most of the human race just as we said we would."

Whipped into a fine frenzy now, Samael glared at him. Lucifer waited for his aide to finish venting five thousand years worth of pent-up venom. Samael didn't disappoint.

"But *no*." The former Archangel drew out the last word in a taunt and Lucifer's fists tightened. "No, you had to go behind our backs in some fucking slapdash agreement that lets your son have the final say in our future. *Our* future, Lucifer. You remember, the ones who followed you out of Heaven, who believed in you and fought for you?"

Lucifer loosened his jaw enough to query, very quietly, "Are you done?"

Samael drew himself up to his full height, still several inches shorter than Lucifer, and lifted his chin. "Apparently we all are."

Closing his eyes, Lucifer counted to ten under his breath. Samael had been a thorn in his side ever since he'd shown up on Hell's doorstep: hot-tempered, driven by a hunger for power, and possessed of serious control issues. As a former Archangel, however, he'd also been the best battle strategist Hell could ask for, and so Lucifer tolerated him. His patience, however, was wearing thin.

Samael cleared his throat and Lucifer held up a hand, increased his count to twenty, and opened his eyes. Without warning, he lashed out, backhanding his aide across the cheek and sending him staggering against the wall. Samael pushed upright again, resentment glowing in his eyes. A reddening handprint took shape on his face.

"What I remember," Lucifer told him coldly, "is that you chose to follow *me*, Samael, not the other way around. If you're unhappy with your decision, you're welcome to leave anytime. If you stay, however, then you would do well to remember your place—and mine. Do you understand?"

Samael said nothing.

Lucifer nodded. "Good. Then understand this, as well. War has never been my primary objective, and I have never pretended otherwise. It isn't enough to take out *most* of the humans. I want them *all* gone. Every single last one of them. War is inevitable—I know that. But not before I say so. Until then, you need to behave like the fucking military leader you're supposed to be, because if we end up fighting on two fronts, we'll get our collective asses kicked, and you know it."

Returning to the desk, Lucifer took a peppermint from a dish there and tucked it into his cheek before looking back at a glowering Sam. "Like it or not, Seth's presence prevents Heaven from moving against us. Watch him, but don't interfere. If you want to throw yourself onto the swords of your kin once the Nephilim numbers are in place, be my guest, but until then, the agreement—*my* agreement—stands."

Samael stared at him, his jaw flexing. Then, with an effort Lucifer suspected would cost them both dearly at some point, his aide dipped his head with a deference at odds with the rebellion flowing from him.

"Of course," Samael said. "Your *Lordship*."

"VANCOUVER! FOR A holiday? Isn't that a bit sudden?"

Alex sidestepped her sister and stood in front of the open closet, surveying the contents. She'd never been to the coastal city in October, but expected Vancouver's autumn weather would be similar to that of most coastlines: changeable at best. She took down a stack of sweaters from the shelf and carried them to the bed.

"I think you might have been right about me going back to work too soon," she said. "I decided I need a change of scenery."

Jennifer scowled. "I don't believe you. The truth, Alex."

Alex set the sweaters by the suitcase. "That is the—"

"The truth."

Alex crossed her arms. "I hate how you can do that," she muttered. "Fine. The truth is I don't think we're done yet."

"Done? Done with what?"

"Seth is back. He's in Vancouver."

Jen's face paled and she groped for the edge of the bed. Pushing the sweaters away, she sat down and swallowed.

"I see. Do you know why?"

"No."

"He didn't tell you?"

Alex shook her head. "I don't think he can. He's in the hospital out there. They say he has amnesia."

"Amnesia—but he's an—" Jennifer's voice choked off. She tried again. "He's—can he—can his kind even have amnesia?"

"I'm guessing something went wrong."

"And that's why you're going out there? To figure out what?"

"And to help him if I can."

"Don't. It's none of your business, Alex. Whatever's going on is between them. It has nothing to do with us."

"It has everything to do with us. We're the ones they're fighting over." Alex reached past Jennifer to pick out the more innocuous sweaters in the stack. She didn't know what she was walking into in Vancouver, and preferred not to stand out in anyone's memory. As she refolded a brown turtleneck, Jen's hand closed over her wrist.

"I don't care. Let it go. Please."

"You don't mean that."

"If it means keeping you safe, yes, I do."

Alex pushed away the suitcase and sat beside her sister. "I have to do this, Jen. There are things I never told you—"

"It won't change my mind." Jen shook her head stubbornly. "Nothing will change my mind. You and Nina are the most important things in my entire universe and I damn near lost both of you this summer. I will *not* stand by and let you put yourself back in the center of that mess again—I don't care what your reasons are. I'll stop you, Alex. I'll go to Dr. Bell if I have to and—"

"Seth is supposed to stop the Apocalypse."

Jen's throat convulsed. "The Apocalypse isn't real. It's just a myth. A legend."

"Like angels and demons?" Alex demanded, her voice harsher than she intended, making Jen flinch. Alex pushed away a wave of pity. Her sister had to know. She wouldn't put it past Jen to carry out her threat to speak to Bell, and who knew what the repercussions might be? "You saw them, Jennifer. You saw what Caim did to those people. To me, to Nina. That was just the beginning. There are tens of thousands like Caim. If they go to war with the angels—"

Jen's grip tightened on Alex's wrist. Prying her sister's fingers loose, Alex gathered her into a hug and rested her cheek against the gray-streaked brunette hair. "I have to help him if I can, Jen. He saved my life. He may be the only one who can save *all* our lives."

"I know," Jen whispered into her shoulder. "But I don't have to like it."

HE STARED OUT the window at the trees and grass and buildings beyond, at the sky, the clouds, the people, the vehicles. Stared, and recognized none of them. He only had names for them because they had been named to him over the past week; only knew it had been a week because he had been told so.

But he still didn't comprehend what a week meant.

He comprehended little, in fact, of what he'd been told by the people who had taken him in, who placed him in this room, who locked the door behind him. His world began and ended with the four walls that surrounded him, the view out his window, and the few hundred words he had learned in his time here. Before that, there was nothing but emptiness. Darkness.

Pain.

He sucked in a breath, a piercing sharpness beneath his ribs. Pain. The ones who cared for him had used the word— *are you in pain?*—but he hadn't understood its meaning. Now he did. He didn't know how he knew, but he did. Knew it, felt it deep inside. A key clicked in the lock. Looking around, he watched as the woman who had found him, the one who brought him to this place, came into his room. Dr. Riley, she called herself.

"Good morning, John," she said.

That was the name they had given him. He knew it was

wrong but could not correct them. Could not tell them what was right.

Dr. Riley looked at the clipboard she held. "You had another quiet night, I see. But you're still not sleeping much. I think I might prescribe something to help you with that."

He watched her. Listened. Had no idea what she said.

Her face changed to a frown. He knew that word from having been asked by a nurse this morning why he frowned; knew it meant Dr. Riley felt the same inside as he did.

Didn't know what to call the feeling.

"Still not talking, either, *hmm*?" she asked. She put her pen on the paper and made some marks. "Have you remembered anything? A name? A place?"

He turned back to the window. Behind him, Dr. Riley sighed.

"Never mind," she said. "I'm sure it will come in time. In the meantime, you have someone coming to see you this afternoon who may be able to help. A detective from Toronto thinks she may know you. I'm picking her up at the airport at three and then we'll come by to visit, all right?"

Toronto. Airport. Detective. More words without meaning. He watched a bird in the sky. The door behind him opened, closed. The key clicked in the lock once more.

NINE

He found her in the gardens, as Raphael said he would. For long minutes, Mika'el stood at the edge of the trees and watched the One, seated on a swing beneath a massive maple, gently moving back and forth with the breeze. His breath lodged in his throat, refusing to move further. Just as his feet refused to carry him forward, held captive by the memory of harsh words that still lingered after more than four thousand years.

He closed his eyes against the agony of turning his back on her, as fresh now as if it had only just happened. An agony he carried with him every second of every day since leaving her presence.

Preternatural awareness shuddered through him and, without looking, he knew the One had turned her gaze on him. He sensed her stillness, felt her ambivalence. It took every ounce of willpower he could summon to open his eyes and meet hers, and then to make himself walk across the lawn.

"Mika'el," she said as he stopped before her.

The sound of her voice speaking his angelic name

reached inside him and laid bare places he hardly knew anymore. He drew himself tall, against the urge to bow, afraid he might not be able to straighten again to face her. "One."

"You came," she said.

A quiver went through Mika'el's wings, echoing the spasm in his heart. "You doubted me?"

A tiny smile curved the One's lips. "I have never doubted you, my Archangel. Myself, yes, but never you."

She studied him for a long moment, and then rose and brushed her fingers against his cheek. Her touch radiated through his body. His soul.

"I have missed you," she said.

Mika'el's breath snagged in his chest and for a moment, all of eternity stood still, centered in that one, feather-light touch. The first connection he'd had with his Creator since leaving her side.

Countless times in his years among mortals, he had observed the bond between mortal mother and child; a love that drew them together fiercely, completely, sometimes to the exclusion of all around them. He had envied humans that bond, not for its strength but for its smallness, and would have given his soul to be able to reduce what he felt for his Creator to that level. To be free of the anguish caused by her rejection of him. His rejection of her.

Now, with just a few words and a brush of hand against cheek, the One had renewed their connection and reminded him not just of the endurance of that bond, but its beauty, too. The all-consuming intensity that tied them to one another.

His Creator's gaze slid away and her hand dropped to her side. "Walk with me."

Mika'el fell into step beside her, hands clasped behind his back, and together they crossed the lawn to a path leading toward the rose garden. For a long time, silence sat between them, neither comfortable nor uncomfortable, just there. Until the One stopped and faced him.

"He shouldn't have survived."

"Who shouldn't?"

"Seth. He should have died in the transition."

Mika'el's entire being went still. "Excuse me?"

"After Aramael killed Caim, when Mittron came to me to see what punishment the Power would face, I read his intent. I knew the Highest Seraph wished to eliminate the Appointed."

"Wait." He shook his head to clear it. "You *knew* what Mittron intended and you let him continue? But why?"

The One's timeless, ageless face became old and weary and unbearably sad.

"My son had become weak. Too weak to carry out what we asked of him. Something in him had changed. Turned wrong. He hid it from me and I couldn't see what it was. I believe in humanity, Mika'el. I've always believed in them. I would never have suggested the agreement to Lucifer otherwise. You know that. But I no longer trusted Seth's ability to become one of them, to learn to have faith in them as I do. I couldn't allow the transition to go forward."

Mika'el shook his head, unable to believe what he heard. "You wanted him to die." A statement, not a question. "Your own son."

The One's chin lifted a fraction. "There were seven billion souls at stake. Whole and unharmed, Seth would almost certainly have chosen in our favor—at the very least we would have had an equal chance and an additional few years before I—" Her mouth pulling tight, she stopped and gazed into the distance. "I couldn't risk it. I had no choice."

"You *did* have a choice. Then. Now. Six thousand years ago. Stopping Lucifer has always been a choice, but you just don't want to see it."

"It's not that simple."

"It *is* that simple," Mika'el snarled, old angers surging up in him. He stalked the broad width of the path. "The only complication is you. If you had done what needed to be done when all this began—if you had let *me* do what needed to be done—we would not be here now. But you refused, because you wanted to believe in *him*, in his potential. Even when your decision nearly decimated your angels, you would not move against him. Instead, you took away your angels' free will—all that made them individual and unique, so you could try to contain the one who had *chosen* to fall from your grace.

"Even now you engage in some kind of cat-and-mouse game with your former consort," he accused, "and to what end? The hope he might yet change? That he might see the error of his ways? The mortals you created are suffering because of him, One. I've witnessed their torment every day since leaving your side, and now—now you tell me you would have sacrificed your own son for him?"

Mika'el stopped pacing and looked down on her, and then, his voice hoarse, laid bare the depth of his own and Heaven's anguish.

"Why?" he asked. "Why choose Lucifer over all the rest of your creations?"

For a very long time, the One stared past him, her face white and marble-still. Above them, a passing breeze rustled through the treetops, carrying with it the song of a distant bird.

"Is that what you think?" the One asked at last.

Mika'el could not answer past the thickness in his throat, could not tell her it was what all her angels thought. What they'd always thought.

His Creator shook her head. "You're wrong, Mika'el. It is not in my nature—not in my capacity—to favor any one life over another. Every living thing in this universe is a part of me, created from me. Who I am, *what* I am, demands I love them all."

"But Lucifer is evil, damn it—how can you continue to love him when you know what he has done? What he is capable of?"

"Because I must," she snapped, taking up the pacing Mika'el had abandoned. "Because I am the One, and all life flows from me, and I cannot value that life based on whether or not it meets your standards any more than I could based on Lucifer's."

Mika'el's head snapped back at the comparison and the One paused before him, reaching to grasp his hands.

"I'm not saying you're like Lucifer, Mika'el. I'm saying my love is not defined by worth. It simply is." Her voice softened. "As for the mortals, remember that much of the pain they endure is inflicted upon them by their own hands and those of their fellow humans. Not by Lucifer's, and not by mine. Each and every soul on Earth has the capacity for both good and evil, and the capacity to choose between those paths."

"And you," Mika'el grated, "have the same capacity for choice. It is wrong to let this continue, One. No matter how much you *love* him, you cannot continue to sit back and do nothing." A sudden idea occurred to him, reaching down to squeeze his heart in an iron fist.

No. That would be impossible . . .

"You *can* stop him, can't you?"

The One released his hands and returned to pacing. Slower steps this time, with a measure to them—a precision—that made the thought-fist tighten a little more.

"One?"

A dozen feet away, the Creator of the universe stopped, her back to him. She sighed, and then, voice quiet, said, "The short answer to that would be yes."

. . . unthinkable . . .

"And the long answer?"

"The long answer, Mika'el, is it's not that simple."

TEN

Alex slipped her carry-on bag from her shoulder. Setting it on the tiled floor in front of her, she scanned the airport throng for the woman who was to meet her. Fiftyish, Elizabeth Riley had told her. Gray hair pulled back, glasses, wearing trousers—she'd actually called them that—and a white blouse because Alex would be arriving on Thursday and she always wore a white blouse on Thursdays.

Of course.

The crowd parted for a moment. Alex spotted a woman beside a car rental booth who matched Riley's general description but looked more like a hippie grandmother than a police psychiatrist. Her "trousers" were of the baggy, multi-pocketed cargo variety. The white blouse involved appeared to be unbleached cotton. And she wore Birkenstocks.

Alex hesitated. Surely not.

Just before the people around her merged again into a living wall, the woman peered over wire-framed glasses perched on the end of her nose and raised an eyebrow in her direction. Shouldering her bag again, Alex threaded her way over to her.

"Dr. Riley?"

The gray-haired woman tipped back a head that didn't quite reach Alex's shoulder. Sharp blue eyes settled briefly on her scarred throat, and then lifted. The hippie grandmother held out her hand. "Detective Jarvis. It was good of you to come all this way."

Alex suppressed a sigh at the *but unnecessary* hanging unspoken between them. Riley had made it clear during yesterday's phone call she considered Alex's trip across the country to be a waste of time, and that she was thoroughly annoyed at Alex's refusal to share any information over the phone. Better to have her annoyed, however, than to even begin trying to explain a man who didn't really exist. At least not before she confirmed it was Seth.

And figured out how she *might* explain him.

She accepted Riley's handshake. "It was good of you to meet me," she responded. "I hope it wasn't too much trouble. I really could have taken a cab."

Riley peered again over her glasses, her bright eyes determined. "No trouble at all, Detective. It will give us a chance to talk."

Which is why a cab would have been so much better.

Alex inclined her head.

"Do you have any other luggage?"

"Just this, thanks."

With a tight nod, Riley headed for a bank of exit doors at a pace that belied her short stature, Birkenstocks flapping on her feet. Alex followed, hard-pressed to keep up.

Twenty minutes later, they merged with the traffic on the freeway. Perched on a cushion behind the wheel of a hybrid SUV, Dr. Riley peered over her glasses at the road ahead. The interrogation began.

"So, you recognized our John Doe from the photo on the poster."

A steady flow of vehicles passed them, going in the same direction as they were. Alex glanced at the speedometer: sixty kilometers an hour, just over half the speed limit. The drive could take a while.

"I believe so, but I won't be certain until I see him."

"The photo was an accurate likeness."

Alex chose not to respond and instead looked out her window at a flock of seagulls wheeling in the sky. A steady *click-clack* signaled Riley's intent to change lanes.

"How well do you know John, Detective Jarvis?"

"Alex. Please."

"Very well. How well do you know John, *Alex*?"

"Not well. We were . . . acquaintances." Such an inadequate word to describe someone who had pulled her back from the brink of death.

Elizabeth Riley made an impatient noise beside her. "Perhaps I should point out that for someone in your rather precarious position, this kind of evasiveness won't help your cause."

Alex shot a sharp glance at the psychiatrist and met a brief, cool look before Riley returned her attention to the road.

"You didn't think I'd ask questions?" Riley asked. "A detective from the other end of the country calls to inquire about my mystery patient, refuses to answer any of my own queries, and then informs me she's flying out the next day in person. Believe me, I asked a lot of questions."

Staring out her window, Alex cursed her own shortsightedness. Of course Riley would have checked into her. She would have done the same thing in the doctor's place—had done, albeit belatedly, when Aramael had joined their serial-killer investigation a few short weeks ago under the guise of being her new partner, Jacob Trent. Although she suspected Riley's questions may have resulted in a somewhat different outcome than hers had—one that didn't end with finding out the subject of her queries was an angel tasked with capturing demons, for instance.

Riley took an exit off the freeway and pulled up behind the traffic at a stop light. "Don't you want to know what I found out?"

"Not particularly."

"You've been through a lot recently, Detective. Your stability is somewhat in question."

The traffic light changed and they moved forward again, Riley maintaining a precise, three-second gap between her and the vehicle in front.

Alex shot her companion a dark look. "My stability is fine, thank you."

"Not according to Dr. Bell. He was surprised to learn you'd come out here without mentioning it to him."

"I'm on leave, and what I do on my personal time is none of Dr. Bell's business."

"So this is personal, then."

"Is that a problem?"

"Not at all," Riley denied. "As long as you understand that not being here in an official capacity means you have the same standing as a civilian in this matter."

"Meaning?"

"Meaning you will be extended no special privileges, no professional consideration."

"Unless I cooperate?" Alex guessed dryly.

"There. I knew you would understand."

"You're very used to getting your own way, aren't you?"

"Trying to analyze the analyst, Detective?"

Alex lifted an eyebrow. "Trying to interrogate the interrogator, Doctor?"

Riley's lips tightened and she lapsed into silence. Alex turned her attention back to the city passing by outside her window. With the Coast Mountains as its backdrop and the Pacific Ocean on its doorstep, Vancouver touted itself as one of the prettiest urban settings in the world.

She wondered how long it would stay that way if Heaven and Hell went to war.

MIKA'EL DIDN'T SPEAK for a long time when the One finished. With every particle of his being, he wanted to reject what she had told him. Deny it. Erase the very words themselves from existence, as if he had never asked.

He closed his eyes and tried again to wrap his head

around her revelation. Complicated? What she suggested she needed to do to full-out stop Lucifer wasn't *complicated*, it was incomprehensible. Inconceivable.

And he could not—*would* not allow it to happen.

"No." His denial dropped into the silence, surprising him with its harshness. He spun to face the One and shook his head. "No," he said again. "There must be another way."

"I've been putting this off for six millennia while I sought another way, Mika'el. First the original pact, then the agreement which stands now. I hoped, if I just had enough time, that I might find an alternative. There is none."

It took a moment to voice words he would never, in all of eternity, have expected to speak. "Given Seth's damaged state, perhaps Lucifer would agree to a replacement."

The One didn't ask to whom he referred. She didn't need to—not with the shadow that stood perpetually between them. "I considered the possibility. Even if he agreed, however, Emmanuelle never would."

That she was right didn't ease his guilt at the relief that washed over him. Nor did it make the prickle of memories easier to bear. Mika'el roughly pushed away all but the here and now.

"Fine. But this—what you suggest—" He broke off and ran a hand through his hair, his wings vibrating with frustration. He forced down emotion and focused instead on the stark realities contained in the One's disclosure.

"It's out of the question," he said.

The One shook her head. "We're out of choices, my Archangel. With Seth as he is, with the risk he poses, I must act now, while I still can. If my son chooses against us, I will be bound by my word."

"And if the roles were reversed? Do you really think your Light-Bearer would feel any such compunction?"

"What Lucifer would or would not do isn't the issue. My word, my promise, my integrity—those are what set me apart from him."

Mika'el stared at her. "You would really allow him to annihilate humanity if Seth chose against you?"

The One said nothing.

It took everything Mika'el possessed to force the next words from his lips. "You've always intended this, haven't you? Always planned to bind with him. To end your presence."

"Intended it, no. Known it would be necessary, yes." The One smiled softly, sadly. "As I said, there is no other way."

A thought began to take shape in Mika'el's mind. An impossible idea that demanded rejection. Except for the fact it wasn't as impossible as what the One suggested. Wasn't as impossible as a universe left without its Creator. Mika'el gritted his teeth and lifted his gaze to hers.

"One other choice remains."

The shadows in her eyes deepened. She shook her head. "I cannot."

"It is no different than allowing Mittron to proceed with the transition, knowing what you did."

"There is a vast difference between allowing Mittron's free will to unfold and ordering my son's actual assassination. What you suggest is—"

"Necessary," Mika'el grated. "If we're to stop what *you* suggest."

"You ask the impossible." The One's mouth tightened. "I am the Creator of life, not the destroyer."

"Is that your final answer?"

"It is."

The idea that had begun to take shape completed itself, sitting in bold simplicity at Mika'el's center, waiting for him to set it in motion.

"Then if you won't order it, I will."

"HOW MANY?" VERCHIEL rested her forehead in her hand and stared at the top of Mittron's desk. No. Not Mittron's. Hers. For the larger portion of two days now, ever since that cryptic note arrived from the One.

Effective immediately, you are promoted to the Sera-
phim choir and charged with the office of Heaven's
executive administrator.

Verchiel closed her eyes against the impossibility she had
yet to absorb and waited for the reply to her question. The
Principality who had come into the office—*her* office—
cleared his throat.

"Seven hundred and three at last count, Highest," he said,
his voice apologetic, as if he knew the inner turmoil she
suffered over her sudden rise in status and didn't want to
burden her further.

Verchiel squeezed her eyes tighter, ignoring the jolt her
heart gave at the *Highest* title conferred on her. Now was
not the time to think about that. Or to panic about it. Lifting
her head, she regarded the record-keeper. "We're certain
about this?"

"Positive."

Verchiel tightened her lips. "And those actually born?"

"Ninety. With another three hundred expected within the
week."

Dear One in Heaven, he wouldn't. Couldn't. Not with the
agreement still in place. Verchiel made herself nod with the
calm sagacity her new office demanded but she did not feel.

"You will continue to monitor the situation and report to
me," she ordered. "Increase the record-keepers if you need
to. None can go unnoted."

The Principality nodded and withdrew in a hushed whisper of pale gray robes, leaving Verchiel to rest her forehead
in her hand, close her eyes, and deal with the ramifications
of the news he had brought.

Lucifer and his followers mating with humans.

Spawning a new race of Nephilim.

And because of her new position, it would fall to Verchiel
to inform the One.

"You know why he does this."

Verchiel jumped at the sudden voice and lifted her head

to the angel in the doorway. The last angel she had expected to see. Ever. She stared at her visitor, mouth dry and heart going still in her chest. "Mika'el," she said at last.

Heaven's prodigal son, the most powerful of the Archangels, leaned against the frame, clothed in human garments—blue jeans and a white shirt with sleeves rolled up to his elbows. His massive wings filled the space behind him. Without asking permission or waiting for an invitation, he stepped inside and closed the door.

A panicky part of Verchiel, left over from her Dominion status, wanted to bolt from the room, but her new position as Heaven's executive administrator held her to the chair. Feigning calm, she waited for him to speak.

"You know why he does this," he repeated.

"Lucifer?" she asked.

He nodded, folding his arms and leaning against the wall. "Does he need a reason other than to prove he can?"

"No, but in this case, he has one. He raises an army."

She heaved a sigh and massaged her temple again: "He already has an army."

"One he cannot use as long as the Appointed lives. Or if Seth were to choose in our favor."

Verchiel's hand stilled. "He would use the Nephilim against the mortals."

"Because we cannot do anything about them," Mika'el agreed, his eyes grim. "Because the agreement didn't foresee the possibility. *I* didn't foresee the possibility."

He straightened, his arms dropping to his sides, and stalked the edges of the room. "The agreement specifies no attack on mortals as long as the Appointed lives, but it never occurred to me Lucifer might resurrect the Nephilim. We held the race in such low esteem, I didn't consider them to be a threat. Hell, I didn't consider them at all."

Pushing both hands through his hair, he stopped beside a window and stared out. Then he pivoted. "I need your help, Seraph. And your utter discretion."

Verchiel blinked. Nodded.

"The Power who was cast out—I need to find him."

"Aramael?" She frowned. "What for?"

"The Appointed."

"The—" Verchiel stopped as she realized his intent. She shook her head. "No. You cannot—*we* cannot. Mika'el, think of the risk—"

"I *am* thinking of the risk," he said, "and there is more at stake than you know. Especially now that I am aware of the Nephilim."

"But there's still a chance Seth might choose in our favor—" She broke off again, working through a maze of impossibilities. If Seth *did* choose in Heaven's favor, Lucifer would simply turn his wrath on the angels and loose the Nephilim against the mortal world in his stead. If Seth chose Hell's path, the angels would engage the Fallen in an attempt to draw Lucifer's forces away from his murderous campaign on Earth—and the Nephilim would still move against humankind. And if Seth died—she closed her eyes. No matter how she looked at this, each and every path ended in the war they had sought, long and hard, to avoid.

"We can't win, can we?" she asked.

"Not the way we'd hoped, no. But we can try to mitigate the damage."

"By forcing Lucifer's hand? The moment Seth is dead, there will be nothing to stop the Light-Bearer from engaging us in immediate war."

"Except a Nephilim army."

The cold sickness rose again in Verchiel's belly. "He grows their numbers."

"And the longer we put off war, the greater those numbers will become."

"You don't plan to wait for him to strike the first blow."

"I do not."

"The One won't allow it."

"The decision is mine."

"But if Lucifer finds out we've assassinated his son, we forfeit the agreement. What then?"

Mika'el looked over his shoulder. Emerald eyes blazed from a face that might have been carved from granite, it had gone so still. So hard. "Then," said Heaven's greatest warrior, "we face consequences none of us ever imagined. The Power's whereabouts, Seraph. Now."

ELEVEN

Alex clipped her visitor tag to her blazer lapel and fol-lowed Dr. Riley into the elevator. The psychiatrist hadn't said a word since their exchange in the vehicle, other than to issue terse directions when she wanted Alex to do something.

"In here."

"Over there."

"Sign this."

And now, "This way."

Alex's mouth tightened. If the good doctor was trying to wear her down, it wouldn't work. She had ample experience at waiting out the most stubborn of suspects—and little patience with people who tried to get into her head. She'd spent a lifetime protecting her innermost secrets; she wasn't about to cave after a half hour with some shrink who had her panties in a twist.

She settled against the elevator wall, careful to keep her body language non-confrontational. Arms at her sides, rather than crossed; posture relaxed; expression neutral. She thought about the man she was about to see. No. Not a man.

Not if it was Seth, and she was almost certain it was. The picture had been too clear for any doubts, no matter what she'd told Dr. Riley. She flicked a glance at her silent companion. When she could no longer avoid the issue, what would she tell the psychiatrist?

Whatever she decided to say, it wouldn't go over well.

Nor could it be the truth.

The elevator doors slid open and Alex glanced at the illuminated display. Eleventh floor. This was it. She took a deep breath and wiped her palms against her jacket. Dr. Riley's sharp gaze tracked the movement. Alex dropped her hands again, determined not to add to the other woman's arsenal.

They walked down the corridor to the nurse's station. The security guard handed over a key and pressed a button to release a door to their left. Alex raised an eyebrow.

"You locked him up?"

"For his own safety as well as ours. We don't know who he is or where he's from, or that he doesn't have a violent background."

Sudden doubt reared in Alex. She couldn't imagine Seth remaining locked up like this. Maybe it wasn't him after all. Or worse, maybe it was, and something had gone terribly wrong. More wrong than simple amnesia.

How could Heaven's contingency plan save humanity if he had no powers?

Realizing Dr. Riley stood in the open doorway, waiting, Alex hurried to join her. Riley raised an eyebrow, but Alex ignored the unspoken demand for explanation and trailed the doctor into the ward. On the other side of the door, a woman stood, pressed against the wall, dressed in a hospital gown. Sharp eyes peered out from behind strands of gray hair, tracking Alex. Gritting her teeth, Alex wondered if she would ever leave the memories of her mother behind.

Riley touched her arm. "I should have warned you," she said. "Are you all right?"

Alex pulled away from both the touch and the unexpected compassion. Bell had told her? That son of a bitch. She'd have his balls on a platter for this. *Patient confidentiality, my ass.* "I'm fine," she said. "Thank you."

Riley studied her for a long moment, gaze frankly assessing, then nodded. "Right. Let's go meet our John Doe, then, shall we?"

Alex shoved the past back into the mental closet where it belonged and followed Riley. When she got back to Toronto—*if* she got back—she would skewer Dr. Bell for his unprofessional conduct. Reaching the end of the hall, Riley inserted the key into a door on the left-hand side and pushed into a room.

Alex drew a deep breath and followed. Inside, she scanned her surroundings with a cop's attention to detail that was as much a part of her as her own skin. Walls and ceiling painted institution green, floor tiled beige. Ceiling light flush-mounted behind a protective metal grate. Bathroom, no mirror, off to one side. A basic cot in one corner, bolted to the floor. One window, grated, across from where Alex and Riley stood.

And one man at that window, his back to Alex, standing almost exactly as he had when she'd first seen him on her front porch.

Seth.

Alex stared at him, ignoring Riley's watchful presence at her side. He was just as big as she remembered. Just as powerful. And, at first glance, just as imposing. But even before he faced her, she sensed a change in him. An emptiness.

The aura that seemed to reduce the rest of the world's size in comparison to him was gone, along with the overwhelming presence that had once made her want to back away even as it had threatened to draw her in. She met his gaze across the room and saw—nothing. No recognition, no interest, no spark of identity.

He stared at her for several long moments, and then left the window and shambled toward her. Not even his gait remained as she remembered.

Seth on the outside.

Empty on the inside.

Loss tightened Alex's throat. Her last hope, her last possible connection to Aramael, dissolved in the pale afternoon light of reality.

Stopping in front of her, Seth's gaze locked with hers. She waited, and then, without warning, he smiled—a familiar, crooked, quirky half smile—and reached out to brush a strand of her hair back from her face. A bottomless sadness opened in his dark eyes.

"Alexandra Jarvis," he whispered.

Elizabeth Riley's keys hit the floor. Seth's eyes followed the sound, lifted to the psychiatrist, and then grazed over Alex, empty once more. Shuffling back to the window, he resumed his vigil.

Riley cleared her throat. "Well. I guess that settles it. He's who you thought."

Alex nodded, her mouth too dry for speech. She sensed Riley's gaze on her, but couldn't pull her own from Seth's broad back. Couldn't shut down the memories his touch had triggered.

Aramael. Caim. Hatred that had spanned millennia. An encounter with evil that had left her torn and battered and clinging to life by a gossamer thread. Murder. Seth's hands, healing her. And a loss so profound she was certain she would never recover.

"Detective."

Riley touched her arm and Alex jumped, her reverie shattered. She stared at the shorter woman, who peered over her glasses in return.

"Are you all right?"

Alex forced a nod. A smile. "Fine. Thanks."

But she wasn't fine. Didn't know what she was, but it wasn't anywhere near fine. Whatever she'd expected coming out here, it hadn't been the discovery that she was nowhere near as strong or put together as she'd believed. Or that Heaven's contingency plan had failed before it began.

"Hmm. Well, I assume you're ready to talk to me now you've identified our John Doe." Riley stooped to retrieve her keys and, without waiting for an answer, tugged open the door. She stood, holding it wide, and looked askance at Alex.

Alex cast a last glance at the broad-backed man at the window. "I'll be back soon," she said.

The hollow Seth gave no indication he heard.

RILEY LED ALEX to an office tucked away behind the nurse's station they'd passed when they'd come in. Alex declined coffee, accepted water, and settled in to wait for the inquisition, still with no idea what to say that would even half satisfy the questions she saw behind Riley's eyes. The doctor settled into the chair behind the desk.

"Seth Benjamin," Alex offered.

Riley shot her a sharp look. "What?"

"That's his name. Seth Benjamin."

Riley made a notation on a pad of paper before her. "What else?"

They call him the Appointed. He's an angel . . . or something like one. He saved my life. He's here to stop Heaven and Hell from going to war. To save humanity from annihilation.

"Nothing." Alex sighed. Setting the glass of water on the edge of Riley's desk, she leaned forward to rest her elbows on her knees. She rubbed a hand over her eyes. "I really don't know anything about him. He was a—friend of a friend. I only met him a few times."

Riley's gaze burned a hole into the top of her skull. She didn't look up. It was true, after all. Beyond Seth's name and the fact he could heal mortal wounds and disappear in the blink of an eye, she knew nothing about him.

God damn. It would have been *so* much simpler if she'd turned out to be nuts rather than tapping into this whole divinity thing. A nice padded cell somewhere sounded pretty good at the moment.

"And this friend?" the psychiatrist asked.

"He—" Alex waited for the spasm in her heart to pass. "He's gone."

"Gone. As in dead or disappeared?"

A little of both, Alex supposed. But again, a truth better kept to herself. She opted for the answer she hoped would bring fewer questions. "Dead."

"Dr. Bell didn't mention anything about you having lost a friend. Have you told him?"

Alex considered pointing out to Riley that Bell had no business mentioning anything, but decided it was unwise to antagonize the woman. She would deal with Bell later.

"No. It was—complicated. And very personal."

"I see. And Mr. Benjamin? How did he fit in with this friend?"

"I'm not sure. Like I said, I didn't know him well."

"But well enough to recognize his picture and fly across the country on your own *personal* time to see him."

At last Alex raised her head. She sat back in her chair and reached for her water. "Well enough for that, yes."

"And well enough for your name to be the first and only thing he's uttered since we found him."

"Apparently."

"Detective—"

The phone on Riley's desk rang, cutting off what Alex was certain would have been the beginning of a lecture. Not that she would have blamed the psychiatrist. She'd handled enough evasiveness in her own career to know exactly how frustrating it could be. If she were in Riley's shoes, she'd be lecturing, too. Or threatening.

Riley lifted the receiver. "Elizabeth Riley."

Letting her attention drift away from the doctor, Alex studied the room, noting the multiple diplomas hanging on the wall behind the desk, the file cabinet in one corner, the lush greenery sitting on the windowsill, and the lack of any other personal clutter or ornamentation of any kind. Not so much as a vase or a photo stood anywhere in sight. Lifting a brow, Alex looked over her shoulder at the shelves behind her but found nothing except books—in alphabetical order according to author, no less.

Her gaze settled on the file cabinet, its lock button pushed in to secure the contents. *Seth is in there. Everything Riley knows about him. Maybe with details that can help me figure out what went wrong . . .*

A sharp note in the psychiatrist's voice tugged Alex's attention back to the woman behind the desk.

"Well, the ultrasound technician was wrong, then, wasn't she?" Riley said to the person at the other end. "How is she doing?" Her frown deepened. "Of course. Yes, I'll be there in about—" she glanced at her watch, then at Alex. "Hold on."

She placed a hand over the receiver.

"I have a patient who's just gone into labor under somewhat unusual circumstances. She isn't handling it at all well—can you take a cab to your hotel?"

"Of course."

"Five minutes," Riley said into the phone. She hung up and stood. Taking her keys from her pocket, she dropped them onto the desk. "You'll need your luggage from my car. Leave the keys at the information desk downstairs when you're done. And the name of your hotel. And, Detective, just so you understand, we are far from being done here."

Alex reached for the keys, noting that one of the bunch looked like it might fit a file cabinet. She weighed temptation against consequences; the possibility of the Apocalypse against Riley's reaction to finding her rooting through confidential files.

The Apocalypse won.

"Doctor, is there a washroom I can use before I head out?"

Already on her way to the door and thoroughly distracted, Riley waved a vague hand. "Down the hall, first left turn, door on the right. If you get lost on the way out, one of the staff will direct you."

The psychiatrist disappeared out the door. Alex waited, jingling the keys she held, watching the hands on a wall clock inch forward. When five minutes had passed without Riley returning, she stood, took a deep breath, crossed to the file cabinet, and inserted the key. Hoping to hell the doctor didn't have a video camera set up to record patient appointments, she released the lock.

A hand closed over her wrist.

TWELVE

"Jesus Christ!"

Alex wrenched her wrist from Seth's grip, her heart threatening to explode from its new residence in her throat. Dark, fathomless eyes met hers. She drew a ragged breath and sagged against the file cabinet she'd been about to invade.

"God damn it, you took twenty years off my life—wait. How did you get in here?" She glanced past his shoulder at the office door. No attendant waited. She looked at Seth again. "Seth? How did you get out of your room? It was locked. And there's a security—"

"Seth," he repeated, his gaze clouding. His brow furrowed.

"That's your name, yes. Seth Benjamin."

He extended a hand and Alex stiffened when his fingers traced the scars left by Caim's claws. Seth tipped his head to one side.

"Alexandra Jarvis. I know you."

"You remember?"

Again a cloud passed across his eyes. "I don't know remember."

"You don't know—" Alex frowned. What the hell was that supposed to mean? An idea whispered through her mind with diaphanous fragility, dissolving before she could grasp it. She shrugged irritably, certain she was missing something obvious. "Never mind. We have to get you back to your room before someone notices you're gone."

Crossing the room to the door, she peered into the hallway. No one. So no alarm had been raised yet, thank God. She could just imagine Riley's reaction to finding Seth missing from his room. One more explanation Alex wouldn't be able to provide. Turning, she found Seth standing at her elbow. She jumped. "Shit—you have to stop sneaking up on me like that!"

"I don't know shit."

"Yeah. I noticed." Alex ran a hand through her hair. How would she get him past the security guard and the electronically locked door to his ward? And how the *hell* had he gotten out in the first place?

"I don't know Seth Benjamin."

Seth's voice had risen and he moved closer to her. Alex took an involuntary step back. Even without that presence she remembered about him, he was still an imposing figure.

"I know. But I'm sure it will come back to you," she soothed, "and I'll try to help you remember whatever I can. You just need to give it time—"

His eyes snapped black fire and he scowled at her. "I don't know sneaking. I don't know need. I don't know remember!"

Alex went still. The idea returned and settled in her brain. "You don't know language," she whispered. "It isn't that you won't talk—you just don't know how. Shit."

Seth glowered. "I don't know—"

"Yes, yes," she interrupted. "You don't know shit. But I do—and I can help. I don't know how yet, but I'll figure out something. I promise." She glanced out into the hallway again. "Now, however, we really need to get you back to your room."

"I know room."

The relief in Seth's voice sounded so heartfelt, Alex couldn't help but smile.

"Good. How are you on go and stay?"

Ten minutes later, feeling as if she'd just been through a basic dog-obedience lesson, Alex joined Seth by the door, where she'd sent him on a *go* command and then convinced him to stay.

"Right. So do you think we have this straight now?" she asked. "You go to your room and stay there."

"I go. I room. I stay."

She opened her mouth to correct the grammar, then closed it again. Time enough for that later. "Close enough."

"You come."

She shook her head. "Not right now. Later."

Seth looked doubtful. Alex gave his arm a little squeeze, knowing *later* had no meaning for him, trying to impart reassurance all the same.

"You go now. I'll come later," she said.

Dark eyes looked into hers, still barren of the angel she had known, but no longer entirely hollow. "Promise?" he asked.

"You know promise?"

"I know promise."

"Then yes. I promise."

He smiled. Trust—although he wouldn't know the word—settled across his expression.

"I go now."

And he did.

Alex stared at the emptiness vacated by Seth. She'd been so focused on the language issue she'd forgotten the whole angelic thing. Forgotten she dealt with an otherworldliness she still hadn't quite come to terms with. Lifting a hand to push back her hair, she stared at its tremble and tucked it into her jeans pocket instead. Hell. An angel without a memory who still retained his powers. That couldn't be good.

She wondered what other talents Seth might have discovered beyond his Houdini act. What other talents he even possessed. Her scars prickled. Could he still heal? Still bring people back from the brink of death? A host of potential conflicts raced through her mind at the possibility. If he should display his talents to others—

Hell.

Alex headed for the file cabinet. One crisis at a time, she told herself. Communication first, then worry about the rest. She tugged Riley's keys from the lock, no longer caring what observations the psychiatrist might have made. Not after what she'd just figured out for herself.

Heaven's contingency plan was screwed unless she could find a way to fix him.

SETH WATCHED FROM his window as Alexandra Jarvis walked to the waiting vehicle and got in. He touched his throat, tracing lines like those he'd seen on her. *Pain.* He frowned at the sensation—at the idea it contained which he couldn't quite grasp. The vehicle below began to move away.

He curled his fingers into his palms, discomfort fluttering in his belly. He wanted to go with her but held himself still. While he didn't fully understand the *later* she had spoken of, he did know her promise to return. And, though he couldn't have said how, he did know her. Knew her touch, knew her eyes, knew the feeling—named or not—that had surged in his breast when he met her gaze.

Which was more than he could say about anything he'd seen or experienced since he'd opened his eyes and stared at Dr. Riley for the first time.

The car carrying Alexandra Jarvis disappeared around a corner and Seth moved his hand from his throat and placed it against the grated window. He also knew the energy he'd found waiting inside him when Alex had left his room, the energy that let him think himself to her side. Stretching his mind ever so slightly, he tested it again. Metal and glass dissolved beneath his touch to let in the fresh, salt-tinged breeze. The discomfort at his center gave way to another feeling—again unnamed, but this time simply right.

Breathing deeply, Seth settled in to wait.

"DR. RILEY?"

Tearing her gaze from Melanie Chiu's draped form on the steel table, Elizabeth took in the grim expression of Aaron Warner, the obstetrician who had joined her. A pallor underlay his skin and he still wore bloodied scrubs.

"What happened?" she asked, tipping her head toward the table.

"Beats the hell out of me," Warner muttered. He shook his head, staring past her at Chiu's covered body. "I've never seen anything like it. A week ago the ultrasound said she was only six months along, but that baby was as fully developed as any I've ever delivered. And it came so damned fast—"

His voice trailed off into silence, broken only by the sound of a trolley passing by in the corridor outside. Warner swallowed.

"It ripped her apart from the inside," he finished hoarsely. "It broke her pelvis, for God's sake. She bled out before we could mop up enough to see what to clamp. We just couldn't move fast enough."

"And the baby?"

"A girl. She's fine. Perfect. Tested ten on both Apgars." Scraping off the cap he still wore, Warner tossed it onto a pile of soiled linens in the corner, then placed his hands on his hips. He scowled at the bed. "What the hell was this, Dr. Riley?"

Elizabeth crossed her arms against a sudden chill. "I wish I could tell you. Ever since Melanie was admitted, she insisted she didn't have sex until the second of September. That's three weeks ago yesterday."

Warner flicked her an impatient look. "That's impossible."

"I know." She sighed. "There had to have been some kind of trauma she was hiding; something she blocked out."

"You still thinking rape? Maybe someone gave her GHB."

"Maybe, but it's unlikely. If it was Rohypnol, she would have remembered flashes by now, at least of the events leading up to the rape. There's also the possibility of incest. Whatever it was, chances are we'll never know. Not now. Do you know if anyone has called Child Services about the baby?"

Warner nodded. "Pediatric wants to keep her for a few days of observation, but someone is coming to start the paperwork tomorrow. Did you want to speak to them?"

"What's the point? With Melanie gone, I can't offer them anything." Elizabeth stepped out of the way of a maintenance worker wheeling a bucket and mop into the room. "But if her family ever shows up, make sure someone calls me."

ALEX SET HER suitcase on the desk and surveyed the hotel room, from dingy walls to dingier carpets to questionable-looking bed linens. It sure as hell wasn't the Ritz, but she'd chosen it for its proximity to the hospital, not its level of luxury. Besides, she'd stayed in far worse when working undercover.

She pulled open the curtains and looked out through a window in need of washing. A narrow parking lot separated her from the solid brick wall of the neighboring building. Lovely. Good thing she wasn't here for the scenery any more than she was for the luxury.

Leaving the curtains open, Alex tugged the cell phone from her waist and glanced at its display. It was already six o'clock, which made it nine in Toronto. She should give Jen a call, she supposed, to let her know she'd arrived safely and see how Nina was doing. She should, but she really didn't want to face her sister's questions about Seth and what she planned to do. Because the truth was, she hadn't the faintest idea. Knowing Seth had lost his capacity for language was one thing; figuring out how to fix it was quite another. Alex set the cell phone beside her unopened suitcase and scrubbed both hands over her face.

Even if he could speak, there was still the little matter of his memory—or more specifically, the lack thereof. What would it matter if she could communicate with him if she didn't know what the hell to tell him? Heaven's contingency plan, he'd called himself once before, but a plan for what? What exactly was he here to do?

God, what she wouldn't give for a little divine intervention right about now. Swallowing against the tightness building in her throat, she pressed her lips together and unzipped the suitcase. No. She'd promised herself she wouldn't go there. She *couldn't* go there. Not when the memories were still so fresh. Not when they made her want to curl up into a ball and cease to function.

And sure as hell not when the fate of the world might hinge on figuring out what to do about Seth.

Abandoning the suitcase and scooping up her phone, she headed for the door. Food, she decided. Food, and then sleep, and then a plan.

Saving the world would just have to wait.

THIRTEEN

Elizabeth traveled through the hospital corridors on auto-pilot, her mind churning at the events surrounding Melanie Chiu's death. And that baby.

A shudder rippled through her. The infant had already been removed from the room when she arrived, but she'd gone to the nursery after she'd left delivery. A healthy girl, perfect in every way except one: her apparent age. Elizabeth would have sworn on her own life the baby was at least two weeks old instead of mere hours.

But that was as impossible as the story that had existed only in Melanie Chiu's head. Tucking back a strand of hair, Elizabeth wished she had pushed Chiu harder, insisted the young woman delve deeper for the truth. But hindsight was always twenty-twenty, and it was too late for should-haves. Whatever trauma Chiu had hidden from Elizabeth—hidden from herself—they would never know.

Pushing into her office, Elizabeth tightened her lips at the arbitrary fragility of the human psyche, at how completely a mind could protect itself from memories it couldn't handle. It never ceased to amaze her how some people could

suffer the most horrific of events and emerge relatively
unscathed, while others folded like a house of cards. And
then there were those like John Doe, whose mind had folded
in on itself with a totality she had never encountered. An
absoluteness that challenged not just her, but the dozen or
more colleagues with whom she'd consulted.

With a clinical curiosity, she wondered for a moment
where Detective Jarvis sat on the spectrum, and then shook
her head. She had enough patients on her hands without
looking for extras—Alex Jarvis was already under compe-
tent care and didn't need her help. Doe, on the other hand . . .

Reaching her desk, she looked down at the name she'd
scrawled across the pad of paper. Seth Benjamin. A clue to
Doe's identity, and the beginning of a whole new set of
questions. Questions such as how he and Detective Jarvis
were connected; why Jarvis downplayed that connection
after flying three thousand miles to see him; and what other
secrets the detective hid, not just from Elizabeth, but from
her own doctor. Her fellow cops. Scowling at the way her
thoughts kept coming back around to the Toronto detective,
Elizabeth settled into the chair and lifted the phone's
receiver. Hugh Henderson answered on the first ring.

"It's me," she announced. "Chiu had her baby. And I have
a name for John Doe."

Henderson heaved an exaggerated sigh. "You really aren't
going to deal with Daniels on the Doe thing, are you?"

"No."

"Hold on." Papers rustled across the line and then Hugh
said, "Fine. Start with Doe. What do you have?"

"The detective from Toronto flew in this afternoon. She
identified him as Seth Benjamin."

A pause, and then, "That's it? No date of birth?"

"Just a name."

Hugh grunted. "I'll pass it on to Daniels, but he probably
won't find much. What else did she tell you?"

"Absolutely nothing."

"What do you mean, nothing? Does she know him
or not?"

"She says she only knows his name."

"But you think she knows more."

"A lot more. He recognized her. Called her by name."

"I thought he didn't speak. That he had that aphrodisia or whatever you called it."

"Aphasia. And he did. Until he saw her. Her name is the first and only thing he's said."

Hugh sighed. "Hell. All right, tell me where she's staying and I'll have a talk with her in the morning. She may be more willing to speak to a colleague."

Elizabeth snorted. "I doubt it, but be my guest."

"And Chiu? You said she had the baby? How is it? *What* is it, boy or girl?"

"Girl. Nine pounds, five ounces."

"Ouch. That had to hurt. Chiu is what, ninety-eight pounds soaking wet? Is she all right?"

Elizabeth leaned back in her chair and stared at the ceiling. "She's dead. The attending obstetrician said the birth was so fast they didn't stand a chance. The delivery room was like something out of a horror movie."

Hugh went quiet on the other end of the line. Then, softly, he said, "Shit. Poor kid. And the baby?"

"Alive." Elizabeth hesitated, loath to say more, as if by not disclosing details, they wouldn't be true. But Hugh knew her too well.

"And?" he prodded.

"The baby was full term."

"Didn't the ultrasound last week put it at six months?"

"It did." Elizabeth closed her eyes and massaged at a spot just above the bridge of her nose. "The technician must have screwed up. It happens."

And it had to have happened this time, because as Warner had said, the alternative was simply impossible.

The silence at the other end of the phone drew out so long that Elizabeth opened her eyes again. Frowned. "Hugh? Are you still there? Did you hear what I said?"

"I'm here. And yes, I heard." His voice had gone low and gruff, as if he didn't want to be overheard at his end. "Liz—"

That damned nickname again. Elizabeth scowled. She really was going to have to break him of that. Before she could frame her usual objection, however, Hugh knocked all thought of nicknames from her head.

"Liz, Chiu might not be the only one."

WORD WAS DEFINITELY getting around.

Aramael eyed the three Fallen Ones forming a semi-circle around him and then sized up his surroundings. With a twelve-foot-high chain-link fence at his back, a deserted warehouse parking lot stretching beyond his stalkers, and not another soul in sight, his chances of escape looked bleak. Weariness crept over him. Three of them, one of him. Bloody Hell. If his last few demises had been painful, this one was shaping up to be downright brutal.

His predators drew nearer. Aramael tensed, curling his hands into fists. He'd tried a variety of responses to these attacks, and had learned death came fastest when he fought hardest. His ego took less of a beating when he resisted, too. He launched himself at the nearest Fallen One, his fist connecting with a cheek. A foot merged with his rib cage in retaliation, driving out any satisfaction.

Aramael landed on his knees with a grunt. He staggered upright, but another blow in the small of his back sent him down again. They didn't give him another opportunity to rise.

Knowing any attempt at self-protection would only prolong matters, Aramael resisted the urge to curl into a ball. He tried to determine where each of his attackers stood, not because he could do anything to them, but because it distracted him from his bones splintering, his body turning to pulp. The now-familiar red haze began to descend and he braced for the unpleasant sensation of death.

A gust of wind drove grit into his mouth. Shouts came. Cries of pain that weren't his. And then . . . nothing. Nothing but the sound of his own harsh breathing in his ears. His own blood rushing through his veins and dripping onto the pavement.

He waited for the blows to resume. Then, when they didn't, for his body to begin its inevitable healing. Bones knit together, internal organs stopped bleeding, ruptured vessels repaired themselves. The haze receded. Aramael cracked open his eyelids and stared at his enemies, scattered on the pavement around him. He frowned. *What the hell—?*

When enough of his pieces had moved back to where they belonged, he pushed himself gingerly into a sitting position, surveyed the Fallen Ones, and then raised his gaze to a form perched atop the fence. His jaw went slack. Cold fingers of fear—true fear—wrapped around his belly.

Dropping to the ground, the Archangel stalked toward him, silent, watchful, grim. Aramael climbed to his feet and, heart thundering, eyed the warrior. Disbelief shocked through him.

Over his entire existence, he'd rarely had more than a glimpse of any of the reclusive Archangels—other than when Raphael and Uriel had thrown him out of Heaven—but he didn't remember seeing this one at all. If he wasn't mistaken . . .

The Archangel stopped a few feet away and folded his glossy black wings against his back. Aramael drew tall.

"I won't go without a fight," he snarled. "I don't care who ordered it."

The Archangel raised an eyebrow. "I've seen you fight," he responded. "Forgive me if I'm not that concerned."

Aramael glared at him. The Archangel was right. He couldn't even best a Fallen One and he wanted to stand up to one of Heaven's enforcers? Even at the peak of his angelic strength as a Power, he'd been no match for an Archangel.

Especially if this Archangel was who Aramael thought he was.

"So is this how it ends? She changes her mind and, just like that, I'm exiled to Limbo?"

"If that were her wish, then yes. That would be exactly how it would end."

Aramael wiped at the blood trickling from his nose. Details about the newcomer began to filter through. *Wings folded.* Archangels only folded their wings when they were relaxed. *Expression bland.* No Heavenly fire glowed in the green gaze regarding him with such—disdain? Aramael bridled anew and drew himself to his full height.

"You have issues with me, Black One?" he challenged.

The Archangel's wings unfurled ever so slightly at the slur. A reference not to the color of his wings, but to the black souls his kind were said to possess. Souls burned by Hellfire itself when they forced Lucifer across the barrier between Heaven and Hell, into the realm the One had allowed him. An unsubstantiated rumor, but one that nonetheless enjoyed widespread belief among angelkind.

"Watch yourself, Power," the Archangel drawled. "I may not exile you to Limbo, but I'd be quite happy to let these three at you again." He furled his wings. "And to answer your question, any issues I might have are irrelevant."

"Then suppose you tell me what is relevant."

"My task. And yours."

Aramael frowned. "Task?"

"Your Creator needs you, Aramael of the Powers." The Archangel smiled tightly. "And judging by the company you keep, you need me."

FOURTEEN

Alex paused, coffee cup halfway to her mouth, as a man slid into the restaurant booth opposite her. Showing none of her surprise at the intrusion, she ran a cop's gaze over him. Early forties; closely shorn dark hair salted with gray; an off-the-rack suit sitting across his shoulders in a way that hinted at regular exercise. She raised an eyebrow at the sunglasses hiding his eyes.

"Vancouver PD, I presume?" She took the sip of coffee he had interrupted, and then set the cup on the table beside the remains of her breakfast.

Her uninvited companion's lips curved upward. But only slightly. "You sound like you were expecting me."

"Not really. But I'm not surprised Riley sicced you on me."

The man hadn't removed his sunglasses yet, and Alex steeled herself against a surge of annoyance at the intimidation tactic.

"How did you know where to look for me?" Pretending idleness, she flipped the page of the newspaper she'd been scanning.

"You needed breakfast. On a cop's salary, you wouldn't be going anywhere fancy. This is the closest place to your hotel."

Not bad.

"Hugh Henderson," he added. "Detective, Sex Crimes. Aren't you going to ask why I'm here?"

"I'm guessing Riley hopes you can get more information out of me than she did." Alex sighed and rested her chin in one hand. "And that you ran Seth's name and came up dry."

The sunglasses reflected her own gaze back to her. After a long moment, Henderson slipped them off and tucked them into the inside pocket of his suit jacket. Light glinted off the plain gold band he wore on his left ring finger. Hazel eyes regarded her coolly.

"You knew we wouldn't get anything."

Alex nodded.

"So that's not really his name, then."

Alex moved her hand up to rub a temple. How to phrase this so she didn't dig her current hole any deeper? And so Henderson didn't accompany her back to the airport and put her on the next flight home?

"It's the name I know him by," she hedged.

Henderson's gaze narrowed and several long seconds passed. "Twenty-eight years," he said finally.

"Pardon?"

"That's how long I've been a cop. Twenty-eight years." He paused as a waitress approached with a coffeepot and refilled Alex's cup, waving her off when she reached for his. When they were alone again, he looked up with a knock-off-the-bullshit expression. "I know evasiveness when I see it, Detective, and I don't give a rat's ass if you're here unofficially or not. I don't appreciate having a colleague try to snow me."

Adjusting her estimate of his age a few years upward, Alex looked out the window at the pedestrians on the sidewalk. A child in a yellow raincoat gave her a shy smile and wave as he trotted past the restaurant at his mother's side. She watched the bright spot of color until parent and offspring disappeared from sight. A hard lump settled in her throat.

If she couldn't help Seth after all, if he couldn't stop the coming war, what would happen to humanity? What would happen to Nina, already so fragile, and all the yellow-raincoated children of the world?

She swallowed the lump.

"Thirteen years," she said, returning her gaze to Henderson. "That's how long *I've* been a cop. I don't snow colleagues."

Henderson toyed with a spoon on the table before him. "But you still won't give me answers."

"I can't."

"There's a difference between can't and won't, Detective Jarvis."

Alex held his gaze without blinking. "I know the difference, Detective Henderson."

A flush of color rose from beneath Henderson's collar. Alex heaved an inward groan. Great. That was all she needed to do, piss off a cop in his own jurisdiction when she had no real business being here in the first place—no business she could discuss, anyway. She leaned her elbows on the table and threaded her hands into her hair, imagining herself in Henderson's shoes and knowing she'd react in exactly the same way. She had to give the man something. Some tidbit to appease him.

Henderson cleared his throat. Alex held up one hand to forestall him, leaning her head sideways into the other.

"You know about the serial killer we had in Toronto last month."

A blink acknowledged the sudden change in subject.

"Seth—Mr. Benjamin was—" Alex hesitated, framing her words with utmost care. *A tidbit, not a five-course meal.* "He was instrumental in the solving of the case."

Henderson waited and Alex had to grit her teeth to keep herself quiet. She decided she preferred being on the business end of that particular interrogation tactic. More seconds passed. A tiny glint of humor moved across Henderson's gaze, an acknowledgement of the stalemate.

"Instrumental how?" he asked.

She had to force the words out. "I can't say."

The flush returned and crept upward, staining Henderson's jawline. "Is there anything you *can* say, Detective Jarvis?"

"Mr. Benjamin didn't want his involvement widely known. He gave us no information about himself and we were in no position to force the issue."

"And I can confirm this by talking to—?" The Vancouver detective's voice was tight.

Alex recalled Roberts's offer when he'd shown her Seth's photo—*call me. I'll do what I can*—and hoped to hell he'd meant it.

"My supervisor." She sighed. "Staff Inspector Doug Roberts."

ARAMAEL INSPECTED HIS image in the mirror and then tossed the damp, crumpled paper towel into the garbage can. He hadn't been able to wash away all the traces of his latest beating, but at least his appearance wouldn't draw too much attention anymore. Especially not in this place.

He dodged the door as a man pushed into the bathroom and staggered toward the row of urinals along one wall. With a grimace, Aramael stepped into the narrow corridor, trying not to breathe too deeply of the stench of beer and misery oozing from the walls. A throb of music from the strip club overhead accompanied him back to the shabby basement bar.

His gaze traveled the half dozen patrons lining the stools along the counter, each seeking refuge from the world in varying states of inebriation. It was no wonder the Archangel had chosen this place. Most of these mortals had already turned from their Guardians, making it unlikely that a Fallen One would wander in to disturb the tête-à-tête he had requested. A tête-à-tête he'd made clear he wanted kept secret.

Aramael's gaze settled on a set of wing tips jutting over the top of the booth at the far end of the room. Threading his way past a battered pool table and the clients seated at the bar, he slid into the seat opposite the Archangel. Not a single head turned to mark his presence.

The Archangel surveyed him, toying with one of the glasses on the table. "Not much better, but you'll do. We'll have to see about getting you a clean set of clothes. That's Scotch, by the way." He nodded at the glass in front of Aramael. "You looked like you needed it."

Aramael ignored the drink. "*We* aren't doing a bloody thing until *you* tell me what the hell is going on. And who you are."

"You know who I am."

"No." Aramael paused. "But I suspect."

"My name is Mika'el."

So it *was* him. Mika'el. Legend among his own kind, the most powerful of all the Archangels, rumored to have defied the cleansing of free will among the Heavenly host and to have been banished to the mortal realm for his insubordination.

Aramael stared at the angel on the other side of the booth, wondering what the sentence had done to him, contemplating the eternity he himself would endure here. A sliver of dread pierced his heart. Even if he did manage to find Alex, and even if he were to reestablish what had been taken from them, and even if she lived an extraordinarily long life, at some point she would be gone and he would find himself just like Mika'el, living a life of eternal solitude.

He backed away from the abyss behind the thought. He didn't need to go there. Not yet. Picking up the drink, he swirled the amber liquid in one direction, then the other. "The stories were true, then."

"That would depend on the stories."

"You defied the One and were banished to Earth."

Mika'el snorted. "Wrong on both counts. I didn't defy her, and I left of my own accord."

"Because—?"

"We had a disagreement."

"A disagreement," Aramael repeated. "You left Heaven, left the One's side, because you didn't like something she said?"

Mika'el's eyes narrowed. "You of all angels should know things are never as simple as they appear."

Touché.

"Can I ask what the disagreement was about?"

"We're not here to discuss me."

One look at the Archangel's iron-hard jawline assured Aramael he didn't want to pursue the subject. "Fine. Then what are we here to discuss?"

"Seth has transitioned to the mortal realm, but things—well, let's just say things didn't go as planned."

"Mittron." Aramael bit out the hated name as a statement, not a question.

"Mittron," the Archangel agreed.

"You know?" Aramael frowned. "Then the One must, too."

"The Seraph has already faced Judgment."

Savage satisfaction sparred with disappointment in Aramael's belly. As glad as he was the Highest had gotten what he deserved, he had very much wanted the pleasure of seeing to Mittron's punishment himself. Very much.

He took a swallow of Scotch. "Limbo?"

"I didn't ask."

He grunted. Whatever it was, it could never be harsh enough. Never begin to equal the damage the Seraph had caused. He raised an eyebrow in Mika'el's direction.

"So what is this all-important task the great Mika'el was pulled from retirement to tell me about?"

Mika'el ignored the dig. "The Appointed transitioned as an adult rather than an infant."

Aramael stared at the Archangel. "An *adult*? But that

means he could make a decision at any time, without a chance to get to know them."

Except Seth *had* gotten to know some of them. However briefly, he'd at least met Alex and her colleagues and family—a tiny fraction of humanity but enough, with luck, to give him some perspective. A damn good thing, too. Aramael's gaze returned to the bar. Because if Seth had seen only *this* as humanity's potential . . .

"It gets worse." Mika'el grimaced. "He has no memory."

In a few brief words, Mika'el told Aramael what Mittron had attempted—and failed—to do. Shock rocked Aramael to the core. *So much for context.* "Bloody Hell," he breathed. Reaching for his glass, he downed the contents and waited for the burn to pass. "What is the One going to do?"

"There's nothing she can do. Not without forfeiting the agreement."

"Which would give Lucifer free rein over the mortals."

"It would."

"There must be *some* way to stop the Appointed."

Mika'el stayed silent, his gaze unfaltering. Slow realization unfurled in Aramael's mind. He shook his head, first in disbelief, then in denial.

"She wouldn't ask that of me," he said.

"She isn't asking it of you. I am."

The Archangel was serious. Aramael struggled to breathe. To remain in his seat and not launch himself across the table at the warrior who held his gaze. "I'm not a murderer."

Again Mika'el said nothing.

From the far side of the bar came the clink of a glass, the crack of pool balls colliding. The steady thump of music drifted down from the club above.

"I am not a murderer," Aramael repeated through teeth clenched as tightly as his fists.

But the churn at his center had begun to give way to clarity. To sick, awful certainty. The Archangel was right. Heaven couldn't leave the Appointed in such a position of power in his current state. There was no telling what kind of damage had been done to Seth's soul during Mittron's botched attempt to transition him. The risk in letting him make a choice in this state was simply too great. It made sense to eliminate him.

Just as it made sense that Mika'el had come to Aramael. To the one angel no longer connected to Heaven who might take on the task.

His fingers tightened around the empty glass. Breathing deeply, he let the wretchedness permeating the bar seep into his every pore. Sudden bitterness burned in his chest. Had he not sacrificed enough already? He'd lost everything he had once been, everything he'd known, and for what? To save *these*? These, whom she called her children and deemed worthy of protection from Lucifer at the cost of her own son? At the cost of first Aramael's soulmate, and now his very soul?

He gathered himself to leave. To rise from his seat and tell Mika'el what he could do with his *task*. But something greater than anger held him in place. Something greater than him.

"Does she know?" he asked quietly.

"She knows."

"And she is all right with the idea?"

Mika'el didn't answer.

Aramael stared at the empty glass in his hands. Felt the echoing emptiness in his belly. "There is no other way?"

"None we can afford."

"So is this an order, then?"

"You've been banished, Aramael. I have no authority to order you. I can only ask—and remind you of the part you played in this whole mess."

Aramael flinched. Physically. Viscerally.

"You prick."

"I state nothing but the truth, Power."

The truth, the whole truth, and nothing but the truth. *So help me, One.*

Aramael's gaze slid to a point beyond the Archangel's

shoulder. It *had* been his fault. Giving in to his feelings for Alex, losing control of himself, taking a life. All choices he had made. All leading to this. All demanding he put the memory of Alex behind him and accept Mika'el's task. He cleared his throat. "Will I have help?"

"As much as I can give."

Wondering if the words were as hollow as they sounded, Aramael grunted.

"One more thing," Mika'el said. "We think the Appointed retains his powers—"

"Great."

"—and we know he remains immortal."

"You can't be serious. I don't have the ability to take that from him."

"You have been given what you need."

Frowning, Aramael pulled into himself for a moment, examining his center. He found none of the energies he had once taken for granted. No connection to Heaven; none to the One. He opened his mouth to tell the Archangel so—and then paused.

Wait. That. What was that?

A tiny pulse, buried deep in his core, new, unfamiliar, and, when he reached out to touch it, surging with promise. Aramael drew back, startled. Wary.

His eyes narrowed on Mika'el. "What the hell is that?"

"It is enough. Call on it when you're ready. But you only get one chance."

"And if I mess up?"

"I think," said Mika'el, "we both understand that's not an option."

FIFTEEN

"I s it him?"
Alex balanced a load of books in one arm, pinned the cell phone against her shoulder, and fished in her pocket for her room key as she exited the elevator. "Nice to hear your voice, too," she told her sister dryly. "And yes, the flight was great, thanks. Right on time."

"Is it Seth or isn't it, Alex?"

Alex's fingers closed over the key. "It's him. He has amnesia, but he seemed to recognize me."

"Seemed?"

Entering the corridor to her room, Alex noted that management hadn't yet replaced the burned-out bulbs she'd mentioned to them. In fact—she slowed her steps to let her eyes adjust to the gloom—she'd venture to say at least one more had burned out since she'd left a couple of hours earlier.

She sighed, then answered Jen's question. "He said my name when he saw me."

"That's it? Nothing else?"

"Nothing." Alex grimaced. "He hasn't said anything since he was found."

"Is he injured?"

"No, I think—" Alex shifted her load and poked the hotel room key at the lock on her door. It missed. "Hang on a sec, Jen."

She bent to peer through the gloom and wrinkled her nose at an un-nameable odor rising from the carpet. Maybe that was why management hadn't replaced the lights—they were trying to hide whatever caused the smell. Two books slid to the floor.

"Oh, for chrissake," she muttered.

"Something wrong?" Jen asked.

"Just trying to get into my room." Alex succeeded in mating key to lock and straightened again. Three more books toppled from the pile. "Hell. Jen, can I call you back in a few minutes? I'm dropping stuff all over the floor."

"It's all right. Nina and I are going out for lunch anyway. We're celebrating her meds being cut. Last night was the first night she didn't fall asleep in her dinner."

Alex paused for a moment, giving Jen her full attention. "That's fantastic news," she said. "I'm so happy things are getting better."

"Happy enough to visit us when you get back?"

If I get back.

"Of course. I'll come straight there from the airport. Promise. Give Nina a hug for me, all right? And, Jen—" Her voice caught.

"What, sweetie?"

If something happens . . . if I can't fix Seth . . . if I don't make it back before things go wrong . . .

"Nothing. Just—nothing. I'll call you in a couple of days, all right? Love you." Before her sister could respond, Alex flipped the phone shut and reached for the doorknob.

"You lied to me," said a woman's voice behind her.

Reflex sent Alex's hand to her hip where her gun should have been. By the time she remembered it wasn't there, her brain had identified the voice—and she still wanted the gun.

She looked over her shoulder at Elizabeth Riley, who was obviously spoiling for a fight.

Wonderful. Lips tightening, Alex pushed open the door and carried the remaining books into the room. She set them on the dresser and glanced at the bedside clock. Ten past two. Six hours since Henderson had visited her in the coffee shop. She wondered how many of those hours Riley had spent in the corridor, lying in wait for her return.

She turned back to the psychiatrist, who still stood outside the room, arms crossed and expression belligerent. "I didn't lie."

"Seth Benjamin doesn't exist. You gave me a false name. What would you call that if not a lie?"

Squatting to retrieve the fallen books, Alex regarded Riley wearily. She'd known Henderson would tell the shrink about their conversation, but had hoped for the day to go over things in her head, collect her thoughts, get her story straight. Hell, to come up with a story at all.

Books in hand, she stood up again. "You'd better come in."

Riley glared at her over the tops of her glasses for a moment and then followed her into the room. Closing the door, Alex motioned toward the only armchair, a battered piece near the window that dated back at least to the sixties and looked to have been rescued from a Dumpster.

"Have a seat."

She deliberately withheld the *please*, and the narrowing of Riley's eyes said the doctor knew it. Good. It served her right for turning out to be a bulldog in a hippie-grandmother disguise. Dropping onto the edge of the bed, Alex waited for the psychiatrist to take a seat in the chair.

"I didn't lie," she said again, when Riley had settled. "I gave you the only name I have for him. I also told you I didn't know him well. I never ran his name myself."

"What about your mutual friend? Did you run him?"

Alex looked away, staring at the gilt-framed landscape on the wall. Wondered, with a moment's idle curiosity, what might have come from running an angel's name through the police computer system. Would he have had a criminal record? A driver's license? Outstanding parking tickets?

"I knew him," she answered. "I didn't need to run him."

"Detective Jarvis—"

"I didn't *need* to run him."

Riley studied her in silence. Taking off her glasses, she polished them with the bottom edge of her blouse. She slid them back into place. "Well. I can't say it was nice to meet you, Detective, but it certainly was interesting. I hope you have a safe trip back to Toronto."

Alex's head jerked up. "I'm not done here."

"Oh, but you are. Quite done."

Shit.

"Seth recognized me," Alex reminded her. "I can help you reach him."

Riley gave a short bark of laughter. "You think I would trust you to do that? You have evasiveness written all over you. Your secrets have secrets. And there is no way in hell you're going near my patient unless you come clean and start giving me some answers. Straight ones." She held up a hand as Alex opened her mouth to object. "Don't. Unless you're ready to talk—really talk—I'm not interested."

Rising, Riley headed for the door. Alex stared after her, impotence paralyzing her throat. She had to stop the other woman, but the psychiatrist wanted truths she wouldn't believe even if she did hear them.

Truths that weren't Alex's to speak.

Riley was halfway across the room, then all the way, and then reaching for the doorknob.

Alex stood up from the bed. "I know why he isn't speaking."

The psychiatrist turned the knob. "So do I. It's called aphasia. Global aphasia, to be precise."

"That means he doesn't know language?"

The rigid lines of Riley's back gave evidence of her internal struggle as she hesitated at the door. At last she released the knob, folded her arms, and faced Alex. "Yes. We just don't know why. There are no signs of physical trauma, no signs of stroke or disease—the CAT scan came back clean and the neurologist can't find anything."

"Wait—you *tested* him?"

A sardonic brow shot up toward Riley's hairline. "We're doctors. That's what we do."

"And the tests came back—"

"All normal."

Alex fought back the need to hyperventilate. If Seth wasn't human, how was that possible? Had whatever caused his amnesia—or aphasia or whatever Riley wanted to call it—somehow changed him physiologically? Seeing Riley reach again for the doorknob, she said rapidly, "He can learn."

"I've had a speech therapist working with him every day for the last week. He hasn't said a word."

"He said my name. He can learn."

Riley looked wearily over her shoulder. "Detective Jarvis—"

A trill interrupted and the psychiatrist muttered an oath and shoved her blouse out of the way to unclip the phone from her waistband. She flipped it open. "Elizabeth Riley."

Alex moved to gaze out the grime-streaked window. Not out of any sense of consideration for Riley's privacy, but to give herself time to drag the fragments of her mind back together again. Seth, undergoing medical tests. Tests that showed him to be normal—human, even. But she'd seen otherwise. She'd watched him disappear. Knew he still had at least some of his powers.

As for language, she'd heard him speak. Was certain he had the capacity to relearn speech. But if she couldn't tell the shrink about the come/go/stay lesson that had taken place in her office, how the hell would she convince her? Alex massaged the ache beginning in her temple. She could so use a drink right now.

"What do you mean, gone? How can it be gone?"

The sharpness of Riley's voice snapped Alex's attention back to her. She leaned against the window frame as the other woman's brow furrowed.

"Well, it must be somewhere—maintenance must have removed it and forgotten to tell you. Do we have another room for him? Just move him there, then, and I'll do the paperwork in the morning. And make sure you report this to Admin—I want to know who's responsible." Riley snapped the phone shut and stared at it a moment before she replaced it in its holder.

"Trouble?" Alex asked.

"The window and security screen are missing from John Doe's room."

Shit. Alex focused all her energy on not reacting, saying instead, "You could ask him what happened if you'd let me work with him."

"And why exactly do you expect to have more success than the speech therapist?"

"Has he said the therapist's name?"

Riley's nostrils flared and she stared at Alex, her expression giving no clue to what went on behind the sharp eyes and wire-framed glasses. Steeling herself, Alex held her gaze. She willed the woman to accept her offer and not press further for answers she simply could not give. Riley's eyes narrowed, slid away, dropped to the stack of books on the dresser.

"Interesting reading material."

Three illustrated encyclopedias. Two illustrated dictionaries. Several children's books to teach reading skills. Alex shrugged. "They're for Seth. I thought it might help."

She didn't add that it had damned well better help, because if windows and security screens were disappearing from Seth's room, she needed to establish communication sooner rather than later.

Riley picked up one of the dictionaries and flipped through it. After a moment, she set it down again and tugged open the door. "Tomorrow," she said without looking back. "Nine a.m. I'll meet you at the nurse's station. Bring the books."

SIXTEEN

Aramael braced himself against the wall, chest heaving, bricks rough beneath his palms. Probing the inside of his mouth with his tongue, he connected with a loose tooth and sent a sideways glare at the Archangel waiting for him.

"Tell me again how this is supposed to help?"

Mika'el paced the plank floor with the slow, lazy watchfulness of a predator waiting for its chance to make the final kill. A smile ghosted across his face. "I've seen you fight, remember? The Fallen Ones will keep coming after you unless you give them reason to leave you alone, and I can't stick around to act as your nursemaid."

"So your solution is to beat the crap out of me before they do?"

"If you'd learn to keep up your guard, I wouldn't be able to hit you as often."

"Maybe not, but you'd hit just as hard."

"No harder than you can. Once you start landing as many blows as you take, you won't make such an appealing target, believe me."

Aramael dodged a right jab. Mortar crumbled to the floor

of the deserted warehouse as Mika'el pulled his fist out of the wall. He scowled. It seemed to him the Archangel was enjoying the lesson far more than he should.

"But that's the problem, isn't it? I *can't* hit as hard as you. Or them."

Mika'el caught back a left hook in mid-swing. "Pardon?"

"I said I can't—"

"I heard you. I just didn't believe *what* I heard. Is that what you think? That you can't hit as hard as a Fallen One?"

Aramael scowled at him and pulled the neck of his T-shirt down to expose the ugly, ridged scar on the back of one shoulder where Mittron had torn away his wings. "Maybe you missed the part about me being thrown out of Heaven and stripped of my powers."

"I didn't miss anything, smart-ass." Mika'el scooped up a towel from the corner and tossed it to him. "But I think you may have misunderstood."

"Misunderstood what?"

"Regardless of what happened, you are still—and always will be—an angel. You are a superior being, physically equal to each and every Fallen One in the universe. With the exception of Lucifer, perhaps."

"But Mittron—"

Mika'el raised an eyebrow.

Aramael sighed. Right. Mittron, architect of this entire mess. "So what did he forget to tell me?"

"The only powers stripped from you were those connecting you to Heaven: your ability to move between realms or communicate with your kin, or to call on energies that were never yours to begin with. Everything else is as much a part of you as breathing—your immortality, your ability to heal yourself, your physical strength. Mittron could no more take away those than he could turn a human into an immortal. It simply isn't—and wasn't—within his power."

Aramael spat on the towel and rubbed away the dried blood from his already healed lip. He walked across the dusty floor and stared out the window at the street below, thinking back over the month he'd spent as a punching bag for any Fallen One who tracked him down.

Thirty days' worth of reasons to hate Mittron a little more. It really was too bad he'd never have a chance to repay the Seraph.

Down the block, the driver of a delivery van unloaded a rack of bread at a corner store. Traffic noises drifted in from the city: a siren, a horn, a truck rumbling along the pavement. Aramael's breathing slowed, evened out. Could Mika'el be right? He focused inward for a moment but found nothing but frustration. If he did retain any part of the angelic, he sure as hell couldn't feel it. He just felt *puny*.

He scowled at his faint reflection.

But if it were true . . .

"You're sure." He looked over his shoulder. "You're sure I'm as strong as they are."

"Positive."

"If I do fight back the way you say, what's to stop them from calling on their own powers?"

"It's unlikely they will. We had a few days after the pact fell where the Fallen Ones believed they had free rein in the mortal world, but your former colleagues convinced them otherwise. Things have been quiet again for almost three weeks and should remain so as long as the agreement stands. The Fallen Ones are sufficiently cautious that you won't face anything more than you can handle."

Aramael grunted. "So you're telling me—"

Mika'el smiled with grim satisfaction. "I'm telling you that, with a little work, you can kick a Fallen One's ass from here to Hell and back again."

Aramael dropped the towel onto the windowsill and turned to the Archangel.

"Then what are we waiting for?"

ALEX PRESENTED HERSELF at the nurses' station at 8:57 a.m., books in hand, as ordered. Elizabeth Riley waited for her beneath the clock on the wall, fingers tapping against crossed arms. The psychiatrist wore cargo-style pants again, and a blouse the color of a summer sky. Without a word, she led the way down the corridor, Birkenstocks slapping against gleaming linoleum. Following, Alex wondered if Fridays were standard blue-blouse days.

"I trust you slept well?" Riley broke the silence at last.

With the ease of habit, Alex told the same lie she'd been telling since Caim had very nearly killed her. "Fine, thanks."

"Your hotel isn't too noisy? You've hardly chosen a place conducive to sleep."

"Maybe not, but it's all I can afford if I'm going to be here for a while."

Riley's expression clearly said she didn't think a long stay necessary—or likely, but her grunt was non-committal. Stopping in front of a door, she slid a key into the lock. "Time to put your theory to the test."

She pushed open the door and stepped inside, only to come up short. "What the hell—?"

Alex peered over her, gaze sweeping the empty room, heart sinking. She pushed past Riley to make sure Seth wasn't out of view in one of the corners. Nothing. Her heart sank. *Lord, Seth, I told you to stay . . .*

"They must have moved him again." Riley muttered something under her breath and then added, "Wait here. I'll find out what's going on."

She returned thirty seconds later, a nurse in tow. She shot a grim look at Alex. "No one moved him. We're doing a sweep of the floor and we've notified security."

Standard procedure. But not standard circumstances. An image of Seth, cornered by security guards, sprang to Alex's mind—along with visions of a half dozen messy outcomes. Shit, this was so not good. Before she could think of a way to express her reservations, however, a voice hailed from down the corridor.

"Found him!"

The same relief that flashed through Alex crossed Riley's and the nurse's faces. Following them to where an orderly stood outside another room, Alex stepped inside, leaving the three in a heated debate about negligence and dereliction of duty.

Seth turned from the gaping, empty window space and smiled his pleasure at seeing her. "Alexandra Jarvis." He waved his hand at his surroundings, looking satisfied. "I room," he said. "I stay."

In the room to which she'd told him to return, the one where she'd first seen him. Of course. With a twinge of regret, Alex glanced over her shoulder where Riley read the riot act to the blameless nurse and orderly, and then she smiled at Seth.

"Yes," she agreed. "You stayed." She held out the bag of books she carried. "I brought you something."

Seth left the window and strolled over to join her. He reached into the bag and took out one of the illustrated dictionaries, turning it over to examine it. "Something?" he asked quizzically, holding it up to her.

"A book. A dictionary."

He frowned.

Alex took out another book. "Book," she said again. "A story."

A third. "Book. An encyclopedia."

Seth's bafflement only appeared to increase, however, and so she put back the two books she'd taken from the bag and held out her hand for the one Seth held. She flipped through the pages, stopping at the letter *b*. "Book," she said, pointing to the illustration and then hefting the volume in her hands. Another point to an illustration, and then to the cot along the wall. "Bed."

Seth's gaze narrowed.

Alex thumbed through more pages and pointed to the door outside, where Riley had gone silent and watched intently. "Door."

Flip, flip, flip, point. "Window."

Flip, flip. She pointed from the book to Riley and then to the nurse. "Woman."

Seth's finger touched her gently, mid-chest. "Alexandra Jarvis. Woman."

Alex looked up into black eyes lit with understanding. Lit with a faint glimmer of *Seth*. She caught her breath, a frisson crawling up her spine. She'd been right. He was still in there. He just didn't know how to get out.

"Yes," she agreed. "I'm a woman, too."

His gaze lingered on hers for a long moment, and then dropped to the book in her hands. Alex held out the dictionary to him and he took it gently, almost reverently. "Book," he whispered.

"Yes," Alex said. "Dictionary."

Seth went to the window, leaned a shoulder against the frame, and began flipping through the pages. But just as she was giving herself all kinds of mental pats on the back and feeling more than a little smug, Seth's reverence turned to frustration.

"I don't know book," he accused, his tone one of betrayal. He slammed the cover shut and threw the dictionary on the bed, his dark eyes sparking. The bed bounced under the impact—or did it?

The cot legs hovered above the floor. Shit. Alex cast a quick glance at Riley, but the doctor was frowning at Seth and didn't seem to have noticed anything odd. Yet. Crossing to Seth's side, Alex took his fisted hands into her own, prying his fingers from his palms.

"It's all right," she soothed. "At least this tells us I'm right about the language thing. I didn't expect you to be able to read."

"I don't know *book*," he growled, curling his fingers around hers in a tear-inducing grip.

Swallowing a wince, Alex kept her voice even. "I know. But *I* know book, and I'll teach you. I promise."

"Detective Jarvis, a word, please," said Riley.

Alex ignored her, holding Seth's dark, turbulent gaze with a steadiness she hoped would mask her rising unease. Seth Benjamin may have saved her life once, but what did she really know about him? Aramael had described himself as a not-nice kind of angel . . . What if Seth was of that same breed? With no memory of who he was, no checks and balances built into him the way Aramael had . . .

Agonizing seconds dragged past. At last Seth's grip relaxed, restoring circulation to her tortured digits; he might not comprehend her words, but he seemed to understand her intent. Behind her, someone exhaled in a rush. Alex offered up a quick, small prayer that the sound would cover the muffled thud of the bed dropping back to the floor.

She gave Seth's fingers a light squeeze. *Please, please let Riley have stayed focused on Seth and not the bed.* "Much better," she said. "We'll figure this out, all right? Together. You just have to be patient and wait."

Heaven's contingency plan looked unconvinced.

"Wait," Alex repeated. "You stay here, you wait, you be patient."

"Detective." Riley's clipped voice held a distinct, unhappy edge.

Alex squeezed Seth's fingers a final time and then turned, her gaze flicking over the little group still in the doorway. Riley, who seemed intent on boring a hole through Alex with her hostile glare. The nurse, staring at Seth with a perplexed frown etched between her brows, most likely still trying to figure out how he'd been moved without her knowledge. And the orderly, whose gaze was fixated on the bed.

He'd seen.

Alex slanted a glance toward the cot and winced. The bolts that had secured the bed to the floor now lay free of their moorings, scattered across the tile. First the window grate, and then Seth's disappearing act, and now this.

Not good. Not good at all.

A hundred possible outcomes to the situation raced through her mind, all of them ending with Seth, of unknown and possibly uncontrollable powers, going up against a curious and frightened system. Not just *not good*, but downright dangerous.

She had to get him out of here. But how?

And to where?

She spun back to Seth, the seeds of a vague, desperate plan beginning to form. "Wait," she said in a low voice, looking pointedly toward the window and knowing she had about three seconds to get this across to him. "Watch. When you see me, come."

"Come?" he echoed, taking a tentative step toward her.

"Not now," Alex hissed. She looked back at a visibly irritated Riley. "Later. Watch now," she pointed toward the window, making sure her gesture was hidden from the others. "Be patient. Come later."

"Detective," Riley grated.

Alex stared into Seth's eyes, willing him to understand. "Come later," she repeated. "When you see me out there."

"Detective Jarvis," the psychiatrist snapped, "either come with me now or I call security."

"Coming," Alex said. "I'm coming."

SEVENTEEN

Dancing out of Mika'el's reach, Aramael watched the Archangel swipe blood from a split lip. It marked the second blow he'd landed in this session; the second Mika'el had failed to block. And the Archangel had not yet touched him. Hard satisfaction burned in Aramael's chest.

Mika'el regarded him with a mixture of ruefulness and approval. "You have learned well, Grasshopper."

Grasshopper?

Mika'el waved away the question before Aramael could ask it. "Never mind. Human thing. It just means I think my job here is done."

Aramael lowered his fists. "Done? You're not taking me to Seth?"

"If you're capable of slipping past an Archangel's guard, you're ready to take on a few cocky Fallen Ones." Mika'el stepped past him and picked up a towel from the floor by the wall. "I told you I had better things to do than baby-sit you."

"I don't need a babysitter. But when I find Seth—"

The Archangel shot him a narrow look. "I cannot help you with Seth, Power. You must know that."

"I knew you expected me to—" Aramael paused. Gritted his teeth. "I know I must kill Seth, but you said—"

"I said I would give what help I could. This was it."

A flush of anger started at Aramael's toes and spiraled upward. He supposed a part of him had suspected as much, but he hadn't wanted to ask. And would have preferred not to know.

He wrestled with his reaction. It made sense, of course. While Mika'el may have been absent for four and a half millennia, his connections to Heaven were still strong. Traceable. The Archangel couldn't be seen to have anything to do with what needed to be done. The alternative, however, stank.

"So that's it, then. I've become the sacrificial lamb."

"It may not go that way."

"Fuck you, Mika'el," Aramael snarled. "That's exactly how it will go. These little tricks you taught me"—he waved at their informal fighting ring—"may work on the Fallen Ones, but they won't even slow down the Appointed. Seth has his powers. I only have one shot at this, which means I'll have to wait until he is fully engaged in wiping out my own immortality before I can move against his. My chances of surviving this are infinitesimal. You know it."

He struggled with his breathing, facing at last what he hadn't dared think about when the Archangel had first assigned this task. What he had tried so hard to ignore ever since. At his center, the core of loss he carried, the place that marked where he had once held Alex, became a gaping hole.

If he didn't survive this, if he died—and he almost certainly would—he would never have the chance to know her again. Never know if what he thought he remembered had been real. If it could have been revived.

He would never know if faith could restore love.

"You know what you're thinking isn't possible," Mika'el said.

Aramael shot him a filthy look. "What, now you're a mind reader?"

"I recognize the symptoms. You're not the only one to lose a soulmate."

"I didn't *lose* her. She was taken from me."

Mika'el's gaze narrowed. "Just how much of her do you remember?"

Aramael looked away. "Enough to know what I no longer have."

"You never had her in the first place," the Archangel pointed out. "And you never can. She is a mortal, Aramael, and you are and always will be an angel of the Sixth Choir. A Power. What happened between you has already caused unparalleled damage. The cardinal rule banning interaction between angels and mortals is there for a reason."

"Fuck the cardinal rule. Heaven threw me out, remember? The rules don't apply to me anymore. Especially once I've done what you ask."

"Assuming you survive, the rules do apply," the Archangel corrected. "If you choose otherwise, you choose to fall."

"This, coming from the angel who has asked me to assassinate the Appointed."

"That's different."

"Is it? If I go through with this, Mika'el, I'll compromise my own soul. I'm pretty sure that will result in my fall."

"And what if it does?" Mika'el stood tall, aloof, every inch one of Heaven's warriors. "What if you do have to sacrifice yourself in order to stop Armageddon and save humanity? Will you deny your Creator, Power? Turn your back on her and her children?"

"Like you did?" Aramael shot back.

Before the last word had fully left his lips, he found himself against the wall, feet dangling, with Mika'el's hand wrapped around his throat. The Archangel's black wings spread wide. Aramael saw each individual feather, sensed the power pulsing through them. He swung at the Archangel defiantly. Missed. And with new insight, understood he had only landed those blows against the other angel because

Mika'el had let him. He might be able to fight off a Fallen
One, but with or without powers, he could never hope to
take on one of Heaven's warriors.

"You know *nothing*!" Mika'el spat. "I have given my life
to her a hundred thousand times over. I begged her to let
me—" He broke off and his fingers tightened, digging into
Aramael's larynx.

Aramael's lungs screamed for air and the world began
to fog over. Then, as suddenly as the Archangel had seized
him, he let go. Aramael slumped to the floor, blood rushing
to his head, gasping for breath. Slowly his vision cleared
and he sat up. Mika'el stood on the opposite side of the room,
looking down onto the street from the window, his wings
once more folded against his back, his shoulders sagging.

Silence reigned for a long moment, broken only by the
rasp of air through Aramael's throat. The Archangel turned
to him, his gaze flat. His voice flatter. "Your Creator needs
you, Aramael of the Powers. Once you have completed your
task, should you survive, then your choices are your own.
Be ready to leave at midnight. I'll take you as far as I can."

In a rush of feathers, Mika'el was gone. Aramael stared
at the empty space left behind, the Archangel's parting
words lingering in the air. Then he pushed to his feet.

Mika'el had begged the One to let him—what?

"IT'S TUCKER," SAID a voice when Henderson answered his
cell phone. "From Homicide. You know that girl you were
looking for? Katherine Gray? We have her."

"Have her?" Henderson echoed. "As in—?"

"She's been identified as the Jane Doe who hit the pavement two nights ago. The coroner hasn't signed off on anything yet, but it looks like suicide. Twenty stories down,
headfirst."

Tucker's voice droned on, but the rest of his words disappeared inside the sudden buzzing in Henderson's head as
he dropped into his chair. *Suicide*. He stared at Gray's driver's license photo on his desk, and the birth date jumped out

at him. His stomach twisted. She would have been twenty-seven next month. Five years younger than—the twist in his stomach became a heave and he gritted his teeth. Another needless death that he could have prevented. *Should* have prevented.

"Henderson? You still there?"

"Yeah." Hugh swallowed a mouthful of bile and wiped a palm over his clammy forehead. "Yeah. I'm here. The coroner is sure about the ID?"

"Dental records are a match."

Fuck. His hand moved over his cropped head. God almighty, he hated this job sometimes. He rubbed his jaw, digging deep for the cop in him, needing it to process the news. He found only memories. Recriminations. Nightmares.

Suicide.

Fuck, fuck, fuck.

"Right," he said. "Thanks for letting me know. Make sure I get a copy of the report, will you?"

"Sure thing."

"Wait. What about the baby? She was pregnant."

"Like I said"—Tucker's voice went grim—"twenty stories. It'll be in the report."

Hugh stared at the phone long after he hung up. Another mother and child dead because of him. Because he hadn't paid enough attention, hadn't seen the warning signs. Not even Liz could argue his responsibility this time.

His gaze moved to a stack of messages one of the admin assistants had placed on his desk. The name on the top slip of yellow jumped out at him. Father Marcus, St. Benedict's Parish. The assistant no longer scrawled the word *again* across the top of the message, but it was still there. Unseen. Accusatory. Father Marcus had called every month for the last ten years, ever since Laura and Mitchell had died.

Unable to bring himself to speak to the man who represented the Church that had abandoned him and his family when they needed it most, Hugh had never called back.

He reached for the message, crumpled it, and then

hesitated. Smoothing it out, he stared at the X through the box marked *urgent*. A last-ditch effort to gain his attention? He toyed with the paper. Tapped it against the desktop. Then, jaw going tight, dropped it into the trash can.

Urgent or not, he still wasn't ready to go there.

RILEY HAD MISSED her true calling, Alex decided as she sat in the psychiatrist's office, waiting for the doctor to wind down. The woman would have made a great cop with her lecture punctuated by *overstepping your bounds*, *out of your jurisdiction*, and various other references to turf and territory.

Alex endured the ordeal with as much patience as she could muster, her attention straying to the shelves behind Riley's head and then to the seconds ticking by on the watch strapped to her wrist. How long would Seth wait? *Would* he wait? What if he turned up here, now, out of the blue? How the hell would she explain that to Riley?

Realizing her leg jittered up and down under her sweaty palm, she made herself take a deep breath and focus on stilling it. Christ, how long was this going to take?

"—understand?" Riley finished, her brows arching sharply upward and her eyes cold as she peered over the glasses perched on her nose.

Shit. Understand what?

"Of course," she said. "You're absolutely right about everything, Dr. Riley, and I apologize for having over-stepped the way I did. I never meant to cause trouble."

Riley glowered. "And?"

"And—?" Wasn't that enough?

"And you'll tell me everything you know about Seth Ben-jamin. No more secrets."

Alex's face went still. She glanced again at her watch. Ten minutes since she'd left Seth: she sure as hell hoped he had the gist of *patient*. She looked up at Riley again, search-ing for words—no, for sheer inspiration. But before she could open her mouth, the doctor rose from behind the desk, her face a closed, hard mask.

"Get out," Riley ordered.

"Excuse me?"

"I've been a psychiatrist for thirty years, Detective Jarvis. I know when someone is preparing to lie to me and I am sick to death of your evasiveness. Get out. We're done."

Argument didn't even cross Alex's mind. As she raced for the elevator, however, she couldn't help but reflect on the track record she seemed to be establishing where shrinks were concerned. First Bell had thrown her out of his office, and now Riley. It was almost enough to give an angel-seeing, demon-surviving cop a complex. If she'd cared.

Ten minutes later, she pulled the rental car to a stop in a no-parking zone alongside a fence thick with ivy and peered through the leaves at the hospital. Her heart sank. So many windows, all so far away. No way would she be able to spot Seth at one of them, and with that damned fence in the way, he couldn't see her or the vehicle, either.

Resting an elbow on the steering wheel, she threaded her fingers through her hair. What the hell was she supposed to do now? For a second, she contemplated climbing the fence, perching atop it, and waving to get Seth's attention. A brief second, because the next image that came to mind was one of her trying to convince the local constabulary she really hadn't gone off the deep end.

Despite what Riley and Bell might otherwise tell them.

She dropped her head back against the headrest and stared at the ceiling. *Think, damn it, Jarvis. There must be some way—*

"I come now?" a deep voice inquired from beside her.

EIGHTEEN

"Are you okay?" Liz Riley asked. "I can clear my schedule if you need to talk."

Hugh rubbed a hand over his eyes. The vague tension touched off by the conversation he'd had with Detective Jarvis's boss had escalated into a full-fledged headache with the news of Katherine Gray's suicide. Opening his top desk drawer, he rummaged inside for the acetaminophen he kept there.

"I'm fine," he answered Liz. "Generally pissed at myself, but fine."

"Then what are the pain killers for?"

He pulled the receiver from his ear for a second and gave it a sour look. Then he tucked it back into the crook of his neck and opened the pill bottle—a two-handed job because of the childproof lid. "What are you, psychic?"

"I can hear the bottle."

"I have a headache. I'm fine."

"I've known you for more than ten years, Hugh. It's in your voice. You're not fine."

"Then I'll *be* fine once the headache is gone." Tossing back two tablets, he reached for the cold coffee on his desk and grimaced at the congealed cream floating on its surface.

Liz sighed. "You're not responsible for Katherine Gray, Hugh. Any more than you were responsible for—"

"Don't." The word came out harsher than Hugh intended and he scrubbed an impatient hand over his head. She still didn't get it, and no matter how good a shrink she was, she'd never get it because she hadn't lived it. But even if she hadn't been able to take away the guilt or the horror, she'd given him the tools to survive and, for that, he was grateful. Which made him sorry he'd snapped. "I know you're trying to help, Liz, but I'm fine. And you're not my doctor anymore. So do us both a favor and let it go, all right?"

"Damn it, Hugh—"

"Let it go."

Liz muttered something he didn't ask her to repeat and then heaved another sigh. "Fine. So was that it? Just the news about Katherine Gray?"

Leaning back in his chair, Hugh put his feet up on the desk and crossed them at the ankles. He stared at his shoes. Should he tell her about the conversation with Staff Inspector Roberts in Toronto? About the distinctly woo-woo flavor of a discussion he still couldn't quite believe he'd had with another cop? Would it help to share what Roberts had told him about Seth Benjamin? His gaze slid to the trash can. Or to confess to ten years of ignored messages?

"Well?" Liz prodded.

"That was it. Just Gray."

"Hugh—" The psychiatrist broke off. "Hold on, something's up here."

A quick, muffled conversation took place at the other end of the line, and then Liz's voice came back on.

"Do you mind if we finish this later? We're in lockdown. One of the patients has gone missing."

"Benjamin."

"How did you know?"

After all Roberts had told him? How could he not know?

"Lucky guess," he said. "Go. Let me know if you need help."

* * *

SHE'D REALLY PAINTED herself into a corner this time.

Alex stared across the hotel-room bed at Seth, still clad
in hospital pajamas, and cursed her recently acquired ability
to act without thinking through the consequences. What had
seemed like the only option at the time had taken on omi-
nous overtones now that she looked back on her actions.
Riley would be livid, Henderson would be just as pissed,
and if the court put out a detention order for Seth, Alex
would face charges of contempt.

Taking a deep breath, in through the nose and out through
the mouth, Alex reined in her overwrought nerves. No one
knew, she reminded herself. No one *could* know. Riley had
seen her leave the psych ward alone; Seth's room would have
remained locked; the security cameras in the hospital and
the parking lot would show nothing. No connection between
her and the missing patient. For now, they were safe.

For now.

But Alex still faced the problem of a powerful amnesiac
angel. And the question destined to dog her every step: *now
what?*

She cleared her throat. "Are you hungry?"

Seth regarded her with a calm she would have liked to
own herself. "No," he said. "Thank you."

He was learning fast.

Her gaze dropped to the books he clutched in his hands
and a smile tugged at her mouth. "Would you like me to
help you with those?"

Seth frowned at the books. "Those?"

"The books. Would you like to learn the books?" They
might as well get right to it. The faster he learned, the sooner
she could tell him what little she knew of him. For all the
good it might do if he still didn't have his memory.

He held out the books to her. "Yes."

Alex glanced around. The only potential work surfaces
were the dresser with the television on it and one small desk
in the corner where she'd set her suitcase. The room, she

realized, was barely adequate for one person, let alone two. A move to something bigger, however, would draw Riley and Henderson's attention, so they'd just have to make do. With a sigh, Alex shifted her suitcase to the floor and tugged the desk out from the corner, positioning it beside the bed.

"Come," she said to her student, patting the faded bedspread. "Sit."

BY THE TIME they took a break several hours later, Seth had proved himself not just an apt pupil, but a phenomenal one. He blasted through the reading books, retaining everything he learned on the first try, and was halfway through the second illustrated dictionary when Alex returned to the room with their take-out chicken dinner and an armload of clothes she'd picked up at a nearby discount store.

He looked up with a frown as she closed the door. "Magnet," he said, holding up the book in his hands and pointing to a picture. "What is attract?"

Alex dropped the room key on the dresser beside the television, her exhaustion-fogged brain struggling for a definition he would understand. "Something that pulls another thing toward it," she decided.

"What something?"

"A force of some kind. It's invisible—you can't see it." She set their dinner on the desk and then placed her wallet beside it, flicking open the clasp. "This is a magnet. See how this piece pulls the other side toward it? That's attraction."

She demonstrated a few times and then, with a smile, handed the wallet over to a captivated Seth while she unpacked the deep-fried chicken, french fries, and coleslaw. Hardly her dinner of choice, but the fast food place had been the closest thing still open and she hadn't wanted to leave Seth to his own devices while she hunted down something less artery clogging. If only she'd left him playing with a magnet in her absence, he might have remained occupied for hours.

"Alex, you are a magnet, too?"

Alex looked over to find Seth frowning again. "Why do you say that?"

Seth's gaze lifted, meeting hers with an intensity that sent a curl of warning through her belly. "You attract me."

Oh. Alex's memory leapt back to a moment when she'd stood outside a church-turned-slaughterhouse, her hand on Seth's arm. Something had flared between them in that instant. An unexpected something she had all but forgotten, that returned now with a shocking swiftness. The already small room shrank ten sizes. Setting down the box of french fries, she opened her mouth, then snapped it closed again when no sound emerged. She groped for the chair and sank into it, searching for a response.

Seth preempted her efforts.

"Why?" He studied her, his dark eyes curious and warm. Too warm. "Why do you attract me?"

Change the subject, she told herself. *Distract him.*

Seth, however, had other ideas.

"Do I attract you?" His voice dropped, roughened, and his words slid over Alex like raw silk, catching on her every heightened nerve ending.

Alex curled her fingers into the chair arms. Hell. She'd just lost her soulmate, the world was on the verge of annihilation, she had somehow managed to become the savior of the savior, and her answer to the whole mess was a rush of hormones?

Her cell phone shrilled into the taut, expectant silence and she damn near vaulted from the chair. Hand shaking, she tugged the phone from its case and flipped it open.

"Jarvis," she croaked.

"You'll notice I'm doing you the courtesy of calling instead of coming to your room," a gruff male voice said.

"Detective Henderson?"

"He's missing."

Caught off guard by Henderson's abruptness—and still reeling from Seth's questions—Alex almost forgot to play dumb. She bit back her well-rehearsed but too-early denial just in time. "He who?"

"Coffee," Henderson replied. "Same place as before. Five minutes."

The connection went dead. Alex lowered the phone, stared at it, and then snapped it shut. Son of a bitch. She might be considered one of the best interrogators on the Toronto police force, but she had met her match in Vancouver's Hugh Henderson. The man changed direction so often and so quickly she found herself hard-pressed just to keep up, let alone keep her wits about her.

Tapping the phone against one knee, she went over the terse conversation again. She suspected Henderson's comment about calling instead of coming to her room had been more veiled threat than courtesy. If she wasn't in the coffee shop in—she glanced at her watch—four and a half minutes, she'd guarantee he'd be at the door in six.

She looked over at Seth, relieved to find the intensity in his gaze replaced with curiosity. At the very least, taking a break to see Henderson would give her time to decide how she was going to handle the attraction issue.

She hoped.

"I have to go out," she said. "Just for a little while. Will you be okay here?"

"I come?"

In spite of her current stress level, Alex's lips quirked. Tomorrow they'd have to do something about grammar. "Not this time. I have to go alone. You stay here and read, and—" She broke off at a sudden idea and rose from the chair. Going to the television, she switched it on, hoping it was one of the things in the hotel—unlike hallway light bulbs—that worked.

A picture sprang to life on the screen. Success. She turned to Seth. "This is a television. I don't know if there's satellite or not, but there should be enough on to keep you occupied for a while. You change channels with these buttons." She pressed the up arrow and then the down, and

Seth's eyes narrowed on the television. "And this is for volume."

Louder. Softer. Seth's eyes widened and he reached for the control. Alex smiled.

"Just don't turn it up too loud, all right? We don't want to disturb the neighbors."

"Neighbors?"

Right, he hadn't reached *n* in the dictionary yet. Was still at *m*. *M* for *magnet*. Alex's cheeks warmed again.

"The people in the rooms around us." Lifting her wallet from the desk, she tucked it into her jacket pocket. "So we have this straight, right? I go, you stay?"

Seth flicked the channel upward several times and grinned. "I stay," he agreed, and settled in to investigate his new toy.

NINETEEN

Alex stripped off her rain-soaked jacket and slid into the booth across from Henderson. She shook her head at the approaching waitress. Her jitters were bad enough without adding caffeine to the mix. Clinging to the questionable calm she'd managed to impose over herself on the short walk from the hotel, she met the Vancouver detective's eyes. "Well?" she asked. "I'm here. Now what?"

"Now you tell me who he really is and why you're hiding him in your room."

Balling sweaty hands into fists under the table, Alex readied herself to lie through her teeth. She'd make a lousy criminal. "I assume you're talking about Seth, Detective, in which case I've already told you all I know about him, and what do you mean hiding him? Are you telling me he's *missing*?" She allowed her voice to rise with what she hoped was the right amount of concerned indignation.

Henderson's gaze didn't so much as flicker. "When you clench a hand, there's a corresponding muscle movement as far up the arm as the shoulder," he remarked. "You might want to watch for that in your interviews. It's a dead give-away of nerves."

Alex's fists tightened before she could stop herself. She knew that, damn it. She'd just been so focused on keeping her face still—she scowled at her colleague. "I know how to conduct an interview, Detective Henderson. What I don't know is what I'm doing here."

Leaning back on the bench seat, Henderson toyed with a spoon on the table until Alex was tempted to snatch it away and rap it across his knuckles. She swallowed, remembering a time when she'd wanted to do something similar to Aramael. When she'd sat in another coffee shop a lifetime away and witnessed the beginning of the end of the reality she thought she'd known.

"Benjamin disappeared from his room," said Henderson.

Wrenching her mind back to the present, Alex stepped into semi-rehearsed territory. She frowned. "When?"

"They noticed the absence at dinner."

"Who the hell left his door unlocked?"

"No one. It was still locked."

Alex paused for effect and then drawled, "He's missing from a locked room and I'm responsible. What, I waved my magic wand and poof, he disappeared?" She flapped away Henderson's response and, not wanting to push her luck too far, switched tactics. "Never mind. What about the cameras? They're all over that ward—they must have caught some-thing."

"That's the problem. They didn't. They show everything else, but no Benjamin. Not so much as a glimpse of him. He was in the room, and then he wasn't." Setting aside the spoon, Henderson leaned forward, placing his elbows on the table. His gaze held Alex's for a bare second before sliding away, up toward a television suspended from the wall over the counter.

Alex wondered whose idea it had been to question her this time: Henderson's or Riley's.

"I spoke to your supervisor."

Another topic change. "Oh?"

Henderson's gaze skipped back to hers. It moved away again. "You didn't tell me Benjamin saved your life in that fire."

Caution prickled up Alex's spine. "I don't know what you're talking about."

"Roberts saw Benjamin standing in the flames when you staggered out. You were bleeding and burned. He didn't have a mark on him." Henderson continued to look toward the television. "And before you say it, I asked. Roberts swears he wasn't seeing things."

Alex waited, certain he wasn't yet done. Her gaze traveled over the lines of fatigue etched around his eyes and the scruff along his jawline, the look of a cop working too many hours. One who had seen way more than any person should have to see and yet continued to do his job because someone had to. She thought about Roberts, a cop just as dedicated as Henderson, who knew so much more than she'd realized and had risked his reputation to share the information.

For her sake.

Was she ready to take the same risk?

Henderson sighed and flicked another glance her way. "Your staff inspector made some pretty bizarre statements, Jarvis. I'm not sure what I'm supposed to think."

Welcome to the club.

Crossing her arms on the table, Alex hunched her shoulders. "Detective Henderson—" she began.

But Henderson cut her off with a wave of one hand as he slid out of the booth. He crossed to the counter and called to the waitress. "Turn that up, will you?" He gestured at the television.

The waitress demurred, citing rules, but stopped when Henderson flashed his badge. With a shrug, she stood on tiptoe and raised the volume on the television. The female news anchor's voice filled the late-night quiet of the coffee shop. ". . . yesterday's report of unusual pregnancies occurring in China has triggered a flood of similar accounts from around the world. Dozens of families and medical personnel have stepped forward in the last twenty-four hours, claiming to know of babies delivered a mere *three weeks* after conception. As bizarre as the claims are, however, even more unsettling is the fact that none of the mothers have survived childbirth. The medical community is at a loss to explain the phenomenon, and scientists are scrambling to find answers. In the meantime, several religious groups . . ."

Henderson's cell phone shrilled and he unclipped it from his belt, signaling to the waitress to lower the volume once more. "Henderson. Yeah, I just saw. No, I'm with Detective Jarvis."

He met Alex's gaze and mouthed. "Riley."

Wonderful. Alex tuned out Henderson's side of the phone conversation and stole another look at the screen over his head. A list of countries had appeared, each with a number beside it. Russia, four; India, six; China, seven; Australia, two; the U.S., eight; Canada, three; Mexico, five—the list went on. Alex frowned. The hair on the back of her neck prickled and a half-formed idea slipped across her mind.

"I have to go."

Alex jumped as Henderson materialized at her elbow and took down the coat he'd hung on the rack beside the booth. She nodded at the television. "What's that all about?" she asked.

"Other than the weirdest damn shit I've ever seen?" He shrugged into the coat and scooped up a set of keys from the table. "I have no idea."

Alex raised an eyebrow. "So why the interest?"

Already three steps away, Henderson twisted around. He stared at Alex, a muscle in his jaw twitching. Alex waited.

"A case I'm working on may be connected," he allowed. He lifted his chin toward the evening news. "Two, actually. Both claimed they'd been raped. One died giving birth a couple of days ago. We thought she was just a messed-up kid, but now—" He broke off, frustration stamped across his brow, and then muttered, "Now I don't know what to think."

"And the other?"

Gray tinged Henderson's skin and the Adam's apple bobbed in his throat. "Suicide," he said. "Two nights ago."

A shiver crawled down Alex's spine and the half-formed notion resurfaced in her mind, twining with Henderson's revelation. "What about the babies?" she called after him.

Henderson looked over his shoulder. "They're holding the first for observation. The second died with the mother. And Riley just called to say they may have a third in ER."

Alex stared again at the television screen as Henderson shoved open the door and stepped out into the night. The elusive idea began to take shape. Solidified. Brought her out of her seat with a "Son of a *bitch*!" that turned heads.

Henderson hunched past the coffee shop window, head down and collar up against the driving rain. Rounding a corner, he disappeared from sight. Alex hesitated for a split second and then bolted after him.

She caught up with him as he pulled open the door of a nondescript, dark blue sedan. "Detective Henderson, wait—"

Stooped to slide into the car, Henderson hesitated and then straightened again. Rain plastered his short-cropped hair to his scalp and ran in rivulets down his face. He frowned at her over the roof of the car.

"What is it?"

Alex hesitated. *Seth.* She should get back to Seth. But she needed to know if she was right about the pregnancies. About—she pulled her coat closer against the weather's onslaught. The hospital wasn't far. It would take her a half hour, tops. She'd be there and back well before the television had lost its charm. If Henderson agreed.

She swiped a drip of water from her nose and raised her voice over the rain. "I want to come with you."

Henderson's eyebrows joined over his nose. "Why?"

"These girls, the pregnancies—you're sure the news report is right?"

"You know something."

"I have an idea. But I want to confirm it before I say

anything. I need to talk to the girl." *Before I throw away my career, what little respect you have for me, and my apparent sanity, all in one shot.* "Please."

Henderson stared at her for a long moment and then, without a word, he slid behind the steering wheel and closed the door with a thud. Taking his silence as agreement, Alex pulled open the passenger door and climbed in beside him.

"WHAT DO YOU mean, he's gone?" Lucifer looked up from his writing and scowled. "Gone where?"

Samael shrugged. "We have no idea."

"He can't have just disappeared—" Breaking off, Lucifer stared at Sam, then set aside his pen. "He disappeared."

"The way the humans tell it, yes."

"He has his powers."

"It looks that way."

Lucifer rested an elbow on the chair's armrest and tapped a finger against his mouth. "Well, well. Now I'm really curious. Anything from the Guardians?"

"Nothing. If I had to guess, I'd say they're as much in the dark as we are, but they're not saying a word about any of it, not even among themselves."

"But no trace of Heavenly presence near him."

"Unfortunately not." Samael folded his arms and leaned against the door frame. "And believe me, I've been watching."

Lucifer did believe him; no one would be happier than Sam to find an excuse to cry foul so he could at last go to war. "Contain yourself, Samael. If things have gone as awry as I think on Heaven's end, you may well be engaged in battle sooner than I'd planned."

"What do you think happened?"

"Something catastrophic. Seth's transition as an adult and his amnesia are mistake enough, but to retain his powers? I suspect all of Heaven is in an uproar over this."

"Huh," Sam muttered. "Maybe that would explain it."

Lucifer raised an eyebrow. "Explain what?"

"There's been a Judgment. I haven't been able to find out against whom, yet, but it might be connected to this."

Lucifer's heart clenched. Judgment. There hadn't been a Judgment since his own, six thousand years before, the very memory of which still turned his core to ice. Lucifer forced a swallow and fixed his aide with a glare. "And you didn't think to mention this to me because . . . ?"

Another shrug from his aide, this one containing a distinct air of arrogance. "You've never been all that detail oriented. I didn't think you'd care."

Lucifer watched the fingers of his right hand curl into a fist atop the leather-bound journal on the desk. "Again, Sam?" he asked, his voice soft. "The warning the other day wasn't enough? You tread a dangerous path these days, my friend."

"Better than the imaginary one you tread," Samael retorted. "Damn it, Lucifer, open your eyes. With or without the Nephilim, we're still going to have to fight the same war and suffer the same losses."

"But without them, we cannot hope to take on the mortals as well."

Samael studied him. "You're certain that's your reason for hesitating?"

"It is my reason for biding my time," Lucifer agreed through his teeth. "And you might want to be careful where you're going with this."

Samael heeded the warning for all of a second before he continued as if Lucifer hadn't spoken. "Because you know she'll never take us back. She can't, and you're an idiot if you think otherwise."

Lucifer slammed his fist against the desktop. Polished mahogany cracked through and a half dozen peppermints bounced from their bowl. Samael rustled his wings, angry frustration warring with a watchfulness that told Lucifer the Archangel knew he had overstepped. Again.

His aide's expression turned sullen. "Forgive me," he muttered. "I go too far."

"Yes," Lucifer agreed. "You do."

He hated that the former Archangel was right—hated even more the weakness in himself that wished otherwise, even after all this time. Lucifer pushed back from the desk. Needing a moment to gather himself together after Samael's accusation—for that's what his aide's words had been—he picked up the journal he'd been working on and slid it into place on a shelf behind him, the last in hundreds exactly like it but for the numbers on their spines. One thousand and eleven of them now, an ongoing memoir begun as a labor of love. A record of every thought, every action, every reason for doing all he had done. All he would do. Because he was damned if he would be held responsible for anything more than loving too much or too deeply.

Damned, too, if he would allow his upstart aide to usurp the conflict begun in the name of that love. As powerful as Samael was, as much responsibility as Lucifer had been willing to let him take on, only one of them was truly in charge—and the former Archangel could not be allowed to forget it.

Lucifer swiveled. "Apology accepted, but I want you to remember what I said the other day because I meant every word of it. Until I say otherwise, the agreement stands and no one lifts a finger against my son."

He strolled across the room to stand before his aide, face mere inches away. A flush spread across Sam's cheekbones and his eyes slid away to stare at a point beyond Lucifer's shoulder. Lucifer grasped the Archangel's face in one hand, fingers digging into mahogany-dark flesh, and forced the golden gaze back to meet his.

"If you do anything to interfere, anything at all to cross me, make no mistake, Samael. I will crush you."

TWENTY

Alex stood by the nurse's counter in the emergency ward, fingers drumming out her agitation against the polished surface. Catching an annoyed glare from a doctor at the far end, she pulled her lips tight in apology and slid both hands into her pockets. A dozen feet away, the exchange between Henderson and Riley continued unabated.

Alex grimaced again. Riley's eyebrows had damn near disappeared into her hairline when Alex had entered the ER at Henderson's side. The shrink hadn't even acknowledged her presence. Had simply taken the Vancouver detective's arm, drawn him aside, and without lowering her voice, demanded, "What the hell is she doing here?"

Glancing at the clock above the counter, Alex felt her nerves wind a little tighter. She'd already been here ten minutes. Was Seth still watching television? Was he getting restless yet, wondering where she was? Would he go looking for her if she—

"Detective."

Riley's cold voice jolted her back to the present. She

looked down into the hostile blue eyes and tried not to think about how easily this woman could sink her entire career. One phone call from Riley to Alex's own department shrink, and Alex would spend the rest of her working life writing traffic tickets. If she were lucky enough to keep her job at all. Her fingers curled inside her pockets.

Just tread lightly, Jarvis.

"Follow me." Riley led the way down the corridor, the ever-present Birkenstocks slapping against her heels.

An unhappy-looking Henderson fell into step behind her and Alex flashed him a quick look. "Well? Is this one like the others?"

"Not on the surface."

Alex frowned. "Can you be a little more specific?"

"We've had two prior victims. One claimed she had been raped by someone posing as her boyfriend, the other that she had no recollection at all of even having sex. This one—" Henderson nodded his head toward the door beside which Riley had stopped to wait for them, scowling. "This one was brutalized."

Alex stopped walking. Hell, she'd left Seth alone for nothing. "So it's not related, then."

"There's more." Henderson stopped beside the psychiatrist and looked back at her. "She and her boyfriend had taken a vow of abstinence. Boyfriend showed up at her door last night and started getting pushy. She resisted, he insisted. One thing led to another and he raped her."

"I'm sorry, but I don't see the connection—"

"She claims that, about halfway through the attack, he changed."

Cold trickled down Alex's spine as Riley's scowl deepened to a glower. "Changed how?"

Henderson's mouth went tight and he stared at the floor for so long without answering that Riley cleared her throat and spoke instead.

"She claims he changed into someone else, Detective Jarvis. A stranger. With wings. She says he was an angel."

*   *   *

"SO." HENDERSON SNAPPED his notebook closed and stuffed it into his jacket pocket. "I'm ready to hear that idea you had."

Alex stared down at the girl in the hospital bed. Beyond what Riley had already told them on their arrival, they'd gleaned little else from the traumatized victim. Now that the sedatives had kicked in, they wouldn't get anything more, either. Which left them with Jenna Murphy's fantastical claims, a pregnancy test that had come back positive after a rape that had occurred only a few hours before, and more questions than answers.

Oh, yes, and an increasingly hostile Riley, who maintained the pregnancy test proved nothing and argued that Jenna had probably lied about her virginity and been pregnant already.

Alex wished the shrink could have been right. She would have given anything, in fact, not to know otherwise. She breathed carefully, the air icy in her chest. But she did know. What was happening, what the pregnancies were, what Lucifer was doing. She knew, and couldn't begin to describe her horror.

A new race of Nephilim.

The first salvo in a war between Heaven and Hell.

Henderson waited, facing her across Jenna Murphy's bed, Riley at his shoulder. Without looking up, Alex felt the shrink's assessing stare. If she and Henderson had been alone, if the psychiatrist hadn't been there, Alex might have told him. He needed to know what was happening, what was coming. Everyone needed to know.

But Riley *was* there, and unlikely to leave if asked, and if Alex started spouting off about certain legends and myths being true but not quite as everyone imagined—about Heaven and Hell being real and on the verge of wiping out the human race—she had no doubt she'd find herself on the next plane back to Toronto, leaving Seth on his own, with no one to run interference for him while he figured out who he was. What he was. What he had to do to stop the Apocalypse.

Alex's heart stuttered to a halt under the sudden, massive weight of realization. *I'm all he has. I'm the only one in the world who knows about him.*

"Detective?" A thread of steel wove through Henderson's voice.

She sucked in a ragged breath. She had to get back to the hotel. Had to make Seth understand, make him remember. Because if anything happened before then, if anything happened to *her* . . .

She pushed back hair still damp from the rain. "It's nothing," she told Henderson. "Sorry to get your hopes up, but I was wrong."

"Alex, does any of this have to do with—" Henderson broke off, glancing sideways at Riley. Indecision crossed his face and then his jaw flexed. "It's not just coincidence, is it?"

"What's not?"

"The pregnancies. Your serial killer. Benjamin. It's all connected somehow, isn't it?"

Despite Riley's presence, if Henderson had looked at Alex, if he'd met her gaze for even an instant, she might have caved. Might have believed him capable of accepting her words, even if he didn't understand them. But the way he stared fixedly down at the girl in the bed, the way his body had gone rigid and his fingers clenched around the pen he held—everything about him spoke of denial.

Looking away from the other detective, Alex met Riley's gaze one last time. Without another word, she left the examination room and headed for the exit, trying to focus on what she could do to help Seth remember, and not dwell on the fact that she had no idea *what* he needed to remember. That she knew nothing beyond what he had told her in parting a short month—and an entire lifetime—ago.

Heaven's contingency plan, he'd said. But a plan for what? And even if she knew, even if he remembered . . .

All those babies.

A whole new race of Nephilim.
What if it was already too late?

HUGH STARED AT the space vacated by Alex Jarvis for long seconds, debating whether to go after her. Whether he wanted to. By the time Liz cleared her throat beside him, claiming his attention, the Toronto detective had been gone long enough to make the decision moot—and his relief palpable.

Because if he were honest, he was so not ready to hear Jarvis's idea. Not yet.

He looked down at Liz, who stood with arms folded over Murphy's chart, and raised an eyebrow, inclining his head toward the door. Nodding, Liz detached herself from the wall, hung the chart at the foot of the bed, and led the way into the corridor.

"Well?" he asked as the door closed behind them. "What do you think?"

Liz snorted. "You've got to be kidding. You want me to venture a professional opinion on this?" She waved at the room they'd just left. "Not a chance."

"I'll settle for an unprofessional one."

"Fine. Every single one of those girls was—*is* delusional. Except they're not." Liz poked a strand of hair back into the coil at her nape and scowled at him. "Their stories are obviously invented. Except they're not. And the pregnancies are impossible. Except—"

Hugh held up a hand. "I get the picture." He rubbed a hand over the end-of-day stubble along his jaw. "Has anybody figured out how the hell it's happening?"

"Theories range from environmental causes to superbugs to the next step in evolution—and the religious extremists have a whole other take on things. But the truth? We have no idea." Liz went quiet for a moment, and then asked, "Do you really think she knows something?"

"Who, Jarvis?"

"No, the Tooth Fairy," Liz snapped. "Of course, Jarvis."

"Yes, I think she knows something."

"Then why didn't you go after her?"

"Because I'm not sure I want to know what it is."

Liz was silent for a moment as an orderly pushed a man in a wheelchair past them, chatting about an upcoming hockey game. A doctor coming from the opposite direction deftly sidestepped the chair without looking up from the clipboard she carried, and continued on her path.

"We need to know."

Hands in pockets, Hugh scuffed his toe against the gleaming linoleum floor. "Do you believe in God?"

The psychiatrist blinked behind her wire frames, but her expression remained neutral as she allowed the abrupt change of subject. "I believe some people need to believe in a higher power," she allowed. "For comfort, for security, for direction—for a multitude of reasons. And I believe it's normal to seek that ideal when faced with an unknown, such as we are right now."

A smile curved Hugh's lips. "Very diplomatic, but it doesn't answer my question. Do *you* believe?"

"I've never seen the point. But that doesn't diminish what you're obviously going through right now."

"I spoke to Jarvis's supervisor in Toronto."

Irritation crept into Liz's voice. "You can be a difficult man to converse with sometimes, Hugh Henderson. What does Jarvis's supervisor have to do with this?"

"He told me things. About Seth." Hugh leaned back against the wall as an orderly rolled a gurney past them. "Things a part of me would prefer not to be true. The same part that doesn't want to go after Jarvis right now."

"Like what?"

Hugh extracted a hand from a pocket and scratched again at his jaw. "Benjamin saved Jarvis's life."

"From the serial killer. Yes, I know."

"Do you know about the fire, too? About how he sent her out of an inferno and stayed behind in the flames—only to turn up on your porch a month later without so much as a scorch mark?"

Liz stared over her glasses at him, eyebrows tugging together. "I should think it obvious he found another way out."

"Just like he found another way out of a secure room?"

"I'm not sure what you're suggesting."

Hugh detached himself from the wall. "Nothing," he said, because he wasn't suggesting anything, really. Couldn't bring himself to do so. He shook his head and said again, "Nothing. Just pointing out another in a long line of fucking impossibilities."

Blue eyes examined him as they might an interesting specimen. Or a patient. Then Liz shook her head and muttered, "I can't believe I'm doing this."

"Excuse me?"

The psychiatrist pressed her lips together, tapped a toe against the gleaming floor, and then straightened her spine with a snap Hugh was surprised wasn't audible. "There's something you should see," she announced. "Come with me."

She took him up several floors in the elevator, into the heart of the hospital. Hugh glanced at the sign on the ward doors as she pushed through, ever-present sandals slapping against her feet in the evening quiet.

"Maternity?"

Liz's lips tightened again. "Wait."

She strode ahead of him to the glassed-in nursery and slowed her steps, peering into the room filled with bassinets and squalling infants. As they neared the end of the window, she stopped and lifted a hand.

"There." She pointed.

"There what?"

"Third bassinet from the left, front row."

Hugh looked at the chubby baby, identified as a girl by the tag on the foot of her bassinet, and felt an involuntary tug at the corner of his mouth. A less pleasant tug at his heart. He gave himself a second and then cleared his throat. "She's cute," he said as the black-haired baby returned his interest and waved a rattle in his direction. "But isn't she a little old to be in here?"

"How old do you think she is?"

Hugh clenched his hands in his pockets. "Is there a purpose to this?"

"I know this is difficult for you, but humor me. Please."

Difficult? She had no idea.

Hugh studied the baby in the bassinet, now waving her arms and kicking at her blanket with enthusiasm. He thought back to Mitchell at this stage, remembering how he'd loved listening to his son's squeals and gurgles, how he'd loved holding him, breathing in the baby-sweet scent, watching the awe and wonder unfold at every new discovery.

Remembering how he'd come home to the awful silence one day. The stillness of both mother and child.

A touch on Hugh's sleeve jolted him from the past. He swallowed, holding himself rigid against the tremor running through him. All this time and it still felt like yesterday. His nostrils flared with his inhale.

"Six months," he grated. "She's six months old."

The same age Mitchell had been when he'd died.

Liz said nothing.

Glancing down, Hugh raised an eyebrow. Liz Riley, hard-assed shrink, gnawing on her lip like she hadn't eaten in a week? He caught her arm, made her face him. "All right, what's going on? Why did you bring me here? And what's with the baby?"

Liz folded her arms across herself and hunched her shoulders, appearing to deflate before his eyes. With a final nibble at her bottom lip, she said, "She's Melanie Chiu's daughter, Hugh. She's less than three days old."

Hugh wondered if the message from Father Marcus was still in the trash can by his desk.

TWENTY-ONE

"So this is it." Aramael stared out at the moonlit waters. The Strait of Juan de Fuca stretched between where he stood on the coast of Washington State and where he would find Seth. Where he would kill and probably *be* killed in a bid to save the mortal race—and a woman on the other side of the continent whom he would never see again. Squinting through the dark, he shot a disgusted look at Mika'el, who had returned long enough to start him on his journey. "This is your plan. You want me to swim that."

"It's either that or cross-country. Water is the shorter route, and time is of the essence."

"If time is of such import, take me through the border— I'm sure you could sway a guard or two. Oh, wait, I forgot," Aramael drawled. "That might draw attention to your presence and Heaven can't get its hands dirty."

It was for that same reason they'd just traveled twenty-four nonstop hours by car. Superior physical ability or not, every joint in Aramael's body made its opinion known with regard to that journey, but he'd rather face another like it than swim the distance Mika'el asked of him.

"At least let me take the car and try getting through on my own."

The Archangel shook his head. "You'd never succeed. Travel between the mortal countries is difficult enough these days even with proper documentation. Try going through border control without it and you'll find your ass in jail faster than you can blink—and that would just be the beginning of your nightmare."

It seemed Mika'el had a negative answer for everything. He also had a point. Even if Aramael were able to escape a mortal prison, the ensuing hunt for him would make getting to the Appointed more complicated than he cared to think about. And more time-consuming than they could afford.

"What about once I'm on the other side? I'll be getting out of the water in a densely populated city, with no mortal identification of any kind. How do I keep from getting my ass tossed into jail there?"

"Stay on course and you'll get out of the water on Vancouver Island," Mika'el corrected. "It's closer and you'll be able to land near a small community. You'll have a better chance of remaining undiscovered there while you get your bearings."

"And then I get to Vancouver how?"

"Be creative."

Aramael grunted. Scowled. "I'm still going to end up in a densely populated city with no identification."

Mika'el heaved an exasperated sigh and returned his scowl. "Then I suggest you don't draw attention to yourself until you get to Seth."

Aramael's mouth twisted. *Get to Seth*. Now there was a fucking understatement for what he'd been asked to do. He sighed. "That's your advice. That's the best you can do. Swim and don't draw attention to myself. Can I at least have a boat?"

"Not from here. Too great a chance of being seen by the coast guard. Speaking of which, duck if you see them while you're in the water. And move fast. Every second you delay gives Seth more time to regain full control of his powers. Your best chance is to get to him before that happens. "

"I know what my best chance is, Archangel. But you want this to happen quietly, remember? That means I have to get past hospital security without knocking the place apart, because if I cause a scene, the Guardians will notice, and if they notice, you can bet your wings Lucifer will, too. And I don't remember anyone *here* volunteering his assistance."

Mika'el's jaw tightened. "Careful, Power."

"Or what, you'll smite me?" Aramael asked bitterly. "I don't recommend that, it won't end well. Trust me, I know."

The two of them fell silent. Aramael stripped off his shoes and socks, shirt and jeans. Bundling everything into the shirt, he secured the load with his belt, hoping he wouldn't lose it all in the water. No matter how small a community he ended up in, emerging on the Canadian shore clad in nothing but underwear wouldn't help his stay-out-of-jail agenda.

"Aramael."

He would have ignored Mika'el and just walked into the water and not looked back, but something in the quiet of the Archangel's voice made him meet the emerald gaze one last time.

"For what it's worth, you're right," Mika'el said. "You're not a murderer. I'm sorry you must become one."

HUGH CLIMBED THE stairs toward the stone edifice towering above him, wiping sweaty palms against his jacket. Pulling open the heavy oak door, he stepped into the cool, dim interior of St. Benedict's. He'd stood outside for almost twenty minutes, battling a racing heart and sweaty palms, waiting until he was sure he was ready for this. But as the door swung shut and the tomb-like silence enveloped him, he knew he'd made a mistake.

He should have called instead.

More than a decade had gone by and he was nowhere

near ready to be back here. Would never be ready. He turned to make his escape but the door handle eluded him in the gloom.

"Fuck." He groped along the wood. Could they not provide decent lighting in this place?

"Can I help you?" a man's disapproving voice asked.

Adrenaline jolted through Hugh's veins. He curled his fingers into his palms. Abandoning his escape efforts, he turned to confirm what his ears had already told him. He knew that voice. Would have known it anywhere, even after all this time.

"Father Marcus. I wasn't sure I'd find you here at this hour."

A burly man stepped out of the deeper shadows of an archway, still robed from evening Mass. He squinted through the gloom. "Hugh?"

He stretched out a hand toward the wall and the sconces lining the foyer grew instantly brighter—as did the priest's lined face. He smiled with delight and came forward to envelop Hugh in a bone-crushing bear hug.

"It *is* you. I'd given up hope of ever seeing you back here." Father Marcus pulled back and clapped his massive hands onto Hugh's shoulders, adding a shake to his greeting that nearly knocked Hugh's two-hundred-plus pounds from his feet.

In spite of his inner turmoil, Hugh couldn't help a small smile as he endured a second hug before extricating himself and stepping back. "It's good to see you, too, Father."

The priest snorted. "What's this Father nonsense? You and I were and always will be friends, Hugh, no matter how much time passes. Call me Marcus as you always have." Marcus's eyes grew sober as he studied him. "You look well."

The tightness returned to Hugh's chest. The door at his back beckoned. Reminding himself of the reasons that had brought him here, he reached deep and stood his ground. Fleeing wouldn't make the last ten years any easier. Nor would it provide the answers he'd come for.

"Thank you," he said. "But I'm not here for personal reasons. Do you have time to talk?"

"Always. Let me lock up so we're not interrupted."

Stepping out of the way, Hugh watched the priest take a key from the same niche beside the door in which he'd always kept it, regardless of the many times Hugh had discussed security issues with him. Hugh shook his head but remained silent as the giant dead bolt clicked home and Marcus returned the key to its hiding spot.

"Sanctuary or my office?"

Hugh's palms went damp. Whether he knew it or not, Marcus offered a bitch of a choice: the place denied his family because of the circumstances of their deaths, or the one in which he'd turned his back on Church and faith? He stared past the priest into the vaulted expanse of the sanctuary. The old but still-fresh bitterness rose in his chest. Once again he considered flight; once again he smothered the urge.

"Office," he said.

If Marcus noticed the strangulation in his voice, he didn't comment, only motioned toward the archway on the left, the beginning of the passage that ran the length of the church to the offices tucked away at the back. Minutes later, Hugh found himself seated in a room that hadn't changed in . . .

Well, a long time.

He refused the offered coffee and waited for Marcus to take his seat behind the desk. Then, not wanting to give the priest the opportunity to steer the conversation into personal waters, he opened his mouth. Marcus beat him to it.

"Thank you for coming. I can't tell you how difficult this decision was—or how many of the Church's laws I am breaking," the priest muttered, staring down at his folded hands on the desk. "If the bishop had any idea . . ."

Hugh made a rapid adjustment in his thought process. Of course. Marcus's message. He couldn't very well admit he hadn't come because of it. Pushing aside his own questions for the moment, he cleared his throat. "Your message said it was urgent. What's going on?"

"The pregnancies."

Hugh blinked. Foreboding crawled down his spine. The priest couldn't mean . . .

"What pregnancies?"

Faded blue eyes lifted to his. "*The* pregnancies, Hugh. The ones on the news, in our own city, all over the world."

He did mean. The air snagged in Hugh's lungs and refused to move. He coughed. "You know something about them?"

"I know they've happened before." The priest's face had gone haggard. Suddenly Marcus looked every second of his age. "Six thousand years ago, give or take."

MIKA'EL TOOK HIS place at the table, Raphael on his left, Gabriel to the right, the others continuing the circle from there. Uriel, Azrael, Zachariel. Technically, each of them held an equal role in council, an equal seat in the hall; there was never to have been a leader here, never to have been one Archangel with more authority than another. And yet all eyes still turned to Mika'el, just as they always had.

He stared down at his fingertips resting on the plain wooden surface, worn smooth over thousands of years of polishing. Expectant silence settled over the gathering. Lifting his gaze, he let it travel the room, meeting each of his fellow Archangels' eyes, pausing at the gap in their circle where the traitor Samael had once sat, forcing himself to move on.

"The pact is broken," he said. "The agreement will not stand. We go to war."

The rustle of multiple wings whispered through the hall, rising to the vaulted ceiling. One of the gathered—Mika'el didn't see who—coughed.

"But Seth lives," Azrael objected.

Mika'el's jaw flexed. He stared at the other Archangel. "The agreement will not stand," he repeated.

Silence dropped across the table as the Archangels absorbed the impact of his words. Then Zachariel frowned.

"What you are suggesting—it is an enormous risk."

"Perhaps," responded Gabriel, the only female among them. "But given the circumstances, would it not be a greater risk otherwise?"

The caution behind the exchange told Mika'el his fellow warriors knew exactly what he had left unsaid and understood the critical need to keep silent about it—even in their own meeting place. Even in Heaven. He glanced again at the hole in their midst that marked a betrayal from which they had never recovered.

"Is it to be one of us?" Uriel asked, and wings rustled again.

Mika'el shook his head. "One no longer connected to us."

Curiosity sat heavy behind their eyes, but no one asked. Most, if not all, of them would figure out that Aramael had been tasked with the Appointed's assassination, but they would not speak his name. Wouldn't even hint at it. Samael's treason had taught them well.

Across the table, Zachariel cleared his throat. "What now?"

Mika'el gritted his teeth and closed his eyes, bracing himself to step fully back into the role he had forsaken almost five thousand years before, a role he had never thought to fill again. The weight of the One's disclosures pressed in on him with the force of a collapsing star. He opened his eyes and surveyed the grim faces of his fellow Archangels again.

"Now," he said, "we plan."

TWENTY-TWO

"Well, well. A once mighty Power stooping to theft. What is the world coming to?"

Aramael's fingers stilled in their unraveling of the knotted rope holding the boat to the pier. He straightened with slow deliberation. So. They'd found him, had they? It had taken them long enough—he'd been expecting them since Mika'el left him on the Washington shoreline. Or maybe they'd just waited until he'd crawled out of the water and they didn't have to get wet to come after him.

Pivoting, he faced the Fallen One leaning against a lamppost a few yards away in a pool of light. Only one. Good. It would be his first fight since Mika'el had declared him capable, and he hadn't looked forward to taking on multiple enemies when he tested the theory that his strength equaled theirs.

Aramael studied the leather-clad figure. He'd seen that craggy face before. He searched his memory and his mouth drew tight with satisfaction. Estiel. How fitting that one of the Grigori, the choir of angels that started the whole downfall mess, should be the first Fallen One to encounter his newly honed fighting skills.

He shifted into a wider stance.

"Let's skip the small talk, shall we? I'm on a tight deadline."

Estiel gave a bark of laughter. "I heard you were still pretty cocky. We haven't beaten it out of you yet?" He straightened. "I guess we'll just have to try harder. But not faster. Deadline or no deadline, I plan to take my time. I want to enjoy this."

Aramael waited for Estiel to stroll forward. When the Fallen One stopped a scant few feet away, he lashed out with all the controlled fury taught to him by Heaven's best. Estiel's jawbone gave way beneath his fist with a satisfying crunch. The Fallen One staggered backward, surprise flaring beside pain in the flat black gaze.

Regaining his balance, Estiel pushed his jaw back into place and narrowed his eyes. "You've been practicing."

"And you're still talking too much."

Estiel feinted left and then caught him in the gut with a solid right. Something inside Aramael ruptured and began to bleed, but he shut out the pain and danced away from a second blow. Leaning into Mika'el's training, he drew into himself until he found the angel still there. The strength. The sheer power that came with being who he was.

What he was.

In quick succession, he delivered punishing hits to Estiel's gut, ribs, and—when his enemy spun away to avoid him—kidneys. Estiel crashed to his knees on the pier. Without pause, Aramael aimed a vicious kick into the Fallen One's belly, sending him a dozen feet sideways.

Surprise in the dark gaze turned to disbelief as Aramael stalked across the boards to stand over him. Estiel slithered away but came up short against a post. Curled into a ball, eyes glazed with pain, he glowered at Aramael.

"You wouldn't." His lips twisted into a sneer. "You're of Heaven. You can't."

"Haven't you heard?" Aramael growled. "They threw me out. And I already have."

He brought down his foot on the Fallen One's skull. Felt it turn to pulp beneath his boot. For a long few seconds, he stood amid bone shards and gray matter and pooling blood and stared at what he had done, examining the cold ease with which he had done it. At last he turned from his enemy and went back to the task of stealing a boat to take him to Vancouver.

It didn't matter that Estiel wasn't really dead, or that Aramael could no longer take an immortal life—at least, not this one. Nor did it matter that the Fallen One would rise again and go on to tell his compatriots of the new and improved version of their nemesis, or that they were certain to come after him again, perhaps in numbers that would make fighting back impossible, even with what Mika'el had taught him.

None of it mattered except the truth at the core of it all.

Releasing the boat from its mooring, Aramael leapt onto its deck. Mika'el had been wrong about him becoming a murderer.

Because he couldn't become what he already was.

SETH STOOD AT the bedside, staring down at Alex. Even in sleep she looked tired, still carried that frown between her eyebrows. His hand curled at his side, alive with its own desire to reach out and smooth away the lines of concern.

Because he recognized it as concern, now. Understood she worried. About him, about what she had watched on television with him—a newscast, she had called it—before she finally fell asleep in the chair beside him as day moved back toward evening. Knew it had been right to move her to the bed then, but would be wrong to touch her in her sleep now, without her permission.

After thirty-one straight hours of watching the world through the eyes of the box on the desk and manipulating it to pick up on energy signals it normally wouldn't, he knew all that and more: different languages, places, events, people . . . But for every one thing he learned, more questions had arisen. Thousands of them, burning in his brain, demanding answers. Demanding he fill the void that remained within him.

Alex had done her best to provide those answers. She stayed by his side for twenty-seven revolutions of the clock, watching, answering, breaking only for food and bathroom and the occasional stretch that had drawn his attention away from the pictures to her lithe, curved form.

Her voice had grown hoarse and her eyes had taken on a bruised look until, finally, she had drifted into sleep.

Seth had moved her then, placing her in the bed the way he had seen it done on television. Arranging the pillows. Tucking the covers around her. Always feeling her warmth. Her pull on him.

An attraction, she had called it. The people on television had given it other words, too. Love. Need. Want. Desire. Alex had explained the emotions to him when he asked, along with myriad others—anger, rage, jealousy, sadness, hope—but her words had only served to feed his curiosity. And his growing, unsettled awareness of the differences between them. Between him and her and those like her.

He may have woken up in this world, but he became more convinced by the minute he didn't belong here. Memory issues aside, he felt no familiarity with any of what he saw, any of what he learned. No connection.

Except . . .

Alex moved in the bed and Seth's gaze returned to the blonde hair splayed across the pillow, the tiny frown pulling at her forehead, her length hidden beneath the covers. At his core, he felt again the stir to which he was becoming so accustomed.

Except.

Why the connection to her—and only her? What was it about this woman that drew him so inexorably toward her? Why did it feel so right? So inevitable? How did he fit into her life?

Did he fit?

Alex shifted under the covers once more and he waited, but she only breathed deeply and settled again. With a sigh, Seth lowered himself into the chair at her side and prepared to wait a little longer for her return to him.

ARAMAEL EYED THE burly security guard lumbering down the corridor and expelled a hiss of air. Bloody Hell, the last thing he needed was a confrontation with a mortal. The door of the stair exit to the left of the nurses' station opened and another guard stepped into the hallway.

Bloody, bloody Hell. So much for in and out discreetly.

He regarded the nurse on the other side of the counter who, judging from the satisfied line of her mouth, was the instigator of his approaching difficulties.

"Something I said?" he asked. It had taken him the entire night and most of the day to cross the water, ditch the stolen boat along an empty stretch of coast, and make his way—mostly on foot—this far. He hadn't expected to gain unchallenged access to Seth, but neither had he expected this level of resistance.

"I've told you three times we don't have a Seth Benjamin registered here, sir, and that if you didn't leave, I would have you escorted from the building." She shrugged. "You didn't leave. Here's your escort."

Aramael worked to keep the scowl out of his own expression. While he didn't have much experience with sweet-talking the mortal race, he assumed some kind of pleasantry would be required, particularly when he needed cooperation rather than to make an enemy. The burly guard approached at a steady pace, hand moving to rest atop the baton hanging from his belt. Jaw aching, Aramael forced a smile.

"Look, I'm not trying to cause trouble—"

"Well, you're certainly succeeding."

"I just need to find a patient you're supposed to have here. His name is Seth Benjamin, but he can't remember who he is. Maybe he—"

"He has amnesia?" the nurse interrupted.

"Yes."

Her expression cleared. "Then you want John Doe."

Who?

About to shake his head and start over again—for the fourth time—Aramael paused when another nurse stepped in and whispered something in the woman's ear. The current bane of his existence raised an eyebrow.

"Well, that explains it." She held up a hand to the security guards. "You're right. John Doe was identified as Seth Benjamin. I've been off for the last three days and haven't reviewed all the charts yet. Who did you say you are?"

"A friend." Aramael reined in his impatience as a shadow of displeasure crossed the nurse's face at his tone. He took a deep breath. Just a few more minutes and the threat of Seth would be removed. Humanity would be safe for a little while longer. If one didn't count the coming Armageddon. "So, may I see him?"

"Nope."

Aramael's hands curled into fists. He pulled them from the counter and stuffed them into his pockets. "But you've just said he's here—"

She shook her head. "I said you were right about the name. But he's not here."

Oh, for the love of—

He unlocked his jaw to ask in as neutral a voice as he could manage around his increasing annoyance, "Do you know where he is?"

"Gone," said a new voice. "And you haven't answered the question. Who are you?"

Aramael looked down at a woman who had come from behind him. Middle-aged by human standards, she had an air of authority about her despite her casual dress. Sharp blue eyes returned his study, traveling over him from head to toe and back again, and then narrowing on his face.

"Just a—" He broke off as her face tightened. As if by some unspoken signal, the burly guard moved to the woman's side and Aramael felt the other guard's presence loom to his right. He hesitated, reviewing his options. While he might overpower the two guards and make his escape as easily as he breathed, his chances of getting back in to see Seth would be markedly lower if he did—and the disturbance would draw the exact attention he wanted to avoid. On the other hand, the woman obviously knew Seth, and if she couldn't connect him with the Appointed, she might at least give him information he could use. Time, he reminded himself dourly, being of such an essence.

From the dregs of his former existence, he pulled a name. "Jacob Trent," he said. And then, hoping to inspire confidence, he added, "I'm a detective with the Toronto police."

The woman scowled. "Are you serious? What, she knew I'd turf her out on her ass and so she sent you? Well, you can tell her I said—"

"She?"

"Alexandra Jarvis, of course. I know you're working with her."

"Alex is *here*?"

The woman went quiet, a dozen questions milling in her eyes. In his shock, Aramael could decipher none of them. Nor could he summon even the flimsiest of arguments when she lifted her chin.

"I think you'd better come with me," she said.

He thought so, too.

TWENTY-THREE

Alex opened her eyes to find Seth standing over her, silhouetted against the faint light coming in the window behind him. Jolting awake, she struggled upright against the pillows and then stilled. Pillows? Last thing she remembered, she'd been sitting in the chair, watching television with Seth and trying to answer his many, many questions. She pushed back her hair. Outside the hotel window, the afternoon she'd left behind had become dusk, accounting for the deep shadows in the room.

She cleared the sleep from her throat. "How long was I out?"

"About four hours," his voice rumbled in reply. "Not long enough if the required eight hours per twenty-four is correct."

A smile tugged at her lips. Along with reacquiring more or less full language skills at an unnerving rate over the last thirty-six hours, Seth seemed to have accumulated a fair bit of trivia. "It's correct, but I'm sure I'll survive. I've made do with less."

"Because you're a cop."

Alex remembered the conversation that had followed on the heels of the *Law & Order* episode they'd been watching; remembered, too, Seth's concern when the discussion had turned to the dangers of her job, and from there to the topic of mortality. The exchange had exhausted her with its complications. She suspected she'd gone to sleep out of sheer self-defense. Which reminded her . . .

"You put me to bed."

The shadowy Seth nodded and Alex resisted the impulse to switch on the bedside lamp. She didn't want to see what was going on in those black eyes right now.

"Thank you," she said instead.

"You're welcome."

Silence fell, awkward and too big for the room. Alex cleared her throat again. "You must be getting hungry."

"I am, but not for food."

Alex's heart took up residence in her throat. "Excuse me?"

"Relax," Seth drawled. "I'm in no position to pursue a relationship with you at the moment."

That did it. Alex rolled over and vaulted from the bed on the other side, knocking a lamp over in her frantic search for a switch. As she stooped to retrieve it from the floor, all the lights in the room illuminated at once, freezing her in place. She closed her eyes, stopped counting at thirty, and stood up again, setting the lamp back on the night table.

"Something I said?" Seth asked. He'd changed into the clothes she'd bought for him and pulled his hair back into a familiar ponytail. He looked just like the old Seth. The supremely attractive old Seth.

"No. Yes." Alex pulled her sleep-fuzzed brain together. She should have bought him something other than what she remembered seeing him in. Something other than the black that so enhanced his imposing stature, making it seem like he filled half the hotel room. Her mouth twisted. His memory might not have come back yet, but that presence of his—the one she'd had no business noticing in the first place and certainly had no business remembering now—had. In spades.

"Kind of," she allowed in response to his question. "It's just—we had a similar conversation once."

Seth's gaze sharpened. "This attraction between us isn't new, then."

Alex balled her hands into fists. He'd been a hell of a lot easier to manage *without* the language skills, damn it. "No. It's not."

"But something kept us apart."

Alex took a moment to formulate a response, straightening her shirt and tucking it back into her pants. She slanted a covert look at Seth, noting the astuteness she remembered had also returned to the dark gaze. Which meant he wasn't going to let her get away with anything less than the truth.

Hell.

She nodded. "Yes."

"Who am I, Alex?"

"I don't know."

Black eyes narrowed. "You're lying."

Alex sighed. "No. I'm prevaricating." Combing her fingers through her tousled hair in an effort to restore it to order, she met his gaze squarely. Openly. "I really don't know who you are, Seth. All I have is what little you told me when we met the first time, and a whole lot of supposition I've come up with on my own, the accuracy of which is highly suspect, I'm sure."

"I need to know."

"I agree. But not yet."

Frustration marred the dark brow. "Why not?"

"You need more information first. Context for what I—"

Someone banged at the door and Alex froze, words and all. Her eyes flicked to the bedside clock. Shit. It was too late in the day for housekeeping, and that was no polite knock—which meant it had to be either Henderson or Riley, neither of whom would be a good thing.

Catching Seth's gaze, Alex put a finger to her lips and he nodded his understanding. Thank God for education by television. She waited while he moved silently around the corner, out of sight of the door, and then scanned the room to be sure nothing of his presence would be visible. Their unwanted visitor hammered again.

Alex peered through the peephole and scowled as her suspicions were confirmed. Riley. She took a deep breath, mustering herself for the inevitable verbal battle with the psychiatrist, and pulled open the door. Whatever she might have said died in her throat when a second figure thrust aside the doctor and stared down at her with cold gray eyes in a face she thought she'd never see again.

Her heart stalled in mid-beat. *"Aramael?"*

HUGH LISTENED TO the voice mail message left by Liz Riley three times before enough of it filtered through Father Marcus's words to make sense. Even then, it kept jumbling up with what the priest had told him, so that Liz's voice seemed to fade in and out of Marcus's in his head.

"Hugh, it's me," her message began.

"Documents exist. Scrolls," Marcus's voice echoed.

"There's been a new development," said Liz.

"No one outside the Church knows of them. Most in *the Church don't know."*

"Someone came looking for Seth Benjamin at the hospital—he claims he's a police officer."

"They tell a story of women becoming pregnant and giving birth within a matter of weeks . . ."

"He says he's from Toronto . . ."

"The children grew at phenomenal rates and developed inhuman powers . . ."

"And claims he knows Alex."

"Hugh, the scrolls claim these children were the product of angels lying with women . . ."

"We're heading to her hotel now. Detective Trent—that's his name—thinks she's hiding Seth."

"They were the Nephilim . . ."

"I need you to call me when you get this message—or better yet, just meet us there."

"And the Church thinks it's happening again."

"End of message," the automated female voice informed him. "To listen to this message again, press one. To save this message for a period of seven days, press nine. To delete it—"

Hugh disconnected. He stared out the windshield of his sedan at the evening street, alive with vehicles and people. A familiar world that had, in the space of a short conversation with a man he hadn't seen in more than ten years, become a place he no longer recognized.

Angels lying with women.

A place that made even less sense than it had before.

Angels.

His jaw went tight. Reaching beneath his seat, he pulled out the dashboard cherry light, switched it on, and steered into the traffic. Alex's hotel was halfway across the downtown center. With luck, he'd be there before Liz made it out of the elevator.

"ARAMAEL," ALEX SAID again. Her tongue felt thick and heavy in her mouth, as if it didn't belong. None of her felt like it belonged, in fact, because none of this could be happening. She dug her fingers into the unforgiving door frame until they ached, but not even they felt real.

Aramael of the Sixth Choir of angels, Power, hunter of Fallen Ones, cast from Heaven for killing his brother to save her, standing now before her in a seedy hotel in downtown Vancouver. Alex stared at him, hungry for the details that had already begun to fade in her mind. His height, his powerful build, the aura of strength and raw magnetism she remembered from their first meeting.

"How did you find me?" she asked.

"I didn't," he said. "I wasn't looking for you."

Alex's entire being flinched from the denial. From its implications. Aramael's gaze met hers, cold and flat, shutting her out with an absoluteness that cut to her core.

She'd been shot once, in her sixth year on the job, at a domestic dispute turned ugly. Her vest had saved her from death but not from the bullet's impact, which she'd decided

at the time felt rather like being kicked in the chest by a
horse—agonizing, paralyzing, stunning. She realized now
it had felt more like this. Like looking on the other half of
her very essence and seeing him gaze back without concern.
Without emotion. Without any of the recognition that had
once flared between them.

At the far end of the corridor, the stairwell door closed with
a distinctive metal clang. Alex dragged her gaze from Aramael
and looked toward the sound, but no one emerged to intrude
on a reunion she had never dared let herself think about. One
that sure as hell wouldn't have gone like this if she had.

She swallowed, twice, and willed her lungs to function
again. "I see," she said. "Then why *are* you here?"

Aramael stepped closer, staring past her into the hotel
room. His scent, warm and spicy and—heavenly, for want
of a better word—wrapped around her. Fighting not to close
her eyes and fall into him, Alex gritted her teeth and turned
her spine rigid against need.

Aramael looked past her, through her, nodding toward
the hotel room. "I'm here for him."

Pulling the door against her side, she blocked his view.
Aramael's gaze returned, shadowed with a darkness, a turmoil, she had almost forgotten.

Had wanted to forget.

Her cop's instincts bristled to life. Something was wrong.
Very wrong. She took a firmer grip on the door. "Who?"
she asked.

Aramael shook his head. "Don't. Neither of us need sink
to a level of playing games."

"Fine. Then why are you here for him?"

"So you *do* have him," Riley interjected. "I *knew* it."

The psychiatrist tried to push past Aramael, but he held
out an arm, blocking her path.

"This isn't mortal business," he said.

Riley opened her mouth to object, stopped, and looked
at Alex, the faint beginnings of uncertainty shining from
behind her wire frames.

Alex forced her gaze back to the remoteness in Aramael's eyes. "Answer me," she said. "Why do you want to see Seth?"

"It isn't mortal business," he repeated.

Riley took a second step back, and then a third.

Alex lifted her chin. "I'm not just any mortal," she reminded him. "Not after all that's happened."

His expression turned impossibly colder. "Yes," he said. "You are. Now let me pass."

Fighting off the paralysis of sheer, soul-deep agony, Alex shook her head. "Not unless you tell me what's going on."

"I can't."

"Bullshit." Slamming the hotel room door shut, Alex scowled and crossed her arms. "The evasive routine doesn't work with me, remember? It never has and never will. Either tell me what's going on or leave. Your choice."

Aramael stared at her. "You can't stop me."

"Maybe not," said a new voice, "but I can."

Alex was certain all three of them—she, Aramael, Riley—looked down the corridor in perfect unison. Any other time, she might have found that amusing, but right now, as she stared at the gun in Hugh Henderson's hands, she failed to see much humor in any of this.

"Liz, move away from him and come here," Henderson ordered, jerking his head to the side. Riley did as directed, her face a study in utter confusion. When she was within arm's length, Henderson reached out to tuck her behind him. He raised an eyebrow at Alex. "Are you okay?"

"I'm fine, but—"

Henderson released Riley's arm and held up his hand. "Am I understanding this right? Do you have Seth in your room?"

Oh, for the love of—Alex sighed. How much more complicated could things get? She glowered at Aramael, nodded defeat at Henderson. "Yes. He's here."

"Okay. We'll deal with that later. Right now I need you to move over here with me." Waggling his fingers at her, Henderson scowled at Aramael. "And I need *you* not to move," he added. "In fact, I'd strongly suggest you don't even breathe."

"Detective Henderson," Alex began.

"Don't." Henderson shook his head. "Not so much as a word, Jarvis. I'm sick to death of the whole cloak-and-dagger thing you have going. I want answers and, with or without your cooperation, I plan to get them. Now get your ass over here before I decide to arrest you, too."

TWENTY-FOUR

"We've found him."

Lucifer looked up to find Samael standing in the doorway, wings outspread in obvious excitement. "That was quick."

"And unexpected." Coming into the office, Sam glanced back as his wings knocked into the door frame. He tucked them into place against his shoulders. "You remember the Power who broke the pact?"

Once again, Lucifer set aside the journal he had been working on. He popped a peppermint into his mouth. "Caim's twin. Yes. What about him?"

"You knew he was cast out into the mortal realm without his powers? Some of the ranks have been toying with him, exacting a certain—revenge for what they perceive to be his sins against their colleagues."

"I care about this why?"

"Patience, oh Mighty One." Samael grinned, obviously enjoying himself. "I'm getting to that."

Lucifer glowered at the overt use of the nickname he

knew was murmured behind his back. "You're pushing your
luck, Archangel," he warned.

Samael waved a dismissive hand. "Whatever. Just listen.
Qemuel was the latest to go after the Power. He was follow-
ing him, waiting for his opportunity to strike, when the
Power went to a hotel to meet a woman."

Whatever? Lucifer's fingers curled around the pen he'd
begun to wish was Samael's neck. "That might make the
Power a potential recruit," he acknowledged tightly. "But I
still don't see—"

"She's the Nephilim Caim tried to kill."

Sam's smile took on a whole new level of satisfaction.
Lucifer waited, sensing more to come. His aide didn't
disappoint.

"And she has Seth."

The pen in Lucifer's hand snapped in two, sending a
spray of ink across the desk. A stain spread over the page
he'd been writing. It couldn't be. The consequences were
too great; she wouldn't dare move against him that way.
Wouldn't risk—

"You know what this means."

Lucifer fought down a sour rush of sickness and held up
discolored fingers for silence. There had to be another explanation. She was the One, the Creator, the single constant in
the whole of the universe. A fine film of sweat broke out
along his forehead. She wouldn't break her word like that.
Couldn't. Not when her word was all he had left. Not when
he counted on that word to give him the time he needed to
finally rid himself of that plague she called her children.

He raised his gaze to Samael's gleeful face. The expecta-
tion behind it. "That's it? That's all we have?"

Samael's smile faded. "We have an angel in direct contact
with the Appointed," he said. "One of Heaven's own, interfering with your son. Violating the terms of the agreement."

"Did Qemuel see them together? The Power and the
Appointed?"

"Not exactly, but—"

"Then how do we know the Power was there for him and not for the woman?"

Temper darkened his aide's face. "And Seth just happened to be there?" he snarled. "You can't seriously think this is all a coincidence. The One's mark is all over this."

Agony lanced through Lucifer's chest. He felt certain that his very heart had begun to bleed. Wondered if it had ever stopped. "It doesn't matter," he said.

"It doesn't—" Sam stared at him.

"Without proof, we cannot demand her forfeiture and if we move prematurely, we'll be the ones forfeiting instead of her."

"What does it matter? Either way, we go to war."

"Agreed, but we go to war on our terms, not hers." The black smear on Lucifer's skin shrank and disappeared. He looked up at his nearly apoplectic aide. "I haven't come this far only to see my plans for humanity crushed by your impatience, Samael. I don't care what it looks like, I've made my decision. We wait until we have the Nephilim in place and we do nothing to jeopardize the agreement. Is that clear?"

Black wings opened with a thunderous crack and the papers stacked on Lucifer's desk scattered in the draft. Lucifer narrowed his eyes, but the Archangel either didn't notice the warning sign or chose to ignore it. Slamming his hands onto the mahogany surface, Samael leaned down.

"Fuck that," he snarled. "I am *done* waiting. Done waiting for her, done waiting for Seth, and especially done waiting for you. We have ample cause to declare the agreement broken. You can do whatever you'd like with the mortals, but *we* are going to war."

Lucifer stared at a drop of spittle clinging to his aide's bottom lip. Slowly, wearily, he climbed to his feet and looked across at his aide's fury. Then, without warning, he struck, shoving the desk with a single, mighty thrust across the room, Samael with it. The Archangel struck the wall with a grunt amid a shower of peppermints launched from their dish. Pinned, he lifted his chin as Lucifer stalked toward him, his startled gaze turning first wary, then sullen.

But not afraid.

Not yet.

Nostrils flaring, Lucifer reached across the desk, grasped his aide by the throat, and lifted him up and over to dangle in front of him, feet several inches above the floor. Samael clawed at the fingers cutting off his air, his eyes widening.

"I warned you, Samael," Lucifer said. "So many times I warned you, but still you chose to ignore me. And now I have endured your insolence long enough."

The former Archangel's arms flailed as Lucifer threw him across the room. He crashed into one of the bookcases, splintering three shelves and sending their load tumbling to the floor around him. Lucifer followed.

His aide dragged himself upright, shock and uncertainty flickering across his face. "Lucifer, I—"

A backhand sent the Archangel staggering into another waterfall of books. Lucifer followed, relentless in his pursuit. Another slap split Samael's cheek. A third and fourth, each delivered with measured but increasing force, transformed his eyes to pools of blood.

Samael scrambled to get away, scuttling across the floor on hands and knees, his wings dragging through the wreckage of the room. The stench of fear oozed from his pores to hang in the air, but still Lucifer didn't stop. Following the Archangel, he delivered blow after punishing blow until Samael lay at his feet, weeping in agony, shattered beyond recognition, his wings in tatters.

Done at last, Lucifer crouched at his aide's side. He rolled what remained of Samael's head toward him. Blood seeped from the Archangel's eyes, mingling with tears. Shaking his head, Lucifer wiped away the crimson trickles.

"I'm sorry it came to this, Samael, truly. But I need to be sure you've learned your lesson."

Samael mewled a plaintive response.

"No." Lucifer shook his head again. "No, there's one more thing I must do to be certain. This will hurt, but you need to hold very still or I might make a mistake. Quiet, now."

He plunged a hand into Samael's chest. The Archangel

arched and writhed beneath the new assault, a thin, high-pitched scream emanating from the gore that had once been his mouth. Lucifer reached deeper, deeper, until his fingers closed over a tiny sphere, hard as marble. He smiled.

Withdrawing his hand, he wiped the orb clean on a part of his sleeve not already covered in Samael's body bits and held it up for his aide to see. The Archangel fell silent except for the gurgle of air passing through the fluids in his throat.

"Beautiful, isn't it?" Lucifer asked, admiring the swirl of light pulsing between his thumb and forefinger. "Hard to believe something so small can contain all you are, the very essence of your immortality."

He looked down at Sam again, letting his smile fade. "You do know I can take it from you anytime I wish, don't you, Samael? That I can destroy you with just a twitch of my fingers?"

He tightened his delicate hold by the slightest fraction and a whistling hiss broke from Sam.

Lucifer nodded. "You understand. I'm glad. Now understand this, Samael formerly of the Archangels." He enclosed the sphere in his fist and terror shot through Sam's eyes. "Understand that, while you might be useful to me, I do not need you. I never have. So if you ever so much as breathe discontent again—if you so much as *think* it, I will not stop. I will kill you."

Rising to his feet, he dropped Samael's immortality onto the floor. It rolled to a stop by his aide's mutilated fingers.

"I'm going out," Lucifer said. "When you're done putting yourself together, make sure you clean up the mess. And get me more peppermints. You've ruined mine."

TWENTY-FIVE

"**D**amn it, Jarvis, I'm not kidding," Henderson growled. "I will arrest your ass in a heartbeat if you don't get over here."

"Hugh, what in God's name is going on?" Elizabeth Riley hissed.

"Let me handle this, Liz. Just stay back. Jarvis, I gave you an order."

Focusing on Aramael's back, on the way his shoulders flexed and then stilled, Alex didn't dare look up at the others. The cold in her settled deeper. He was waiting. The moment she moved from the door—

"I can't. He'll go after Seth."

"If he so much as twitches, I promise I'll shoot. Now move."

"I know you're trying to protect me, Henderson, but I'm not the one he's after."

Aramael's shoulders tensed again and Alex frowned, an un-nameable something tugging at her mind. A question that wouldn't quite take shape.

"For fuck's sake, Alex," Henderson growled. He sighed

and reached for the handcuffs clipped to his belt. "Fine. Have it your way." He waggled the gun at Aramael. "You. On the ground, face down, hands away from your body."

Aramael didn't move and a frisson of warning ran down Alex's spine. If she didn't put an end to this standoff, it was going to get ugly. No matter what Aramael's reason for being here might be, he would never allow himself to be taken into custody. Couldn't allow it.

Shooting a quick glance past him to where Henderson was beginning to look downright pissed, she pitched her voice low enough that only Aramael could hear. "You need to get out of here. Now."

Aramael met her gaze over his shoulder. "I can't."

"Look," she said through clenched teeth, "I get you have an agenda of some kind, but neither one of us needs the kind of attention you'll bring if you're taken into custody. Now get the hell out of here while you can."

Not that having him disappear into thin air would be much better, but at least he wouldn't be around for questioning.

"You don't understand," he said, gray eyes boring into hers. "I can't."

"You—" She stopped. Stared at his shoulders. Willed herself to see them there, rising beyond him, flexed, powerful, iridescent with their golden fire. But there was nothing. Her gaze moved to his again.

"Your wings," she whispered. "Aramael, what happened to your wings?"

But even as she asked, she knew. Felt the answer come together in her head like the pieces of a puzzle.

"You can't stop me," he'd said, and yet he'd remained there, in the hallway, allowing her to block his access to Seth. Had remained solid, and present, and unmoving. Had done nothing about Henderson, or the gun, or the threat of arrest.

A tiny muscle flickered near Aramael's ear, the only movement in a body that might otherwise have been stone. Winter's barren chill stared back at Alex from his eyes.

"I need to see Seth," he said.

"No." Alex shook her head. The doorknob pressed into the small of her back. "No. You need to tell me what the hell is going on."

"I told you, I can't."

As if he hadn't spoken, Alex looked past him to Henderson. "I'll trade you," she said. "Him for Seth."

Henderson's gun dropped several inches. The Vancouver detective gaped at her. "Come again?"

"I need to talk to Ara—him." Alex tipped her head toward Aramael. "And I need someone to watch Seth for me until I get back."

"Back from—watch—" Henderson lowered the gun to his side and stared at her as if she'd suggested they join forces in knocking off a bank. "Damn it, Jarvis, this isn't some kind of negotiation here and I am not your on-call babysitter. I overheard Ara-whoever he is uttering threats and I am arresting him. *And* I'm taking Seth Benjamin into custody, *and* I'll be questioning you, too. End of fucking discussion."

Alex curled fingers into palms. "Remember when you spoke to my supervisor? To Roberts?"

"What the hell does that have to do with anything?"

"Remember what he told you about Seth?"

"Of course, but—"

She uncurled one finger and lifted it to point at Aramael. "He's like Seth."

"Alex."

Aramael's snarl made her flinch, but she held her ground, because she had to know. She had to find out what he wanted with Seth, to know if she was right about him hunting. And if he was, *why*. Which meant getting him away from here, alone, to answer her questions—any way she could.

Henderson's scowl deepened. "Like him how? Connected to the serial killer case, you mean?"

"That—and whatever else Roberts said."

Henderson hadn't told her much about his exchange with her supervisor, so Alex could only guess at what Roberts had divulged, but the Vancouver detective's reticence about the conversation—and the sudden gray tinge in his face now—hinted at a certain level of detail. She waited for him to process her words.

The Adam's apple in Henderson's throat bobbed as his thumb toyed with the safety on his gun. He stared, first at her, then at Aramael. At last he cleared his throat.

"You know how this sounds."

Alex nodded.

"You know how your supervisor sounded. How Father Mar—" He broke off.

Father? As in *priest*? A priest who knew what, exactly? Alex bit back the questions. *One thing at a time, Jarvis.*

"I know how it sounds, yes."

"But you still want me to believe you—to believe this." He waved his handcuffs at Aramael.

"Just accept it's possible. Let me talk with him."

Riley put a hand on Henderson's forearm and he started, looking down at her as if he'd forgotten she was there. An entire unspoken conversation seemed to pass between them before Henderson grunted. Riley looked mutinous.

"Ten minutes." Henderson lifted his head to look at Alex. "You have ten minutes."

"Alex—" Aramael began.

"Don't," she said. "I didn't create this mess, Aramael. You did. I just bought you ten minutes of as much anonymity as you're going to get. Whether you get more time or not depends on what you tell me. Either way, you're not going near Seth unless you convince me I should let you. Got it?"

Her wingless soulmate's mouth went tight. Frustration flashed through his eyes, but he nodded his acceptance and Alex reached for the knob.

"Shit," she muttered. "It locked itself." She raised a hand and knocked. "Seth? It's Alex. I'm locked out. Can you open the door for me?"

Silence.

She knocked again, louder this time. "Seth? Open the door."

No response.

Making a fist, she pounded. Hard. Harder.

"Seth! Damn it, Seth, answer me!"

Henderson joined her, hammering louder. "Seth Benjamin, open up."

Still nothing.

"No way we'll force it without a ram," Henderson said. "Liz, get the manager. Tell him it's an emergency and make sure he brings the—"

Aramael's hand reached between them—Alex would have recognized the strong, tanned forearm anywhere—and shoved the door inward, sending it to the floor with a crash, frame splintered. A slack-jawed Henderson stepped away from the angel. Tightening her lips, Alex pushed past into the room. A second later she confirmed what they already knew.

"He's gone."

TWENTY-SIX

Seth moved through the streets with long, angry strides, his gaze flicking from one example of human devastation to another. He'd learned the word while watching the news with Alex the night before; she had explained it as the wreckage remaining after some kind of disaster. While the news had used it in the context of an earthquake on the other side of the planet, it was the word that came to mind as he viewed the world before him now.

Devastation.

Men and women of all ages stood in the street, sat against lampposts and brick walls, and sprawled among boxes and garbage like so much litter on the sidewalk. Studying each as he walked past, Seth saw no life in the eyes that followed his progress, no hope in the faces. A new feeling stirred inside him, something he couldn't put a name to, but knew was the opposite of the attraction that pulled him to Alex.

Alex, who would be able to explain what it was he witnessed here. Alex, who had restored his ability to communicate again, sheltered him, taught him to trust—and then betrayed him.

Seth's chest burned. He felt—he didn't know how he felt. Didn't know how to identify whatever caused this fire in him and left the sour taste on the back of his tongue. Alex would be able to help him identify that, too, of course, but she was otherwise occupied right now. With the man who had been outside the hotel room door with Dr. Riley. The man she had accused of being *like Seth*.

Seth hadn't been able to see who she referred to, but her meaning had been clear and had supported his growing suspicions: if *he* was like Seth, then *Seth* was not like others. Not like the ones who had found him and locked him in the hospital. Not like the ones he watched on television or read about in the newspapers or books. Not like the ones he walked past now. Not like Alex.

Seth was something other. Something different. But what? And why did the knowledge make him ache inside, as if he had lost something vital, something he needed to complete himself? More important, why hadn't Alex told him when he had asked? Why had she been about to hand him over to the ones he'd escaped while she talked to another who had come for him?

The churning at Seth's center intensified. He scowled at the thousands of other questions stirring along the edges of his consciousness.

A scuff against concrete snagged his attention as a patched and faded man shuffled after him. An unfocused gaze met his, hesitated, then dropped to the sidewalk as the man veered to the left and crossed the street. Seth stared after him.

"It's a shame, isn't it?" a voice remarked from the shelter of a doorway.

Distracted, Seth looked around as a figure stepped from the shadows onto the sidewalk, his blond head shaking in apparent sadness. Apparent, because Seth would have sworn the sentiment wasn't genuine. His gaze narrowed on the newcomer.

The man strolled closer, stopping a few feet away. His eyes, a startling, intense purple under the streetlight, settled on Seth. "Such a waste, when they fail like this."

"They?"

"Mortals." The man nodded toward the street. "Humans. The One's precious children."

Seth shook his head. "I have no idea what you're talking about. These are adults, not children—and who is this One?"

The purple gaze sharpened on him. "You still haven't remembered, have you?" the man murmured.

A vague uneasiness crawled over Seth's skin. Suddenly missing the comfort of Alex's presence, he felt the urge to return to her. A nagging curiosity held him. "Do I know you?"

"Yes and no." The stranger smiled, and a pure and steady light seemed to shine from his face. "I am like you."

"Like me how?"

"Of another realm, another world. More than they have ever been or can hope to be." The man indicated the street scene again.

"I don't understand."

Another smile. More light. "Then walk with me, Seth born of Heaven and Hell, and I'll explain."

Something in the stranger's voice—or was it in the way his odd inner light turned cold?—made Seth uncertain he wanted to hear what this man had to tell him. *Heaven and Hell?*

He shook his head. "I need to get back. Someone is waiting for me."

"A woman. I know."

Seth scowled. "How do you know? Who are you?"

"I am Lucifer. Bearer of Light, ruler of Hell, former help-meet of the Creator of All." Lucifer's purple gaze became wry. "And I'm not just like you, Seth Benjamin; I *am* you—or half of you, anyway. You're my son."

HUGH CAUGHT HOLD of Liz's wrist as she made to follow Alex Jarvis and the stranger—Aramael—down the street. The psychiatrist opened her mouth to object, but he shook his head at her, focused on the cell phone against his ear.

Waiting. Wishing he'd thought to do this as soon as he'd hung up from Alex's supervisor yesterday.

"Okay," the voice at the other end came back on the line. "I've got it here. It's a sizeable file, though—you sure you want the whole thing?"

"I'm sure."

A sigh. "I'll have it copied and couriered to you tomorrow."

Liz tugged at his fingers and he tightened his grip, shooting her a warning frown.

"Tonight," he told the voice. "Rush."

A heavier sigh, followed by a grumble. "Why not? It's not like I have a family to go home to or anything. Fine. I'll send it tonight. You'll have it by noon."

The line went dead. Pocketing the cell phone, Hugh frowned at Liz, who still pulled at his grasp. "Simmer down, Doc. I gave her ten minutes, remember?"

"That was *before* she lost my patient again," she retorted. "I want to know what the hell is going on, Hugh. Why are you suddenly on Alex Jarvis's side? And what the hell did she mean about this—this *friend* of hers being like Seth? He told me he worked with her in Toronto."

Hugh drew her to the side of the hotel entrance, away from the crowd that had gathered: management, guests, cops who had responded to the disturbance of doors being knocked down and guns being drawn. He grimaced. It would take him a month of Sundays to write up all the reports he'd have to file on this. Pushing aside the thought, he focused on the irate psychiatrist.

"Alex didn't lose Seth, and you know it. He disappeared on his own, just like he did before." He waved her silent when she opened her mouth to argue. "Let me finish. I think the friend, this Aramael, did work with her," he said, "and with Seth. At least on the serial killer case. But not as a cop."

Liz stopped trying to tug free. Her eyes narrowed. "You're referring to what the supervisor told you."

"Yes."

"You know that's insane."

"Yes."

"You have no proof."

"I've requested the case files from Toronto and—" Hugh stopped and compressed his lips. He'd damn near told her about Marcus just then—had only just caught back the story of secret scrolls and divine beings and superhuman half-breeds. As good a friend as Liz might be, she was still a department shrink and wouldn't hesitate to file a report on him if she thought he'd lost it. Which she almost certainly would if he blurted out a story like the one Marcus had told him.

No, when he told her what the priest had said—*if* he told her—he'd have to make sure she was at least somewhat receptive first. In the meantime, he needed to keep her away from Alex Jarvis. He shook his head in answer to Liz's statement. "I'm not expecting much in the way of extraterrestrial testimony, so no, I have no proof. Only my gut."

Liz remained silent for a long time, staring down the sidewalk at Alex and her companion. At last she shook her head. "I spend my days trying to help people who have delusions like this."

"Disappearing from a locked room isn't a delusion, Liz. It's a fact. It happened. Just like all those impossible pregnancies happened. Just like Chiu's baby happened."

Just like Katherine Gray killed herself because she couldn't handle whatever was growing inside her and Jenna Murphy may very well be telling the truth about her attacker.

Hugh didn't speak the last part, but Liz's stare—weighing, considering, wavering—told him she was thinking about the other young women, too. Just when he believed she might relent, however, might allow herself to buy into even a fraction of what he had begun to suspect, she pulled free of his hand.

"You do what you have to. I'm going back to the hospital."

"That's it? Life doesn't fit your parameters so you're going to pretend it's not happening? You can't just keep running away like that."

"I'm not running away," she said, "but I can't accept what you're saying, either. This wouldn't be the first instance of mass hysteria, Hugh. Or mass hallucinations. The human mind is extraordinarily complex."

"You don't really believe that."

"I believe exactly that. Science—"

"There are some things in this world science can't explain. Alex—"

"Alex Jarvis is even further into this delusion than you are. I'm sorry, but if you intend to follow her down this path, you'll have to do it without me." Stalking away, Liz looked back over her shoulder a final time. "Let me know if . . ."

"If?" Hugh prompted when her voice trailed off.

Liz's flat blue gaze met his. "If you decide you want to talk," she said. "Professionally."

TWENTY-SEVEN

A lex led Aramael down the sidewalk to the far end of the hotel. When she'd put enough distance between them and Henderson and Riley, she stopped and shoved her hands into her pockets. A handful of pedestrians hurried past them. Even at half past seven, most carried briefcases or computer bags—stragglers leaving their offices after another long workday.

"He's serious about the ten minutes," she said, nodding toward Henderson. "So start talking."

"It's not that easy. There are things happening you know nothing about."

"You mean the Apocalypse?" She almost laughed at Aramael's surprise. Almost—except, again, it just wasn't funny. "Seth told me. Before, when he knew who he was. He called himself Heaven's contingency plan, but he wouldn't tell me anything else, so I haven't been able to help him remember. I thought that was why you were here, that you'd come to remind him, to make him better. But I was wrong, wasn't I?"

"Yes."

The sheer simplicity of his answer took away her breath. She warned herself to stick with the issues at hand—the important, concrete ones, not the nebulous, don't-want-to-go-there ones.

"What happened, Aramael?" she asked at last. "What changed?"

Aramael's expressionless gaze met hers. He didn't pretend to misunderstand, didn't avoid the question. "I protected you," he said. "There were consequences."

"Your wings."

"Yes."

Alex swallowed. "What else?"

"My realm, my Creator, my powers." A shadow crossed his face. "You."

"Me?"

"I remember you as my soulmate, but that is all. What connected us is gone."

A knife slid between Alex's ribs and pierced her heart. She drew a careful breath around the pain, pausing for a moment to examine it. Deep, but not as deep as she would have expected. If she'd expected any of this. Did it make her a terrible person, that she wasn't devastated by his revelation? That she felt not just sadness, but an odd sense of relief that an angel no longer loved her with an intensity capable of destroying the world? She exhaled the breath she'd drawn.

"I see. Will it come back?"

Long seconds passed before, voice quiet, Aramael responded, "Knowing why I am here, would you want it to?"

She stared at him for a moment, not wanting to answer. Not wanting to *know* the answer. "So I was right, then. You're hunting him. Why? Didn't your One send him to stop the war?"

"She did, but something went wrong. Seth isn't—" Aramael hesitated.

"He isn't Seth," Alex finished. She leaned against the hotel's brick wall and tilted her head back to stare at a streetlight that had flickered to life above them in the gathering gloom. "He's not whole."

"Then you've seen it."

"Yes, but he's getting better. He can communicate again, and he's learning unbelievably fast, and—"

"He's dangerous."

Head still tipped back, Alex stared down the bridge of her nose at Aramael. "So just because an angel needs a little help, he's being exiled to this Limbo place? That hardly seems like a Heavenly thing to do."

Aramael looked away from her glare. "He cannot be helped, Alex. Seth is—" He paused. "He's like one of your nuclear missiles, already in flight and without a guidance system. The only difference is that he becomes more powerful with every minute. If we don't stop him now, he is potentially capable of taking out the entire human race."

Alex blinked at the analogy. "That's one hell of a threat," she said at last.

"Yes. It is."

"Is your One not capable of fixing him?"

"Capability isn't the problem." Aramael sighed and looked down the sidewalk to where Alex had already noticed Henderson edging toward them. Riley was no longer with him. "Do you remember the pact I told you about between Lucifer and the One? There was a follow-up agreement that involved Seth. Under it, neither side can interfere with his intended purpose on Earth."

Alex estimated they had a minute, tops, before Henderson's sideways shuffle brought him within earshot. "Will you please stop talking in circles?" she hissed. "Just tell me what the hell is going on so I can decide whether I want to help you or let Henderson arrest you."

Aramael's eyes closed and his shoulders flexed. Alex looked toward Henderson again. *Fifty-five seconds.*

"Seth is the One's son."

She turned her stare on Aramael.

"His father is Lucifer," he continued rapidly, shooting his own glance toward the approaching Vancouver detective. "When he was born, Lucifer and the One reached an agreement under which, when the time was right, Seth would be reborn into the mortal realm. He was to live among you until he reached adulthood and then, through his own choices, make the final decision regarding humanity's fate. A path of good would have required Lucifer to finally step aside and leave the mortal world alone. Permanently. Any war that might occur then would be between Heaven and the Fallen and would not involve mortals."

"And a not-so-good path?" she croaked.

Aramael's mouth drew tight.

Holy fucking hell.

Alex swallowed several times, trying to pull together the scattered fragments of her thoughts—and reality—when all she really wanted to do was run. Hard, fast, and as far away as she could get. Failing which, puking her guts out seemed a reasonable alternative.

Henderson was halfway down the sidewalk.

"You're telling me Seth is the Second Coming?"

A brief impatience flashed across Aramael's face. His mouth drew tight, but he nodded. "If that's how you want to think of it."

"What went wrong?"

"His transition—courtesy of a traitor."

Heaven had traitors? The cop in Alex opened her mouth to ask for details, but she snapped it shut again. She already had enough information to guarantee nightmares for the rest of her life, short as that was shaping up to be; any more would make sleep itself impossible. She focused on following Aramael's words through to their conclusion.

"So, because he's already an adult, any choice he makes now will stand."

"It will."

"What do we do?"

"I find him. Stop him."

"No." She shook her head. "None of this is his fault, Aramael. He's a good man—angel—whatever the hell he is. I've felt it in him. Seen it. He saved my life, damn it."

"He remembers none of that."

"But I do. He isn't responsible for whatever went wrong with his transition, and he's recovering. Quickly. He's held back his powers—he hasn't once struck out at anyone, not even when he was caged up in the psych ward." She surreptitiously rubbed thumb against fingers that still bore the marks of Seth's grip from yesterday. *An anomaly,* she assured herself. *Born of frustration.*

She pressed on. "He's already learned so much. He's trying to learn more. His mind is intact and if we can trigger his memory, he might remember why he's here, do what it is he's supposed to do. Isn't that what you want? What your One wants?"

"You care for him."

Alex flinched from the accusation she imagined behind the words. Imagined, because given what Aramael had told her, it certainly wouldn't be real. Not anymore. Tucking away the velvet-over-silk memory of Seth's voice and the feelings it stirred in her, she met her soulmate's gaze with a level one of her own. "I owe him my life," she said. "But that's not what this is about."

Aramael regarded her in silence for a moment before looking away. "Nor does it change what must be done. If he makes the wrong choice, knowingly or otherwise, humanity will be lost. I cannot let that happen."

"And without him, we'll be caught in a war between Heaven and Hell," Alex snapped. "Seems to me the odds are pretty even at this point."

A few feet away, Henderson cleared his throat. "Time's up, Jarvis. My turn to ask questions."

Alex ignored him and continued to glare at her soulmate. "I won't let you take him, Aramael."

The exiled angel's gray eyes turned hard and his mouth

thinned. A tiny muscle pulsed in his jaw. He shook his head, a slow back-and-forth movement. "You still don't understand, do you?"

"Understand what?"

"That you have no say in the matter. When I said this wasn't mortal business, I meant it. I can't make you help me, but neither will I let you stop me."

TWENTY-EIGHT

"We've lost Seth."

Mika'el's hand stilled and he stared for a moment at the pen he held, weariness rising in him. Some things never changed. A mere two days he'd been back in Heaven, and already he had been cast once more in the role of de facto leader—the Archangel all others went to when they didn't want to disturb the One but needed a near-final authority. The role had never been sanctioned, but neither had it been forbidden—and so it had endured. Even in his absence.

He raised his gaze to an agitated Verchiel standing a few feet inside the doorway of his borrowed office.

"Again?" he asked wearily before waving away the question. "What happened this time?"

"The woman—the Nephilim—Aramael's soulmate—" Verchiel's hands fluttered upward with each attempt at explanation.

Mika'el held back a sigh. "Spit it out, Verchiel. What about her?"

Pausing, Verchiel clasped her hands before she responded. "She reached Seth before Aramael did. Her interference slowed him and, by the time he had access, Seth had disappeared."

Mika'el frowned. "What does she want with the Appointed?"

"From what we can piece together, she is trying to help him regain his memory."

"And we didn't anticipate this interference because . . . ?"

"She lives thousands of miles from where he was found and we had no reason—" Verchiel sighed and, closing her eyes for an instant, pinched the bridge of her nose. "It never occurred to us."

Mika'el swallowed a biting observation about the efficiency of the new Seraph's administration. It would be easy to lay blame at Verchiel's feet, but it wouldn't be just. She didn't deserve it—not with all she'd taken on in the last weeks. Better to remain focused on the real problem of their missing Appointed. He set down the pen and sat back.

"We must have had reports from Guardians who have seen him elsewhere."

"We've alerted everyone, but there's nothing."

"Not even a hint? A rumor?"

The Highest shook her head.

Rising, Mika'el sent the chair thudding into the bookcase behind him. "Will this never end?" he muttered, striding around the desk.

Verchiel leapt out of his way. "What are you going to do?"

"Find him." Mika'el paused to glower at her. "Preferably before Lucifer does, if he hasn't already."

"Do you think . . . ?"

"It's possible. But it's also possible Seth has simply gone off on his own somewhere, and until we know otherwise, we need to be looking for him."

"Shall we send others to search as well?"

"No. There's still a chance Lucifer doesn't know he's missing, and the last thing we need is to alert him."

"But where could he have gone that no Guardian has seen him?"

Mika'el started for the door again, speaking over his shoulder without breaking stride. "Two possibilities: a nest of Nephilim or a place where Guardians have been renounced. Since the first doesn't exist that we know of—yet—I'm betting on the second, of which humanity has many."

"Wait!" Verchiel's voice stopped him just outside the office. "The woman may be able to help you."

"The Naphil? How can she help?"

"She was the last to speak to him, so he may have told her something. She is also a police officer, so she will know the kinds of places you mean. He could be anywhere, Mika'el. You cannot hope to find him on your own. Not in time."

Mika'el hesitated. Verchiel was right. They couldn't afford to waste time in aimless pursuit. Neither, however, could they afford to further complicate matters. The question was, which path carried the higher risk? He tipped back his head against the knot of tension forming at the base of his skull and closed his eyes. Whatever choice he made, the ultimate destination would remain the same; he just had to ensure they minimized the damage incurred along the way. He unclenched his jaw and looked back at the Highest Seraph.

"Where do I find her?"

ALEX'S CHIN LIFTED and, too late, Aramael remembered the defiant streak in her that had both attracted and aggravated him. He knew she would take his words not as the statement of fact they had been, but as a personal challenge.

The first words out of her mouth confirmed his misgivings.

"Like hell I won't stop you," she retorted. She turned to their spectator and jabbed a thumb in Aramael's direction. "If he so much as twitches, shoot him."

The man's jaw went slack. "Excuse me?"

"You heard me. And be prepared to move fast. I don't know how much of his power he still has."

"Alex." Aramael grated the warning through clenched teeth.

Their companion choked, recovered, and echoed, "Power?"

"Don't," said Aramael, his gaze locking with Alex's.

She shook her head. "No. You don't get to keep your secrets anymore, Aramael. Not with all that's going on. Besides, given what Henderson has already heard, I'll only be filling in the blanks."

"Think of the panic. Think of what your world would look like if it knew about ours, about what is going on in its very midst."

"If it knew God had abandoned us, you mean?"

Aramael raised a brow, startled by the savagery behind her words. "The One has not abandoned her children."

"Bullshit. There's a whole new race of Nephilim being born as we speak—" Alex broke off when he recoiled. "You didn't know?"

"That's impossible." A return of the Nephilim? Mika'el would have told him . . . wouldn't he?

"It's all over the news. Dozens of babies all over the world. And your One is not only letting it happen, she's sent you to stop the only angel—being, whatever the hell you want to call him—who might be able to end it. Who might be able to stand between Lucifer and the human race."

From the corner of his eye, Aramael saw the man who had joined them cross himself, forehead to chest, shoulder to shoulder, and then draw his weapon from its holster.

"The One didn't send me. I act alone."

"Then don't do this. Give me a chance to fix Seth, because without him there will be war, and humans will be caught in the middle of it. You've seen how fragile we are, Aramael. We won't last. We *can't* last if that happens."

"The risk is too great. As long as Seth lives—"

Shock flared in Alex's eyes and, too late, Aramael realized his mistake. Fucking Hell. He should never have remained here, letting her draw him into discussion, putting him on the defensive. He should leave—now, before he made things any worse. Before the betrayal in summer-sky-blue eyes wrapped any further around a heart that could not be allowed to feel again.

But Alex's whisper held him immobile, fists clenched at his sides.

"You told me you can't take life," she said, and Aramael flinched from the accusation in her voice. "You said you can't destroy, that it would upset the balance."

"I've already upset it," Aramael said, his voice harsh as he remembered Mika'el's accusation. His truth. "Now I need to restore it."

"By killing again?"

"With Seth as he is, the odds are too heavily in Lucifer's favor."

"So you decided to kill him."

"Yes."

"I don't believe you. I know you, Aramael. You're not a killer."

"No," he snarled, "you *don't* know me." He seized her shoulders, only just refraining from shaking her, ignoring the gun suddenly thrust into his face.

"You don't know any of us. Get it through your head, Alex. We're not like you. When I said what happened between us was a mistake, I meant it. It was a colossal, monumental error made by an angel who believed he could manipulate the universe. He was wrong. *We* are wrong. I murdered my own brother because of you. Did what no angel can do. *Ever.* Now all of humanity will pay the price of my sin unless I can stop the Appointed."

"But Caim was an accident," she whispered. "This is different. Deliberate. Like it or not, I do know you—and you wouldn't do this on your own."

Aramael stood in silence for a moment, remembering

Estiel on the boat dock. How easy it had been to crush the
Fallen One's skull beneath his boot, how easy it would have
been to finish the job if he'd had the power to do so. What
would Alex think if she knew what he had done? What he
had been capable of doing?

Staring at his hands on Alex's shoulders, he let himself
feel her warmth, her life . . . and wished with every particle
of his being this could have ended differently. More, that
it had never happened at all. Down the block, movement
caught his attention as a figure emerged from beside a building, massive black wings unfurled behind it. Aramael went
still.

Mika'el.

An undoubtedly pissed Mika'el in search of expla-
nations.

Aramael's grip on Alex tightened for a moment. He
wrestled one last time with the desire that called to him,
the duty that owned him, and then, letting his hands fall
from Alex, he reached out to pluck the gun from the man's
grip.

"I've changed," he said, looking down as he pulled the
clip from the gun's handgrip. He emptied the bullets into
his palm. "I'm no longer of Heaven and no longer bound by
the rules that once governed me. What I do, I do alone." He
handed the pistol and clip to Alex and met her gaze a final
time. "And what I'm going to do is stop Seth."

Dropping the bullets at her feet, he strode down the
sidewalk to where the winged figure had stepped out of sight
again.

"Aramael!"

Alex's voice, calling his name, wrapped around his heart
and pulled, but Aramael didn't break stride. She called a
second time, and then a third, with anger and betrayal and
an underlying note of agony that pierced to his core. The
cords around his heart went taut and, for a breath of an
instant, Aramael faltered. Wondered. Wished.

Gritting his teeth, he continued walking. Another dozen

steps along, the connection to Alex snapped with a sudden-
ness and completeness that left him stunned. Bereft. Certain
he had nothing more to lose, he rounded the corner into
an alley and came up short against Mika'el's soot-black
wings.

TWENTY-NINE

Alex didn't know how long Aramael had been out of sight before a hand on her arm jolted her back to reality. A reality where the angel she should never have known was hunting the one being who might save humanity . . . unless she pulled herself together enough to stop him.

Sucking in a great, shuddering breath, she loosened her death grip on Henderson's gun and handed it back to him. A semi lumbered by, making the sidewalk vibrate beneath her feet. Henderson took his weapon and silently began loading cartridges back into the clip. Alex glanced down. She hadn't even noticed him stoop to retrieve the bullets; she'd been too busy watching Aramael walk out of her life for a second time.

The sidewalk blurred and she lifted her hands to scrub angrily at tears she refused to shed. Blessedly, Henderson said nothing. She hunched her shoulders against a chill gust of wind.

"Is he really trying to kill Seth?" Henderson asked.

Swallowing hard, Alex settled for a nod when the lump in her throat wouldn't move out of the way of her response.

A city bus rolled by on the street, swirling dust in its wake. A siren wailed to life in the distance.

"Come on," said Henderson gruffly. "I'll buy you a coffee."

"No. I have to find Seth."

"Ten minutes won't make a difference. It'll give you a chance to pull yourself back together."

"Ten minutes might make all the difference. I'm fine," she snapped, muttering a belated, "Thank you."

"Then let me put it this way. We're in a city of almost two and a half million people. Trying to find an ordinary man is like looking for the proverbial needle, but one who can disappear at will? Trust me, Jarvis, without help, you don't stand a chance."

She fixed him with a resigned eye. "And you'll help, but only if I answer your questions first."

Slinging an arm across her shoulders, Henderson guided her down the sidewalk toward the coffee shop that had become their informal meeting place. "Your deductive reasoning is pretty good, Jarvis. You should think about becoming a detective or something."

MIKA'EL WHIRLED, WINGS taut and feathers razor-edged with anger, slicing Aramael's cheek as they whispered past. "Well?" he demanded. "What happened?"

Aramael stepped back warily, swiping at his bloodied face with his sleeve. "Seth wasn't in the hospital. I had to allow a mortal to take me to him. He was with Alex."

"Alex?"

"My—" Aramael bit back the word *soulmate* and said instead, "The Naphil woman."

The emerald gaze fastened on him with an intensity that seemed to see through to his very soul. Worse, to the weakness that had made him hesitate. Made him unable to push past Alex into the hotel room to take Seth when he might have done so.

"Fucking Hell," said Mika'el, drawing himself tall and

flexing his wings so that alley litter swirled in eddies around their feet. "You still have feelings for her. Why didn't you tell me?"

Aramael stared at a graffiti symbol spray-painted on the brick wall, listening to the wail of a siren drawing closer. "I didn't know until I saw her."

Until I looked into her eyes and remembered everything about her. About us. As if I had never forgotten any of it.

Mika'el waited a moment and then raised an eyebrow. "That's all you have to say about your failure?"

Aramael bristled. "I *failed*," he snapped, "because Seth wasn't where he was supposed to be and no one told me otherwise. Why the hell didn't you tell me Alex was involved in this? And why didn't you tell me about the Nephilim children being born?"

"The Nephilim are Heaven's concern," Mika'el said coldly. "Not yours. As for the woman, we didn't know she was involved. We never considered the possibility."

Wings rustling in irritation, the Archangel paced a few feet down the alley. Aramael waited, hands clenched and pride stinging from the unsubtle reminder that, regardless of the task he'd been set, Heaven wanted no connection to him. Heaven's warrior paced back again. The siren grew nearer.

"We need to find Seth. We don't know where he is," Mika'el said at last. "We think—hope—it means he's somewhere that has no Guardians. The woman may be able to help us."

"I doubt it. She knows why I'm here and has sworn to stop me."

"She knows? How the hell—" the Archangel waved away the question. "Never mind. Did you at least tell her why?"

"I did, but she thinks she can save him." Aramael repeated Alex's arguments to Mika'el but kept to himself the part about her caring for Seth. *Because it doesn't matter,* he told himself. Not because it would hurt too much to admit. Out in the street, the deep blare of a horn joined the siren.

A fire truck sped by the end of the alley, red from its dome lights splashing bright across the Archangel's face, dull across the black of his wings. The siren's clamor faded into the night. "What about the woman?" he asked. "Your feelings—"

"My feelings have been dealt with."

Mika'el stared at him, weighing, judging. Aramael wondered if the Archangel could see the emptiness in him that he felt. If he could see the raw remains of the connection severed when Aramael had ignored his soulmate's call.

"I hope you're right," Mika'el said finally. "In the meantime, it will be best if we split up to look for the Appointed. You go on your own, and I'll try to reason with the woman." About to leave, the Archangel swung around again, his green eyes brilliant with a hard, determined light. "No hesitation this time, Power. If you find him, do what you must."

"And if you find him first?"

"I'll get word to you."

"What about Lucifer? If he realizes—"

Mika'el paused at the mouth of the alley and looked back over his shoulder, mouth tight.

"Let's cross that particular bridge to Hell when we come to it, shall we?"

"I'M NOT INSANE," Alex said without preamble, as soon as the waitress departed. She wanted nothing more than to be out on the streets, looking for Seth before Aramael found him first, but Henderson was right. She needed help. And judging from the way he settled into the other side of the booth, he meant what he said about getting answers first.

Henderson reached for the sugar and a little tub of cream. "I'm listening."

Alex glanced around the coffee shop. Apart from the waitress and a couple by the door, too involved with one another to notice anyone else, she and Henderson were alone. Before she could think better of it, she launched into her story. She kept her voice expressionless, staring into her coffee as she spoke, and tried not to think about the impossibility of her words.

About whether or not Henderson would believe them.

Angels. Demonic serial killers. Heavenly treason. Forbidden soulmates. Murder. Broken agreements. Failed contingency plans. Nephilim children. Assassination orders.

The Apocalypse.

When she finished, silence settled over the booth, so absolute she could hear the swish of water in the dishwasher behind the counter, the ticking of the clock above it. Long seconds dragged by. Elbow braced on the table beside her now-cold coffee, Alex rested her forehead in her hand and waited for her colleague to say something. Anything.

At last Henderson cleared his throat. "I am so glad," he said fervently, "that Liz didn't stick around for this."

Alex choked back a laugh. It was hardly the response she'd expected, but she had to concur. She doubted she would have been able to say half of what she had in front of the disapproving Dr. Riley. Or that Riley would have believed any of it.

"Does that mean you believe me?"

"It means I don't necessarily think you're certifiable," Henderson allowed. "But Christ, Jarvis. Angels? Demons? The Second Coming? Those are some pretty out-there stories."

"And the pregnancies?" she retorted. "Those are normal?"

Henderson toyed with his spoon.

"You've seen it with your own eyes." Alex glared at him past her supporting hand, trying not to think about how desperately she needed someone besides herself to know what was going on in their world. Someone to believe her. "The news reports, Seth disappearing from his hospital room and the hotel. How else would you like to explain what's going on?"

"That's the point. I'd rather not explain it at all. I'd rather it all just went away."

Alex closed her eyes. "Welcome to my world," she muttered. "But like it or not, I think the Apocalypse is upon us unless we can stop it, my friend."

"Armageddon."

"What?" She peered past her fingers.

Henderson slouched over his coffee mug. "The war. It's called Armageddon, not the Apocalypse."

"What the hell's the difference?"

"The Apocalypse is the drawing back of the veil between us and Heaven. Armageddon is the final war that results. Not that it matters, because I think you're right."

She gaped at him. "You do?"

"The Church knows about the Nephilim."

"What church—wait, *the* Church? But how the hell—how did they—how did you—" Alex made herself stop. Gritting her teeth, she counted to three, about as high as she could remember the order of numbers at the moment, and then glared across the table. "Talk."

"An old friend called me today. There's a set of scrolls dating back six thousand years that describes pregnancies like the ones happening now—and the children that resulted. No one knows about them. The scrolls, I mean."

"Obviously someone does. Jesus, Henderson, what kind of friends do you have?"

"Impossibly loyal ones," her companion replied.

Alex decided to pursue the cryptic remark another time. "If they're such a secret, why did he tell you about them?"

"Information like this has a way of surfacing despite efforts to the contrary. He's concerned that if it gets out . . ." Henderson compressed his lips.

Following the unfinished sentence to its conclusion, Alex went still. Holy God. He was right. Chaos wouldn't even begin to describe what would happen if word got out about the scrolls—about the Nephilim, the angels, Lucifer.

If the world knew what she and Henderson knew, Armageddon wouldn't be about Heaven and Hell going to war, it would be about humanity imploding. Destroying itself in complete and utter panic.

Before she could fully absorb the realization, the sound of a cleared throat beside the table drew her attention. Glancing sideways, she saw a low-slung belt dividing blue jeans from a white shirt. In the same instant, she became aware of an energy radiating toward her. Her heart stumbled. *Another angel.* She knew the thought to be true even before she raised her gaze to the black wings spread wide behind the stranger who had joined them.

Even before she met brilliant green eyes in a deeply tanned, exquisitely carved, and ferociously scowling face.

THIRTY

Another angel.

Once again, Alex wanted nothing more than to turn tail and run. Might have done so, if the newcomer hadn't stood in the way of escape.

Prying her tongue from the roof of her mouth and forcing a calm she didn't feel past the stutter of her heart, she asked sourly, "Which one are you?"

The angel looked to her companion and then back to her. Ignoring her question, he demanded, "How much have you told him?"

"Everything I know."

A deep sadness flared in the angel's eyes and, just for an instant, Alex regretted the exposé of secrets he and his kind had guarded for so long. Then she gave herself a mental shake. *They* had caused the current situation, not humans, and she was damned if she'd feel guilty about doing everything she could to save her world from their screwups.

"Is there something you want?" she asked.

Resignation replaced sadness.

"Seth," he said. "I need your help finding him."

Alex scowled. "No."

"Uh, Jarvis?" Henderson leaned across the table. "Do you know him?"

"Only that he's one of them. Apart from that, no. But it doesn't matter"—she shot their visitor a cold look as Henderson slumped back in his seat, jaw slack—"because I'm not going to help him kill Seth."

The angel fixed her with a frosty stare of his own. Behind him, the amorous couple had left the coffee shop and the waitress stood at the far end of the counter, refilling sugar dispensers and shooting resentful glances between their group and the clock above the coffee machine.

"I don't think you appreciate the consequences of allowing him to live."

"I appreciate he's our only chance of preventing a war humanity cannot survive."

"Some of you *will* survive Armageddon," he disagreed. "If Seth lives and chooses the wrong path, however, I guarantee not a single mortal soul will survive Lucifer."

Alex ignored a wheeze from Henderson. "How the hell do you know he'd make the wrong choice? If you'd give him half a fucking chance—"

The angel cut her off with a dismissive gesture. "Aramael told me your arguments."

"But you don't care."

A painful kick connected with her ankle under the table even as a flash of anger lit the emerald eyes. Alex's mouth went dry. She had seen firsthand the kind of damage Caim and Aramael had wrought. What part of it not being wise to mouth off to superior beings was she having trouble with? She reached for her cup and took a swig of cold coffee, blaming the tremble in her hand on a shudder of disgust, avoiding Henderson's accusatory glare.

Setting down the cup again, she forced her gaze back up to the angel. "I'm sorry," she said. "That was uncalled for. I'm just—"

"Frustrated?" the angel supplied, and she blinked. Had that been a note of compassion in his voice?

"Angry." Terrified, too, but she was damned if she'd admit it. She linked cold fingers together. "Why do you need help finding Seth? Why can't you find him yourself?"

The angel's gaze sliced to Henderson and then back. "Everything?" he clarified. "Including what Aramael told you?"

"All of it."

Looking irritated but resigned, the angel motioned for Henderson to make room. The other detective slid as far away as the bench would allow. Folding his wings against his shoulders, the angel sat beside him. Henderson didn't appear to notice the brush of feathers against his side.

"Unfortunately, we lost our connection to Seth when his transition went wrong," the angel said. "We've been relying on the Guardians of those who come into contact with him to track his movements since then, but after you took him from the hospital, we didn't even have that. We should have been able to pick up on his trail again once he left your care, but no one has seen him. We're hoping that means he's gone to a place where humans have renounced their Guardians."

Henderson cleared his throat and joined the conversation. "Hoping?"

The angel slanted a look in his direction. "The alternative would be far worse."

Alex considered asking, then filed the idea under the too-much-information heading, shook her head to warn off Henderson, and followed the obvious thread. "What human would renounce a guardian angel?"

"One whose choices have led to him or her losing all hope. In this instance, many of them, probably living in a community. As a police officer, you would know where such a place might be."

Alex exchanged glances with Henderson, who nodded.

"It's a big city," he murmured. "I can think of a few places that might qualify."

She looked back to the angel. "I'm still not helping you."

"Not even when you are partly to blame for the mess?"

Alex's jaw dropped. "Excuse me?"

"Aramael told you your relationship could never happen."

"What does that have to do with anything?"

The angel's eyes had become chips of green ice. "He killed Caim for you."

Alex's face flamed. For a split second, she simply stared at the angel, too stunned to breathe, let alone speak. Then she found her tongue. "You're blaming *me* for Heaven's screwup? You son of a bitch."

"I told you, I need your help."

"And what, you thought you could guilt me into it? Go to hell."

"You don't know what's at stake—"

"I know I'm not helping you kill Seth Benjamin," she snarled and, ignoring Henderson's choke and another kick, she slid out of the seat, only to come up short against a broad, immovable chest. "Get out of my way."

Dark anger seethed in the green eyes, but before the angel could respond, Henderson scrambled out from behind the table and tugged her away.

"Are you fucking out of your mind?" he hissed. "If this guy is what you say he is—"

"Oh, he's what I say he is, all right. A goddamn—"

Henderson's free hand clamped over her mouth and, startled, Alex transferred her gaze to him. Steady eyes regarded her. "Done?" he asked.

Alex scowled at him and then slumped, nodding. Henderson removed his hand.

"Good. Now. Speaking honestly, what are the chances he's right about Seth being a danger to us?"

Alex eyed him belligerently. "You're taking things awfully well, you know." Far better than she had when she'd tumbled into her own alternate reality. Better than she was now, for that matter.

"Blame it on my Catholic upbringing," Henderson retorted. "Now answer my question."

She huffed. "I don't know. But without him, we're screwed."

"You really think we can sway him in our favor?"

"I think it's worth a shot."

Henderson held her gaze for another second before he nodded. "She'll do it," he said to the angel. "She'll help. So will I."

"I never said—"

"On one condition," the Vancouver detective added, his voice raised over hers.

Alex gaped at him. The angel raised an eyebrow.

"You give her twenty-four hours with Benjamin and then re-evaluate the situation before you make a decision."

The angel looked from Alex to Henderson and then back, annoyance giving way to defeat. "Done," he said, his gaze holding hers. "But you will honor my decision."

Alex opened her mouth to give her own opinion of the deal. She snapped it shut again when Henderson's fingers dug into her arm. No matter how much she hated it, he was right. She stared at the floor.

"Done," Henderson told the angel. "And I know where to start looking."

"And that, oh esteemed son, is the full story." Lucifer sat on the bus stop bench, his arms spread wide along its back and legs stretched before him. "Everything you always wanted to know about the human race and then some. Are you impressed?"

Seth stopped pacing to lean against a telephone pole. "Far from it," he said. "But that was your intention, wasn't it?"

Lucifer smiled. "You catch on fast."

Seth said nothing, mulling over all his self-proclaimed father had told him, weighing it against what he had already learned on his own in the short time he'd been here on Earth.

A realm, Lucifer would have him believe, far removed from his own.

A car pulled up to the curb a few dozen feet away and a woman detached herself from a wall to saunter over to the open window. No, not a woman—a girl. No more than a child, really, aged by makeup and the life she led. He could feel her suffering from here, the craving that wracked her wasted body. She got into the car and he watched it pull away again.

"She'll be dead before the year is out," Lucifer observed. "Another shining example of humanity's potential."

Seth shot him a narrow look. "You don't like them much," he said. "Why?"

"You need more reason than this?" Lucifer waved a hand at the street.

Following the gesture, Seth took in the nighttime vignette lit by streetlamps and neon signs, headlights and the splash of police car dome lights. Yawning black holes punctuated the garish brightness, alley mouths gaping between buildings, leading to places darker than the night itself. And everywhere, people. In cars, on foot; sitting or standing in doorways; sprawled on the sidewalk or street where they had fallen. People who were drunk, high, insane—or preying on those who were.

The very air reeked with their despair.

With their decay.

Again that feeling, as yet unnamed, washed over Seth. A shudder followed in its wake.

"Revulsion," Lucifer said, watching him.

"What?"

"That's what you're feeling. Revulsion. Disgust. Repugnance. Humans have many words for it, but they all mean the same thing." Lucifer gazed out over the street again, his expression distant. Cold. "They all mean this. The definition of humanity's reaction to their own failure."

"But not all humans are like this."

"Aren't they? Those who are tucked up in their homes with their tidy little lives, pretending all is right with a world that crumbles around them—are they really any different? You've seen the news. This isn't just here, it's everywhere. In every city, every country, every single corner of this pathetic world," Lucifer bit out the words. "It isn't new, either. I've lost count of how many times history has repeated itself. Civilization after civilization creates this putrefaction in its center. Creates it, ignores it, tries and fails to purge it through violence or a hundred other means, and is eventually swallowed by it. All because they are so damned arrogant, so certain they cannot fail."

Seth tried to fit Alex into the picture painted by Lucifer but couldn't. Down the street, a police car and an ambulance pulled up beside a man writhing and shrieking on the street, a victim of drug-induced demons. He remembered the newscasts, with workers digging out those buried in the rubble of an earthquake, doctors tending the people of a country devastated by illness.

"You're wrong," he said, watching the paramedics. "There are some who work to better their world, to help."

Lucifer gave a soft, humorless chuckle. "There have always been some like that," he agreed. "A handful of do-gooders trying to stem the flow of futility. Look how well they're doing. Wars have become greater, weapons more destructive, cities like this more rotten than at any other time in human history. The very planet is threatened by the actions of the masses. Do you really think a paltry few can make a difference?"

"Perhaps they can't," Seth said with what he considered perfect reasonableness, "but who are we to say they don't deserve the chance?"

Purple eyes riveted on his. Narrowed. Turned to ice. "Bloody fucking Heaven," Lucifer spat. "You've fallen in love with the woman."

THIRTY-ONE

S nagging the set of car keys sailing through the air toward
her, Alex scowled at Henderson as he strolled in the wake
of his missile. About bloody time he got back. She'd been
cooling her heels on the sidewalk for what, ten minutes?
She'd understood his need to make a few arrangements, but
this was ridiculous. Henderson forestalled complaint.

"We're good to go," he said. "I've put out Benjamin's
description with an order not to approach him under any
circumstances. If anyone spots him, they'll call me."

"And you'll call me."

"I'll call you," he agreed. He nodded toward the angel
pacing the sidewalk a short distance away. "You going to
be okay with him?"

"I'll be fine." She heard the edge in her voice and reined
in her irritation. The Vancouver detective was doing his
best, and a few more minutes wouldn't make a difference.

Unless it meant missing Seth by that length of time.

Henderson nodded. "All right. The keys are to my vehicle." He pointed to his blue sedan, parked up the block.
"There's a GPS in it, already set to get you to Cambie and

Hastings. Park west of Cambie and walk along Hastings from there—the place is like a rabbit warren with all its alleys, so it's best to go on foot. I'll pick up another unmarked car—I have a ride back to the office waiting for me—and then I'll head down to Main and walk up from there. This is for you."

He held out what looked like a jacket, bundled up.

Alex shook her head. "Thanks, but once I start moving, I'll be warm enough with what I have."

Henderson reached for her hand and stuffed the bundle into it; Alex's fingers closed over something hard within the folds. She raised an eyebrow.

"That's my spare. Don't you dare get out of the car without it."

It was on the tip of Alex's tongue to remind him of whose company she'd be traveling in, but instead she accepted the bundle—both because it was easier to do so and because it might, in the long run, prove wise to be carrying.

"You check in with me every half hour," Henderson reminded her of his earlier instructions. "And if anything looks remotely like it's going south, you get the hell out. Immediately. Understood?"

"Thirteen years on the job," she reminded him. "I've seen my share of shit, Henderson."

"Maybe. But you're not in uniform and you haven't seen Downtown Eastside at night." He poked a finger into her shoulder. "Every half hour or I send in the cavalry. Clear?"

Without waiting for an answer, he stomped down the sidewalk. Instantly, the angel was at Alex's side.

"*Now* can we go?"

Alex looked up at him. For the first time, she realized he was taller than Aramael, though not quite as broad-shouldered. Even lacking her former soulmate's breadth, however, he had an air of authority about him, a power in the way he moved and spoke, that left her with no illusions as to which of them ruled over the other.

And she'd called him a son of a bitch.

Damn, Jarvis. Way to choose those battles.

"The car is over here," she said, leading the way.

Ten minutes later she pulled over to the curb, a block away from the intersection that marked ground zero for Vancouver's skid row. Before she'd even switched off the engine, she understood what Henderson had tried to tell her. She'd heard of Downtown Eastside, of course, had even watched the documentaries put together by the Vancouver Police Department's self-named Odd Squad, the beat cops who walked the area every day.

But nothing could have prepared her for the reality.

Or for the shock of realizing that a naïve and uninitiated Seth would have no understanding of this as an example of humanity.

In grim silence, Alex reached into the backseat for the jacket Henderson had given her. Angelic sidekick aside, she had no intention of going unarmed into those streets. Unwrapping the gun, a thirty-eight—no holster and too big to carry in a pocket—she leaned forward to tuck it into the back of her waistband. It wasn't comfortable, but it was there if she needed it.

She looked at the angel seated beside her, his face still, his eyes missing nothing of the street before them. "Ready?"

They got out of the car and Alex pushed the lock button on the key fob as she joined him on the sidewalk.

"We have a lot of territory to cover," she said, tucking the keys into her jeans' pocket. "Are you able to sense him in any way?"

"If I could, I wouldn't need you."

Deciding arrogance must be an angelic trait, Alex swallowed her preferred retort with difficulty. She gave her companion a tight smile. "Then I suggest we set a search pattern and try to stick with it."

"Agreed." He pointed into the alley beside them. "We'll start there."

With a sigh, she followed him across the sidewalk and into a darkness so absolute it swallowed them whole. She paused to let her eyes adjust, then had to jog to catch up with the angel, who hadn't broken stride and seemed oblivious to both the dark and the detritus through which they moved.

Making herself match the angel's pace, she followed a few feet behind him, scanning doorways and makeshift living quarters tucked into the shelter of Dumpsters, catching glimpses of the people who lived in their shadows, broken and lost in ways she couldn't begin to fathom.

Not a single gaze lifted to hers.

Alex stuffed her hands into her pockets, then took them out again and flexed them at her sides. If she needed to reach for her weapon, she didn't want to get hung up on the way to it. Henderson had been right. She'd worked cases in the worst neighborhoods Toronto had to offer, but this—this outdid them all. She picked up the pace and caught up to the angel. If Seth were down here somewhere, seeing this, and anything happened to push him into making the choice of which Aramael and her surly companion warned . . .

Suffice it to say she needed to get him the hell out.

"Are you all right?"

She glanced at the angel in surprise, hearing that note of compassion again. "Fine. Just a little taken aback by all this."

"And worried about Seth seeing it."

"Yes."

At the end of the alley they headed left down the street toward another hole in the light, past teenage girls selling themselves to feed needs they couldn't escape, past men and women of every age sprawled on the sidewalk in drug-induced stupors. Alex's nails dug into her palms.

The next alley was wider, lit well enough to see the used hypodermics and condoms littering the broken, filthy pavement—and the deathly pallor of a man propped in a doorway. The angel stopped beside him for a moment, staring down, then turned away.

Alex hesitated. "Wait. I think he may have OD'd."

"He did." The angel took her arm and steered her away.

She tugged free. Turned back. "Are you sure he's—"

"Yes."

Damn. Shoulders slumping, she reached for her cell phone. "I'll call in a report."

"There's no time. He will be found in the morning and we need to find Seth *now*."

Still she hesitated. Leaving anyone like this, homeless or otherwise, was just wrong.

"Naphil." The angel waited until she looked at him. He shook his head. "Nothing can be done here. Leave him. I'll have the Guardians see to it that a patrol comes through here at first light."

Again that compassion, so out of place in a being that exuded such a harsh authority. But he was right. Casting a final glance at the prone figure, Alex fell into step beside him. "May I ask you something?"

"You may, but it doesn't guarantee an answer."

"Why do you call me Naphil like that?"

"Like what?"

"Like the word leaves a bad taste in your mouth."

"I didn't realize I did so. I'm sorry I offended you."

"That's not an answer."

They passed a woman sitting on a concrete step, her arm tied off and blood trickling from where a needle still pierced a vein. She didn't look up. Alex's gaze lingered on her. She'd never seen so much misery in one place. How, in today's world, could human beings be allowed to fall through the cracks of society like this? How the hell did the beat cops deal with it day in and day out, knowing that, in most cases, their help would be too little and far too late?

And we call ourselves civilized.

"How much do you know of your kind?" the angel responded to her question.

She shot him a hard look. They neared the end of the alley now, and his features were clear in the increased light. Calm, expressionless, devoid of the distaste she'd read into his words.

"I'm not a *kind* of anything. I'm as human as anyone else on the planet, and I'd never even heard of the Nephilim before—" Her voice hitched a little as she caught back words all too bound up in memories. *Before I met Aramael. Before Caim held me and made me call for my soulmate from a place of pain I hadn't even known existed.* "Before all this," she finished.

"At this point I suppose you may be right, although your line will always carry the taint of their blood."

"Thanks so much."

He shrugged. "It's a simple fact, Naph—"

"Alex," she said. "Just call me Alex."

"Defender of man," he murmured.

"What?"

"That's what Alexandra means. Oddly appropriate, don't you think?"

Alex had no idea how to respond. The street opened before them, a dozen feet away.

"I am Mika'el," the angel continued. "Michael, if you prefer."

Alex's foot caught on a chunk of broken pavement. A strong hand closed around her arm, preventing her from sprawling headfirst in the filth.

She stared at his hand. Swallowed. Looked up—way up—to the angel. "Michael as in—the Archangel Michael?"

He nodded.

Seriously? Alex pushed back a strand of hair. Her knowledge of angel lore was limited at best, and she wasn't even sure how much of the lore was accurate to begin with, but wasn't Michael supposed to be—

"The most powerful warrior in Heaven, yes."

Alex took a step back and nearly fell over the same chunk of pavement. She righted herself and knocked away his helping hand. "Please tell me you can't read my mind," she growled.

"Only your face," he said. "Based on my knowledge of humanity's legends about me, your look of panic made your thoughts transparent enough."

An explanation somehow lacking in the reassurance she'd wanted. Turning, Alex led the way onto the sidewalk and toward the next alley.

"So which do you prefer, Mika'el or Michael?" she asked the Archangel she'd called a son of a bitch only a short while before.

He considered the question as if surprised she'd asked. "Michael," he said at last. "I prefer Michael."

"And are you?"

"Am I what?"

"Heaven's most powerful warrior."

She didn't know what was more telling, his prolonged silence or the harsh "yes" that followed, but his antipathy toward the label could not have been more obvious. Nor could the unspoken warning not to question further have been more clear.

They traversed the next alley without speaking. It occurred to her that Michael hadn't answered her question about his distaste for the Nephilim, but in the face of her increasing edginess, it didn't seem important enough to pursue. Where the hell was Seth? What if he wasn't even down here, and they wasted their time? Twice she pulled her cell phone from the clip at her waist and flipped it open to be sure she had service and hadn't missed a call from Henderson. Nothing.

Then, halfway down the block to yet another alley, the phone rang. Alex had it open and against her ear before its second trill. "You found him?"

"No sign yet, sorry," came Henderson's voice. "I'm just checking on you."

"Oh, hell. I forgot to call you."

Henderson waited, then said dryly, "Apology accepted. Where are you right now?"

Alex squinted, searching for a street sign. "Hastings. A little west of Abbott. You?"

"Heading your way from Main. You still have our friend with you?"

"Of course."

"Good. Then I'll talk to you again in a half hour. When *you* call *me*."

The call went dead and Alex met her companion's questioning look. "Henderson," she said. "Checking in."

Michael nodded.

The cell phone rang again.

"Now I have him," said Henderson.

THIRTY-TWO

"What do you mean she's not human?" Elizabeth Riley asked, staring at Melanie Chiu's baby. The three-day-old girl sat in a playpen, unsupported, and waved a rattle at her gleefully, two pearly white nubs visible on her bottom gum. Uneasiness trickled down Elizabeth's spine, but she stubbornly thrust it away. "What the hell is she, if not human?"

Dr. Gilbert, the on-call pediatrician, thumbed through several pages of a chart as if searching for an answer. Then she flipped the chart closed and handed it to Elizabeth with a sigh.

"See for yourself," she offered. "She's half human, but we've never seen anything like the other half of the DNA. The lab is going crazy trying to identify it. A lot of labs are."

Elizabeth shot her a sharp look. "A lot of labs?"

"Around the globe." Gilbert toyed with the ponytail draped over one shoulder. "All the babies born from the accelerated pregnancies are testing with the same type of DNA and we haven't been able to find anything that remotely matches it. We thought at first it was just a mutation, perhaps caused by something viral, but it's more than that. It's completely foreign. Some governments are isolating the babies for study, which means our information pool could dry up in a hurry. I'm already getting the brush-off from certain quarters."

"You can't be serious. That sounds like something out of a science fiction movie."

"A bad one," Gilbert agreed. "Especially when you add in the rumors of aliens. UFO sightings have quadrupled in the last week."

"Wonderful," Elizabeth muttered. "If we keep this up, we *will* have mass hysteria on our hands." She gave Chiu's baby a final once-over and then turned away. "Let me know if they figure out what's going on, will you?"

Out in the corridor, she took her cell phone from her pocket and dialed Hugh's number, waiting while the call went straight to voice mail. The tone sounded and she spoke, her message terse. "Half the Chiu baby's DNA has never been seen before. I'm still not buying your theory, but—oh, hell, just call me when you get this, will you?"

She hung up, closed her eyes, and leaned against the wall letting the sounds of the maternity ward wash over her. Newborn wails, a woman's laugh, the squeak of rubber shoes down the linoleum hallway. Then, gathering her resolve, she marched toward the elevator and her office. While Gilbert might be getting the brush-off, Elizabeth had a good twenty years on the pediatrician and wasn't above using her seniority to get what she wanted. And what she wanted right now was answers. She didn't care if she had to call in every favor ever owed to her, she was getting to the bottom of this.

VERCHIEL PAUSED AT the greenhouse door, braced herself, and then pushed inside. The One looked up from trimming a bonsai tree, her expression of welcome fading as Verchiel approached.

"More good news, I see."

"Apologies, One, but I thought you should know this."

The One's hands stilled in their task for a second, and then she continued pruning.

"Seth?" she asked quietly.

"No. He's still missing. It's the Nephilim children. The mortals have identified them as not fully human and have begun studying them."

"At their level of science, that is to be expected."

"Some governments have involved themselves in the studies."

Snip. Snip. Snip.

"Are any of the children old enough to have shown their abilities yet?"

"Not yet."

"But it is only a matter of time." The One stepped back to study her handiwork, her head tipped to one side. "Only a matter of time before they realize what the Nephilim are capable of and begin to think of them as potential weapons. Before they try to turn those weapons against one another."

"That's what we're afraid of."

The silver head nodded. "Thank you, Verchiel. You were right to come to me."

Verchiel hesitated for a moment and then, realizing she had been dismissed, inclined her head and departed. A few steps away from the greenhouse, the sound of shattering glass made her duck to one side as the One's pruning shears sailed past to land in the shrubbery. Verchiel stared after them for a long time before she transferred her gaze to the gaping hole in the greenhouse's formerly pristine side.

Witnessed the hunched shoulders of the figure within.

And felt the edges of Heaven itself unravel a little bit more.

HENDERSON HAD HIM. *They* had him.

Alex's heart leapt into her throat. "Has he seen you?" she demanded.

"No. He's talking with someone. Male, tall, blond. Looks like they're arguing."

"Where are you? Is it faster for us on foot or should we go back to the—" Alex jumped as the phone was plucked from her fingers. She opened her mouth to object, but Michael held up an imperious hand and she subsided, listening to his instructions in confusion.

"Make sure you're standing somewhere they can't see you," he told Henderson. "Then look around at where you are and notice the details. All of them. The buildings, names, cracks on the sidewalk, everything you can. Hold the images in your mind and stay focused—good. I have it. We'll be there in a second."

Michael snapped the phone shut and handed it to her. "This may be unpleasant," he said, "but it's the fastest way."

"What . . . ?" Alex's words died on her lips as Michael's wings unfolded behind his back. Pitch-black, with almost twice the span of Aramael's, they were at once breathtaking and humbling, magnificent and terrifying.

And they were moving forward as if to ensnare her.

Alex stumbled back, but Michael caught hold of the hand she put up in defense, using it to pull her toward him. She landed against his chest with a force that knocked the wind from her lungs. Before she could catch her breath to protest, his arms wrapped around her, holding her tight against him.

His wings followed, closing over her head and enveloping her in a cocoon of feathers. Then Michael's body turned molten, becoming a liquid heat that poured through her, changed her, became her . . . And the entire world fell away in a rush of vibration. An absence of anything she had ever known. Ever been.

Alex had barely registered her lack of self when she stumbled at the sudden feel of pavement beneath her again. She felt herself thrust upright, the protection of angelic wings torn from her, their loss brutal. Ice crystallized in her veins.

Henderson stared at her as if she were an apparition, reaching to steady her when she stumbled against him. "Christ, Jarvis," he muttered, his pallor assuring her he had seen everything. Including Michael's wings. "What the hell was that?"

Alex opened her mouth to respond, but her voice seemed not to have followed her to where she stood now. Pressing her lips together, she shook her head.

"Where?" Michael demanded of Henderson.

"The other side of the street, about a half block down. By the bench."

Michael looked in the direction indicated and inhaled sharply. He went still for a moment, then drew tall, seeming to increase in size. A scowl darkened his face.

"Lucifer," he spat. His powerful wings unfurling behind him again, he shot Alex a steely look. "Stay here."

Alex shook off Henderson's hands and the residual disorientation. *Lucifer?* That couldn't be good. Through sheer force of will, she made her throat muscles respond again, albeit in more of a croak than actual speech. "I'm coming with you."

A ferocious glare stopped her in her tracks. "I said stay."

A shiver went through her. Not fear, exactly, but something very like it that made her want to give in to the command. She shoved the urge aside. Seth was out there and, judging by the look on Michael's face, he would die unless she went to him.

He might die anyway, but she couldn't think about that.

She caught hold of the Archangel's sleeve. "That wasn't our deal, Michael."

"Michael?" Henderson half choked behind her.

Alex ignored the other detective. Couldn't have answered if she'd tried as Michael's gaze lifted from her hand on his sleeve.

"Circumstances have changed, Naphil."

Holding tight to her determination, Alex lifted her chin.

"We had an agreement. I get twenty-four hours before you make a decision."

Hard fingers grasped her wrist and Michael jerked her into the shelter of the building at the edge of the lot. Taking her chin in his hand, he twisted until she looked down the street.

"Do you see him?" he snarled. "Do you see your precious Appointed? And the one standing with him?"

Alex found Seth first, his familiar figure standing tall and straight, his hands tucked into the pockets of the jeans she'd bought for him just yesterday. Then her gaze went to the man with him, taller even than Seth, blond hair shining under the streetlight above, making him seem almost luminescent.

She tried to nod, couldn't against Michael's grip. Whispered instead, "I see."

"*That*," Michael said, "is Lucifer. The one being we could not allow to gain access to the Appointed. His presence changes everything, Naphil, and it makes any agreement between us null and void. Do you understand?"

Alex stared at the luminous man down the block and her heart shriveled in her chest. Lucifer. Seth's father and would-be destroyer of all humankind. She could only imagine what poison he had fed Seth, how he had tainted their one chance at preventing the coming war.

Taking her silence as compliance, Michael released her. "Good," he said. "Now stay."

Wings half-open, he stepped out of the lot and stalked toward the duo beside the bench. Alex's gaze shifted to Seth.

Seth, whose identity and destiny had been stolen from him by a traitor. Seth, who had saved her life and shown her such gentleness, such compassion. Who stood now, arms crossed and body half-turned from the father he should never have known, oblivious to the approach of one sent by his own mother to—

Alex stiffened. Stared.

Seth, who displayed the body language of one who

rejected both what he heard and the person from whom he heard it.

"The *Archangel* Michael?" Henderson croaked behind her.

Alex didn't answer.

She was too busy chasing the Archangel in question.

THIRTY-THREE

Lucifer heard the rustle of feathers in the same instant he felt the Heavenly presence—both too late. He knew it even before he whirled and found the Archangel, black wings spread wide, not two dozen strides away. More than close enough to have already seen him.

Shock tightened his throat. Swift fury, self-directed, followed. How could he have been so careless? He'd known they would be watching over the Appointed, damaged as Seth was—damn it to Heaven, he'd been the one to warn Samael of the risks. Had told his aide to keep away from Seth, not to do anything to jeopardize their plans . . . and now he himself had ruined everything. Bloody Heaven, how stupid could he be?

Forfeiture.

After all this time, all this effort, the mortals were going to survive. Even if he refused to withdraw from their realm as promised, they would survive. Because no matter how many his followers managed to take out before Heaven stopped them, they would never eliminate them all. There were just too many.

Sickness filled him. Not even the Nephilim could help. The angels would know of the infants by now and, with the agreement broken, would do everything in their power to keep the Fallen away. The army he had created would remain untrained. Impotent.

Useless.

"Who is that?" Seth asked at his shoulder.

Lucifer grimaced. "A messenger," he said. "For me. Wait here."

He walked to meet the Archangel, a small start of surprise kicking through his veins as he moved close enough to recognize him. Mika'el? Since when had he returned to the One's side?

"You have broken your agreement with the Creator," the Archangel announced when Lucifer reached him.

Lucifer let his gaze travel over Heaven's warrior with a deliberateness that made Mika'el stiffen and gave Lucifer time to hide his own bitter turmoil.

"Well, well. If it isn't the prodigal son."

Mika'el scowled. "You will hand the Appointed over to me."

"Seth is free to go wherever he likes," Lucifer said with a shrug. "I have no hold over him."

"You have tainted him."

"I educated him."

The Archangel's scowl deepened. "Interference contravenes the terms of—"

A small whirlwind of human flesh burst past the black wings and planted its feet wide on the pavement between them, back to Lucifer, facing Mika'el. Lucifer stared at the creature, tasting its presence and then raising an eyebrow. Nephilim blood. Faint, but still in its veins.

"You gave your word," it snarled at the Archangel.

Lucifer's other eyebrow shot up. Not just any Naphil, but one with an apparent death wish. He waited to see how the Archangel would respond.

Mika'el glared at the Naphil, fury blazing from his eyes. "I told you to wait."

"And I told you I'd help you find Seth only if you didn't harm him," the creature snapped back. "You gave me twenty-four hours. You *agreed*."

Lucifer's brows snapped together. Harm Seth? He reached out to shove the creature aside, but Seth beat him to it, stepping into the fray and taking the creature's arm.

"Alex? What are you doing here?"

Seth looked down at the creature with concern, his grip on it gentle as he drew it aside, and understanding dawned in Lucifer. So this was the mortal Seth had fallen in love with, the woman who stood in the way of him reaching his son. But what had she meant about harming Seth?

He stared over the woman's head, meeting the Archangel's guarded gaze. His watchfulness. Lucifer's breath stilled.

She wouldn't.

Mika'el's expression hardened.

She couldn't.

The Archangel glanced at the woman, fury flashing through his eyes. Fury and—despair? Betrayal slammed like the fist of Heaven itself into Lucifer's gut.

She had. After all her talk, all her holier-than-thou lecturing, the One had gone back on her word. Had breached their contract. Had forfeited the human race to him. Her mortal children, his to destroy at last. All of them, without Heavenly intervention.

Euphoria surged . . . and came up short against Mika'el's flat, uncompromising gaze. Lucifer hesitated. That was not the look of defeat he'd expected.

"We need to talk," Mika'el said. "Privately."

Drawing his wings against his back, the Archangel stalked down the street. With a last glance at Seth— accompanied by a shudder of disgust at his son's continued physical contact with the woman—Lucifer followed.

"Harm him?" he growled, the moment they were out of earshot. "The One sends you to kill the Appointed and you dare accuse *me* of interfering?"

"She didn't send me to kill him. The decision was mine."

"Semantics, Archangel, and you know it. You could not

do this without her knowledge and therefore her implicit consent. Whether you planned to kill him yourself or have the Power do it, you have still broken the agreement. According to the One's own terms, I demand forfeiture."

The Archangel said nothing. He stared back at Lucifer with a fierce, ugly hatred, his entire body as rigid as stone. Lucifer eyed him. Mika'el was strong. Stronger than the others. They had tangled before, and if it hadn't been for the One's interference, Lucifer may not have faced a simple exile to Hell.

But the One's warrior didn't move except to shake his head. "I'm afraid not, Light-Bearer. Whatever may or may not have been intended, the Appointed remains alive and well and neither the Power nor I have so much as spoken to him. On the other hand, I have witnessed *your* interference with my own eyes. The only one who has forfeited, therefore, is you."

"Except you have no idea what passed between us and therefore you have no proof." Lucifer gave Mika'el a tight smile, watching him struggle with the truth of his words. In the back of his mind, an idea began to form.

"Then we are at war."

The satisfaction in the way Mika'el spoke the words sent a frisson of uneasiness down Lucifer's spine. For six thousand years, the One had done everything in her power to maintain peace, and now her Archangel gave every impression of spoiling for a fight. Why? What had changed? What could have made war the most appealing alternative all of a sudden? He narrowed his eyes.

Without warning, his thoughts snaked back five thousand years, to the signing of the agreement. The only meeting with his Creator that he'd had since he had left her side, rife with the unspoken. Rife with secrets. He remembered what he had suspected, even then . . .

"You're trying to protect her."

If he hadn't been watching so intently, he would have missed Mika'el's flinch. But he was watching, and he saw, and then he knew.

Everything in him went cold. His blood, his heart, his soul, the tiny sphere that held his immortality. He'd gone around and around the idea a thousand times after signing the agreement, had very nearly driven himself mad wondering at its truth before finally dismissing it. It had been too unthinkable, too impossible.

And apparently real.

With a clinical distance, Lucifer's mind flipped through the facts. The One, the all-powerful Creator, could not stop him without sacrificing herself. Mika'el would do anything to stop that from happening, even if it meant leading Heaven's angels against their kin in another war. Because the Archangel could not destroy Lucifer himself, however, he would ultimately fail.

Which left only the question of when.

Not yet. Not until I'm done.

The idea that had begun forming gelled into completion.

"There's just one problem," he said slowly. "The agreement still stands."

Mika'el snorted. "And how do you figure that? You've just spent the last two hours or more corrupting the Appointed's thinking in every way you can."

"And you intended him harm. We both erred, Mika'el, and such errors can only have the effect of canceling out one another."

"You're insane if you think I'll agree—"

"You have no choice," Lucifer snapped. "Don't you get it, Archangel? I know what she has to do to stop me, and if you push me into war before I'm ready, I'll see to it she has no choice. You'll lose her."

The lines about his mouth white with tension, Mika'el stared at him. "You're serious."

"I've never been more so."

"And what of the Nephilim army you build? I'm supposed to simply ignore that?"

"Again, you have no choice. Like it or not, the agreement stands. Strike a blow against me or any of my followers, and you will be in contravention, at which point I will demand forfeiture." Allowing a moment for his words to fully hit home, Lucifer stretched out his wings, ruffled the feathers into place, and folded them closed again. He smiled. "Now, shall we discuss terms?"

THIRTY-FOUR

"Let me get this straight." Alex ended her pacing with a swivel toward the little group waiting for her: Seth, Henderson, Michael. "He wants to leave the agreement in place. Knowing you planned to—"

She broke off, shooting a quick look at Seth. He didn't know about the assassination order yet and, in her opinion, never needed to. Despite the fact she had all but announced the fact in front of both him and Lucifer just a few minutes before. Tightening her jaw, she looked at Michael and amended, "Knowing what you planned to do. And you're okay with the idea."

"I didn't have an alternative." Arms folded across his chest, Michael glared at her, his accusation clear. "But please, if you have any better ideas on how to run the universe, I'm all ears."

Alex bit back an invitation for him to go screw himself—not, she hazarded, the kind of thing one said to an Archangel, especially when he was right about this predicament being her fault. If anything, she owed him an apology for announcing his intentions to Lucifer. But how the hell did one even begin to apologize for a mess of this magnitude? Far better to try to fix it. She raked her hair back from her face. "After all I've heard about Lucifer, it just doesn't sound like the kind of thing he'd do, which makes me wonder what he's really up to."

A flicker in Michael's gaze suggested he knew something he wasn't sharing, and his sideways glance at Seth said this wasn't the time to ask. Curbing her impatience, Alex switched tacks. "How do we know he won't go after Seth the minute you turn your back?"

"We don't."

"But you're still not staying."

"He wouldn't agree to that. He did, however, agree to Aramael."

A little of the air in Alex's lungs left in an audible hiss. She swallowed. "Aramael? But he has no powers. How—?"

"In the interests of *peace*"—Michael bit out the word—"the Light-Bearer has also condescended to allow the return of some of Aramael's powers to him. The Power will be permitted to watch the Appointed to ensure none of the Fallen Ones approach or try to interfere until he is ready to make his choice."

Alex fell silent, digesting the idea. Sifting through its implications. Aramael, staying with them. Remaining close. Watching over her once more. She brought her wayward thoughts up short. No. Watching over Seth, not her. This had nothing to do with her.

Seth cleared his throat. "We could avoid all of this," he said. "I'm happy to make my choice now in favor of humankind."

Alex's heart gave a leap. Why hadn't she thought of that?

But Michael shook his head. "I wish it were that simple, Appointed. Unfortunately, you are not ready."

"I don't understand. I know what I want."

"The choice isn't something you make with your mind, or even your heart," Michael said, "but with your essence. Your soul. It will happen instinctively, unconsciously—and without your control."

"How long will that take?" Alex asked.

"We cannot say. It could be hours." Michael looked at her. "Or it could be weeks or months."

Weeks or months of living in a state of limbo? Of not knowing if humanity would continue or be crushed by Lucifer's army?

Seth's hand settled on her shoulder. "Are you all right? Your skin has changed color."

Squeezing Seth's hand, Alex forced a smile. "I'm fine. It's just a lot for us mere mortals to take in, that's all."

A glance at Henderson backed her up. He looked as pale as she felt, maybe more so. And he didn't even have to cope with the soulmate aspect. His gaze met hers.

"You'll need somewhere to stay. I have a spare room. Nothing fancy, but it's yours if you want it. He"—he nodded at Seth—"can have the couch."

Politeness dictated she decline. Weeks or months seemed far too much to ask. Reality, however, gave her pause. After the busted-down-door incident, she doubted the hotel would welcome her back. Even if they did, she couldn't afford to remain there—or in any hotel—indefinitely. Henderson's offer would at least give them somewhere to stay long enough to figure out their next step, maybe even to arrange taking Seth back to Toronto with her.

"You're sure?" she asked.

Henderson met her gaze, his hazel eyes steady. "I have never been more sure of anything in my life," he replied. "Or less so. Come on, I'll take you and Seth back to your car."

He started down the sidewalk, Seth by his side, but when Alex made to follow, Michael held her back. "There's one last thing I need to speak to you about."

"If it's Aramael, you can stop worrying. Whatever I might feel for him, I've no intention of following through on it. Something about the end of the world being nigh has dampened my enthusiasm."

Michael fell silent for a moment. Then, his voice quiet, he said, "The soulmate system isn't perfect, Naphil."

Her gaze flew up to meet his again, but now it was his turn to look away, into the distance. She frowned.

"What's that supposed to mean?"

"Sometimes the soulmate you're destined to have isn't the best match for you. Sometimes . . ." He paused. "Sometimes lives are too separate. Too much has happened on each of your individual paths, too many responsibilities get in the way, too many choices are made by one that the other cannot agree with."

Alex looked down the street to where Seth and Henderson had stopped to wait for them beneath a streetlight. She met Seth's dark gaze, watched his brow furrow. Could he hear what Michael was saying?

"He hears nothing. I've made sure our conversation is private," Michael said, and again she wondered if he could read her thoughts. "You're the only one who should decide who to be with," he continued. "The only one who *can* decide."

She swallowed. "What are you saying?"

He expelled a long gust of air. "I'm saying Seth needs you, Naphil. More than Aramael ever can or will."

She gaped at the Archangel. "But he's—I'm—It's—"

"Forbidden? Normally, yes. But these aren't normal times. Right or wrong, the Appointed loves you, and if you can see fit to return his love, it may well save your race."

Alex scowled. "Forgive my skepticism, but who the hell do you think you're kidding? A few hours ago you told me my involvement with an angel *caused* this whole mess. Now you want me to believe getting involved with another will clear it up again? Make up your mind, Michael. You can't have it both ways."

A dark flush stained the Archangel's cheeks. He looked away. "I may have been wrong to blame you, but—"

"*May* have?" she interrupted.

"*But*," he continued, his eyes glittering, "it changes nothing. I need you to do this."

"Why should I trust you? If you'll sink to the level of blaming me for causing fucking Armageddon, how far will you go? No." She shook her head. "I won't let you turn whatever may or may not be between me and Seth—now or in the future—into another means to your end." Pushing past the Archangel, Alex started toward Seth and Henderson.

Hard fingers seized her arm, spinning her around. Michael glared down at her. "He gave up who he was for you," he snarled.

Shock rendered her speechless for a moment before she found voice enough to stammer, "He—what?"

"He tried to give up his responsibility, his powers, his destiny—everything—because he had fallen in love with you. The transition was altered at his request so he could be mortal. So he could be with you."

Alex stared toward Seth again, her mind numb. No. It wasn't true. Couldn't be true. The son of the One and Lucifer had abdicated his place in Heaven because of her? Such a thing wasn't even in the realm of possible.

Then why did he know me when I arrived at the hospital? Why was my name the first thing—the only thing—he spoke? Why did he follow me to Riley's office? Trust me so implicitly? Ask me if I was a magnet?

Oh, dear God.

Michael's grasp tightened. She glanced down at his fingers on her arm and then back up into the emerald eyes, softer now, with a hint of the compassion she'd seen in him before.

"How?" she asked. "Why me? First Aramael, now Seth. What is it about me that made this happen?"

"I'm not sure. Something in the Nephilim line from which you come that has survived time, perhaps. But whatever it is, you need to use it. You need to make it work for us."

"You mean I need to use it against Seth."

"For him," Michael corrected. "He wants this from you. He is weak, Naphil. He needs you to make him strong."

For a moment, Alex considered it. There was, after all, something already there. A pull between them, a magnetism.

How difficult would it be to actively pursue what lay beneath that attraction for the good of humanity? But even as the idea crossed her mind, she rejected it.

"No." She shook her head again, this time with purpose. "I disagree. He's stronger than you think he is and I won't use him like that, Michael. It would be wrong—and it could very well backfire on us if he found out."

"Naphil—" he began.

Alex cut him off, her voice hard. "I said no. I've already done enough damage in this whole fiasco. I'll be damned if I'll risk adding to it." She shook off the Archangel and started toward Seth again but spun back after only a few steps. "Oh, and by the way?"

Michael waited.

"My name is Alex, not Naphil. Get it right."

VERCHIEL JUMPED AS the office door crashed open and the Archangel Mika'el's presence—and seething fury—filled the room.

"He knows," Mika'el grated. "Lucifer knows."

Verchiel blinked. "I'm sorry. I don't know what you're talking about."

"That's because no one is *supposed* to know," the Archangel spat, coming into the room and slamming the door shut behind him with enough force to split the oak from top to bottom. Mika'el glared at the door, then at Verchiel. "No one," he reiterated with a growl. "And yet the Light-Bearer does."

The Archangel paced the carpet in front of Verchiel's desk, shoving a chair out of his way. She waited, telling herself it was to give him time but knowing it was because she dreaded what he would say. Two full crossings of the room. A fist driven into a wall. A snarl of frustration. Then Heaven's greatest warrior rounded on Verchiel and, in a few terse words, shattered her world.

"The One cannot stop Lucifer without sacrificing herself."

The room fragmented into shards of sound and light. Dust motes floating in a ray of sun. The rush of blood in her ears. Mika'el's bleak emerald gaze. The sound of his ragged breathing.

Whatever she expected, it hadn't been that.

"That cannot be," Verchiel murmured finally.

"It can't, but it is. When the One created Lucifer, she intended him to be a partner, a helpmeet. She made him very near her equal. Doing so required a significant portion of her own power to be transferred to him. So much that the only way to stop him is to bind their energies together."

"Meaning . . . ?"

"Meaning he would cease to exist on a physical level. And so would she."

Agony shafted through Verchiel's core. An agony so complete, it stole her very sense of self. A world without the One. A universe without its Creator. No word existed to describe how impossible the concept was. How unbearable.

"She would never do it," she whispered.

Mika'el stalked to the window and leaned his hands on the ledge. He stared out into the gardens, his face dark.

"Mika'el?"

"She already considers the possibility," he answered at last.

"Then you must stop her." *You*, not *we*, because they both knew that only Mika'el was strong enough to stand up to the One. Verchiel lifted her chin. But she could help. "What can I do?"

He met her gaze over his shoulder. "I find myself in an untenable position, Verchiel. You might want to reconsider before you ask to join me there."

"There is no consideration necessary, Mika'el. I love her as much as you do. Tell me."

The Archangel regarded her a moment longer before looking back out into the garden. "Lucifer insists the agreement remain in place."

"But he will continue to build—"

"The Nephilim army, I know."

"The One—"

"Doesn't know. She cannot."

Verchiel's inhale this time was involuntary, making her cough. "You're not going to tell her?"

"Now you understand why my position is so untenable." Mika'el turned at last from the window, leaning back against the ledge and crossing his arms.

"Is there *any* way out of this?"

Mika'el sighed raggedly. "I thought if we struck the first blow, we could weaken Lucifer enough to remove him as a threat, at least for several thousand years. It would have given us a chance—given *her* a chance—to come up with another solution. Unfortunately, we no longer have that option."

Verchiel stared at him. How had Heaven ever come to this? How could she not have seen what was happening? All those moments when she had witnessed something more than sadness in the One, something more than she understood, and she had never said anything. Never asked.

"About all we have working in our favor at the moment is Seth having fallen under the influence of the Naphil," Mika'el continued. "She may yet be able to persuade him to choose in our favor. That would at least buy us some time."

"To do what?"

He raised bleak eyes to her. "I don't know."

She nodded, an odd calm stealing over her. "If you're wrong, if Seth should choose against us . . ."

The Archangel's jaw went tight and his gaze slid from hers. "I won't let that happen. But I need your help, which means you need to make a decision."

"Tell me what you need."

"Send for Aramael." He dropped a parchment, taken from the folds of his shirt, onto the desk. "This will restore some of his powers. He is to watch over the Appointed."

She stared at the roll. At the seal of the Office of the Archangels holding it closed.

"It's not as refined as hers, but it will do what it needs to do," Mika'el said quietly.

"They—all of you—?" She looked up. Only working together, with all six in agreement, could the Archangels have raised the kind of power needed to restore another's abilities.

"They've decided, too. We're going to save her, Verchiel. We must."

She swallowed. "And when she realizes that Seth lives? What we've done? Acting on our own like this, Mika'el, it amounts to—" She broke off, unable to make herself say the word.

Mika'el's face took on the hard planes of stone. Standing tall, he crossed to the fractured door and pulled it open. "It's treason," he said heavily. "We know."

THIRTY-FIVE

Aramael eyed the stoic Archangels by the door. Talk
about déjà-vu. They may have requested he accompany
them this time, rather than ripping him out of the mortal
realm without warning, but his soul still cringed from the
memory.

He shoved his hands into his pockets, pacing from one
side of the office to the other. Stopping in front of a bookcase, he stared at the row of books at eye level and listened
to the clock mark the passage of time. Tried to focus on his
surroundings rather than think about why he'd been brought
here.

About what might be coming.

Or what had passed before in this same place.

Could they not have taken him somewhere else? Did it
have to be here, where everything that had defined him,
everything that *was* him had been so violently stripped
away? A shudder ran through him and the scars on his shoulder blades burned with the remembered fire of their loss.

Then, just as he couldn't endure it any longer, the door

opened behind the Archangels. Aramael braced himself and faced the newcomer.

Air gusted from his lungs.

"Verchiel?"

A hint of a smile curved the Dominion's lips. Aramael took in the scarlet robe that had replaced her usual purple. No. Not the Dominion. Not any longer.

Digging deep for a semblance of protocol, he inclined his head. "Highest," he murmured. "My congratulations. I had no idea."

"Under the circumstances, there was no way you could know." Verchiel looked to the Archangels. "My thanks, Raphael. Uriel. I won't need you anymore."

The Archangels nodded and withdrew, with the ebony-skinned Raphael casting a last look over his shoulder that assured Aramael he had neither forgotten nor forgiven how Aramael had called him bastard at their last meeting. An apology down the road might be in order . . . assuming Aramael was still around to issue one.

The door closed, leaving him alone with Verchiel, who crossed to the desk and laid down the cloth-wrapped bundle she carried, then came forward to take his face in her hands and stare into his eyes.

"Forgive me," she said. "I am so sorry for everything you have had to endure, Aramael, and all because I was too weak to stand up to Mittron. To think for myself, as you accused."

Aramael blinked, unsure if he was more taken aback by her touch or her words. He didn't know whether angels of the other choirs reached out to one another in this fashion, but they sure as hell didn't do so with Powers. Not that he carried that rank any longer.

As for the apology . . . Mouth twisting, he pulled away from Verchiel's touch. "Is that why I'm here?" he asked. "Because of your conscience?"

The Dominion—no, the Highest Seraph—winced, her blue eyes clouding over as she withdrew a few steps. Without answering, she walked around the desk and settled into the chair. "Now that Lucifer has found Seth—" She broke off at his start of surprise. "You didn't know?"

"Last I heard, Seth was missing and Mika'el blamed me. *They*"—he tipped his head toward the door through which the Archangels had disappeared—"weren't exactly forthcoming when they came to fetch me."

"Mika'el and the woman found Seth in the company of Lucifer."

Her name is Alex. Aramael bit back the automatic correction. It was time he went back to thinking of Alex that way himself—as the woman. The Naphil.

Instead of the soulmate he would never have.

"Then we are at war."

Verchiel shook her head. "More like an impasse. Lucifer knows about the plan to remove Seth."

"And he didn't demand forfeiture?"

"Given he was found in the Appointed's company, he couldn't."

"But if both sides have reneged on the agreement . . ."

"That's his reason for insisting it still stands."

Cold trickled down Aramael's spine. "The Nephilim."

"You know—?" Verchiel caught herself. "Yes, well, that's why we have no choice but to play along for the moment. We need time to decide what to do."

"But his time with the Appointed—we have no idea what Lucifer told him or how Seth will react. You take an enormous risk."

"A calculated one," Verchiel corrected. "Whatever Lucifer told Seth appears to have been adequately mitigated by the woman. At least for now. Lucifer has agreed to let her remain with Seth, to replace the mortal influence he would have had if things had gone the way they were supposed to."

The muscles in Aramael's throat tensed. "She has that much influence?" he asked, careful to keep his voice neutral.

Verchiel looked away, her forehead creased. "There's really no easy way to tell you."

"Tell me what?"

"Aramael, Seth caused his own flawed transition." Verchiel's gaze didn't quite meet his. "He tried to give up his place, his destiny, in order to become mortal. So he could be with the woman."

Aramael walked to the window and braced himself against the frame, one hand on each side, staring into the gardens below, the woods stretching beyond them. He'd suspected Seth's feelings for Alex when the Appointed had been brought in to help him protect her from Caim. Suspected, but had no idea of their intensity. Even if he had known, he'd been in no position to do anything about it.

Just as he wasn't now.

He aimed a narrow glare over his shoulder at Verchiel and growled, "You do know that whatever punishment was meted out to Mittron, it can never be enough to pay for what he set in motion."

To his surprise, the Highest blanched.

He frowned. "Something I said?"

"Mittron pays dearly for his sins," Verchiel said softly. "He will do so for eternity."

In a few clipped words, she told him of Mittron's Judgment, of how he had been exiled to the mortal realm and sentenced to feel the agony of every soul lost to the Fallen Ones for as long as Heaven and Hell battled for dominion. Aramael didn't hear anything past *mortal realm*.

Mittron wandered Earth? The same Earth to which he himself had been sent? The mortal world wasn't a small one, but given an eternity, it was possible—reasonable, even—that their paths might cross. A dark anticipation curled through Aramael. Perhaps he and the one responsible for his suffering weren't done yet after all.

"—know it will be difficult, but you're the only one Lucifer would agree to."

Verchiel's voice penetrated his thoughts and he made himself look over his shoulder at her. "Sorry, what was that?"

"I said—" Verchiel broke off and then, her voice becoming terse, gave him what he was pretty sure was the abbreviated version. "We need someone to watch the Appointed, Aramael. To make sure Lucifer and the others keep their distance. He agreed to have you do so."

"*Me?*" All thought of Mittron and possible revenge evaporated. "First you want me to kill him and now I'm supposed to protect him?"

"Not protect. Simply watch. The Light-Bearer deemed you most likely to keep your own distance from the Appointed and so not bring any Heavenly influence to bear on him."

Aramael absorbed this new revelation. If nothing else, Lucifer had an excellent understanding of the mechanics behind soulmates. The Light-Bearer was right. Knowing what Aramael did about the Appointed's feelings for Alex, he would just as soon slug Seth as speak to him. Which pretty much guaranteed he'd keep his distance.

He closed his eyes and rolled his head against the tension in his neck. Another Guardianship role. He sure as hell hoped this one turned out better than the last.

He glared at the new Highest Seraph. "So I'm to keep my distance and what, throw rocks if I see Lucifer or a Fallen One? I'm somewhat incapacitated, remember?"

"Lucifer has agreed to let us restore limited powers to you."

"*Lucifer* agreed?" Dropping his hands, Aramael rounded on Verchiel. "Are you kidding me? Since when does the Light-Bearer run Heaven?"

Verchiel bristled. "He does no such thing."

"Doesn't he? You've just told me it was his idea to let the agreement stand, and now you're letting him decide how much power you return to me. What the hell is that, if not letting him call the shots?"

Rising, Verchiel leaned toward him, resting her hands on the desktop alongside the wrapped bundle. "It is none of your business," she informed him coldly. "I have set you a task, Aramael. Do you accept it or not?"

Well, well. The Dominion—no, the Highest Seraph—had

grown a backbone. And she was hiding something. Aramael eyed her narrowly. "You're not telling me something."

Verchiel waved him silent and dropped into her chair again, one hand massaging her temple. "I'm telling you everything you need to know," she said, her voice reverting to its usual even tones. "Everything I can. We know this is a temporary solution at best. We know Lucifer plans to grow the Nephilim as long as the agreement remains in place. We *know*. But every moment of peace we can buy gives us another moment to figure out what we're going to do about it. Another moment in which humanity can continue breathing and the universe hasn't been ripped apart at its very seams."

Lowering her hand from her forehead, Verchiel reached for a scroll on the edge of her desk and held it out to him. "The ability to communicate with Heaven and your kin," she said, "and the ability to move freely in the mortal realm. Follow Seth, watch him. Call for help if you need it."

Aramael stared at the offered document with its unfamiliar seal. His mouth became a desert. After the last such paper he'd been handed, it took all the will he possessed not to step back.

"That's it?" he asked. "That's all *Lucifer* will allow me?"

"It's what Mika'el forced him to agree to. You'll have that"—Verchiel set down the roll and nudged it toward him—"and the safeguard Lucifer knows nothing about, the one chance you have to take Seth's life if you need to."

Aramael's mouth twisted. Wonderful. Limited powers and the ability to remain a murderer. Flexing his fingers, he walked forward to take the parchment. Its intent flooded him the moment he touched it, its power rushing in to fill the emptiness he had carried with him since the One's decree had left him bereft of all he had ever known. Ever been. Harsh and jagged—perhaps because it sought to restore something the One had never intended for him to have again—it settled into his soul.

And left him aching for that which remained missing.

He crushed the used paper in his fist, staring at it. Hating its limitations. Then, dropping it onto the desk, he lifted his gaze to Verchiel's once more.

"Thank Heaven for small miracles," he said, and didn't even try to hide his bitterness."If we're done here, I believe I have a job to do."

Verchiel's voice stopped him near the door. "There's one more thing."

More? What more could there be? Turning back to the new Highest Seraph, he went still, his gaze riveted to her desk. To what lay on her desk. An eternity passed in the space of a breath.

At last he looked up, into Verchiel's suspiciously shiny eyes. Without a word, he unbuttoned his shirt, slid it from his shoulders, and presented his back to her. Eyes closed and head bowed, he waited to be rejoined with the wings Mittron had ripped from him.

THIRTY-SIX

Seth stared down at the lights of the city twenty stories below, stretching as far as he could see in all directions. Behind him, the door slid open and Alex stepped from Detective Henderson's living room onto the concrete balcony. She joined him at the railing.

"Are you all right?" she asked.

"Apart from not remembering any of what I learned about myself today?" He rested his forearms on the rail and linked his fingers. "Or learning it in the first place? I'm just great. You?"

Alex either didn't notice or chose to ignore the heavy sarcasm in his words. "You must have questions."

"More than I can begin to ask."

"Why don't we start with what Lucifer told you?"

Seth snorted. "Would you like to begin with his fall from Heaven or how no mortal is worth the air he or she breathes?"

"You probably know more than I do about the former. As for the latter, I think you've already seen enough to know otherwise. There are good people in the world, Seth, and if

I can say that, doing what I do for a living, you know it's true."

Seth went silent for a moment. Glancing sideways at Alex, he asked, "What did he want to talk to you about?"

"Michael?"

He nodded.

Seconds ticked by. So many of them, he began to think she wouldn't answer. Then her hands curved over the rail beside his, close enough that her warmth radiated to him.

"He wanted to talk about us."

"You and me?"

"Yes."

Seth listened to the even cadence of her breathing. "Are you going to tell me what he said?"

"He said you have certain . . . feelings for me. He wanted to know if I returned those feelings."

"How does he know what I feel?"

"I think it's part of the whole Heavenly angel thing." Alex met his gaze with a little grimace. "It's actually quite annoying."

Seth's mouth curved and he looked away, back out over the city lights. Weighing his words, he wondered how much he might be able to ask this time, how far Alex might let him go before she closed herself off to him again. He wished he knew the social parameters in this situation.

He cleared a gruffness forming in his throat. "And do you? Return my feelings?"

Alex's fingers tightened on the railing and the tiny instant of levity that had existed between them disappeared. Her gaze became distant. "A month ago, a Fallen Angel named Caim started killing people in Toronto, where I live. He was looking to murder a Nephilim, hoping to ride the soul back to Heaven. Don't ask me how it was supposed to work, it's just what I was told. Anyway, I apparently have Nephilim blood in me and, because I was investigating the murders and likely to come in contact with Caim, Heaven got nervous and decided I should be protected. They sent an angel—

a Power—who was to guard me and at the same time hunt the Fallen One. Things didn't work out the way they were supposed to. The Power couldn't do both tasks at the same time, so they sent you to take over the protection part."

"Aramael was the Power?" Seth asked quietly.

"Yes."

"But he was more than that."

Alex's voice went hard. "Aramael turned out to be my soulmate. The connection between us interfered with his ability to hunt. When they sent you, he was finally able to go after the Fallen One, but Caim got to me and you couldn't protect me after all. Caim made me—" She swallowed. "Caim was Aramael's brother. He claimed Aramael had betrayed him and he wanted revenge. He wanted him to see me die. He made me call for Aramael, and Aramael ended up killing him—an unpardonable sin in the One's eyes. He was stripped of his powers and cast from Heaven."

You couldn't protect me.

Seth had gone cold at the words, shock threading through him. He had failed her? But if he was the son of Lucifer and the universe's creator, then how . . . ?

Alex's hand closed over his forearm, silencing his questions beneath a wave of sensation. Seth's heartbeat turned heavy.

"It wasn't your fault," she said. "There were other things going on, complications. There was nothing you could do to stop him. Besides, you came back. After Aramael was taken by the Archangels, you came back. You saved my life."

Small comfort, given what she must have endured at the Fallen One's hands. Seth stared at the slender fingers against his skin. What she perhaps still endured, if the despair he'd seen in her eyes was anything to go by. Lifting his free hand, he took her fingers in his and traced them with a thumb.

"Was that the sum of our connection?" he asked. "The fact I failed to prevent your pain but redeemed myself by saving your life?"

Alex inhaled sharply. Somewhere in the apartment

behind them, the soft chime of a clock marked a quarter
hour.

"No," she said at last. "There was more. An attraction."

"But you had a soulmate."

"Yes."

"And now?"

Alex stared down at their hands and then tugged her
fingers from his. "Now I don't," she said. "It changes
nothing."

HUGH FISHED A tie clip out of the valet tray on his dresser
top. Clipping it onto the end of the tie he'd slung around his
neck, he stared at his reflection. With the whole world having shifted beneath him the way it had last night, he found
it unsettling that nothing about him reflected the change.
He still woke at 6:45 a.m., still donned a suit and a clean
shirt, still wore one of the ties Laura had bought him the
Christmas before she'd—

His fingers tightened on the fabric. He thought again of
what he'd learned from Alex and Father Marcus the night
before. What he'd witnessed for himself. Armageddon. Was
such a thing even possible? Truly? If it were . . . His gaze
fell on the photo on the dresser, lingering on the face of the
smiling woman holding a baby. His son.

Armageddon.

"Son of a bitch," he murmured at his image. He looked
again at the photo. Maybe Father Marcus had been right.
Maybe things really did happen for the vague, unknow-
able reasons the priest had tried so hard to convince him
existed. Maybe Mitchell and Laura were better off dead,
because if they'd lived, how would he have protected them
from what he knew with gut-congealing certainty was about
to unfold in the world? For that matter, how the hell was
he supposed to protect anyone from what he'd seen last
night?

Angels. Archangels. Lucifer. Armageddon.

Bloody hell.

Reaching into the top drawer, Hugh withdrew the crucifix that had lived there since his church had abandoned his wife and son. He picked up his keys and cell phone from the night table. No new messages. Nothing more from Liz, even though he hadn't yet responded to her call about the Chiu baby's DNA, and nothing from Marcus. A good thing if it meant that the news of the scrolls was still under wraps; a bad one if it meant Marcus himself was.

He'd call later to find out which. For now, though—he gave his reflection a wry grimace. For now he couldn't keep avoiding Alex. Or the son of God.

"YOU LOOK LIKE you had a long night."

Alex looked up from her coffee as Henderson strolled into the kitchen and settled onto the other stool at the countertop bar. He wore a fresh suit for the first time since she'd met him and looked like he'd had far more success at the sleep thing than she had.

She smothered a yawn. "You've no idea."

"Saving the world getting to you?"

"For a start."

Henderson reached past her to remove a mug from a hook beneath the cupboard. "So what is this thing with Seth?" he asked, nodding toward the living room and the sound of the television.

Alex didn't pretend not to understand. "There's nothing with Seth."

Henderson poured coffee into the cup, added sugar, stirred, and raised calm eyes to hers. "Bullshit. You were like a cat on hot bricks when we got back to the apartment last night. Something is going on."

"Fine. Then whatever it is, it's none of your business."

From the corner of her eye, she saw his eyebrow ascend. He watched her in silence for a moment and then shrugged. "Have it your way."

He looped a chain around his neck and tucked something inside his shirt. Alex caught a glimpse of a wooden cross before it became hidden beneath the fabric. It was her turn to raise an eyebrow.

"None of your business." Henderson smiled tightly.

Alex tinked the spoon against the mug in response and favored him with a dour look. "If you're having second thoughts about letting us stay here, just say so."

The Vancouver detective opened his mouth to respond, hesitated, and snapped it shut again. His expression went from belligerent to weary. "That's not it," he said, sighing. "I'm happy to have you here. Really. I was just worried about the consequences of everything, of all of this—well, you know."

She did know. And she believed him. Alex let her shoulders relax and took a sip of her coffee. They sat in silence for a few moments, listening to the sounds of the television float in from the living room. A military documentary, by the sound of it. Great. Alex massaged at the ache between her eyebrows. More questions she couldn't answer. "So what are you up to today?" she asked at last.

Henderson shrugged. "Following up on two more rape-pregnancy cases that came in yesterday. Catching up on paperwork. I'm expecting a copy of your serial killer file later today."

Alex frowned. "A copy of the file? Why?"

"While you're playing babysitter, I need to start pulling together enough ammunition to convince the earthly powers-that-be of what's going on." Henderson looked across at her, his eyes sober. "The secret is going to come out, Alex. It's just a matter of time."

"About that—you're sure he was real, this friend of yours with the scrolls?"

He stared at her. "What kind of question is that? Of course I'm sure he's real. I've known him for more than twenty years."

Alex waved away her words. "Never mind. Sorry. The

last priest I had dealings with turned out to be a Fallen One in disguise. It didn't end well." Ignoring the curiosity sparking in Henderson's eyes, she sipped her coffee. "You trust him, this Father Marcus?"

"I've tried to pretend I don't for the last ten years, but yes, I trust him."

She left the first part of that comment alone. "How did he find out about the scrolls? Has he seen them himself?"

"He trained as a curator before he took his vows. In exchange for ten years of working in the Vatican, they gave him his choice of post."

"And he's sure these are authentic." Alex knew Henderson would have asked all these questions of the priest himself, but couldn't stop herself. The questions—and the investigative thinking behind them—were familiar. Calming.

"Positive."

She lapsed into silence for a moment. The sounds of battle in the living room raged on.

"Even if the news about the scrolls doesn't get out for a while," Henderson said at last, "these pregnancies have already caused a stir. It's only going to get worse. Every nutcase on the planet will be crawling out of the woodwork and if we're not ready for them, we won't need Lucifer's help. We'll just have our very own Armageddon. There's already some weird-ass stuff going on. Reports of certain governments confiscating the babies from their families and putting them into research facilities. You don't happen to know what they'll find, do you? What's special about these kids?"

Alex shook her head. "I never thought to ask. I'm willing to bet it won't be good, though. For the babies or for us. Damn it to hell," she muttered. "Trust humanity to react like this."

"Kinda makes you think the old boy has a point about us, doesn't it?"

"Where certain people are concerned in this world, he

does have a point." Alex stood and dumped her coffee into the sink. "You're right about getting our facts assembled, but we're treading very, very thin ice here. It would help if you could get Riley on board to attest to the possibility we're not completely nuts."

"I'm working on it, but she's tough. She wants hard evidence. As will everyone else." Henderson paused and his eyes narrowed. "You're holding out on me. What do you have that I need to know, Jarvis?"

Alex reached for a pad of paper and pen hanging beside the wall-mounted phone. She did have something he needed to know. Something that had occurred to her the second she'd figured out the Nephilim connection, back when she'd still been invested in a keeping-secrets agenda. She tore off one of the miniature sheets and jotted down a name and phone number, then held it out to Henderson. "That's the coroner in Toronto. He has some DNA evidence that should help."

Henderson took the paper, his gaze becoming sharp. "DNA?"

"It's all in the file, but this way will be faster. It might be what you need to convince Riley. When Caim was on his rampage in Toronto, he left behind a claw in one of the vics. The DNA was never identified. You need to have them compare it to Chiu's baby."

Henderson's expression flickered for an instant—probably at the word *claw*—or maybe because she hadn't handed this over sooner. But he said nothing, just nodded, folded the paper, and tucked it into his breast pocket. Then he tipped his head toward the living room.

"So what's your plan for the day?"

Alex crossed her arms and leaned a hip against the counter. "No idea. He's determined to learn everything he can. Maybe we'll hit a bookstore or library sometime today so he can do some reading but, beyond that, I'm clueless."

"Sounds like a good start." Henderson stood and pushed the stool back into place. "I have to run. I'll see you later."

"Henderson?"

He paused in the doorway.

Alex offered him a lopsided smile. "I suggest you practice the words before trying to get anyone to side with us. Being able to actually say *angel* will go a long way to explaining things."

THIRTY-SEVEN

From Power to this.

Aramael stood in the shadow of a massive tree trunk as Alex and Seth stopped to watch a group of children clambering over playground equipment. Could she really think to influence the Appointed with a morning walk along the shore, a few hours at a bookstore, and now another stroll through a park? Though Heaven knew this was better than having them return to that damnable apartment, where they had both spent the previous night in the same room together, as they had done at the hotel—

Aramael inhaled sharply, nostrils flaring. Damn it to Hell and back, *why* could he not stop thinking of her in that way? He knew—with every atom of his essence—that he would never have her. *Could* never have her. But as Seth reached to brush back a strand of her hair, the knowledge did nothing to stop the ache in his chest that became more pronounced with every wretched minute he was forced to watch them.

"Struggling, Power?" a deep voice inquired beside him.

Startled, Aramael whirled to face Mika'el. Great. He'd been so wrapped up in his own misery he hadn't even sensed the other angel's presence. Now he could add humiliation to his growing list of emotions he wasn't supposed to have. He glowered at the Archangel.

"What do you want?"

Mika'el crossed his arms and leaned against the tree. "A progress report would be nice."

"If I had anything to report," Aramael snarled, "I would have done so. *This*"—he jutted his chin toward Alex and Seth, now settled on a park bench, his arm extended behind her, her hair brushing his sleeve—"this is all I have. They walked, they talked, they read, he watched hour upon hour of television, and that's it." He swallowed, and the knife in his throat sliced all the way to his belly.

"No activity from Lucifer or the Fallen Ones?"

"None."

"That you've seen."

Aramael bristled at the not-so-subtle dig. "None," he repeated in a growl.

"You are keeping your distance."

The knife gave a savage twist. "Yes," he said, but he could hear the hoarseness in his voice. All night he had wrestled with the desire to go to Alex, if only to stand at her bedside and watch the even rise and fall of her chest in sleep, the peace of her features . . .

"Aramael."

"I've kept my distance, Black One," he snarled.

The slur made Mika'el's wings extend almost halfway before he caught himself and folded them against his back again. For a long moment, the Archangel stared past him without speaking. Then, voice cold, he said, "Just remember your part in this mess, Power, and see you continue to stay away. Your interference at this point could well be the tipping point from which we could not recover."

The Archangel departed in a soft swirl of dust, leaving Aramael to his vigil.

* * *

"YOU'RE RESTLESS."

Alex paused in her pacing of Henderson's living room floor and looked over at Seth. "I'm sorry. Am I disturbing you?"

Seth had paused the documentary he watched and now set the remote on the table. Rising from the sofa, he strolled across the room to join her, as comfortable in his current environment as though born to it instead of having learned it all in just a few short days. Reaching her, he leaned a shoulder against the sliding glass door to the balcony and slid his hands into his pockets.

"What's wrong?"

"Nothing." She grimaced. "I'm just not very good at not doing anything."

"I don't understand. We walked, we talked, we read. Are you bored with me?"

"No! No, it's just—" She hesitated, trying to frame her words to eliminate any misunderstanding. As at ease as Seth seemed to be with the world, he still lacked the nuances of language and tended to take things too literally.

"I miss my job. Miss being in control. Miss working to solve things."

"You wish you could solve me."

"I wish I could be of more help to you."

"So I could make my choice and we would be finished."

"That's not what I meant."

"What *will* happen then?" Seth's black eyes took on the intensity that always sent a sliver of unease through Alex. "To us. Do we just go our separate ways? Will you forget about me and expect me to do the same about you?"

Alex's breath snagged at the base of her throat. "I don't know what will happen in the long term," she said. "Heaven may have other plans for you. Other expectations. But whatever happens, I do know forgetting you would be impossible."

"But you still don't want a relationship with me."

"Want doesn't come into it."

"Then you do want me."

Dear God, he could make things difficult. Alex waited for the live-fish-in-her-gut feeling to subside and then tried again. "You have to see how different we are, Seth. I'm just a mortal and you're—"

The cell phone at her waist trilled.

"Leave it," Seth commanded, but she had already flipped it open, only too glad of the intrusion.

"Jarvis."

"You happen to catch the news today?" Henderson's tight voice asked.

"No, why? What did I miss?"

"The crazies are crawling out of the woodwork. Some guy stabbed a pregnant woman on the street in Houston, Texas. Mother of two, six months along with her third. Both she and the baby were DOA."

Alex threaded fingers into her hair and tightened her grip until pain twinged through the roots. "Christ."

"He claimed she was carrying Satan's spawn and he was carrying out the Lord's orders. He has a history of mental illness. Thinks the angels talk to him. Said the Archangel Raphael told him—"

"Stop." Alex sank onto the edge of the couch and rested an elbow on her knee, burying face in hand. Angels. Again with the fucking angels, just like her mother. She took a long, slow breath.

"You okay?" Henderson asked.

She closed her eyes. "Ever notice how often the voices that tell these people to kill come from angels?" she asked.

"Until you mentioned it, no. What's your point?"

"Between that and the number of wars fought in the name of God, doesn't it make you wonder what life would be like without all this religious bullshit?"

Henderson grunted. "And I thought I was jaded. Don't you think you're being a little extreme?"

"My mother killed my father and herself when I was nine, Hugh. Because the angels told her to. I found their bodies."

"Shit," Henderson said quietly. "I didn't know. I'm sorry."

Alex waited until she was sure her voice would respond and then said gruffly, "It was a long time ago. But yeah, when it comes to religion, I might be just a little extreme."

"Then I'm guessing it might be a little much to ask you to check on a priest for me."

She lifted her head. "Father Marcus?"

"He isn't answering his phone. Three new cases just landed on my desk and I can't get away."

"Can't you send someone else to check on him?"

"I've read the Toronto file, Jarvis. If something has happened to him—something like Father McIntyre . . ."

"You'd like to know first."

"I don't know what difference it would make—it would still have to be reported—but yes. I'd like to know first."

Alex didn't question his logic. Or his paranoia. If anything like Toronto had happened to Father Marcus, a heads-up would be a definite advantage. Emotional rather than practical, perhaps, but still very real. "Text me the address," she said. "I'll let you know what I find."

Flipping the phone shut, she looked up to where Seth waited by the glass doors, his dark eyes watchful. Assessing.

"That was Henderson. There's been an incident."

"I heard."

"Ah." Alex stood and tucked the cell phone back into its holder, its vibration announcing Henderson's text as she did. She cleared her throat. "He wants me—"

"I heard that, too. I didn't know about your parents. I'm sorry."

A flare of grief blindsided her. Blinking back unexpected tears, she responded gruffly, "Like I told Henderson, it was a long time ago. Would you mind very much if I went out for a while? It should only be an hour or so."

"Would it make you happy?"

She remembered their interrupted conversation and returned his smile. "It's not quite what I had in mind, but it will do for now."

"Do you want me to come with you?"

She hesitated. Cringed from the hurt in his eyes.

"Go," he said.

"It's not that I don't want you—" Hell. That sure hadn't come out right.

A half smile curved Seth's lips. "I know."

The live fish returned to Alex's gut. Heat rising in her cheeks, she took her coat from the closet. "Will you be all right on your own here?"

"I may go for a walk."

"Alone?" Alex's voice came out sharper than intended and she flushed again. "Sorry. I just worry about you."

Seth chuckled outright. "You do know how odd that sounds, don't you? Given that I'd be much better equipped to deal with a Fallen One than you would be?"

"I know, but—"

"I've no interest in speaking with Lucifer again even if he does try to reach me, Alex. I promise. Besides, they assigned your soulmate to be my watchdog, remember?"

Alex stilled at the underlying edge to Seth's voice, but when his expression remained relaxed—bland, even—she decided she had imagined it.

"Go," he said again. "I'll be fine."

Silently she put on her coat and gathered her things. Keys, gloves, wallet. She considered going into Henderson's room for the spare weapon he'd shown her stored there, but decided there was no point. The priest scenario was going to play out in one of two ways. Either Father Marcus would be just fine—the more likely finding—or she would walk in on another scene like the church in Toronto.

A crucifix, mounted on the wall behind a flimsy wooden dais. Upside down. The body on it not of plastic or wood or plaster, but of bone and tendon and shreds of putrid flesh—recognizable as human only by its general shape.

Alex gritted her teeth. Either way, a gun wouldn't help, and certainly wouldn't be worth the risk of having to explain why she carried one off duty and out of her jurisdiction if she happened to be caught with it. Hand on the doorknob, she looked over her shoulder at Seth and met his steady black gaze. His words ran through her mind again: *"Then you do want me."*

She couldn't keep running away from him. Or from herself.

"I'll be as fast as I can," she said. "Then . . ."

"Then?"

"We need to talk."

ARAMAEL STRAIGHTENED FROM his leaning post against the ventilator housing on the rooftop and stared at the apartment across the street. The two presences he'd been monitoring had divided, moving floors apart, the distance between them continuing to grow. What the hell?

He moved to the edge of the gravel roof. He could still sense Seth in the apartment, but Alex—his gaze flicked to the street. Far below, a door opened and a woman emerged onto the sidewalk, heading toward a parking lot. Alex was leaving. Alone. Without Seth.

And Lucifer knew about her.

Tension coiled through Aramael. The thread of connection he'd tried to dismiss earlier returned, back as if it had never been gone. He closed his eyes as Alex got into a vehicle, started it, and pulled onto the street. The thread began to draw taut, pitting desire against duty once more.

Fucking Hell, would he never be rid of Mittron's curse? Every time he thought himself cured of his soulmate, every time he was sure he had his feelings under control—feelings he should never have had in the first place—his soul betrayed him yet again.

Gritting his teeth, he fought the urge to abandon the Appointed and follow Alex. The thread stretched tighter, thinner. Grimly he rode out the certainty he would be ripped in two, clinging to the knowledge that he had survived walking away from her once and could do so again. He had no choice, because giving in to this just wasn't an option. It had never been an option, and it was damned well about time he came to grips with the knowledge.

The car carrying Alex disappeared around a corner. The strings around Aramael's soul stretched beyond agony, reached breaking point, and snapped at last. Breath returned. He waited, making sure the connection was really gone—again—and then turned back toward his post, only to come up short in stunned surprise.

"Seth? How the Hell did you get here?"

Arms crossed, the Appointed scowled at him. "More to the point, what the hell were you so focused on that you didn't notice?"

THIRTY-EIGHT

"It's a match."

Elizabeth looked up as the pediatrician, Dr. Gilbert, marched into her office and flopped into the chair across the desk from her.

"It's not an exact match, of course," Gilbert continued, "but the same genetic makeup is there, and—"

"Wait." Elizabeth held up a hand to stop the flow of words. "I assume you're talking about the Chiu baby's DNA, but you've lost me. A match to what?"

"The DNA results the coroner in Toronto sent out." Gilbert raised an eyebrow and prompted, "From the serial killer case they had a month ago? It isn't exact, but it's close enough to tell us it came from the same kind of . . . being."

Coroner? Serial killer? Elizabeth brushed the questions aside in favor of the one making her eyebrow arch the highest. "Being?"

Gilbert rested an elbow on the arm of the chair, her knuckles against her mouth, and stared at her. Then, moving her hand to play with the stethoscope hung around her neck, she said, "The Toronto DNA came from a claw, Dr. Riley."

Elizabeth gaped at the pediatrician, certain she couldn't have heard right. Gilbert grimaced.

"Yeah, that was my reaction, too. But the coroner there was adamant that's what it is."

"A claw. As in from an animal?"

"Not one that's in any database, no. Or one that normally roams the streets of Toronto, either, I'm guessing."

"But that's impossible."

"Also my reaction. And the coroner's. He was shocked as hell to get the police request." Gilbert seemed to recognize Elizabeth's confusion and elaborated, "Detective Henderson of the Vancouver PD called the coroner this morning. The coroner faxed him the results, he forwarded them to our lab, and the tech called me an hour ago. I just spent the last half hour on the phone with the coroner confirming everything."

"*Hugh* Henderson?"

"Someone you know?"

"He's handling Melanie Chiu's file."

"Well, he's going to love this. Toronto has three more babies just like ours. The coroner just finished the autopsy on the mother of the last one, born yesterday. After Henderson requested the DNA from the case, the coroner had the children's hospital there compare the babies' DNA with the same claw. He got the same results we did. We're in the process now of forwarding the comparisons to all the other labs looking into this."

A cold, hard knot settled into the middle of Elizabeth's chest, right where her heart resided. Hugh had found the proof she'd demanded. Concrete evidence that made it impossible for her to keep looking the other way.

Gilbert cleared her throat. "There's one more thing. We don't have results, yet, but we've taken a DNA sample from an amnio on the rape victim brought in the other night."

"You did an amnio on her? She consented?"

"Child services came in with a court order."

"Child—?" Elizabeth gaped at the younger doctor. "You've got to be kidding me. What kind of idiot judge would sign an order like that?"

Gilbert's fingers curled around the stethoscope. "I'm guessing the same kind that would sign an order letting them take the Chiu baby away from her grandparents this morning."

ARAMAEL WATCHED SETH stroll toward the edge of the roof and look out across the night-lit city. The sound of an aircraft passing overhead mingled with the ceaseless, muted traffic rhythms from below, filling the silence stretching between them. Aramael waited.

"Well?" the Appointed asked over one shoulder. "You haven't answered my question. What were you so focused on that you couldn't sense me?"

"And I'm not going to answer you, either. Under the terms of the agreement, I'm not even supposed to speak to you."

"Fuck the agreement."

"You already tried." The words slipped out before Aramael could think better of them and Seth's gaze sharpened.

Darkened.

"What is that supposed to mean?"

"Nothing. It means nothing." Damnation. Mika'el would have his head for this.

"It means something, or you wouldn't have said it." Seth turned away from the city to face him again. "Either you tell me or I go in search of Lucifer and ask him. Your choice."

Aramael's jaw flexed. Seth's memory might still be missing, but his personality had certainly returned in force, complete with the arrogance Aramael remembered. The air of superiority that expected others to fall in with his wishes, and that told Aramael he meant every word of the threat he'd just uttered.

He sighed. "You know about the transition, how it was supposed to go. How it failed."

"Go on."

"You made it fail."

"Excuse me?" Seth scowled. "Why would I do that?"

"Because of Alex. You tried to give up your destiny and transition as a mortal adult so you could be with her. Unfortunately, the Highest Seraph didn't have the capacity either of you believed he did and so we find ourselves here."

Seth stared at him. "I tried to give up who I was for her?"

"More *what* you were, but yes. You did."

"Does she know this?"

"I have no idea."

The Appointed paced slowly along the edge of the roof, one arm crossed over his chest, the other hand lifted to rub thumb across bottom lip. "I need to tell her," he said softly. "This will change everything."

Alarm made Aramael's center still. "It changes nothing, Appointed," he disagreed. "You still need to make a choice. It would be better if Alex didn't know."

Seth flashed him a vicious look. "You'd like that, wouldn't you?"

"That's not what I meant."

"Isn't it? I've felt you, you know." Hands clenched at his sides now, Seth stalked toward him with measured, deliberate steps. "I've felt your desire for her, Power. Your connection to her. I know how you hate seeing me with her, how it twists you up inside."

For an instant—an agonizing, frozen-forever-in-time instant—Aramael stood again in Alex's kitchen, her body pressed to his, her lips crushed against his with a hunger that matched his own and demanded his surrender. Remembered need shuddered through him. With an effort that threatened to rip the heart from his body, he stepped out of the memories and back into reality. Into his standoff with the Appointed.

"She is my soulmate, Seth," he said simply. "She will always *be* my soulmate. I can't change that, and I can't help what I feel for her."

Seth stopped before him and a subtle energy crackled between them, making the air sharp and alive. "Then maybe you should try harder," he suggested, his voice cold. Eyes colder. "Because you cannot have her, Aramael. Now or ever. Act like my Guardian to your heart's content, but stay the fuck away from Alex. Understand?"

Without waiting for a reply, the Appointed was gone. For several long seconds, Aramael scowled at the space Seth no longer occupied, trying to extricate reason from the tangled mass of resentment and fury. Trying to remind himself he was here to watch over the Appointed, not take him out as he'd first been assigned.

Pulling his mind into himself, he centered it and reached to connect again with Seth's presence in the apartment across the street. It wasn't there. He tried again. Nothing. The apartment was empty. Aramael cast his awareness in an ever-widening circle. Several blocks; the entire city center; the populated coastline; as far away as his abilities would allow. Still nothing.

Shock, icy with foreboding, settled into Aramael's core and he stared out across the sparkling lights of the city. Bloody fucking Hell.

He'd lost the Appointed.

Again.

ALEX ROSE FROM her chair as a robed, middle-aged man detached from the post-Mass stragglers and came toward her. With an effort, she returned his warm, welcoming smile with a tight one of her own. She'd been waiting for almost forty-five minutes and her patience threshold was headed rapidly downhill.

"Father Marcus?" she asked.

"Father Sebastian, actually."

"Is Father Marcus here?"

"I'm afraid not. Is there something I can help you with?"

"Do you know where I can find him?"

"The mid-Atlantic, I would think." The priest smiled again but there was no corresponding crinkle at the corners of his eyes this time. "He was called to Rome. He left this morning."

Tension crept across Alex's shoulders. The cop in her didn't like phony smiles. Her narrowed gaze swept over Father Sebastian, noting the careful stillness in his face, the tightly clasped hands. Was he who he said he was, or—? She thought of how Caim had once fooled her and, almost involuntarily, looked past the priest into the church's belly to where a crucifix was suspended on the wall behind the altar. Only the standard figure hung there, reassuringly carved of inanimate material.

She expelled the breath she'd held and went back to studying the priest. He looked human enough, but it was damned unnerving to know that she would never be certain. Never be able to tell. With anyone.

Shrugging off the disquiet crawling over her skin, she said, "That was fast. He didn't mention anything last night."

Father Sebastian's hands tightened a little more. "You saw him last night?"

"Is that a problem?"

"Of course not. Just—who did you say you are again?"

He was a man protecting a secret, she decided, but most likely on human orders rather than supernatural ones. She shook her head. "No one. It's not important."

Pushing through a group still clustered by the door, she stepped outside. Eyes closed, she stood for a moment and let the oppressive weight of the building slide from her. Her shoulders slowly moved away from her ears and back into their normal position. It had been twenty-three years since her last church visit and anything less than double that would be too soon for her next.

Sighing, she opened her eyes again. Henderson, leaning against the car she'd parked curbside, lifted a laconic hand. Alex paused mid-step, then continued down the stairs.

"I thought you were too busy to come."

"I was. I am. Liz called me."

"About—?"

"In a minute. I take it Marcus is alive and well?"

"And on a plane to Rome, I'm told."

Henderson blinked. "Rome. Do we know why?"

"No, but if we were to guess that certain parties are trying to limit the potential of a news leak, I think we'd be right." Alex rubbed at the back of her neck. Her shoulders might have returned to a normal height, but they'd left her stiff as hell. "It's a good thing, I suppose."

"And probably too late."

Her hand stilled. "Riley's call?"

"You were right. We have a DNA match to the claw. Chiu's baby, Murphy's fetus, three others in Toronto."

"How's Riley?"

"Pissed as all hell."

Alex frowned. "Because we have solid evidence?"

"Because Child Services has taken Chiu's baby here and all three in Toronto. I'm assuming other governments are doing the same."

It took a moment to absorb the impact of the news. Another to consider the implications. "You think someone knows the Church's secret."

"I think it's a good possibility." Henderson slumped against the car. "And even if they don't, they'll figure it out soon enough. Hell, I know these kids aren't entirely human, but they're still babies. Can you imagine what they'll be put through?"

Alex stared out at the street, watching the traffic without seeing it. "We're a determined bunch, aren't we?"

"Excuse me?"

"If there's a way to prove Lucifer right about us, we'll find it."

Henderson grunted. "It makes you wonder why he—sorry, *she*—bothers with us."

"Because like all good mothers, she loves her children," a deep voice said behind Alex. "All of us. In spite of our faults."

She whirled, staggered, and came up short against a broad chest. Strong, tanned hands gripped her arms. Steadied her. *Michael.* She knew even before she looked up into the emerald gaze. Just as she knew when she saw the fine tension around his mouth that something more had gone wrong. Her heart dropped.

"Seth?" she asked.

"He and Aramael had words. The Appointed has gone missing."

THIRTY-NINE

Entering the apartment, Alex threw her keys onto the hall table and stalked across the room to Aramael. Her granite-jawed soulmate's eyes turned bleak as they met hers. Her step didn't slow.

"What the hell did you say to him?" she snarled.

"Nothing he hadn't already guessed," he said, his voice quiet. Even. Holding a calm he didn't deserve.

Alex fought the impulse to slug him, shake him, do something to break that implacable detachment. "Specifics, damn it," she said through her teeth.

Aramael's mouth went tight.

A few feet away, Michael cleared his throat. "The Appointed has guessed at Aramael's continued feelings for you."

God damn. There was that horse kick in the chest again. Dropping her gaze, Alex swallowed and waited for the shock of pain to subside so she could breathe. So he'd lied to her. He did still feel something, and she was finding out now? Like this? When she had already begun, in spite of her best intentions, to care for another? When she couldn't even take the time to decide what the revelation might mean to her?

If it meant anything at all . . .

Lifting her chin, she stared at Aramael. "Exact words," she said, her voice harsh against her own eardrums. "What did you tell him?"

The gray eyes closed for a moment and then opened onto a pain Alex had never seen before. "I told him that you will always be my soulmate," he said, quiet truth in both voice and words. "And that I can change neither that nor the way I feel about you."

She thought of how she had put off talking to Seth, how she had avoided involvement with him. While she'd meant what she'd told him at the time, about not daring to become entangled with him after all that had happened with Aramael, she'd intended to change that. But he didn't know, and now, after hearing such a declaration from the angel he considered his rival, she could only imagine what he thought of her excuses.

"Naphil—" Michael began.

"*Alex!*" she shouted. "My goddamn name is *Alex*."

Aramael put a hand toward her and she slammed it away. "Don't. You've done enough damage. Could you not see how fragile he is? Could you not have lied, just this once? For him? For the world?" She blinked back tears of fury and despair. "For *me*?"

"He would have known," he said softly. "He couldn't help but sense what I feel for you." A gentle hand brushed a tear from her cheek. "What we feel for each other."

Alex waited for the jolt that should have come with his touch, with the words she had longed to hear only a day ago. Instead, she found hollowness where her heart should have been. She tried to replay what he'd said, thinking she might have been too stunned to respond, but instead of her soulmate's voice, she heard that of the Archangel Michael.

Sometimes the soulmate you're destined to have isn't the

*best match for you. Sometimes lives are too separate. Too
much has happened on each of your individual paths, too
many responsibilities get in the way . . . too many choices
are made by one that the other cannot agree with.*

Alex shuddered as the truth of the words settled into her
soul . . . along with the truth of the rest of what he'd said.
*"Seth needs you, Naphil. More than Aramael ever can or
will."*

Curling her nails into her palms until pain lanced through
her hands, she reached deeper than she thought possible for
a strength she never knew she had. Beyond anything that
might have been and all that could never be, until she
reached what simply was. Then, with a quiet finality, she
raised her gaze to Heaven's Power and said, "Felt, Aramael.
What I felt. Past tense."

Shock stared back at her from his eyes, becoming first
denial and then raw agony as seconds stretched into an eternity. The soulmate she had denied swallowed. Once, twice,
a third time. Then, without word or sound of any kind, he
vanished.

After another eternity, Alex turned away from the emptiness left behind him. "Now what?" she asked Michael.

"I want you to remain here, in case Seth comes back."

"I can leave him a note."

"It's best if you stay. He knows where you are."

*He'll come back if that's what he wants. If he isn't dam-
aged too badly already.*

Alex glanced out the window at the vast city, the vaster
world beyond, where Seth could be anywhere. "Michael, if
he thinks—"

"I'll check back when I can."

And yet another angel vanished from her world.

"HE'S LEFT THE apartment."

Lucifer raised an eyebrow at Samael. "Already? I wasn't
expecting it to happen quite so fast."

His aide shrugged a shoulder that still moved crookedly

after their encounter. "Perhaps it was just time for things to work in our favor."

"That's what I love about you, Sam. Ever the optimist. We're sure his watchdog is nowhere near?"

"Positive."

"What about Mika'el and the others?"

"Very much occupied in looking for him but not even close."

Lucifer shook his head. "I really didn't expect him to make it this easy. Far be it from me to spurn such a gift, however." Strolling past the desk, he took a peppermint from the dish, clapped Samael cheerfully on the shoulder, and headed for the door. "You have my back, Archangel. Remember you're guarding it with your life."

SETH STARED DOWN into the dark, swirling waters below the bridge. Traffic flowed behind him in a steady hiss and swish of rubber against wet pavement, oddly calming in its rhythm. He glanced to the right, at the still-lit windows spread across the city, marking tens of thousands of buildings sheltering hundreds of thousands of mortal lives. Mortals who struggled with the same feelings he did, who fought internal wars on a daily basis, wrestling with joy and agony and a hundred other emotions that could, in a heartbeat, turn their lives upside down.

As Aramael's words had done to him.

"She will always be my soulmate."

He tightened his fingers around the rail and waited for the twist of pain to subside. Was the Power right? Were he and Alex intrinsically, eternally mated to one another? Was that why she had held Seth at arm's length with such unflagging steadfastness, because she felt as Aramael did and just didn't know how to tell him?

But if that were so, if her connection to the Power was still so complete, why would she have intimated desire for Seth? Why would she have hinted she might want a relationship with him if she didn't think it possible?

He scowled at the city lights and the inhabitants hidden behind them. It was beyond his understanding how they survived turmoil such as this without driving themselves insane. He might be doing them a favor if he chose Lucifer's path. At least he'd be putting them out of their misery.

Except it wasn't that easy because he'd also be depriving them of their joy, the utter contentment they felt, as he did, in those brief moments where the universe itself seemed to smile on the complicity between them and the ones they loved. The moments that made everything else fade away into inconsequence.

Such a moment might be his again if he were back with Alex now, instead of standing out here. One way or another, he had to face her, to find out whether or not Aramael's truth extended to her. He needed to apologize for ditching his Guardian and disappearing the way he had, because she was almost certainly furious with him over that.

Sighing, he stepped away from the rail and strode toward the city center until he reached the shelter of an archway over the sidewalk where, taking advantage of being hidden from traffic, he could step from the bridge into the apartment where Alex would be waiting.

THE APARTMENT DOOR opened and then closed, but no voice hailed. Alex paused, halfway out of the shirt she had worn for too many hours that day. Henderson was working overtime—Seth? The steady footfall of steps moved toward her room. *Thank God.*

Even before she'd completed the thought, her heart did a series of barrel rolls, effectively wiping out her relief. So much stood between them. Where did they even begin? The knob turned on the bedroom door and she hastily slid her arms back into the limp blouse she'd been about to discard. Doing up the buttons, however, became an impossibility when the door swung open. Her fingers became thumbs and she clutched at the fabric, expelling a hiss of air.

Seth stood in the doorway, filling the space with his height and the breadth of his shoulders, his face in shadow. Silent. Staring. Clutching her blouse closed with both fists, Alex pried her tongue from the roof of her mouth.

"You're back. I was worried."

He leaned against the door frame.

The fragments of a thousand questions ran through Alex's mind, none settling into completion. There was too much she wanted to know. Too much she needed to say. She took a deep breath.

"Are you all right?"

Without responding, Seth's shadowed form straightened again and began a measured pace toward her. Alex's pulse turned staccato.

"I know what Aramael told you," she said. "I want to talk to you about it. About us."

The lamp beside the bed flickered and went out, plunging the room into dark relieved only by the glow of city lights coming through the uncovered window. Alex's breath lodged in her throat. Fingers tightening on the edges of her shirt, she blinked, trying to find Seth's shadow. It advanced toward her, each step causing another kick of her heart against her ribs.

Seth stopped, inches away, and uncurled her fingers, one at a time, from the fabric she gripped.

"We should talk," she tried to say, but her tongue had turned to stone and she could only wait as Seth's hand curved behind her neck, grasped her hair, and tugged back her head. She stiffened for an instant, taken aback by the edge of aggression, but then his mouth was at her throat, his body against hers, and his hands in so many places she couldn't keep track. Couldn't think past the sensations jolting to life along her every nerve, her every fiber. The truth that had finally dawned when she had faced Aramael and heard his words and known, with utter and absolute certainty, that Michael was right. Seth needed her.

As much as she needed him.

The blouse dissolved beneath his touch, sending a rush of cool air along heated skin. She placed her hands against Seth's shoulders, but his grip on her only tightened.

"Seth, wait. Slow down. Not like this."

Catching both her hands in his, he pushed her against the wall and bent his head to her breast. Alex's eyes closed and she gasped, arching against him. His tongue flicked, teased, tormented, moved to the other side. Heat began to build in her belly, filling her with its heaviness, its demand.

She pulled her hands free, clinging to him now, need overriding all else. Seth's mouth trailed up her throat and along her jaw and then, at last, claimed her own—

In a kiss that tasted of peppermint.

Alex froze.

She'd given Seth a peppermint at the hotel two days ago. He'd spat it out almost instantly. Hated the way it burned his tongue. Hated the taste.

Seth wouldn't taste of peppermint.

Oh, fuck.

The mouth—*not Seth's*—pulled back from hers, moved to her ear. "Something wrong?" it whispered.

Alex fought down the panic snaking through her gut. Mind racing, she made herself hold still and endure the hot breath. If she stayed calm, if she caught him off guard and went for the eyes first—

Hard fingers snagged her arms before the idea completed itself. Pulled her from the wall. Flung her onto the bed. Caught her legs when she would have kicked and rolled away.

"This would have been so much more pleasant for you if you'd stayed cooperative," said her attacker. A Fallen One.

One like Caim.

He sat down beside her and brushed back her hair with gentle fingers. The peppermint scent enveloped her, clogging her nose. The sickness of terror filled Alex's belly, rose into her chest, spread through her limbs. Her heavy, immovable limbs.

Seth-who-wasn't-Seth smiled in the light coming from the window. He touched his hand to her forehead. "Sleep," he whispered. "It will be over soon."

The world went dark.

FORTY

"You son of a bitch."

The snarl reached through the haze in which Alex drifted and jerked her back into consciousness. Raising a hand to her clouded head, she blinked, staring at the ceiling above her, trying and failing to get her bearings.

A low, nasty chuckle reached her ears.

"Did you really think you had a chance?" a voice demanded. Aramael's voice, but with a snarled edge to it Alex had never heard before. "Soulmates are forever, Appointed. Surely you've figured that out by now."

No. That was wrong. They'd talked about this already.

Alex rolled toward the voices and lifted her head. "Aramael? What are you doing?"

Two heads swiveled toward her. Aramael's, his gaze cold as it swept over her, and Seth's, fury blazing from eyes as black as the night. Alex choked on the air suddenly stuck in her throat. Her stunned gaze traveled Aramael's height, taking in the disheveled hair, the unbuttoned shirt and unbuckled pants. She looked down at herself. At her nudity, all too evident amid the tangled bedcovers. The last of her confusion fell away, leaving utter clarity in its wake.

"No." Grabbing the sheet, she pulled it around herself as she bolted from the bed. "Seth, it's not what you think—"

"It's exactly what you think, Seth," Aramael mocked.

"He's lying. It's not him, Seth. It's not—"

Seth knocked away the hand she put out to him. Alex swayed on her feet, made herself remain upright. Forced herself to meet his gaze.

His hurt.

His betrayal.

The beginnings of his hatred.

"You asked me to trust you," he said, his voice raw with anguish, "and I did. I trusted you with my soul."

"Wait," she said, desperation lacing her voice. "Listen—"

But as she reached for him again, the sheet slipped, exposing her nakedness, and Seth's gaze turned vicious. "Go to hell," he said. "Both of you."

And then he was gone—and so was the false Aramael— and only Alex remained, alone in the silence, the stillness. At first, she stared at the space where Seth had been, too shocked to take in the impossible, too stunned to react. Slowly, memories began to filter through.

Memories of Seth-who-wasn't-Seth.

A Fallen Angel's hands.

His heat.

His breath.

Horror and revulsion filled her as every fiber of her being recoiled from the remembered sensations. Staggering into the bathroom, she vomited, wretchedly, violently, into the toilet.

Then, feeling the violation of her body in its tenderness and knowing what had happened after the Fallen One had rendered her unconscious, she threw up again—and again, and again, until there was nothing more. Nothing left. She curled into a ball on the floor amid the tangled sheet that had fallen from her and wept slow, silent tears of defeat.

Fractured images surfaced, flashes of her father's body lying in a pool of blood on the floor. The knife in her dying mother's hand. Caim's many, many victims. Her own niece's mutilation. Father McIntyre's rotting body hanging from an inverted cross. Caim's hand tearing out her throat, ripping through her chest.

All that she had lived through, all she had survived, only to come to this . . . rape at the hands of a Fallen Angel. The utter inability to defend herself against it.

Alex curled tighter.

And then, like a life raft in the midst of a sea, came the thought of Seth. Seth, who deserved so much more than what he'd just witnessed. Seth, for whom she would do anything if she could only erase the betrayal she'd seen in his eyes.

Even if it meant opening her own soul to yet another onslaught.

Drawing the sheet around her shoulders, Alex took a deep, shuddering breath and called for her soulmate.

"AND THAT," SAID Hugh, linking his fingers behind his head and regarding Elizabeth steadily, "is as much as I know."

Elizabeth dropped her gaze to the pad of paper before her. She'd doodled over the same lines so many times the pen had gone through three sheets. "And you believe it," she said.

"I've seen it, Liz. With my own eyes. Wings and all."

Rising from the desk, Elizabeth crossed to the bookshelves and straightened a volume out of line with its shelfmates. "If you were anyone else, I would be arranging a room for you right now. You know that."

Hugh chuckled, a sound oddly lacking in humor. "Are you kidding? There are moments when *I* think I should be committed. But it doesn't make what's happening any less real."

"How many know?"

"You. Me. Alex. I think her staff inspector suspects."

Elizabeth looked over her shoulder to see him grimace

and scrub a hand over his closely shorn hair. "And you felt it necessary to bring me in on this why?"

"If the angels are right and this is just the beginning, we need to start getting ready."

"If there *are* angels," she retorted, "and they're right, then how the hell do we get ready? We don't even know what to expect. Will there be supernatural beings slugging it out on the streets? Are these Nephilim children a threat? Are we going to be involved in the fighting ourselves? How do we prepare for something we don't even understand?"

"Sure as hell not by sitting around on our asses pretending there's nothing wrong." He leaned forward, elbows on knees. "I know I'm asking a lot, Liz. I get that. You'll be putting your reputation on the line. I get that, too. But I could really use your help here. If you add your words to mine, people will start listening. They'll have to."

Elizabeth stared at the clip on his tie, a polished strip of onyx set in silver. More than ten years, she'd known this man, first as a patient and then, gradually, as friend and colleague. She had seen him at his most vulnerable and incoherent following his wife and son's murder-suicide, had supported his painful attempts to reclaim his life, and never once doubted his basic sanity. His innate groundedness. But now?

Hugh's cell phone rang. He pulled it from the case at his waist, his voice impatient as he answered. "Henderson." He listened for a moment and then, gray-faced, took Elizabeth's coat from the rack, scooped up her keys from the desk, and pushed her out the door. By the time she formulated a protest, they were in front of the elevator and Hugh was folding the phone shut again.

"It's Alex," he said. "She's been raped."

FORTY-ONE

Stepping into the apartment, Hugh took in the angels gathered in his living room. He recognized Michael and the one Alex called Aramael, but the third, a crimson-robed woman, was a newcomer. He glanced over his shoulder at Liz.

"You ready for this?" he asked.

She pushed past without answering, taking up a place against a wall. Closing the door, Hugh went to join the group, his gaze taking in the empty kitchen to the left and Alex's half-closed bedroom door to the right before settling on the Archangel Michael. "How is she?"

Alex emerged from her room, her face tight. Pale. "I'm fine," she said. "But Seth isn't. The Fallen One took on Aramael's appearance as Seth walked in, and Seth thought we— that Aramael—" Her voice, flat to begin with, quivered. She stopped, swallowed, and then met Hugh's shock with a steady gaze. "Seth thought Aramael and I had slept together. He's disappeared again and this time we could be in serious trouble. We need to find him before—before—"

"We need," Hugh interrupted, wrapping an arm around her shoulders, "to get you to a hospital."

"I'm not hurt."

Physically. The word hung in the air over them all.

"We need a rape kit, Alex. You know that."

Alex laughed at his words. Genuinely. With an edge of bitterness, yes, but without the hysteria Hugh would have expected. The hysteria that should have been there.

The sound brought the surreal and the real crashing together into a single, radically altered world as nothing else had been able to for Hugh. Not the disappearing Seth, not the bizarre conversation with Staff Inspector Roberts in Toronto or the weirder one with Alex in the coffee shop, not the introduction to an Archangel or learning of six-thousand-year-old scrolls hidden by the Church . . . not even the telling of the tale to Liz.

"I'm sorry," Alex said, seeming to realize how jarring her response had been. "It's just that I've been in your shoes. I remember how hard it is to make that shift."

"It's okay." Hugh took a deep breath and for the first time, looked—really looked—at the angels. Michael, Aramael, and the female, petite and silver-haired, her robe giving her an air of authority. He nodded to her, resisting the impulse to prostrate himself. He still didn't see the wings Alex described, but he had no doubt in his mind she was another of them.

Angels. Celestial beings. Divine creatures from Heaven itself.

In his fucking living room.

"So," he said. "If I can't be a cop, what the hell am I supposed to do?"

"We need you to stay with the woman while we"—the female newcomer indicated her party—"look for the Appointed."

"The *woman*," said Alex, "is going with you."

"No." The female shook her head. "You will only slow us down. You must stay here."

Alex scowled at her. "We've already been over this. I'm not staying anywhere. I'm looking for Seth. I'm the only one he—" She stopped mid-word and paled again. Then she walked toward the one named Aramael, halting halfway to where he stood by the window. "I need to be with you when you find him. You know he won't listen to you. He *might* still listen to me."

Michael responded before the other angel could. "We will come for you when we find him. *If* we need you."

Alex's gaze didn't waver. "Aramael?"

Aramael looked over her head at the others and Hugh saw his gaze meet Michael's. A message passed between the two of them, making Aramael's jaw go hard. Hugh remembered what Alex had told him about her relationship with the angel and his lips compressed in mute sympathy. The angel's pain filled the room, a pulsing energy that was raw and angry and every bit as human as any Hugh had ever felt himself. Perhaps more so.

But the gaze that Aramael turned back to Alex held nothing but grim determination. "Mika'el is right. You should stay here."

Before Alex could react, Michael stepped between them, cold finality stamped across his features. "This will be done our way, Naphil," he said. "You remain here."

Alex crossed her arms and glared at him. "Damn it, Michael, you don't get to tell me—"

A great gust of wind rushed through the living room, making Hugh blink. When he looked again, Michael and the others were gone and Alex was staring openmouthed at the empty space they'd left behind.

"That bastard!" She whirled to Hugh. "Fine. We'll just look for him on our own. If he's anywhere in this city, I'll find him."

"Hold up there, Alex," Hugh called after her when she would have disappeared into the bedroom again. "No way in hell am I dragging you all over the city after what just happened. Let the others find Seth. You need to be checked out."

Alex returned to stand a few feet away, calm, composed, her expression flatly determined. "I don't need a doctor. He didn't hurt me."

"Damn it, Alex, you're in shock."

"He didn't hurt me, Henderson. I wasn't even awake when he—when he—" Swallowing, she made a visible effort to pull herself together. "Look. It happened, I survived, and there are more important things than having my blood pressure taken right now, all right?" She glared at him. "I don't care if I have to go alone and on foot, but I am going to look for Seth."

"Alex," a woman's voice said quietly, and Hugh jumped right along with Alex. He'd completely forgotten Liz's presence, and from the look on Alex's face, she hadn't noticed the psychiatrist at all until now.

Nor did she look pleased to see her.

"Don't you start," she said tightly.

Liz straightened up from the wall, her face wan but determined, and Hugh could only imagine how everything she'd just seen and heard would mess with her logical mind.

"Hugh is right," she said as if Alex hadn't spoken. "You need to be examined."

"I'm not discussing this anymore." Alex started toward her room. "I need my coat."

"Alex," Liz said again, and this time the very quietness of her voice sent a spiral of unease through Hugh's gut.

Alex gave an impatient huff. "What?"

"If this was a Fallen Angel and you're like the other women who were attacked . . ." Liz bit her lip.

Hugh frowned. Liz didn't hesitate. Ever.

The anomaly seemed to have reached through to Alex, too, draining away her impatience. Leaving her watchful. Quiet. Then suddenly horrified.

"Oh, hell," she said.

And she bolted for the bathroom.

THE EXAM ROOM door opened and a middle-aged doctor entered, smiling the impersonal smile of the overworked and exhausted. "Detective Jarvis? I'm Dr. Warner. Dr. Riley asked me to come and speak to you."

Alex accepted the handshake he offered, not because she cared who he was or who had sent him, but because she was firmly entrenched in autopilot at this point, her body functioned on its own. Just as it had ever since she'd emerged from the bathroom at Hugh's apartment, so shell-shocked that her mind felt like it had separated from the rest of her.

Things hadn't improved since arriving in the hospital's emergency ward.

She sat in the chair he indicated. Settling onto a wheeled stool, Warner rolled across the floor to join her, flipping through the chart he'd brought in with him.

"Right, so you've been given the results of the test." Warner glanced up at her to confirm. "You know it was positive?"

Alex's belly stirred. Heaved. Settled again.

Her head nodded.

"The fact it is positive this soon is unusual, of course."

Were all doctors masters of understatement? Was that part of their training or something? Beat-Around-the-Bush 101?

"Unfortunately, it means the morning-after pill isn't an option . . . if, in fact, you intend to abort the pregnancy."

Alex's fingers gripped the edge of the chair until her knuckles ached under the strain, her mind noting the discomfort from a distance. A nice, safe distance she would have done just about anything to maintain. Anything but give in to what a Fallen Angel had done to her.

"Detective?" Warner prompted.

Holding up a hand, she closed her eyes, gritted her teeth, and took a deep, fortifying breath that made no difference whatsoever to the act of bringing mind and body together again, because reclaiming her full sanity in the face of what waited for her was just plain, fucking hard.

Warner's hand closed over hers. One of them, Alex noted, was shaking.

"Are you all right?"

She nodded.

He squeezed her fingers. The tremble was definitely hers.

"I know it can be a difficult decision, Detective, and it isn't normally my job to counsel patients one way or the other," he said, "but to our knowledge, none of the mothers has yet survived giving birth to one of these . . . babies. Under the circumstances, regardless of your personal beliefs, my medical opinion is that you abort the fetus."

Alex's head shot up. Nothing could have completed the joining of mind and body faster than his words did. He thought she hesitated? That she considered letting a Fallen One's child grow in her belly? She yanked away her hand.

"There's no decision to be made," she snarled. "I want it out of me."

Dr. Warner blinked, visibly adjusting his perspective of the situation. "Right. Well, at this stage, the best procedure would be—"

"I don't care what, just tell me when."

Another adjustment. "Fine. I'll go ahead and book an OR as soon as I can. Someone will give you a call with pre-op instructions. If your pregnancy progresses as the others have done, anytime within the first seven days will be fine. That still puts you comfortably within what would normally be the first trimester."

Alex shook her head. "I don't have seven days."

"I know you're anxious, Detective Jarvis, and I understand, but—"

"No," she interrupted savagely. "You don't understand. The thing that did this to me is on the verge of wiping out every human being on the planet. I have one chance to stop that from happening and I need this procedure now so I can get the fuck out of here."

Dr. Warner stared at her. Opened his mouth, closed it, and stared some more. Alex reined in her impatience. Her desperation. Taking a deep breath, she uncurled her fingers and met his astounded, uncertain gaze with a steadiness that took every ounce of her control.

"I know you don't understand," she said. "And I know I sound crazy, but—"

"She's telling the truth," Elizabeth Riley's voice said from the doorway.

Warner looked over at the psychiatrist at the same time as Alex. Alex hadn't heard the door open, and knew she should be pissed at yet another of Riley's invasions of privacy, but right then she was willing to forgive the shrink just about anything. Hell, she would have jumped up and kissed Riley if she trusted her legs to carry her that far. She settled, however, for giving the psychiatrist a tiny nod before turning her attention back to Warner.

Who now looked like he believed she and Riley were both nuts.

Or maybe he just wished they were, Alex thought, recognizing the flicker of unease deep in his eyes and feeling its echo in her own heart. Because he'd seen the mothers and their babies for himself, and he was afraid there might be a grain of truth to her words. Because, like she'd once told Aramael, insanity would be a whole hell of a lot easier than this heart-stopping, gut-churning reality that had become the world's.

At last the obstetrician stood and rolled the stool back to the wall. "I'll book the OR for an emergency procedure," he said.

FORTY-TWO

Alex came out of the utilitarian bathroom to find Elizabeth Riley seated by the bed, flipping through a magazine. The psychiatrist looked up at her as she padded past to the locker and thrust her clothes inside.

"I brought you a toothbrush and toothpaste," she said. "You'll need them in the morning, when you're discharged."

Morning. Alex gritted her teeth at the complexities behind the simple word. Hours spent here, idle, useless, waiting while Seth was out there somewhere, angry, betrayed, potentially lethal. She and Riley had gone three rounds over the matter when Alex learned how long the procedure was going to take. In the first round, she had flatly refused to remain in the hospital that long and Riley had physically blocked her from leaving. Round two had brought Riley's assurance that Henderson had every cop in the city searching for Seth, refuted by Alex's insistence that only she would stand a chance of getting through to Seth.

Round three had resulted in Alex being here now, with Riley's blunt reminder still ringing in her ears. *"If you don't get this thing out of you right now, while you have the*

*chance, you will die—and you're no good to Seth if you're
dead."*

Just because Riley might have won, however, didn't mean
Alex had to like it. Slamming the locker door shut with a
force that drew a frown from a passing nurse, she stalked
past the shrink.

"Have they given me a time yet?"

"They're just waiting for an anesthesiologist to come in."

Alex picked up her cell phone and checked the display.
A little after three. No missed calls. No text messages. No
Seth. Not that any of the angels would let her know, but
Henderson had promised to do so. This was going to be the
longest night of her life. Setting the phone back down on
the bedside table, she studied the other woman. Riley flipped
through pages too fast to even be scanning, let alone
reading.

"I don't need a babysitter," she told the psychiatrist. "I
said I'd stay."

"That's not why I'm here. It's going to be a couple of
hours before you go into surgery and I thought you might
want to talk."

"I'm fine."

Riley set the magazine on her lap. "You were raped,
Detective Jarvis. You are not fine."

Alex walked past her to the window.

Riley remained silent for a moment and then cleared her
throat. "Ignoring it won't change it, Alex," she said gently.

"Neither will talking it to death," Alex muttered, pulling
aside the curtain and staring out into the night.

"You can't keep locking away everything that happens
to you. One day you'll add one too many things and you
won't be able to close the door again and all of it will come
out. Everything, all at once. Trust me, you do *not* want that
to happen."

A shudder crawled up Alex's spine and she scowled, forcing it back down again. Riley was wrong. She'd managed
to keep everything safely locked away so far, and she'd
bloody well continue to do so for as long as she had to,

because with Armageddon pending, she didn't have much choice.

Besides, there was already too much behind her door to risk opening it so much as a crack right now.

"I said I'm fine."

Riley sighed behind her. "Well. I'm here if you change your mind. I will treat anything you say in absolute confidence."

Alex wondered if Riley's idea of *in confidence* was any better than Dr. Bell's had proved to be. Deciding a change of subject was in order, she glanced over her shoulder at the shrink. "So how are you doing with all this?"

Riley picked up the magazine and began flipping through it again, her face expressionless. "I'm struggling," she said at last, and Alex could only guess at the cost of the admission. "It's been a lot to take in."

"I know the feeling."

"Hugh has told me everything he knows, but I still have questions."

"Please. Fire away."

Riley shook her head. "You should sleep."

The suggestion brought a rush of memories associated with the last time Alex had slept. A Fallen Angel's hand on her forehead. His whispered, *"Sleep."* Waking to the aftermath, and Seth's betrayal, and the knowledge of what had been done to her. Of what she carried. Alex made her fingers uncurl from the sudden death grip she had on the curtain. Shutting down thoughts she preferred not to examine, she settled onto the wide ledge.

"I'm not tired," she said. "What would you like to know?"

Astute blue eyes regarded her over wire-framed glasses, but to her great and everlasting relief, Riley made no comment. Instead, she set down the magazine a second time and folded her hands over it.

"All right, here's one. If God exists—" Riley broke off again, then muttered, "I can't believe I even said that."

Alex gave a small smile. "I've been given personal assurance she does, if that helps any."

Both of Riley's eyebrows shot upward. "She?"

"They—Aramael and the others—call her the One."

A moment's silence followed while Riley digested the news. Standing, she set the magazine on the bedside table beside Alex's cell phone before joining her at the window.

"I'm guessing she's not quite the god many imagine." Riley drew back the curtain Alex had released a moment before. Her reflection took on a pensive expression. "The all-powerful one that's supposed to look after us and not let bad things happen."

"I think the all-powerful part is fairly accurate," Alex replied. "But not so much the looking after us. Aramael wasn't big on theological discussions when I asked, but my understanding is the whole free-will thing makes us pretty much responsible for ourselves. Heaven tries to maintain a status quo on our behalf because the Fallen Angels are trying to screw us over, but other than that we're on our own."

Riley's reflection grimaced. "I've always believed that anyway," she said. "But actually *knowing* it's true? Somehow that's just downright depressing." She straightened abruptly. "You know, I don't think I'm ready for this after all."

"I know." An unexpected surge of sympathy softened Alex's voice. "But it doesn't change the fact that it's happening. Or that it's real."

Riley gave her a sidelong look. "Trying to analyze the analyst, Detective?"

Alex chuckled, remembering the first time Riley had asked that question after picking her up at the airport four days—and a whole lifetime—ago. "Nah," she said. "I think the analyst will do just fine on her own once she gets used to the idea."

Riley fell silent for a moment, and then gave Alex's shoulder a squeeze. "Get some rest. They'll be coming in to sedate you as soon as the anesthesiologist arrives. I'll stay in the hospital, so if you need anything, have them page me."

"I'll be—"

"Fine, I know," Riley interrupted. "I get that you're tough,

Alex, really I do. But at some point in our lives, we all need a little help. Make sure you're strong enough to accept it."

"CONGRATULATIONS."

Lucifer looked up at Samael's dry voice and set aside his dog-eared copy of Dante's *Inferno*, the single most amusing literary work to come out of the mortal realm, in his opinion. It had taken a while to get past the sheer arrogance of the idea he would ever welcome any sniveling human souls into his Hell, but since then he'd never tired of reading it. He particularly enjoyed the three-headed version of himself embedded waist-deep in ice, supposedly cast there by the One.

Stretching his feet out to the flames in the fireplace hearth, he lifted a glass from the side table and sipped at the ruby liquid within. "Are these felicitations for anything in particular, or am I supposed to guess?"

The former Archangel shrugged, advancing further into the sitting room. "More for everything in general. Your plan has unfolded with remarkable precision."

Lucifer inclined his head. "It has been rather outstanding, hasn't it? So where do we stand at the moment?"

"Seth has gone to ground in the same area in which you originally found him. The others are searching for him."

"Are any of them close?"

"You know we cannot feel them—" Samael broke off, flinching. "Apologies, Lucifer. I did not mean to speak so sharply."

Leaning back, Lucifer linked his fingers behind his head and allowed himself a small, satisfied smile. He quite liked this new and improved post-beating version of Samael, still a military genius but without those annoying rough edges. He should have reminded his aide years before about who truly ruled Hell; he could have saved himself a great many headaches.

"Apology accepted. Go on."

"We haven't been able to track the angels, but I've set up a perimeter around the Appointed and will let you know as soon as any of them show up."

"What about the woman?"

"The Naphil?" Samael shrugged. "Does it matter?"

Lucifer stared into the pale flames. "I'm not sure. It might. The Nephilim bloodline runs stronger in her than I would have expected at this point. It feels different from any others I've encountered."

"I don't understand."

"She has to descend from one of the most powerful of angels for that to have happened, don't you think?"

"From an Archangel, you mean?" Samael frowned, looking equal parts intrigued and disgusted. "You think *I* fathered her line?"

"You're telling me you didn't dabble?"

"Only once. It was one of the more unpleasant experiences of my life and not one I cared to repeat. She was so insipid and fragile. The mating itself nearly killed her." Samael grimaced. "You really think it possible the woman is of my line?"

"Anything is possible. The question is, does it work to our advantage?"

His aide's expression cleared. "So that was why you took on the task yourself. She carries your child."

"She does," Lucifer agreed softly. "A child that would have been extraordinary regardless, but this . . . this could mean something more. Something greater. Think of it, Sam, my blood mingling with the line of an Archangel." He selected a peppermint from a dish on the couch beside him. "I want to keep an eye on her as well. We'll take the child as soon as it is born. I'll want it raised separately from the others. How are those arrangements going, by the way?"

"We're still working out the details. The mortal world is well connected these days. It makes hiding a large number of infants somewhat difficult."

"I'm sure you'll work something out, my friend. I have every faith in you."

Samael inclined his head a final time and then withdrew. Lucifer heaved a sigh of contentment, leaned his head back on the couch, and closed his eyes. It had taken thousands of years more than he would have liked, but at last he would rid the universe of the One's precious children.

Because with or without agreements or wars or any other unthinkable measures, the One could no longer hope to save the mortals.

FORTY-THREE

Seth slammed his fist into the side of a Dumpster, sending it skidding into a building with a crash that echoed down the alley and sent shards of brick raining down on the pavement. The blow did no good, released none of the pressure building inside him, took away none of the pain or betrayal.

How could she? He had trusted her. Loved her. Believed in her and what she told him about the goodness inherent in humanity. He gazed at his surroundings, at the overflowing piles of garbage, the human refuse, the utter desolation. How could he have believed *this* to be good? How could he have believed *her* to be good?

He longed to flee, to seek out some tiny seed of hope that might counter the growing ugliness at his center, but he didn't dare. They would be looking for him, and this was the one place he knew he could hide, at least for a while. The one place where Guardians were tangibly absent and wouldn't be able to signal his presence to the others. Wouldn't be able to see the rage within him, the seething hatred that threatened to overflow his center, or the anguish that drove him to walk the streets and alleys over and over again, in search of a solace he was beginning to think just didn't exist.

Had never existed.

Seth sent another Dumpster screeching across the pavement in a shower of sparks. A figure scrambled out of the shadows and dropped into an aggressive stance, light glinting from something in his hand. For an instant, Seth tensed, thinking *they* had found him, but then the smell reached him. The thick odor of unwashed skin, old urine, and stale smoke combined with that of alcohol and vomit . . . and mortality. His lip curled.

Revulsion, Lucifer's voice whispered in his memory. *Disgust. Repugnance.*

The man hawked and spat onto the pavement by Seth's feet.

Seth lunged forward and, before the man could react, shoved him the way of the Dumpster. Hard. Almost hard enough to kill him . . .

Almost, but not quite. At the last instant, a thread of regret made him hesitate just enough to weaken his intent and make him catch back a part of his fury. Staring first at his hands, then at the crumpled figure a dozen feet away on the pavement, he wondered what Alex would say if she knew of this.

Hated himself for caring.

Slowly he crossed to the man's side and stared down into pain-glazed, terrified eyes. Eyes that lived because Seth still valued the opinion of the woman who had betrayed him. Spurned him. Lied to him. Self-loathing swelled in his breast. They wanted him to choose whether all of humanity would live or die, and he couldn't even get past the weakness of his own desire and decide for himself whether or not to take a single life.

Was he really so pathetic? So feeble?

The man on the ground scrabbled for the knife he'd

dropped. As filthy fingers closed over the handle, Seth placed his booted foot on the thin, scarred wrist and reached down to pluck the knife from limp fingers. He might not have any memory of who he was, but he had the truth of what he'd been told. The certainty, in the deepest parts of himself, that he was more than mortal. More than Alex. Whatever hold she had on him, he had to break free. Would *make* himself break free. And then—

He hauled the blubbering man upright.

Then he would choose.

For himself.

"WHAT DO YOU mean, postponed?" Alex stared at Dr. Warner, who stared in turn at the floor between them. It was 5:00 a.m. and he'd come into her room just in time to stop the nurse from administering the pre-op sedative. One look at his face had made Alex's heart plummet.

"The anesthesiologist was involved in an accident on the way to the hospital. We're trying to find an alternate right now, but we haven't been able to reach anyone. I'm so sorry, I know how hard this must be—" Warner broke off and reached out to her, his brow knit with concern. "You're not going to pass out, are you? Maybe you should lie down."

Alex brushed off his hand and focused on drawing a breath into frozen lungs. On thinking beyond the *no, no, no, no* running on an endless loop through her brain. On not grabbing the obstetrician by the lab-lapels and snarling, *"Accident, my ass. Find someone and get this thing the fuck out of me—now."*

The coincidence of an accident was just too great, and not to be able to reach another anesthesiologist in a hospital of this size? No way. There had to be something more to this. Something like a Fallen Angel trying to stop her from aborting his child.

"There has to be another way."

"I wish there was, but—"

"Alex." Elizabeth Riley's voice intruded from the doorway, edged with urgency.

Alex looked past Warner and met agitation in the usually calm gaze. "You've heard."

Riley blinked. "You know?"

"Dr. Warner just told me."

Confusion crossed Riley's expression and a surge of alertness chased away Alex's nausea.

"You're not talking about the accident."

The psychiatrist shook her head. "Hugh called. There's a disturbance down in Downtown Eastside. He thinks it's Seth."

Alex had shot to her feet at Hugh's name, pushed past Warner, and already had her street clothes in hand.

"What kind of disturbance?" she asked, motioning to Riley to close the door. Figuring she had nothing an obstetrician hadn't seen before, she stripped off the hospital gown and, with a speed that came from years of responding to middle-of-the-night calls, was dressed again before Warner had even mustered a proper look of surprise.

"Hugh didn't say," Riley answered as Alex slid her feet into her running shoes and stooped to tie them. "Just that he's on his way to pick you up. He said he'd pull into the Emergency bay."

"Wait," Warner objected. "You can't leave, Detective. I need you to remain here to keep our priority for the OR. If we get bumped, I'm not sure when I'll be able to get you in again."

Alex straightened. "There won't be an *again*," she said. "The accident wasn't an accident, Doctor. It was a message from the Fallen—from the father."

A dozen expressions flickered across Warner's face, ranging from skepticism to unease to outright disbelief, culminating in a look that told Alex he once again questioned her sanity. He rocked onto the balls of his feet, hands in pockets, and *ahemm*ed softly. "What kind of message?"

"The kind that tells me no matter how long I wait here,

I'll never be allowed to abort this baby." Alex snagged her coat from a hook behind the door and met Riley's gaze, not daring to think about the truth behind her words. Or the consequences. "I'm ready."

Leaving Warner gaping after them, they traveled the corridors and elevators in silence. Not until they pushed through the doors into Emergency did Riley put a hand out to Alex, pulling her to a stop.

"What you said about not being allowed to abort just now. You really think that's true?"

Outside the glass entrance, a sedan pulled to an abrupt halt, its dome light splashing red into the early-morning gloom. Henderson leaned across the seat to peer at the ER doors in search of her. Alex's pulse, already accelerated, kicked up another notch. This was it. This was their last chance.

If Henderson could get her there in time.

She tugged at Riley's grip. "I have to go."

The psychiatrist's fingers tightened. "You didn't answer me."

"I know it's true."

Riley exhaled in a hiss. "Alex, if you carry this pregnancy to its term . . ."

Alex pulled her hand free. That would be the part she really didn't want to think about. "I know," she said, "but I don't think whoever's behind this much cares."

MIKA'EL LOOKED AROUND as his office door opened without warning and the Highest Seraph stepped inside.

"We have him," said Verchiel. "I've summoned the others."

"Has he . . . ?"

She shook her head. "Not yet, but it doesn't look good. The human police have him cornered in an alley."

The Appointed, cornered? Mika'el's heart pitched down to belt level. *Not unless he wanted to be.* Hell. "He's looking for a confrontation."

"That's what I thought. We're trying to get the Guardians to pull their charges away, but you know what mortals are like when they're in a state of high alert like this."

"Where is he?"

"The area where you found him with Lucifer."

Mika'el grunted. "He stayed that close? No wonder we weren't able to find him." His mouth tightened. "This is it, then. All right, let's get it over with."

Verchiel put a hand out to stop him as he went to step past. "It's not going to be that easy, Mika'el. Lucifer has sentries set up around him. He'll know the minute you arrive."

"That means he knows a Fallen One attacked the woman."

"Of course he does. The attack on the Nephilim woman was deliberate—a way around the non-interference clause. Seth was intended to know. To react this way."

"There must be something we can do."

Tipping back his head, Mika'el tried to think. But no matter how he looked at things, it all came down to one inescapable conclusion. Lucifer had out-manipulated him. He closed his eyes. He had allowed the Light-Bearer to skirt the rules, to get away with brazen disrespect, even to threaten, all in an attempt to protect the One from having to make that final, impossible decision.

And instead it had come to this.

"Mika'el?" the Highest prompted.

He shook his head soundlessly, remaining as he was, letting the knowledge of what was to come settle into him. He waited for it to fill him. Change him. Instead, failure gave way to a quiet, seething righteousness. A determination. No. He would not give up. Not now, not ever. He reached out with every fiber of his existence, allowing the energy of Heaven itself to mingle with his. Reached until he found and embraced the One's own power, taking it within him for the first time in more than four thousand years. Feeling her surprise as he did. Her questions. Ignoring them, he opened his eyes and lifted Verchiel's hand from his arm, giving it a small squeeze as he released it.

"Send the Powers to engage the sentries," he ordered. "All of them."

"All? Even—?"

"All," he said. "Including Aramael."

FORTY-FOUR

Bailing out of Henderson's sedan, Alex took in the scene with a sweeping glance. A dozen police cars were strewn across the street, blockading the alley mouth and all possible chance of escape. Twice that number of officers had taken up sheltered positions behind the vehicles, and an Emergency Response Team van had pulled up across the sidewalk, its back doors wide as members scrambled out.

She turned to Henderson. "Get them out of here."

"Right. And would you like me to drain the fucking Pacific while I'm at it?" he retorted. "It's too late, Alex. You know they won't back down at this stage."

"Then get me in there."

He patted down his pockets and then spread his hands wide. "Sorry, I seem to be missing my magic wand."

"Damn it, Henderson!"

He placed his hands on the sedan's roof and glared at her. "I told you on the way here what it was going to be like. He's in there, tossing around Dumpsters like they're goddamn basketballs. They're not going to let an unknown cop wander in to have a conversation with him."

A resounding crash backed his words, its echo rumbling down the alley and making cops duck behind car doors again. Henderson waited for the reverberation to still before he continued, his voice calmer but no less cutting.

"He's holed up in a blind alley with a hostage and he's not responding to anyone. If hostage negotiation fails, these guys have no choice but to go in there after him, and there's nothing you or I can do to stop them."

"You don't understand. Something changed when he saw me with Aramael. He's on the edge, trying to make his decision, and I think he wants us to force him into it." Alex waved a hand at the gathered cops. "If they go in, he'll kill them."

Henderson stared into the alley. "If we go after him, he'll have reason to take one of us out."

"Or all of you," Alex agreed. "And if he's as far gone as I think, you don't have enough firepower in the city to stop him."

"Fuck," said Henderson. *"Fuck."* He slammed his fist against the car roof and glared across at her again. "You know I'll sound like a lunatic."

"I know."

"Fuck." Pushing away from the vehicle, he strode toward the ERT van, yanking his badge from his pocket.

Alex paced a short, tight line beside the car, her eyes glued to Henderson and the ERT supervisor. She saw it all. The raised eyebrows, the scowls, the glances exchanged between supervisor and nearby team members, the angry gesticulations that all too clearly told Henderson to piss off.

And then the lightning.

Stopping mid-stride, she stared at a sky that had been clear when she'd left the hospital with Henderson—enough so that she'd noticed the crescent moon following them as Henderson drove. Now, the sky that should have been growing pale with an encroaching dawn had instead gone black. A shiver went down her spine. Vancouver weather was famous for its changeability, but this much this fast?

Another shaft of lightning split the sky, then a third.

Just like the storms that had plagued Toronto during

Caim's rampage. The storms that had occurred simultaneously with the murders, earning him the title of the Storm Slasher. Almost as if—Alex sucked in a breath and stared into the still inky-dark alley.

Almost as if Caim had affected the very energy of the world around him whenever he killed. Like Seth seemed to be doing now.

"Got any other bright ideas?" Henderson's sour voice asked. "Because that one went over like a ton of bricks. By tonight, everyone on the force will think I'm a fucking nutcase and I'll be lucky if all I get is—"

His words dropped off into silence as the street dimmed beneath a giant shadow passing over it. The hive of activity around them stilled into an eerie silence and Alex watched all eyes turn skyward. Her mouth filled with dust.

"What the hell?" Henderson murmured.

"It's them." Grabbing the other detective's arm, she swung him around to face her. "They're here for Seth. Whatever you do, don't let anyone follow me in."

"Follow you—Alex, where the hell are you going? Who's here? Damn it, Jarvis, get back here before you get shot!"

Henderson's furious bellow shattered the stillness as she bolted for the alley, bringing the scene back to life. Startled cops grabbed for her, missed, added their shouts to Henderson's. Alex dodged, wove, feinted to the side, and ran like she'd never run before. Behind her, Henderson's voice rose above the others.

"Hold your fire! Goddamn it, don't shoot! She's a cop!"

Ahead of her and to the left, a burly ERT member in full gear was on an intercept course. Lightning split the sky again, illuminating the grim determination on his face. She eyed the police cars blocking the alley, looked back at the ERT member, and calculated her chances of evading him. Her step faltered. Then, reaching deep, she found a final burst of speed and her stride lengthened one more time. Vaulting onto the hood of one of the cars, she slid across it and onto the pavement again. Just a few more feet and—

Powerful arms encircled her, lifted her from her feet, and

swung her around. *No. Damn it, no! Not now. Not this close.*
She shoved at a solid chest, twisted in the iron grip, fought
with every ounce of strength she possessed.

Feathers brushed her cheek.

"Alex, it's me," a familiar voice spoke over her head, and
hands gripped her arms, shaking her. "Stop fighting."

She did, if only out of sheer surprise. "Aramael? You
have your wings back. Thank God! Seth—the Archangels—
you have to help me get in there."

Arms still pinned to her sides, she indicated the alley
with her chin, but Aramael's only response was to tighten
his grip. The hope that had surged in her hesitated, then
shriveled as she raised her gaze to his. ERT members formed
a ring around them, weapons poised, voices bellowing
instructions. Caught up in stony gray eyes, Alex barely registered their existence.

"You goddamn son of a bitch!" She pulled free of Aramael's hands and raised her own to shove at his chest. She
might as well have tried to move the squat brownstone
beside them. Breast heaving, she blinked back tears of frustration. Fury at knowing that, after all she'd done, all she'd
been through, she had failed. Failed Seth, failed the human
race, failed herself.

"I'm sorry," Aramael said.

"Are you?" she demanded bitterly. One of the ERT members reached for her arm and she shook him off with a
vicious, "Back off!" before rounding on Aramael again.
"Are you really? You're getting what you wanted, remember? Seth is about to die. You should be thrilled."

"I never wanted this."

"Because you wanted to do the honors yourself?"

Aramael flinched and his nostrils flared. "This isn't about
me, Alex. I did what I had to do because that's who I am.
What I am. You know that."

"And what about Seth?" she snarled. "Was that something you had to do, too? Tear him apart inside so he would
doubt me and believe the Fallen One's lies? All of this is
still new to him. He doesn't understand. Doesn't know yet

that I care for him." She ignored the flash of pain across Aramael's features and pressed on. "*You* did this to him, Aramael. You owe him another chance."

She glanced past the ERT members surrounding them, past Henderson in furious discussion with the team supervisor, down the alley. What was happening? Had the angels taken him yet? Would she see them go as she had seen them arrive, as a silent, massive shadow passing across her world? Would she feel him go? Her breath rasped in her throat.

She looked up at her soulmate.

Ice crystals had formed in his eyes. "You don't know what you ask."

"I'm asking you to help me. To trust me." Alex reached up and cupped his face in her hands. "I couldn't save you, Aramael. Let me try to save Seth. Let him love me so he can do what he's supposed to."

Aramael stared over her head into the alley, his conflict a palpable, surging energy that enveloped them both. Behind her, the argument between Henderson and the ERT supervisor escalated; around them, heavily armed cops shifted. Agonizing seconds dragged past.

At last her soulmate looked down at her again and took her hands from his face. "You're damned lucky I still have my free will," he grated, "or this wouldn't even be an option."

He raised a hand. Momentary alarm surged through Alex, along with memories of another time he had raised his hand to a human, a time when his wings had come alive with golden flames and a terrible wrath had darkened his features. But the ERT members standing between them and the alley simply staggered backward as if pushed by an enormous gust of wind. No flames. No bodies sailing through the air. Only a half dozen cops pummeled into reverse, trying to regain their balance without dropping their weapons.

Gray eyes met hers again, just for an instant. "I'll hold them off," he said. "Go."

Go to Seth.

Alex turned and ran.

FORTY-FIVE

She found them beneath a single light mounted high on the brick wall that formed the end of the blind alley. Black wings—six pairs of them—formed a barrier beyond which she couldn't see a thing, and the kind of silence reigned where a person truly could have heard a pin drop. Her heart plummeted. Was she too late? Had they already . . . ?

One of the Archangels shifted and the wall of feathers parted. Through them, she saw Seth, his back to the graffiti-covered wall and face twisted with emotions Alex didn't think he had even begun to understand. Ugly intent glittered in his black eyes, and, in his hold, dangled the reason the Archangels hadn't yet struck him down—a quivering, terrified man with a knife at his throat. A knife held by Seth.

"Wait!" Alex lunged through the gap in the blockade and planted herself between the Archangels and Seth. Arms spread wide, she sought and found Michael's face among the others and, ignoring his fury, directed her entreaty to him. "I can talk to him. I can make him understand."

Behind her, Seth grated, "I already understand."

Low, violent energy pushed at Alex's back. She staggered under its force and looked back at him, at the knife in his hand pressed against the man's skin, drawing a bead of blood. At his malice. Her heart shivered but she made herself meet his gaze and hold it without wavering. "It doesn't have to be like this. It wasn't what you thought. Aramael never touched me in the way you think."

"You lie," he snarled. "I saw you. I saw him."

The bead of blood became a line.

"Alex." Michael's voice was cold, commanding, compelling.

It took all the willpower Alex would ever possess to ignore it and continue speaking to Seth. "No. That wasn't him. It was—" She swallowed hard.

"Alex," Michael said again.

She lost it. *"Shut. Up."* She rounded on him. "Just shut up, Michael. You've done enough. More than enough. You and your creator and fucking Lucifer. Seth and Aramael and I are not pawns in some goddamn cosmic chess game!"

"Actually," drawled a new voice, "you are."

Lucifer.

She knew it without looking. Knew from the way six pairs of wings shot open to their full span. The way the energy radiating from Seth was suddenly swallowed by something greater. Something lethal, crackling in the air and tingling along her skin. Her insides went liquid.

Lucifer, six Heavenly warriors, a divine being in a position to annihilate humankind—and her, caught between them all. If it weren't for the death sentence she already carried in her belly, Alex might have at last turned tail and run. But even then—to where? If the human race faced either annihilation on one hand or Armageddon on the other, there would be no safe place on the planet. Perhaps not in the universe.

So she did the only thing she could. She held her ground, continued to shield Seth and his hostage from the Archangels, hoped for a miracle, and tried very, very hard not to flinch from reality. Or from the tiny blue flicker of energy that snapped near her cheek.

"Lucifer." Michael grated the name with such fury in his voice that the walls of the alley trembled, sending a fine shower of dust across the pool of light in which they stood.

"Mika'el. Don't let me interrupt. Please. I believe you were about to forfeit the agreement?"

Lucifer's footsteps signaled his approach and Alex held rigid against the raw desire to simply fold to the ground. Michael's breath hissed out, sending dust motes skidding away from him. "I do nothing more here than end your treachery, Light-Bearer."

As tall and luminescent as Alex remembered, Lucifer stopped at the edge of her peripheral vision. "What treachery would that be, Archangel?" His voice went cold. Hard. "Given you're here to murder my son, what treachery have I committed that could possibly equal that?"

"You're telling me you know nothing of what happened to the woman."

"What woman? Oh, you mean, the Naphil who cheated on the Appointed? Who rejected him and subjected him to unspeakable humiliation?"

Seth inhaled sharply and Alex's gaze swiveled to him. The line of blood across his hostage's throat had become a trickle. "Don't listen to him, Seth. That's not what happened," she said. "I was raped."

Lucifer snorted. "Of course she'd say that. She'd say anything to try and save her race. But you know what you saw, Seth. Her with Aramael, his scent still clinging to her bare skin and the sheet in which she wrapped herself. You know what happened."

Seth's eyes met Alex's, renewed acrimony flaring in their depths. His arm tightened across his victim's chest. The knife shifted in his grasp. Alex swallowed against a tongue three sizes too big for her mouth. More than once she had faced down men who looked the way Seth did now; desperate men on the cusp of making choices they couldn't take back. Choices she and her fellow cops hadn't been able to allow.

The kind of choice Lucifer urged Seth to make now. But this time, with neither weapon nor words, she was helpless to stop it. Or was she? Alex's breathing came to a rasping halt. She tore her gaze from Seth to stare at the luminescent Lucifer, frantically trying to recall everything he'd said, *how* he'd said it.

"Her with Aramael, his scent still clinging to her bare skin . . ."

"That's enough, Light-Bearer," Michael's voice grated.

More blue crackles illuminated the air around them all. Lucifer's doing? Or Michael's?

"Careful, Archangel," Lucifer drawled. "You don't want to start something you can't finish. Such as carry out the One's orders to murder her son, for instance."

". . . the sheet in which she wrapped herself . . ."

At the edge of Alex's vision, Seth flinched.

Lucifer's lips curved upward at the corners. "You hadn't already figured that out for yourself?" he asked his son. He slid thumb and forefinger into the pocket of his jacket and withdrew a round, white object that he popped into his mouth. "I wish I could say such naïveté was endearing, but in truth, it galls me. Are you really so trusting, Seth? So willing to allow others in your life to make your decisions for you? To direct your choices?"

As if he was there. As if he saw . . .

Alex watched Seth's face darken. Saw him believe Lucifer. Saw his decision begin to form. Behind her, the Archangels shifted. Then the scent of peppermint wafted toward her, enveloped her, all but drove her to her knees.

She knew what the Light-Bearer had done. What he tried to do.

"Lucifer—" Michael began.

"Michael," said Alex. Or maybe she yelled it, because the Archangel—all the Archangels—looked startled. Then annoyed. Then just plain pissed. Alex fought off the collective will gathering around her, the desire for her to be silent, and made herself meet the emerald ice of Michael's gaze. "He was there," she rasped. "It was *him*."

Michael's brow creased, then cleared, and then became thunderous. He rounded on the Light-Bearer and the blue crackles multiplied a thousandfold. "She's right. That's the only way you could know how Seth found her."

"You have me," Lucifer said. His amethyst eyes found Alex and he smiled a smile that slithered across her skin like a living reptile. "Or to be more precise, I had her."

Fighting back the tentacles of horror spreading across her mind, Alex tore her gaze from the compelling, awful beauty of God's former helpmeet. She sought Seth's eyes and the comprehension that should have followed his father's admission. Found savagery instead.

"You still thought it was Aramael," he snarled. "You still chose him over me."

Alex recoiled from the accusation and the pain it contained. Had Lucifer's meddling been too much? Could it have pushed a still fragile Seth beyond reach? Her heart twisted.

"Of course she chose him," Lucifer snapped. "Now would you stop being so fucking spineless and slit his throat already? You've made the decision. Now act on it."

"No!" Alex held out a hand toward Seth. "I thought it was you, Seth. Not Aramael. I chose you."

He wanted to believe her. It was in his eyes, in the dark, tortured depths of the soul that stared back at her. A soul that wanted to believe, that fought to do so but in the end, remained too fragmented. A soul that simply couldn't bear the strain.

What remained of the Seth she knew began a slow folding-in on itself.

FORTY-SIX

Without her training, without the edge of years of experience, it might have ended there. With Seth drawing back the man's head and placing the blade under one ear, with a single knife stroke taking the life of one man and indirectly ending billions of others.

But instead, instinct kicked in and Alex lunged forward, catching hold of Seth's hand as his grip shifted. She slammed it into the brick wall. Again and again, until the knife dropped from his startled grasp. Scooping it up, she spun out of reach. Then, her own back to the wall, she faced the entire gathering, breast heaving with the adrenaline aftermath, as startled by her actions as anyone there, staring at the knife she held.

"Oh, for the love of Hell," Lucifer snapped in exasperation. "You stupid, interfering—" He broke off as six pairs of wings snapped wide again. Looking over his shoulder at the wall of Archangels, he heaved a sigh. "Really, Mika'el? You really want to start things now, like this, over a mortal woman? And a Naphil at that?"

"It's over, Lucifer. I demand forfeiture."

Lucifer smiled. He chuckled, then laughed aloud, the sound ringing through the alley and stilling the activity still unfolding on the street beyond. Alex's fingers tightened on the handle of the knife as she caught her breath. Held it. That so didn't sound good.

"Oh, Archangel," the Light-Bearer gasped at last, "you really haven't caught on, have you? I had no idea you could be so slow. I'm so fortunate it was Sam who chose to follow me and not you. I don't appreciate him nearly enough." He wiped at his eyes with the back of one hand and chuckled again. "All right, you win. I forfeit. I won't harm a hair on the head of a single mortal. You have my word."

Words of concession, delivered in a tone of utter delight. Again, not good.

"We had an agreement," Michael snarled.

"And I am honoring that agreement. As per the terms, I will leave the mortals alone. The Nephilim, however . . ." He paused. Smiled the coldest smile Alex had ever seen. "Ah, they'll be a whole other story, won't they? Especially now."

Alex's fingers grew numb and her gaze flicked to Michael. Found him looking livid. No. Apoplectic. Foreboding slipped through her, its presence like the touch of ice-cold silk. She went rigid as Lucifer's gaze settled on her belly.

"I did much more than *take* the woman, Mika'el," he spat. "With her extraordinary Nephilim blood—and it is extraordinary, you know—mixed with mine, the child she carries will be a leader among his kind. A leader of a resurrected race I won't be quite so inclined to fritter away this time."

Through a wave of horror, Alex heard Seth's hissed exhale.

The man he'd held sprawled onto the pavement by Alex's feet. Casting a wild look at the gathering, he scrambled upright and took off as if pursued by the proverbial hounds of Lucifer's realm. The alley swallowed his fleeing footsteps. Silence followed, thick and heavy and terrifying.

Alex stared at Heaven's greatest warrior. *Say something,* she thought to him. *Tell him he's wrong, that you'll save us. Tell him—tell* me *this wasn't all for nothing . . .*

Michael's face had gone gray. "We will fight you," he said.

"Knock yourselves out, Archangel. It won't make a difference. Not anymore. Eighty thousand strong went out among the mortal females last night; we've sown enough seed to create the army I wanted. One you can't touch, that isn't bound by pacts or agreements or any other restrictions. Hell fights, Heaven fights . . ." Lucifer shrugged. "Either way, the Nephilim carry on with their task. With my child"—the Light-Bearer strolled to Alex's side and reached out to slide a hand across her midriff—"leading them."

Alex recoiled. Her gaze met Michael's. Held it. The Archangel's jaw turned to granite and his eyes to chips of emerald ice, but he made no move toward her. No move to stop the Light-Bearer's touch. Her stomach heaved.

"The best part," Lucifer continued softly, "is that I have given you what you wanted more than anything else in the universe. I have saved your Creator from herself. Because not even she can stop the Nephilim now. Her mortal children will be wiped out because of her own rules, her own self-imposed limitations. With no Guardians to guide the Nephilim along her path and no allowances for her angels to take a life in her name, *she* will be responsible for wreaking havoc on humanity, not me. And if I can't be held to blame, she will have no reason to come after me." The Light-Bearer paused. "Actually, Archangel, if you think about it, you owe me. How very ironic."

Then, grasping Alex's chin, Lucifer jerked her face to his. "As for that little plan of yours I interrupted this morning, Naphil, the next time you try it, the accident will be fatal. Try it a third time and many mortals will lose their lives. A fourth, and a city will fall, and so on. You *will* carry my child to term. Do we understand one another?"

Without waiting for a response, he thrust her away, hard

enough to make her stumble and fall against Seth. Arms went around her and tightened for an instant before Seth set her upright and stepped past her.

"Lucifer." His low growl rumbled through the alley. Above, lightning flared blue in response.

His father, strolling toward the wall of Archangels, stopped and glanced over his shoulder. He raised an eyebrow. "Too little, my darling son," he said. "And far too late."

Arms held wide, Lucifer whipped around. Seth jerked backward off his feet, like a puppet on a string, and hit the wall perpendicular to Alex with a grunt. Lucifer's lip curled and he turned away a second time.

"And that's what I get for leaving you to be raised by your mother."

Alex stared at the winded son of the two most powerful beings in the universe. Then at the line of Archangels facing her. All brushed aside without effort, their powers inconsequential in the face of Lucifer's manipulations. Numbness began to replace the horror in her veins. Mind-deep, soul-deep, core-deep numbness.

Perhaps the idea had been brewing for a while in her subconscious. She didn't know. Didn't care. And didn't dare stop to think about it. She just lifted the knife in a hand that felt as dead as the rest of her and turned away so Seth wouldn't have to watch.

Lucifer spoke to Michael now, his voice autocratic. Final. "Give my regards to our Creator, Archangel. And tell her the next move is up to her."

Sliding past the Light-Bearer's shoulder, Michael's gaze met Alex's. It widened the barest fraction, just enough to make Lucifer spin around as she plunged the knife up to its hilt in her belly, aiming low, toward where she knew Lucifer's monster grew inside her. Blood spurted over her hands an instant before white-hot agony drove her to her knees on the filthy pavement.

Lucifer strode toward her, fury blazing from his eyes, and six Archangels moved as one to come between them.

To hold him at bay while the blood spilled from Alex and pooled on the pavement, draining her life with it, and that of the Nephilim child within her.

Alex's hands slid from the knife as Lucifer's luminescence flared again, stretching high over the Archangels' own. Energy sizzled through the alley once more, dancing along her skin—skin that already felt as if it belonged to someone else as she began to grow smaller inside her own body.

"Touch her and I swear you will *beg* to return to Hell before I am done with you," Michael grated.

Lucifer snarled an answer, but his words sounded muted, muffled. Alex felt a distant surprise. Shit, this was happening fast. She must have nicked an artery.

She began a slow slump to the side. An arm slid beneath her and cradled her against a warm chest and a strong, steady heartbeat. Looking up into Seth's sick horror, she tried to smile, but couldn't seem to find her lips. "I had to," she whispered. "I couldn't let him win. Not like this."

His hold tightened. "Tell me what to do. Tell me how to make this better. I can't lose you, Alex. I won't make it alone."

She fought off an encroaching fog. Shook her head. "You can't make it better. Not this time." *It's okay,* she wanted to add, but her voice had disappeared, too, and the effort of searching for it drained her. Her eyes drifted closed, shutting out the alley and bringing a not-unwelcome darkness. The cold seeped toward her core.

"Open your eyes, Alex, damn it!"

Colder.

"Alex, wait!"

Darker.

"Alex!"

Aramael, she thought.

Gone.

FORTY-SEVEN

Seth stared at the body in his arms, mind empty, chest emptier, world at a standstill.

So this was death.

A simple cessation of life. Of being.

Here . . .

And then not.

The reality stunned him.

The finality damn near killed him.

Sucking a breath into lungs paralyzed by loss, he lifted his head. He met the bitter sorrow in Mika'el's eyes, the disgust in his father's. Anger fanned back to life. With a frighteningly foreign detachment, he moved to lay aside the vessel that had been Alex. A hand closed over his arm.

Seth looked around, into the eyes of the angel he held responsible for all that had just happened. Fury licked along the edges of his loss. His jaw went tight, his body rigid.

Aramael gave him a shake. "Did you hear me? I said she's not dead, damn it."

Seth blinked. Scowled. "I felt her go."

"Her soul is still there, but you'll have to work fast. Once it leaves, it will be too late. You can't bring her back after that." Aramael placed his fingertips on the side of Alex's throat. "And for the sake of the One herself, whatever you do, don't save that thing inside her."

Seth looked down at the lifeless form in his arms. "You'll have to do it," he said. "I don't know what to do."

"I can't. I don't have that power. You *do* know what to do, Seth. You're the Appointed. You saved her before and you can do it again. You just have to remember." Aramael looked up, and Seth followed his gaze toward the wall of Archangels between them and Lucifer. The Power's voice went grim as he added, "Before your father does something stupid."

"But I *can't* remember," Seth grated, hearing the agony in his own words. "I've tried, and I can't remember anything."

"You remembered Alex," Aramael said quietly. "Start there. On her porch, meeting her for the first time. She tried to throw us both out."

Seth hesitated a second longer and then pulled into himself, into the opaque swirl that refused to let him pass, no matter how hard or how often he tried. Nothing.

"You were supposed to stay with her while I hunted Caim, but she wouldn't let you," Aramael insisted.

The swirl grew stubbornly thicker. Power built in the air around them. Seth tensed, darting a look at the Archangels between him and Lucifer. Between Alex and the creature who had done this to her.

Aramael's hand tightened on his arm. "Never mind them. Let Mika'el handle it. You need to focus." His voice went tight. "When Alex realized Caim knew where to find her sister, she tried to talk you into taking her there. She didn't want to wait for me. She put her hand on your arm. You felt something. You almost gave in to her because of it."

A tingle passed over Seth's forearm. He stared down, certain fingers had just touched there. The swirl thinned and, just for an instant, he stood on a hot, humid sidewalk, blocking access to a car, hearing a quiet plea. *Come with me if you want, but let me go to them. Please.*

He reached for the memory and tried to seize it, but it was gone again. Frustration returned and he tightened his hold on Alex's body, his fingers digging into the still, unresponsive flesh. "Damn it, I'm *trying*. I just can't—"

The woman in Seth's arms breathed out in a long, low groan, barely audible to his ears, and he stopped short. Stared down. "I heard that," a voice whispered, "and it's good enough for me."

"What?" Aramael asked.

Seth raised his gaze to the Power. "Pardon?"

"You said something. I didn't hear you."

That had been him? But how could he have spoken words he hadn't thought? Unless . . . his center grew still. Unless they had been his words another time, a time before, when he had remembered. When he had known who he was.

Alex, broken and bleeding on the floor of a bedroom, flames surrounding her.

Me, kneeling beside her, begging her to show me some sign of life because I wasn't permitted to bring her all the way back if she was already gone.

The smell of scorched flesh.

My hand, touching her, healing her, taking away the pain.

Seth's fingers closed over something cold and hard and he watched himself pull the knife from Alex's belly. A distant part of him noted a pulse of energy pressing in on him. He pushed the awareness of it away and dropped the blade to the ground. His hand settled over the seeping wound. Heat tingled through his fingertips. Not Alex's heat. His. From somewhere deep within him that he had forgotten. Somewhere that swelled now with remembering.

A soaring, vaulted hall, lined with books and the hushed murmur of many voices.

The bleeding beneath his fingers slowed, then stopped as severed vessels reconnected.

Gardens stretched out before him, a riot of color in some

*places, a deep, cooling green in others, all interspersed with
reflective pools and connected by streams and waterfalls
and meandering paths. A place of unparalleled beauty.
Home.*

Deep tissues, hidden from sight, joined, held, bonded.

*A silver-haired female, luminescent with age and wis-
dom, looked up from a potting bench and smiled at him,
filling his entire being with a tremendous surge of love.*

Fascia knit together. Skin healed.

*A promise, heartfelt at the time but still underlined by
doubt, to honor his word and fulfill the destiny to which he
had agreed. Sadness hollowing a woman's eyes. His mother's eyes.*

A tiny presence, barely clinging to life, tugged at his
attention. He directed his touch away. More memories
flashed through his mind.

*A wooden door. A decision. A co-conspirator. A transi-
tion. Alex.*

Seth's breath strangled in his throat and he stared down
at the woman in his arms. Stared, loved, and—suddenly and
without the fanfare that should have accompanied such a
revelation—remembered it all. Everything. Who he was.
What he was. What he had promised and then renounced
because of a mortal woman.

Because of Alex.

Alex, whose life spark had begun to falter. Seth lifted his
hand from her belly and laid it over her heart, finding a beat
there, but so slow. So frighteningly weak.

Always Alex.

He gathered himself and the very air went still around
him. Focusing, he directed his own life energy down his
arm, through his hand, into her. A pulse moved against his
fingertips, faltered, grew stronger.

"I choose you," he whispered. Alex's heartbeat steadied
into a deep, reassuring rhythm. Beneath them, the earth
rumbled and began to shudder . "I will always choose you."

A Power's fiery wings swept over them as the alley
imploded.

FORTY-EIGHT

"She's coming around."
    Alex's consciousness returned with all the delicacy of a sledgehammer, jolting her into a world filled with noise and confusion. She blinked a few times, trying to orient herself as fingers held her eyelids apart and a beam of light flashed across her eyes.

"Detective? Can you hear me?"

She twisted her head away.

"Can you tell me your name?"

"Jarvis," she croaked. "Alexandra Jarvis."

Why was her voice so muffled?

"Do you know where you are?"

"Vancouver." She put fingertips to the oxygen mask covering her nose and mouth, but a gentle, gloved grip guided her hand to her side again.

"Can you be a little more specific?" the voice persisted. "Where in Vancouver are you, Detective Jarvis?"

She tried to think. Ran through the list of places she'd been. The psych ward at the hospital. The hotel. The coffee shop. Henderson's apartment.

Alex surged upward against hands that tried to hold her down. Ripping off the mask, she sucked for air and choked on a thick swirl of dust.

Henderson's apartment.

Lucifer.

Seth in the alley.

The knife.

"Easy does it, Detective," a calm voice said. "We need to finish checking you out before you get to run around. You were under a pretty impressive pile of bricks."

Alex shook off the hands holding hers and probed her belly. She found the hole in her jacket, the one in her jeans . . . and, beneath the layers of fabric, the scar that marked the passage of the knife. The wound that should have taken her life. Should have taken the life of—

Oh, dear God, no.

With a strength born of equal parts desperation and denial, Alex scrambled up from the ground. Stood, swaying, as two paramedics followed suit and caught hold of her again. Fought them off when they tried to guide her onto a waiting stretcher. That thing couldn't still be alive in her. The Archangels wouldn't have let that happen. Wouldn't have let Lucifer get to her like that. Couldn't have—

Seth. Where the hell was Seth?

Her gaze swept over the ruin surrounding her and she blinked, her jaw going slack. What the hell? It looked as if she stood in a war zone. The walls that formed the sides and end of the blind alley had all collapsed, exposing shattered beams and sagging floors and providing an almost obscene glimpse into the lives of the people who had lived there, who had managed to stay off the streets.

Until now.

Alex swallowed the bile rising into her throat, watching rescue workers and search dogs swarm over the massive piles of rubble. One of the dogs gave a sharp bark and a dozen figures scrambled toward it.

"How many injured?" she asked the paramedics who

seemed to have satisfied themselves with steadying her while she viewed the wreckage. "Was anyone killed?"

"They're still looking," one hedged. Alex shot him a hard look and he added, "Six dead so far. You're the only one we've pulled out alive."

Seth.

She'd barely registered the possibility when a shout went up from the spot identified by the dog. More workers joined the effort and a few seconds later a figure was pulled from the debris, limp, unmoving, still dressed in full ERT gear. A fresh shock of dread jolted through Alex.

"Cops?" she asked through numb lips.

"Five missing."

She sagged and would have dropped to her knees but for the support of the men at her side. All these people, and for what? So she could fail? So she could lose Seth and die giving birth to Lucifer's child? A monster that would lead the other Nephilim to destroy the world?

Firm hands steered her to sit on the stretcher. "Okay, Detective, we're just going to put the oxygen mask on you again for a—"

"Alex."

"Michael!" Alex bounded upright again as a tall figure loomed beyond the paramedics. "What happened? Where is Seth?" She pushed toward him, shaking off the paramedics impatiently.

The Archangel shot a glance at her attendants and Alex half turned to address them, though her gaze never left Michael's.

"I'm refusing treatment," she said.

"Detective—"

"I'm fine. I'll find one of you if anything changes."

After several attempts to change her mind, the paramedics packed up and, heads shaking, departed with their stretcher between them, leaving Alex and Michael alone in their corner of the alley. The instant the men were out of earshot, Alex rounded on the Archangel.

"Where is he? Tell me he didn't choose . . . ?" She trailed off, unable to finish the question.

Michael shook his head, but before Alex could do more than recognize the relief swamping her, he said, "He didn't choose the One, either."

Relief died in her chest, sitting on her lungs with the weight of an elephant. Perhaps she'd been too quick to reject the oxygen mask. She stared past Michael's shoulder at what remained of a building. "Please don't tell me this puts us back to square one."

"More into uncharted territory," Michael said. "He chose you."

"Me?" Alex blinked, and then frowned. "I wasn't one of the choices."

"For him, you were. He had already tried to give up everything for you once, remember."

"Once . . . ? You mean he succeeded this time? But how?"

"Seth attained full power in order to heal you. Once he'd done so, he chose to give up that power in order to stay with you. There were unexpected consequences." Michael gestured at the ruined alleyway and Alex's gaze followed.

"This—this wasn't Lucifer, saving his child?"

Michael shook his head. "No. The child died. This was all Seth's doing. I had no idea it could even *be* done, so I never guessed at the havoc it might wreak."

Another rush of relief traveled through Alex at Michael's first words, only to turn cold when the rest sank in. "It goes beyond this alley?"

"They're calling it an earthquake. The alley sustained the worst damage, but yes, there's more."

The Archangel's hand reached to steady her as she swayed, staring at the destruction. Even if the quake had been small, it couldn't be a good thing—not with Vancouver sitting square in the middle of some serious fault lines. Who knew what else it might have triggered?

"Christ, we have to help." She pinpointed the person who

appeared to be in charge and started in his direction, but Michael's grip brought her up short. Looking up into his set, stoic features, she scowled. "Tell me you're not pulling that whole non-interference thing again."

"The Appointed is already helping, and the Guardians have been instructed to provide more guidance than is usually allowed," he hedged.

"The Guardians." Bitterness edged Alex's voice. She didn't apologize for it. "Your kind bloody well causes this whole, massive mess and now—what? You're planning a fucking vacation somewhere?"

A muscle in Michael's jaw flexed and anger flared in his eyes. "Apart from the fact that it was Lucifer who caused this mess, not us, you forget the war."

She had forgotten.

Could have done without being reminded.

And flatly refused to apologize for that, either.

But still . . . war.

"Already?" she asked, her throat tight.

Michael nodded.

"But Lucifer said—"

"Lucifer has said a lot of things in his lifetime. Few of them worthy of repeating."

Alex looked back at the alley. At the rescue crews scrambling over the piles of debris, the shrouded bodies lined up in the middle of the destruction, the utter devastation caused by Seth's choice. She tried to imagine how much worse it could have been if he'd made a different decision; how much worse it *would* be when powers as great as his began to clash.

Armageddon. It was real. And it was happening now.

"Do we stand any chance at all?" she asked quietly.

"We'll try to confine things to our own realm as much as we can."

His answer-that-wasn't-an-answer was all the more profound for its lack of directness.

"And if you can't confine things?"

"I should get back."

Michael's fingers slid from her arm, but when he would have withdrawn into the shadows, she touched his sleeve. "Wait. What can I do to help?"

"Your part in our affairs is done. Humanity is about to be challenged as it never has before. You will have enough to face here."

"But—"

"Alex." Michael's voice cut across her objection. "You're done."

Alex stared at him, trying to accept his words as he meant them. But she couldn't. Not when she knew about the Nephilim children and a war raging on the world's doorstep, unseen but all too real. All too terrifying. Done? Done how?

"At least tell me what we're facing here," she said. "Tell me what to expect from the Nephilim."

He sighed, seeming to weigh what he might tell her. "For a while, nothing. They must mature first, and—just as it does for any child—much will depend on their environment during that time. Some will be no threat. Others will destroy themselves through their own choices."

"And the rest?"

"The Nephilim are half Fallen Angel. They will have certain abilities the rest of you don't. Greater physical prowess. Sharper mental acuity. The ability to influence human minds. The latter is the most dangerous."

"How dangerous?"

"Descendants of the original Nephilim, hundreds of generations removed and with no real abilities left, have raised entire armies and destroyed millions," Michael said. "I'll leave the extrapolation to you."

"What do we do?"

Heaven's greatest warrior nodded past her and she looked over her shoulder to see a weary, dust-streaked Seth crossing the alley toward her, his gaze carrying an intensity that spiraled through her very core.

"The best you can with what you have," Michael said, "for as long as you have it."

And then he was gone and Seth was there, enveloping

Alex in the embrace she had so long fought against. An embrace that now felt like the only right thing in the entire universe. For long minutes, she did nothing but cling, listening to the steady *tha-dump* of his heart and absorbing his warmth into her own chilled soul. Letting him shield her from the grim new reality of a world she no longer recognized. For equally long minutes, Seth seemed content to hold her.

At last, however, gentle fingers brushed back the hair from her forehead. "He told you."

She nodded against his chest. "Why?" she asked. *Why did you do it? Why did you save me? Why me?*

"From the moment I met you, Alexandra Jarvis, I think you were the only possible choice I could make. I tried to give up my place for you once, but Mittron wasn't strong enough to take my powers from me. Things went wrong." He shrugged and his chest muscles contracted beneath Alex's cheek. "Now things are right again."

Drawing back, she looked up into his black gaze. Met the recognition there. The remembrance. The whole of him, back once more. He nodded in response to her unspoken question.

"I remember everything," he said. "Meeting you, loving you, desiring you as I had never known one being could desire another."

"And your destiny?" she asked. "Do you remember that, too?"

Seth fell quiet for a moment. "Yes. I also remember I would rather have a few short years *with* you than an entire eternity without. The struggle between my parents is theirs, not mine. I thought, hoped, I might be able to ease that struggle, but you were right about us being pawns. Whatever I did, whatever I chose, it would make no difference in a game that is infinite and unending. So if it makes you feel any better, I didn't just choose you, Alex, I also chose not to play their game anymore."

She went still and he smiled down at her. "You wear your

emotions rather plainly, you know. You have guilt written all over you."

"With good reason." Alex pulled away to stare at the chaos in which they stood. "For thousands of years, every-thing between the One and Lucifer was quiet. Calm. Now I've managed to not only trigger Armageddon, but to inter-fere with the one being who might have averted it."

"Not you, Alex, others who used you."

"Semantics."

"Truth," he contradicted firmly. "You were as much a pawn as I was. Besides, what's done is done. We can't change any of it, we can only move forward. Which leaves us with just one question."

She looked over her shoulder to find him looking oddly vulnerable, a little like a small, lost boy—apart from his roughly six-foot-six frame. He quirked a small smile that didn't reflect in the seriousness of his eyes.

"Do we move forward together or alone?" he asked quietly.

Alex studied him, this man who had given up his divinity for her, and for whom she had given up her soulmate. She thought about all they had come through and all they might still have to endure. Then, silently, she held out her hand to him because there could only be one answer. One possibility. One truth.

The best you can with what you have, for as long as you have it.

"Together," she said. "Always together."

As Seth's hand closed over hers, she tucked away the memory of her soulmate in a deep, quiet corner of her heart.

"DOES SHE KNOW?" Aramael stared into the pond, unable to bring himself to meet Mika'el's gaze. He scuffed a toe against the gravel path, sending a stone skipping into the dark water.

"She didn't say anything, so I would guess no."

Lips tightening, Aramael nodded.

"It's for the best," said the Archangel behind him.

Best. Best that Alex knew nothing of his involvement in saving her life, nothing of how he had protected both her and Seth from Seth's own power gone mad. Aramael's hands curled into fists, but he nodded again.

"You still haven't told me how you knew she was dying."

Aramael closed his eyes, the wrench of pain in his chest as fresh now as it had been when Alex called to him from the alley with her dying thought. He gritted his teeth. "Call it a lucky guess."

Mika'el said nothing.

When several minutes had passed and the Archangel still hadn't spoken, Aramael shot a glance over his shoulder to see if Mika'el was even there anymore. Emerald eyes met his, cool and openly speculative. Aramael raised a brow. "What?"

"I need to know that you're able to put your soulmate behind you once and for all, Power. That if she were to call to you again, you could ignore her. Or better yet, not even hear her." Mika'el wiped away a smudge from the polished black chest plate of his war armor. "Because if I promote you to Archangel, I need to be absolutely certain you will be loyal to the One—and only to the One."

"You want to promote me?" Aramael stared at him. "After declaring me responsible for all of this even happening? Why?"

"When I told you at the beginning of this that your Creator needed you, Aramael of the Powers, I didn't lie." The Archangel's eyes had never looked greener. Or harder. "She has kept a secret from us that could cost us her very presence in our lives if we can't stop it from happening. If we're to stand a chance, we need a full complement of warriors. I want you to take the place of Samael."

Looking away into the trees, Aramael took a moment to let the Archangel's words sink in—and to re-master breathing. While a part of him wondered what kind of secret could take the One away from them, he set the question aside in favor of the one he needed answered before he could give his response.

"You haven't answered my question. Why me?"

"The strength of every soul, mortal or immortal, lies in its capacity to make choices. An Archangel's strength is no different, except our capacity extends to making extraordinary choices—such as choosing to walk away from our soulmates for the greater good. Permanently," said Mika'el. "Now, answer *my* question. If your soulmate calls to you again, can you ignore her? No matter what her need might be?"

Aramael shoved his hands into his pockets and stared again into the dark depths of the pool. Even here, in Heaven, the connection remained between him and Alex. A fine thread, like spider silk. Three times now he had held out against it. Had found in himself the ability to endure the agony of having it pull taut, stretch beyond endurance, and break. But Mika'el asked for more. So much more. Could he do what the Archangel asked? Did he have the strength?

Permanently.

An ache settled into his heart and slowly traveled deeper, into his core. His essence. A part of him wanted to deny the Archangel, to reject the very suggestion, but a greater part— a sadder part—knew it was too late. What Mika'el asked of him was nothing more than a confirmation of what Aramael had already decided when he had saved Alex not for his own sake but for hers—and for Seth's.

For the greater good, he had already chosen to let her go.

Aramael turned and found Heaven's greatest warrior holding out a parchment to him. This time, it was the One's seal visible along one edge.

"Welcome aboard, Aramael of the Archangels," said Mika'el. "Now let's move. We have a war to win."

EPILOGUE

"Well?" Lucifer heard the door open, but didn't turn. He didn't need to look around to know it was Samael who entered because, after the last Fallen One's mistaken intrusion, only Sam would brave his current mood.

The door clicked shut and his aide's footsteps crossed the room. "We're ready for them," he said. "The females, too."

Staring out into the barren caricature of a garden, Lucifer clenched his jaw. "All but one," he said.

Samael cleared his throat in a soft cough. "About that—"

Lucifer waved an impatient hand over his shoulder. "I know, I know. I need to let it go, focus on the ones who remain. It just galls me to no end that I didn't see it coming. Didn't anticipate what the bitch would do."

"All may not be as lost as you think."

"Oh, trust me, Archangel, it's exactly as lost as I think," Lucifer said bitterly. "I was there, remember? I saw her stick the knife into her belly. Felt the child—*my* child—die. Saw the ruination of any chance the Naphil would bear another. It doesn't get much more lost than that."

"Unless she isn't the only descendant of my line."

Lucifer snorted. "I'm sure she isn't, but our chances of finding another amid seven billion souls are—"

"She has a sister."

The very universe seemed to still, holding its breath, waiting for Lucifer to absorb Samael's words, to grasp their import and taste the possibilities within them. Another Naphil of Archangel descent. Another chance to produce a child of spectacular ability. A child that would lead the Nephilim to certain, absolute, final victory.

Slowly—afraid that if he moved too fast, he might destroy the perfection of the moment—Lucifer turned to his aide. Samael smiled.

"And a niece," said the former Archangel.

Lucifer smiled, too.

FROM
THEA HARRISON
AUTHOR OF *STORM'S HEART*

SERPENT'S KISS

=== ◆ ===

A Novel of the Elder Races

In order to save his friend's life, Wyr sentinel Rune Ainiss-esthai made a bargain with Vampyre Queen Carling—without knowing what she would ask from him in return. But when Rune attempts to make good on his debt, he finds a woman on the edge.

Recently, Carling's power has become erratic, forcing her followers to flee in fear. Despite the danger, Rune is drawn to the ailing Queen and decides to help her find a cure for the serpent's kiss—the Vampyric disease that's killing her.

With their desire for each other escalating just as quickly as Carling's instability spirals out of control, the sentinel and the Queen will have to rely on each other if they have any hope of surviving the serpent's kiss . . .

"A master storyteller." —Christine Feehan,
#1 *New York Times* bestselling author

"Thea Harrison has created a truly original urban fantasy romance." —Angela Knight, *New York Times* bestselling author

penguin.com